FERVOR

Written and Illustrated By Chantal Boudreau

to a wonderful
friend and
co-worker – I'll
miss you!
— Chantal

Fervor

EAN—13: 978-1-936730-05-6

PREFACE

Dear Readers,

Inspiration can come from unexpected places. While on a hunt for representation, I came across a list of themes that one agent was supposedly looking for. I had nine unpublished manuscripts and a real yen to get some attention from someone in the industry. As driven as always, I decided to take on his challenge. I selected one of his themes and in the course of an hour I had pulled a wide selection of ideas that had been lingering in my mind, and woven them together into a story that matched his demands. I had my plot, my main characters, my title and my outline (which would change somewhat before planning was complete but the basic elements have remained the same.) Of course, the agent in question never even asked for a partial when I queried him with regards to Fervor, but I am still grateful for the initial push that brought Fervor into existence.

Some of the ideas in my book surrounding genetic manipulation originated from a non-fiction book that I had read more than a year before the creation of Fervor. Elaine Dewar's book, The Second Tree: of Clones, Chimeras and Quests for Immorality (Random House, 2004) was a definite influence for me and a source of interest that led me to the Scholars and their experiments. She discussed what extremes man might go to in the name of science and "progress", and questioned the morality of justifying playing God on the basis that it might improve our circumstances. I continue to find her research fascinating.

Another significant influence for Fervor was the growth of social networking. I am in awe of the connections that technology has permitted me to build and I often wonder if someday science might allow those connections to be more direct, from person to person rather than having to use some type of intermediary media. The Connection in my story is merely social networking without the computers, cell-phones or other communication devices, but with other limitations and associated issues.

One of the biggest inspirations for me while I am writing is my music. I normally listen to alternative rock and my playlist for Fervor did include Three Days Grace's "Life Starts Now," but I decided I needed something less mainstream in order to help me capture the unusual flavor that I was looking for, something more indie. I chose Aselin Debison's "Bigger than Me" for a sound with child-like innocence, and Saran Slean's "Night Bugs," for a sound with depth and soul. It was the latter that helped me choose the names "Elliot" and "Francis" for my characters.

Lastly, while writing is a fairly solitary endeavor for me, I want to acknowledge the assistance of my work-in-progress test reader and real-life muse, Barb McQueen, who never fails to bring out the scissors and threaten me when I find myself in need of motivation. Thanks, Barb!

-Chantal

ACKNOWLEDGEMENTS

For test reading: I'd like to thank my primary butt-kicker and real-life muse, Barb McQueen. I'd also like to thank my other wonderful test readers, Ren Garcia, Jonathan Stotlar, and Elisabeth Tilton for keeping me on my toes with questions and constructive criticism.

For moral support: I'd like to thank my very encouraging family, especially my husband, Dale and my kids, Gwyn and Etienne, for putting up with my compulsion to write. I also want to thank my equally encouraging co-workers and manager. Jim, Leanne, Sherry, Marian, Maria, Vicki, Elizabeth – you guys are great! A big shout -out to all my facebook friends too, particularly my writer pals!

Lastly, I want to thank May December Publishing for believing in me. I hope we'll be producing many more books together.

-Chantal

Fervor

CONTENTS

1

AND THEN THERE WERE NONE

All Sam could hear was the screaming, and the screaming was all in his head. He knew that, because, as it woke him, he had tried covering his ears. But it hadn't helped – they were still crying, screaming, shrieking, and wailing. He had tried screaming, too, and while he had heard it inside his mind just like the other voices, what scared him the most was that he had not heard it on the outside as well. He realized at that point that, aside from what echoed loudly through his brain, all that he had was silence. He clutched at his ears, clawed at his bed, and as he hyperventilated, everything went black.

When he opened his eyes again, for the second time that morning, he felt a firm grip on his arm.

Sam was dizzy. The voices were still there in his head, and there were still so many of them, too, but they were much calmer now. Some were louder than others, but most of them were simple whispers and gentle murmurs, like he was listening in on someone else's quiet thoughts. The majority of them seemed to be saying almost the same thing that he was thinking, his own musings blending into the general commotion.

He glanced up, expecting to see the warm brown eyes of Maria – believing that maybe she had woken him, and that he just had not completely shaken himself free from the nightmare yet. The hand on his shoulder, however, did not have Maria's feminine fingers or somewhat swarthy skin. It was a pale hand,

1

larger than Sam's, with squared fingernails that looked slightly chewed. Sam looked up with surprise.

Before Sam could say anything – no, before Sam could *think* anything, the older boy looked into his eyes, put a finger to his lips, and inside Sam's head there was a distinct and obvious *"shhhhhhh."*

Sam obeyed. He could not help but obey. It was as much a compulsion as it was a desire to please the strange blond boy with pale green eyes. Then, the boy talked to him, only he did not move his mouth.

"I'm Francis. I'm here to help you. I'm a Teller, and we have to go to the Gathering. Don't say anything. Don't even think anything. Quiet your mind as much as you can. Then, if you want to say something to me – if you want to ask me any questions – you have to focus your thoughts at me. Think at me. *Do you understand? Nod if you do."*

Sam nodded. He tried to follow Francis's instructions to the best of his ability. Once again, there was that compulsion. The smaller boy closed his eyes, breathed steadily, and tried to calm his thoughts. Others were doing the same somewhere out there in the void in which his mind now floated, Sam sensed it.

When he was sure that his mind was as quiet as he could get it, he opened his eyes again and stared at the pale, blond boy before him. While trying to focus his thoughts, out of habit, he opened his mouth as well to speak. He wanted to ask Francis where Maria was, why he was hearing things in his head, what this strange person was doing in his bedroom. While he could hear what he was going to say in his head, he could not hear it in his ears. He closed his mouth quickly; almost as frightened as he had been the first time that the silence had hit him.

"You won't be able to talk that way from now on," Francis informed him, inside instead of out. *"It's a good thing that you are Connected, but you aren't a Listener anymore. You'll only be able to talk to others through the connection, unless you learn sign language, and you won't be able to make out real*

sounds either. If you want to hear what others have to say, they'll have to communicate to you through the connection."

Overwhelmed by his circumstances, which were more than the typical eight-year-old could endure, Sam started crying. He wanted desperately to understand, but none of this made any sense to him.

Yesterday, he had gone through his usual routine. He had woken up in the normal way, not like this morning. Maria had taken him to school using her magic to guide the hover. Then, he had learned, played, and afterwards, she had picked him up just like she always did. There had been nothing to suggest, the day before, that he would wake up the next morning and everything would be different. But it was.

"Calm down," Francis told him, and Sam felt himself immediately relax. *"I'll try to answer your questions, but you have to use the connection. You have to think them at me – and remember, stay focussed, or everyone will hear you whether they want to or not."*

Trembling slightly, the smaller boy tried to do as he was told. He thought his questions very directly at Francis. Sam felt him cringe, saw the blond youth open his mouth and close his eyes, then rub at his temples.

"Ah! Not so loud. You have a very strong link. That's good, but that means that you will need better controls. Focus is good, too, but don't push so hard. That actually hurt. Try again, but be gentle about it," Francis sighed mentally. Sam decided that it was best if he took it slow, and started with just one question.

"Where is Maria?" There was a tremor to his thoughts as a result of his anxiety, one that he was sure that Francis would be aware of.

"She was your minder? You are too young to remember the first exodus, aren't you? I barely remember it, and I must have at least five years on you. I'm sorry, Sam. She left Fervor. All of the minders did. There are no adults left on the island. They were the last, and now they're gone."

3

Sam's jaw dropped and his little heart fluttered. Maria was gone? No adults left on Fervor? How would he survive? As if he didn't have enough to worry about with this new "connection," as this strangely persuasive boy put it, and his unexpected deafness, he now had a million new questions. Who would take care of him? How would he get food? Who would teach him? Who would make him feel safe? Why did they leave? Why wasn't there any warning? Why hadn't Maria taken him with her?

Sam was so frantic that he forgot to rein in his thoughts. Thankfully, Francis was right there again, watching him with his quirky smile and raising his finger to his lips.

"Shhhhh."

The soothing thought washed over him like a warm bath, and Sam felt himself relax despite a reluctance to let his worry go. He was starting to hate the power that this older boy had over him. He had to know. He needed to know. It was like a small flame of curiosity burning hot and deep inside of him, desperately wanting to flare up and engulf him if it was not fed any answers. He had never felt such a powerful drive to seek out information before – just one more thing to add to the complete and utter chaos in which Sam felt like he was drowning.

"One step at a time," Sam thought. *"Back to the start – back to my first question and work my way forward."*

Francis nodded, and that made the younger boy shudder. He could not think anything without someone else knowing it, or so it seemed. Was it going to be like that from now on? Had he lost all privacy? Was he going to lose his sense of self? There were just more questions, and so far, very few answers.

"If the Directives that the adults left behind for us to follow speak the truth, eventually, we will be able to block others out completely so that we can preserve who we are and share only what we want to. But it will be something that we will all have to learn, and it will take a lot of practice. That's why they left some of us disconnected, to mediate, to help maintain order until we sort all of this out. On the other hand, I wouldn't want

to be them in the long run. They are the Controls. When we finally get this working properly, when things are running smoothly for everyone in the connection, they're going to feel isolated and excluded. They won't feel like they belong on Fervor anymore, and we don't have any way off," Francis assured him.

"What about the hovers?" Sam asked. He noticed that if he managed to hone in on Francis's mind with enough clarity, he could hear feedback from his own thoughts reverberating in the background. It was eerie.

"None of us who were left behind can use them," the blond boy thought with a patronizing edge. *"I don't have the magical training to run one of those things – do you? Anyone old enough to know how to use them is gone now. I think that they arranged it that way on purpose. They set it up to keep us here. They didn't want us to be able to leave."*

Francis's demeanour, which had come across as so peaceful and pleasant despite the oddness about him, seemed to fold in on itself, and for a moment he regarded Sam with an air of melancholy. Then he snapped out of it, and giving Sam that same quirky smile, he offered up a distraction.

"I can see how that might present us with a problem. We have to get to the Hub for the Gathering, and without the hovers, we're going to have to walk. That's a very long walk."

Sam grimaced at this idea. He had been to the Hub, a massive and centrally positioned communal building on the island, only once in his short life, and it had taken more than half a day's travel by hover. If they walked, it would take them several days to get there.

"Why do we have to go? What is this Gathering?" Sam did not want to have to make that trip unless there was no other option.

"You want answers? That's the only place you're going to find them. I can give you some, but I'll only be skimming the surface. I'm your Teller, but I only have leave to tell you so much for the moment. I told you that there would be a lot to

5

learn, and that's where it's going to start. Believe me, you want to go."

Sam gritted his teeth. There it was again. Any time he tried to put up a fight – any time he tried to offer any resistance – it hit him, the blond boy's words hanging over his shoulders like a heavy yoke, a burden that Sam could not possibly hope to escape. If Francis told Sam to believe him, then Sam would. If Francis told Sam that he wanted him to do something, then Sam did. If there were going to be any battle of wills, for some reason, Francis would always come up the winner.

"Why are you here, Francis? Why are you taking me there? What is a Teller?"

Sam wanted to keep it simple and ask only one question at a time, but he found that the thoughts were all tied together, and he could not separate them. It was not as straight forward as talking, this connection. It was difficult to limit what you were thinking at someone.

"That's going to take a lot more explaining than you might imagine. Let's get you ready to go and I can give you some of the details along the way. We have someone else that we have to stop for who will be coming with us to the Hub. She's a Little like you. She's not that far away. I can introduce you now, if you like," Francis suggested. The older boy's eyes went vacant, as if he were staring off into the distance, but that distance lay beyond the confining and bare walls of Sam's room. *"Sarah? Sarah, are you still there? I'm with Sam, just like I told you that I would be. We'll be coming for you soon."*

"Francis?" Sam could barely make out the girl's thoughts, like he was eavesdropping on a private conversation, and only because the older boy was allowing him the privilege. Her thoughts were even more tremulous than Sam's. *"I'm scared. It's so dark, and I can't move without bumping into things. Are you sure Sasha won't be back?"*

"She won't be back, Sarah. She's not on Fervor anymore. Stay where you are. Sam and I can't be your eyes for you until we get there. We'll be leaving here soon. Sam just has to

gather his things." Francis's thoughts always seemed so self-assured, like he had done this before, like he didn't have the same kind of questions that Sam and Sarah had. That in itself bothered Sam.

"Sam?"

He felt the mental tendril extending towards him from the girl, hesitantly. There was something softer and more fragile to the touch of her thoughts that was not there when Francis spoke to him via the connection.

"You're going to help Francis to be my eyes? You can see like he can?"

Answering Sarah was much different from answering Francis. Francis was right there, and the older boy kept his mind wide open to him. To reply to the girl, Sam had to push his thoughts through a tunnel of sorts, a flimsy tunnel that kept out some of the commotion, so that they could hear each other specifically. Her own fear made Sam's feel insignificant. He wanted to make her more comfortable.

"I can see, but I can't hear anymore except through the connection. Don't worry. I'll help Francis to find you, Sarah. You'll be safe soon."

Sam was not sure why, but he honestly meant that. He was fairly sure he knew exactly where she was, and that he would be able to take Francis to her.

"Gather your things – anything that you really want to take with you – because we won't be coming back here," Francis instructed Sam, glancing around the plainly furnished room. *"They'll be assigning us to a house, and it won't be this one. Not enough room for the six of us here."*

"Six?" Sam was puzzled. How did Francis know all of this? It had only ever been Sam and Maria in their boxy little house on the hill. It was not much, he had to admit, with its very simple design and lack of adornment, but it had met their basic needs.

In addition to Maria, he had socialized with others at the school, but he had never lived with anyone else. So far, Sam had counted three – him, Francis, and the timid Sarah – who had for some reason been grouped together. Where were the other three going to come from? The blond boy had been anticipating his question.

"There are three more Bigs, like me, who will be meeting us at the Hub: Nathan, Fiona and Royce. They'll be part of our house-family, too," Francis explained. Just as it had earlier, his expression fell a little, before the older boy realized that he had let his smile slide, and recovered himself. *"And to answer your other question, I know all of this because I'm a Teller. It is the duty of our talent-group. I'll tell you more about it along the way, but I need you to hurry and take what you think you'll need."*

Sam scurried around the small two-bedroom bungalow with bare, neutral walls and ordinary shapes, scooping his most valued possessions into the backpack that he had kept in the past for school. He did not have much to show for his eight years. There were no toys, no pictures on the walls, no trinkets, nothing that was not clearly functional in some way. Maria's obsession with cleanliness had made the place seem almost sterile, as if it had not been bland enough to begin with.

Sam had hesitated for a moment before dumping all of his school things onto the floor to make room for other belongings until he reminded himself that there would be no more school, not in the traditional sense anyway. There were no more minders to take the children there, and no more teachers to teach them. He did keep his sketch pad, and his pencil case, and then he grabbed some clean clothing, shoes, a couple of books, and some food. He also dove into one of the closets and dug through the disorganized pile for a glow torch. He had enough magic in him to make the illuminating device work – it didn't take that much. It was one of the first things that they had taught them to use at his school. The majority of the appliances and bigger devices he did not know how to use. That worried Sam. He hoped Francis or one of the other three Bigs that were supposed to join him were knowledgeable in their use, or their life on Fervor would be a struggle from here on out.

The quiet as he roamed the house looking for the things that he wanted, and the lack of the familiar rustle and clunk of those items was still frightening to Sam. He was bewildered by the sudden hearing loss and wondered at its cause. He had been able to hear Maria's warm tone when she bid him goodnight before he had gone to sleep the prior evening. He had even been able to make out the barely audible hiss as she had extinguished the magic that illuminated his room. That ability was just as much a part of the past as Maria apparently was. He shrugged off the urge to crawl into a corner and to sit rocking and hugging his knees, and instead made his way back to Francis who was waiting for him by the front door.

They stepped out into the lukewarm air of late spring, with a soft breeze blowing off the ocean. Francis turned to look at Sam with those mesmerizing pale green eyes, and grinned.

"The Directives only gave me your location, and even though they did give me all of the members of the house-family's names, they didn't list where I could find them. It is up to you to find Sarah now," he insisted, touching Sam's mind good-naturedly with his own.

Sam's mouth dropped open, and he blinked disconcertedly at the older boy.

"Me? Why me?" he thought.

"The Directives say that we all have to test our gifts now. I'm a Teller, and I've already successfully tested my gift on you and Sarah. As far as I can tell, it's working the way that it is supposed to." Francis said this with a hint of a frown, inside and out. *"I know it makes you uncomfortable. I'm sorry. It's what I have to do. You have to do what you do. You're supposed to be a Finder. I need you to prove to me that your gift is working. Now find Sarah."*

He said it with such conviction that Sam knew that he was not going to be able to refuse him, and the younger boy was correct. Almost immediately, he felt as though he were possessed, driven to find the girl that he had linked with earlier. Knowing in what direction he had to go to find her, but not being able to explain exactly why, Sam started moving. Francis followed behind him eagerly.

After they had been walking for a few minutes, Francis reached out and touched his mind.

"Is it okay if I talk to you, or do you need quiet to concentrate? I know that this is supposed to work for you, but I have no idea how. From what the Directives suggest, the only ones who will truly understand your gift will be others in your talent-group. Only Finders will know what it truly means to be a Finder."

The younger boy paused and looked back at his current companion. *"And only Tellers will know what it truly means to be a Teller,"* Sam thought, trying to hold it in to himself. He believed he saw a momentary flash of hurt – or perhaps it was guilt – in Francis's eyes. He could not be sure if the blond youth had picked up on his thoughts or not, or if that was just a general response to the topic at hand. With a contained sigh, Sam focussed his mind, briefly, on Francis again.

"You can talk to me, but if I want to be sure that we're going the right way, I can't let it distract me too much. If I do, I'll have to stop and reach for her again. As long as I can find her mind, I can find her. I guess that means I could find anybody on Fervor, if I knew who I was looking for."

"Anybody, that is, who was Connected," the older boy corrected him mentally. *"Anybody who isn't a Control."*

Sam considered asking what Francis meant by that, since it was his second time mentioning these Controls, but he realised that, so far, his Teller had only revealed things to him that the blond youth had decided that Sam needed to know. Since they were looking for her anyway, however, Sam assumed that Francis might be more forthcoming about Sarah.

"So Sarah's not a Teller, and I'm assuming that she's not a Finder like me either," Sam remarked, believing that finding would be a rather pointless talent if one were blind. *"And*

10

since I can find her, she mustn't be one of these Controls you mentioned either. What is she then?"

"Your deductive skills are fairly sharp," Francis thought at Sam, with a mental chuckle. *"You had good teachers. You're correct. Sarah's none of those things. Our Control is supposedly someone named Royce. I'm not sure where he is, and you won't be able to find him, but he is supposed to be meeting up with us at the Hub, as are the other two Bigs. No ... Sarah is our Fixer."*

"Fixer? Where are you getting all this from, Francis? You keep talking about these Directives. You have all these strange rules. You know things that I don't about what's going on? How?"

Sam noticed that as he thought these things at Francis, he could sense that there were others in the connection sharing similar feelings while dealing with their own Tellers, probably other Finders like him. This was an experience that was repeating itself across Fervor. It was like a buzzing on the same frame of mind as Sam was on, and the young boy found it very unnerving.

Francis looked unhappy again, and Sam didn't like that. Every time it happened, Sam felt like he was somehow personally responsible – that the blond boy's displeasure was essentially wrong and that the situation needed rectification. There was an unnatural satisfaction in assuring that his Teller's eyes held contentment instead disappointment.

"I told you, Sam. I can't explain everything right now. That's what the Gathering's for. You'll learn a lot there. There will be answers to your questions."

As the older boy's mind touched Sam's, he gestured in the direction that they had been travelling in, along a well-established hover path that passed amongst the trees. He wanted to continue onwards as they discussed things, if it were possible. Sarah would be waiting for them. She was scared and she could barely function without them.

The compulsion for Sam to seek her out was even stronger than the ones generated by Francis's other orders. Sam reached out for her within the connection and re-established her location. Then Sam started moving towards her again.

As they travelled through the shadows cast by the brush, Sam noted two things about what Francis had said that disturbed him. Francis had said that he would learn a lot at the Gathering, but he had not suggested that Sam would learn everything. He suspected this meant that there were things that Francis did know…that would not be shared with Sam. To try to claim otherwise would be a lie, and from what Sam had seen so far, lying through the connection was not an option.

The other thing that bothered Sam was that Francis had said that there would be answers to his questions, but Sam could tell just by the way that the blond boy had thought this at him that there would not be answers to *all* of his questions. Sam did not like that fact either. He did not like it at all.

By nightfall, they had not yet reached Sarah, and the pair had been forced to seek shelter from the cool, damp air of night in the shelter of the overhang of someone's hover garage; their only protection from the elements since neither Sam nor Francis had the knowledge of magic required to work the door device. Sam fell asleep to the murmur of the connection within his head, and the more distinct sound of Francis trying to soothe a distraught Sarah, miserable at the notion that she would have to spend the night as alone as she had spent her day. He pointed out that she was not really alone, and never would be again. She was not happy with this mental reassurance. She wanted to be able to feel someone's touch again, to make physical contact in order to make sure that she had not gone completely crazy as well as blind, and to know once and for all that this was not all a figment of her imagination.

After a fairly unappetizing breakfast of dry bread and fruit juice that Sam dug out of his pack, they set off to find Sarah again. Believing that talking to Francis seemed both pointless and distracting, the two boys walked in contemplative silence, the only real contact either of them making through the connection was to occasionally think at Sarah that it would not be much longer now before they would get to her. Late in the morning, Sam stopped in his tracks and pointed at a house similar to his own small, boxy bungalow. It was equally featureless and neutral in colour, much like the clothing that they wore.

"She's in there. I'm sure of it," he blurted out, glancing at Francis. *"We found her. I found her."*

Puffing out his chest slightly, Sam began to stride up the hill, past Francis, towards the house. As Sam came within arm's reach of the blond boy, Francis purposefully stuck his foot out to trip the smaller boy. The move was completely unexpected, and Sam sprawled onto the ground. He landed hard, grazing the palms of his hands, tearing his pants, and badly skinning his knee. As he managed to drag himself to a sitting position, tears immediately sprang to his eyes. Now the younger child was twice as angry, both for Francis's overtly hostile action, and for the fact that he was now bawling like a baby. Francis was not even looking at him, however. He had left Sam where he sat, and had started for the door to Sarah's house.

"What did you do that for!" Sam raged, with a sizeable push. Francis hesitated in mid-step, clutching at his head.

"I told you not to do that," Francis's thoughts bit back, losing a little of their typical composure. *"That hurts."*

Sam suddenly felt numb, the fury sapped from him by his Teller's words. *"And what you did to me didn't?"* the younger boy complained, with much less force this time. *"Why? Why did you trip me?"*

Francis looked back at him, biting his lip. His pale green eyes held that familiar melancholy again.

"I told you. The Directives say that I have to test your talents. Sarah's a Fixer. I had to give her something to fix," his thoughts revealed quietly.

"But why me? Why not throw yourself to the ground?" Sam demanded, but Francis had already gone back to ignoring him and was in the process of opening the door. Sam believed

13

that he heard the older boy's thoughts vaguely through the connection, echoing something that had been said to him on more than one occasion and was now playing through his mind like a recording.

"First objective is to preserve the ones who uphold the Directives. Without you, this is all for null."

Sam realized what that meant. According to the Directives, he was more expendable than Francis.

Sam waited for his return without budging from the ground, tears still trickling down his cheeks. Francis emerged from the house with a girl who was even smaller than Sam. The waif-like Sarah, who stared vacantly out at the space before her and allowed herself to be pulled along carelessly by the blond boy, had both dark hair and eyes and a thin frame.

"Sam? Francis said that you were hurt..." Her thoughts were very strong now that they were actually meeting face to face – much stronger than their Teller's.

"Here – let me be your eyes," the older boy offered, and then he projected the image that he saw to the slender girl. Sam could see it, too, and it felt weird to see himself through someone else's eyes. He looked so small, his grey eyes sad and accusatory, his light brown hair uncombed and unruly, and his rosy cheeks stained by his tears. Sarah knelt beside him and smiled.

"Is it bad?"

Although Sam knew Sarah had the potential to push much harder than even he could, her thoughts were always so soft, so gentle. He nodded without considering that this gesture would be lost on her if Francis had not chosen to pass it along through his projection.

"Let me see what I can do."

Her mind touched his, and he felt it wrap around the pain and pull it free. Via the connection, she let her magic seep through – into him – and patch the holes that it found there. Moments later, Sam no longer bore any evidence of the damage that Francis's antics had caused. Sarah patted his knee, the hole in his pants being the only thing that remained from his fall. She grinned, even her empty brown eyes shining gleefully.

"Find me a needle and a thread, and I think I can fix those too," she said.

The smaller boy looked over at Francis who was watching them with resignation. Sam was thankful that Sarah would be going with them – someone who was actually more vulnerable than he was. He was also glad that he was not going to be the only Little in their "house-family" as Francis had put it. Things had been hard enough until that point, and Sam suspected that it would be quite some time before they were likely to get any easier.

2

THE HUB

The three travelled together with an awkward awareness of each other's presence. Sarah walked with cautious steps, clutching at Francis's hand, her mind occasionally reaching out to him or Sam for reassurance. Sam walked ahead of them since it was up to him to lead them to the Hub.

According to Francis, all of the children on Fervor were travelling to the communal meeting place purposefully for the Gathering. A few of the house-families had already reached the Hub since they had not had very far to go to get there, and Francis had given Sam the identity of one of the Tellers, Bryan, whom he knew would be already there. The younger boy used the unfamiliar Teller as a beacon, a means of guiding them to the Hub, but Sam did not enjoy having to re-establish the link with this Bryan any time that it was lost due to some distraction. Sam's connection with Francis was not nearly as unnerving as the one with Bryan. Francis's mind was firm and unyielding in some ways, but gentle and calming nonetheless. It was as though the blond boy understood that patience was required to handle the smaller children properly, without causing them undue anxiety.

Bryan's mind, on the other hand, was brusque and rushed, like his connection with Sam was an inconvenience and an annoyance. The link through the connection would be only necessary until Sam was physically close enough to the Hub that he could seek out the large structure instead of having to track a person, which was the more effective part of his gift. Bryan had been somewhat receptive to their initial link, understanding the necessity of the situation, but every time Sam had become distracted and had to look for him again, the new contact was met with mild animosity and a sense of frustration. While Bryan's surface thoughts did not openly state this, in the background Sam could hear his irritated underlying thoughts, quiet and restrained.

"I don't have time for this. The Gathering will be starting soon and there is so much to do to prepare. Why couldn't Francis have directed him to someone else? Why can't the little bugger just focus and stop interrupting me? I told them the Littles would be trouble. Fifty of them – why couldn't they have made do with only two hundred and fifty Bigs? That ought to have been a big enough pool to work with."

It was a swirling mental sigh to Sam – a fog of exasperation hovering at the back of this Bryan's mind. Sam tried hard to ignore it, but it was really difficult. It was as if they were sitting in two different rooms, but had no door between them, and Sam had exceptionally good hearing so that he could still manage to hear what Bryan was muttering under his breath. In a way, it was kind of ironic, considering that in the physical world, Sam was now deaf. He wished he had a proper door to block out those subtle thoughts.

The smaller boy glanced over his shoulder at his two companions. Despite having Francis as her eyes, Sarah still stumbled from time to time, so the older boy maintained a tight grip on her hand to keep her from falling. Seeing Sam look her way in Francis's projected image, she came to a full stop.

"I'm hungry," she declared in a subdued way, directing her thoughts at Sam. There was nothing left in his backpack.

Francis groaned inwardly. This would slow their progress further, but he knew that they could not continue travelling on the mere desire to get to the Hub. This slip of a girl was little more than skin and bones to begin with. If she claimed that she was in need of sustenance, then they would have to oblige her.

"Leave off on seeking out the Hub for the moment," the blond boy instructed Sam, *"Time to test some of your other skills as a Finder. We need food and drink. We'll stop for lunch and replenish our supplies."*

Sam regarded him with puzzlement, but he stopped tracing Bryan immediately – responding as always to Francis's commands with unflinching subordination.

"How?" the younger boy questioned. *"Maria always fetched us food if we needed it while I was at school."*

"There are storehouses across Fervor. There may be one nearby. Otherwise, we'll just break into one of the houses...one that clearly won't be used as one of the family-houses. I'm not asking, Sam, I'm telling. Find us food and drink." Francis's good-natured thoughts steeled slightly, and Sam was willed to obey. He paused, curiously, as things seemed to shift inside him.

One day at school, several months ago, Sam had seen magical projections of bloodhounds at work. What he was experiencing now reminded him of that day. At Francis's prompting, some magic deep within him latched onto an awareness of where food and drink could be found, and Sam was compelled to follow this trail, like scratching at some terrible psychic itch. He scrambled off in that direction, rushing along the most accessible hover paths, and it was all Francis could do to keep up with the smaller boy, especially with blind Sarah in tow.

A few moments later, Sam found himself standing in front of a strange, industrial-looking grey building, unlike any of the houses and schools or community centres that existed on Fervor. He could feel Francis's pleasure embedded in the older boy's thoughts as he and Sarah approached him from behind.

"Excellent! You found one of the storehouses, and quite quickly, too. Your talent is strong," the blond boy exclaimed.

Just as with Bryan, Sam could pick up on the mental murmurings just below the surface ones – the ones he believed

Francis had not intended him to hear. *"I told them the Littles would prove themselves useful. They are better at this than the rest of us. We lucked into it, but they were made that way."*

Made that way. Sam wished that he had not picked up on any of that. Every time that he heard something in the connection he believed to which he was not intended to be privy, it spawned new insecurities, created new anxieties, and led to even more unanswered questions. Why was Francis hiding so much from him and Sarah? Why did he refuse to let them know exactly what was going on?

In the shade of a large pine, they sat and ate without saying much to one another. Sam was just enjoying the relief of not having that pressing feeling that came with Francis's instructions, particularly the compulsion to find things that they were looking for. That drive was irresistible, and Sam had felt trapped by it each time the older boy had demanded that he go looking for something else.

He and Francis were both a little surprised when Sarah, from out of the blue, started asking her own questions part way through the meal. There was always such power behind her mental touch, but at the same time, always so much reserve, perhaps because of her shyness. It took effort for Francis to push his thoughts at Sam, the younger boy was sure of it, but for Sarah it seemed to be second-nature. If the petite girl let go, her push would be a force to be reckoned with.

"What happens when we get to the Hub? Where do we go from there?" she said, nervous and mildly inquisitive.

"Well, first we have to find the Controls," Francis admitted. It was odd, continuing their conversation without having to stop eating, Sam considered. There would be no more concern about speaking with your mouth full. *"Sam won't be able to find them in his usual way, so we'll have to look for where they will be grouped the old-fashioned way in order to locate Royce. Nathan and Fiona will be somewhere in the mix. Sam will be able to lead us to them."*

*"What about testing **their** gifts,"* Sam added, with a hint of resentment. It did not seem fair that he would have to suffer the pain and embarrassment of playing the victim in Francis's tests if the others in their anticipated "house-family" would not have to suffer the same fate. The blond boy's pale green eyes flashed with momentary regret before he turned away from them, looking off towards the direction in which they had been moving before they'd stopped to eat.

"The Directives say that we all have to be tested. Fiona's a Keeper. She'll be difficult to test. Her talent is not that straight forward; it is more passive than yours or Sarah's. Nathan's a Watcher. That won't be easy to test either. His is mostly passive as well and only reactive to very specific situations that will be difficult to simulate," their Teller insisted. The smaller boy did not like the sound of that. It suggested that he might once again end up the pawn in Francis's experimental game.

"What about this Royce boy?" Sam grumbled, his thoughts reflecting some of his displeasure. Francis frowned again, still not facing him.

"Controls can't be tested, and there's no need to. They aren't part of a talent-group in the same sense as the rest of us. They are different." Francis's thoughts wavered slightly in response to the notion of Royce and the other Controls. There was something about them that made Francis uncomfortable, something that he was not sharing with Sam and Sarah.

Francis was evasive again after that, and conversation dwindled. They finished their meal, packed up their new provisions, and Sam reached out to find Bryan again. After getting the expected curt response to his prodding, the small boy reestablished his lines of direction and the three set out towards the Hub again.

* _ * _ *

Sam woke up to the sound of Sarah crying – inside of course, rather than outside. Francis was still asleep, and the younger boy noted a distinct lull in the connection. Most of the people on the island would be asleep at this point in time. That meant that he and Sarah could actually talk in private. The idea intrigued Sam. He had not had any real sense of privacy since he had awoken to the screams, no matter how badly he had wanted it. Francis had said that they would have a lot to learn, and that was the primary purpose for the Gathering. Sam was hoping that this included learning some way of blocking every-one else out, and letting only those desired in.

Truthfully, Sam wanted to run as far away from the other children on the island as possible, not make a conscious effort to move towards them, the way that they had been as they had ad-vanced upon the Hub. The more distance he put between him and another Connected, the more tenuous their link.

"What's wrong?" he said quietly, reaching out to touch her mind as gently as he could manage.

"Oh...Sam. I had a dream. I dreamt that I could see again, and that Sasha was still with me. I miss those things so much. I don't like all the noise in my head. I don't like the way Francis makes me feel sometimes. I don't like all of the chang-es. Why did this happen? Why didn't things stay the way that they were?" she murmured.

"I miss Maria, too, Sarah. I miss being able to hear things. I think Francis knows a lot more about what's going on here than he believes he can tell us. I don't think that he's hold-ing out on us to be mean. I get the feeling that other people are keeping him from saying as much as he wants to, or that he's convinced that by telling us it will hurt us somehow."

Sam paused, letting his thoughts trickle out towards the blond haired boy to make sure that he was still asleep. There was only stillness there, so he continued.

"I can hear some of his thoughts sometimes, ones that he doesn't want me to hear. He was thinking something earlier that made me wonder if you and I are going to be different from the

Bigs, the ones that we'll be living with, other than just in age and size. He thought something about the Bigs being chosen for this, and about the Littles being made. I couldn't understand what he meant, but I think it was important."

"Made...why would he be thinking something like that?" Sarah whispered.

Her vacant stare looked out at the stars, and Sam felt a twinge of sympathy. He could not imagine how difficult this was for her. His issues seemed serious enough, and hers were worse.

"While you were distracted with doing your finding, he and I talked a little as well," she confessed. *"He wouldn't answer a lot of my questions. He said that we had to wait for the Gathering, that there were a lot of things that he couldn't tell me. I could hear whispers of some of the things he was trying to hide. Someone won't let him say everything he wants to say. He's not bad, Sam. He's nice. He doesn't like the things he has to do. It makes him very sad sometimes. It makes me want to help fix him. I can sense that it hurts him, and it feels wrong. The minders were involved with all this, and the other people we never knew, the ones that left before the times that you and I remember. I think Francis was almost as afraid as we are now when it happened the first time."*

Comparing notes, when there was no one else around to eavesdrop, was proving to be useful in Sam's opinion. Francis would likely look upon this conversation with disapproval and order them to stop. Sam did not like being left in the dark. Someone had chosen to mess with who they were, their way of life, and the way that they experienced their world. No one had given them any warning or bothered to ask their permission to do the things that they had done. On the other hand, someone had clearly gone to great trouble to prepare the Tellers, to brief them, to give them some idea of what to expect. It was not fair, especially considering the amount of power that the Tellers had over the other children who had been left behind on Fervor.

"There were a few other things that I picked up on while we were talking – things that still don't make sense," Sarah revealed, her sadness dissipating a little in response to the distraction that talking to Sam offered. *"He thought something about 'stasis' and he wondered how long it would take before we would be ready for 'the Coming.' I don't know which is worse, Sam – the not knowing, for us, or the knowing too much and not being able to share, for Francis."*

"Well I know I don't like feeling dumb, like we should have some idea of what's happening to us, but we don't. I hate needing Francis so much." The smaller boy did resent the older one for that element of dependency. He suspected that Sarah might feel that way even more, considering how bad off she would be without their help. It was at that moment that Francis started to stir.

"He's starting to wake up," Sarah observed softly.

"Can you make me a promise, Sarah?" Sam asked, trying to keep his thoughts quiet, so as not to awaken Francis more quickly. *"Whenever either of us wakes up like this, in the middle of the night, when almost everyone else is sleeping, we'll swear to wake up the other person so we can talk, just you and me, with no one else listening in. Are you willing to do this?"*

"Like we're special friends," she whispered, her thoughts starting to fade.

"Exactly. I think we can trust each other. I've never felt like you were trying to hide anything. That, and everyone else in the house will be Bigs. Us Littles will need to stick together. Don't you think?" he offered.

The dark-haired, dark-eyed girl extended her hand towards him, since she had a general idea where he was, and he took it as an unspoken acknowledgement of their agreement. As they both lay down to go back to sleep again, the feeling that Francis was rousing intensifying, Sam gave her hand a squeeze and closed his eyes.

* - * - *

The Hub

It was two more days of exhausting travel before Sam was finally able to stop tracking the Hub through his link in the connection to Bryan, and instead, focus his finding efforts directly on the massive building itself. It was a huge relief for the small boy to no longer have to disrupt the cantankerous youth by repeatedly making contact after any interruptions en route.

When they finally could make out the giant domed roof of the structure that they were looking for, a thrill ran through Sam, one that he purposefully shared with Sarah. He even went so far as to attempt to project the image that he was seeing to her, despite being completely unpractised with being her eyes. She told him that it was a little bit fuzzy, but for the most part quite good. Francis seemed a little uneasy at this interaction, unsettled at the pair's apparent familiarity, despite the fact that Sam and Sarah had barely spoken over the last few days. He offered Sarah a clearer view of the Hub from his own perspective, and suggested that the Littles try to help him locate Fiona and Nathan through the connection before reaching the actual physical location of the Hub.

Allowing their minds to drift through the connection there, while calling out for their two missing Connected Bigs in the chaos, was not as simple as Francis made it out to be. With the large grouping of children in the immediate area, the connection was thick with thoughts, emotions, and overall confusion. Sarah got nowhere in the pandemonium, and eventually retreated back to what she felt was a safer place, clinging to Francis in both body and mind, but Sam was feeling more adventurous and less insecure than his Fixer companion. He pushed into the middle of the crowd calling out for Fiona and Nathan. He was fairly sure that if he could touch their minds, he could start making use of his talent, and then he would be able to find them with little trouble.

As they neared the huge building, Sam's efforts finally paid off when his thoughts brushed Nathan's ever so slightly. The younger boy was not so sure if Nathan was aware of him,

25

but he latched on like glue, his instinctive desire to find the other boy kicking in instantaneously. Reaching the large double doorway in the entry lounge, he ran into the next crowd beyond, disappearing from view and leaving Francis and Sarah wading in behind him.

"Nathan! Nathan!" Sam called through the loud cacophony that was the connection within the Hub, vaguely reminiscent of the completely disorienting sensation of everyone screaming at once when he had first awoken.

Sam pushed past all of the other minds that huddled in his way. He was feeling dizzy, like he was losing himself in the constant thrum that surrounded him in his head. His heart pounded as he paused, now starting to wonder if there was a physical threat to being in the middle of the throng. People pushed and shoved, many of them searching for someone the same way that he was. Subject to a particularly severe jostle, the small boy suddenly found himself on his knees and in serious jeopardy of being trampled underfoot. That was when a meaty hand settled on his shoulder and pulled him back onto his feet. The same hand then grabbed him by the wrist and dragged him off to one side.

Sam looked the boy who had intervened on his behalf in the eye. He was more than half again as tall as the younger boy, and from all appearances, twice as broad. His eyes were a smoky blue colour, his nose slightly crooked and when he smiled one side of his face lifted a little higher than the other. His square-jawed head was topped with coarse, brown hair that stuck up in various places, as unruly as Sam's was, only thicker and darker.

"You were looking for me, little buddy?"

Sam noted that the larger boy had made no attempt to speak to him with his mouth as well as his thoughts, unlike the majority of the people that milled about them. Nathan had already become accustomed to using the connection as his primary method of communication. That seemed a little surprising to Sam, because this Big, while having a push that offered slightly

26

more force than Francis, nowhere near matched Sarah in his potential for power.

Sam felt something warm trickle across his arm and glanced down to see a rather jagged cut on the hand that gripped him, an open one that was dripping blood. He raised his eyes to the other boy's again.

"Nathan? Francis said we needed to find you and Fiona, so I had to look. What did you do to your hand? We should get you back to Sarah. She can fix that, you know." Sam insisted.

The larger boy gazed at both his hands nonchalantly, and then realized exactly what it was that Sam was referring to. He looked at the cut and frowned.

"When did I do that?" he muttered, more so to himself than to Sam. The smaller boy regarded him with bewilderment.

"I can't feel it," Nathan explained. *"Just like this one."* He rolled up his sleeve to reveal a blistered burn on his forearm that was oozing a clear liquid. *"Or this one."* He rolled up his other sleeve to expose a deep gash lined with a newly forming layer of pus. *"I tried to get a hover going, and I almost had it, too. Then it started to overheat, and, well..."*

Sam contemplated the situation as he led his newest companion back to Sarah and Francis. He was sure that it was not just a coincidence – there was a pattern. Sarah was missing her sight, Sam his hearing, and it was clear now that what Nathan had lost was his sense of touch. As they reached the other members of their "house-family" as Francis had put it, and Sarah began to fix Nathan. Sam eyed the Teller warily.

"So what are you missing then? Taste or smell? You have it pretty easy, don't you, compared to us. What, did they decide that a Teller was too valuable to lose a sense that really mattered?" Sam pushed accusingly. *"Why did they do this to us? You know, don't you?"*

"Smell," Francis admitted, his eyes downcast, and his thoughts and expression filled with that customary melancholy. *"But it's not what you think. You have it backwards. I don't*

27

need to be as strong as you do. Neither does Fiona." He braced himself mentally, shaking off the guilt that Sam had thrown his way and refocused his attention to the things he was supposed to be dealing with at the moment. *"Nathan will be fine. You've only accomplished half of what you need to do here. Go find Fiona."*

Sam gritted his teeth and wished that he were the same size as the blond boy so that he could slug him at that moment, without fear of repercussion, but he doubted he could resist the urge to look for the older girl long enough to make physical contact anyway. His mind immediately returned to the clustering of thoughts within the Hub.

Sam was beginning to understand why it had been simple to find Sarah at the start, and why Nathan had been easiest to find of the two that he had been searching for there at the Hub. The Bigs had weaker links to the connection, with Nathan being the strongest so far. Having that in mind, the small boy directed his thoughts towards something vaguer, something flimsier than what he had found when his mind touched on his other companions.

"Fiona!" he called through the connection, but this time he was hunting for something much different, and having a better idea of what it was that he was looking for made his task that much easier. Unlike Nathan's presence, which had been almost as solid as Sam's own, Fiona's was more like a shadow in the mix, weaker and less substantial. She did not reach out for him in return until he was almost on top of her.

"I'm here," she finally responded, as Sam clambered his way through the obstacle course of gathered minds. He prodded at the faint link that he found there and then latched on to it with equal enthusiasm as he had to Nathan. She was not working her way through the crowd the way the broadly-built boy had been, and Sam had the better sense to skirt the shifting throng this time, not wanting to face the danger of being trampled again.

Once they had made that connection, Sam felt a little more desperate to physically find the older girl than he had Sarah or Nathan. Fiona was not just sad or fearful – she was absolutely heart-sick, like someone had stolen everything from her and had given her very little in return. He had a feeling that she had been rather affixed to the life that she had been living. She had been happy with her family; she was one of the more popular children at school. She had been very satisfied with the way that things were, and he did not feel like she had gained anything truly positive from this change, so hers seemed like an unrewarded sacrifice.

Sam finally arrived beside her and grabbed her hand before she could drift away from him again. He noticed the skin was exceptionally soft and her nails carefully trimmed and filed, not like any of the others. It brought a twinge of loss to his heart, reminding him a little of Maria.

"Here," he said letting his mind push at hers fairly firmly. *"I'm here. I'm Sam. Let me take you back to the others."*

The pretty girl turned to look at him, her expression morose. She was as robust as Sarah was waif-like. Her rounded cheeks were slightly freckled with a rosy glow, and the skin of her face looked as soft and flawless as her hands had been. Her hair hung in long chestnut waves over her shoulders and her eyes were a warm brown with a hint of green at their centres. She was shorter than Nathan, but about the same height as Francis, so a little on the tall side for a girl, Sam would guess. That was assuming that she was about the same age as the other two Bigs.

"What's going on here, Sam? It doesn't make any sense. Martha was gone, and she never came back. Then my brothers told me that I had to come here, and as soon as we made it here they left me. They told me that someone else would come looking for me. They must have meant you."

Sam noted that she was not really trying to communicate with him through the connection. Her mouth moved, as her eyes flashed with panic, but the words that he picked up in her mind were merely an echo of what she has trying to tell him with her physical voice, which he could not hear. She was not making any effort to push at him at all. She was resistant to everything that was happening, still in denial and unwilling to accept the changes.

"Let me take you back to Francis. I think he'll be able to offer you more than I can. He can help you sort it out," Sam offered.

He was more than happy to burden Francis with this responsibility. Sarah and Nathan had been so much more accepting of their situation, despite being as distressed by it as Sam was. Fiona had had several days to let go of the notion that things could go back to what she considered to be normal and adapt to her new circumstances, but she had not. Sam would eventually discover that this was part and parcel with her being a Keeper.

The crowd in the Hub was thinning a little now. The house-families were gathering their members, as dictated by their Tellers, and moving off to one side in small groups. Sam led Fiona back to his own companions and noticed that there was another boy there, almost as tall as Nathan, with black hair and plain brown eyes. The look that this new boy gave Sam was a little menacing, but it was not nearly as unsettling as the other unusual detail about this boy. When Sam reached out to greet him through the connection, the stranger was not there.

While this large boy seemed to direct his attention towards Sam, Francis and Nathan were much more interested in Sam's newest find. Both of the Bigs extended a quiet thought to welcome Fiona, and Sarah, prompted by their responses, followed suit.

"Ah," Francis remarked with a subtle smile, speaking with his mouth as well as his mind in order to include Royce in the conversation. *"This must be our Keeper, Fiona. Sam, this is our Control, Royce. Get to know one another, because these people are your family now. There are no more minders and no more teachers, and from now on, we'll have to rely on one another."* His gaze specifically settled on Royce and Nathan.

"Remember that the next time you are tempted to mistreat any of those that you'll be living with. I am Francis, your Teller. Welcome, all of you, to the Gathering."

THE GATHERING

Now that all of the children that had come to the Hub had settled into organized chaos, the Tellers began directing their groups to various points in the communal hall. As was to be expected, there was no resistance to their commands except for in the case of a couple of the Controls, since those Bigs were not subject to the Tellers' special influence.

Royce, while quiet and stern-looking, did not offer objection to his Teller's orders. He did not look pleased to be there, however, and had not smiled yet, Sam noted. In fact, if the smaller boy had to wager a guess, he fell under the distinction of Royce's least preferred member of their house-family. He was not sure if it was for any reason in particular, such as their inability to communicate without someone else's help, or if there were more to it than that. Sam just knew that, every time his eyes met Royce's, he could see the suggestion of animosity there.

Francis brought his companions over to a flag post that read "thirty-two". Nathan eyed it with curiosity.

"That's our house number," the Teller explained. *"We are only one of fifty house-families. There are three hundred of us on this island, and we have been grouped into house-families of six – one of each talent-group per family."*

"One of each talent-group plus a Control, you mean," Sam remarked, remembering Francis's earlier comments.

"Sam," Sarah hissed softly, giving him a little push. *"You shouldn't be excluding Royce, just because he's not like us."*

"They may not have a gift the way that we do, Sam, but they are still considered a talent-group. I said that they are not part of a talent-group in the same way that we are," Francis replied, using only his mind and not his mouth. The blond boy obviously had chosen to leave Royce out of that part of the conversation just as Sarah had, not wanting to spur the antagonism that their Control seemed to feel toward the smaller boy any further. *"They can still do things that we can't do. They can keep their thoughts private from everyone, not just other Controls. They won't yield to a Teller's promptings unless they choose to, which means they can mediate in any dispute between Tellers and others, and if the connection ever gets too chaotic, like it did when everyone woke up that first morning, and all of the Connected become disoriented by it, it will be up to the Controls to keep things regulated."*

Then it was there again, that quiet little voice inside of Francis's head that he clearly had not anticipated Sam hearing. *"That's the theory, anyway. And the Controls know everything that the Tellers do, in case it ever matters."*

"So we all have our purpose – we all have a knack," Nathan acknowledged. *"All six of us are expected to live together, and learn together, for some strange reason. Are you going to tell us why all of this is happening?"* Again, he spoke only through the connection, but Sam was pretty sure that it was not purposefully to exclude Royce. Sam did note that Royce appeared irked if he sensed that he was missing part of what was being said, as meaningful glances passed amongst those who were Connected. He felt left out. Sam could understand that feeling.

"I can't," Francis said, both inside and out. Those who heard him through the connection knew that he was being truthful. *"There's only so much that I can give you, information-wise. I have to follow instructions – you all know that by now."*

The Teller glanced over at Royce and Sam thought he detected nervousness from the blond boy.

"I thought we were here to learn," Sarah mumbled.

"You are here to learn. You're here to learn about the connection, and how to build walls, so that you can block people out of your thoughts when you want to. You're also here to discover how to set up a door amidst those walls so you can get back out to the connection, and let people in when you need to. You'll find out how to knock once others have their walls and doors set up, so you can let someone else know that you want in, and you'll learn how to push as hard as you can, to break through that door, to be used only in the case of an emergency, when there isn't time to knock and wait for a response. You'll get the chance to practice a little before we leave here, but don't even start to think that you'll manage to perfect these things before we go. It will take a lot of time and a lot of practice," their Teller insisted.

"Years," came the secondary voice that Sam was picking up on. *"It will take years."*

More thoughts that Francis had intended to keep behind his "walls", Sam considered, keeping his own thoughts quiet. Apparently, those walls weren't quite as sound-proof as Francis had believed them to be.

"It would seem that it's going to take longer than years," Sam stated, before catching himself. Three of his five house-family mates turned to look at him, startled, Francis included. The blond boy blushed.

"What did Sam mean by that, Francis?" Nathan demanded. *"How long is this, whatever this is, going to last? Are we stuck here like this for good? What happens as we get older?"*

"It's like we're in prison," Fiona sighed. *"I'm the captive and you five are my cellmates."* She glanced over at Francis, rethinking her statement. *"Well, four cellmates and one warden."*

35

Sam had not intended to start any conflict. It had been
entirely by accident. He felt the other minds about him stirring
anxiously as well. There was friction building amongst the other
groups, too, and it was rising in volume, like some irritating
buzz within the connection. That was when he felt himself
physically being lifted off his feet, by his collar. Everyone in his
group who was Connected had stopped what they were doing,
and all but Sarah were now staring at him.

"Make that two wardens. Royce told us to quit the 'in-
side only' talk, little buddy," Nathan explained solemnly, since
Sam was still unaware of exactly what was going on behind him.
"He said that we have to stop keeping stuff from him, and let
him in on things. I don't think that he likes any of us, but he
seems to have it out for you, especially. He said that he could
see that you were going to be trouble from the first time that he
laid eyes on you. I don't think that I like him, either."

That was when Nathan spoke out loud for the first time
since they had met, his spoken thoughts also echoed in the connection.

"P-p-put him d-d-down, R-Royce," the broadly-built boy
stammered. He moved forward, raising his fists.

"Yes," Francis agreed. *"Put him down. No need for that*
– it's okay, Nathan. We'll settle this civilly for now. We have to
stop excluding Royce from conversations. If my walls still aren't
quite working right, then I needed to know that, and Sam just
gave me that opportunity. To make things easier, why don't I
head off any other questions that I can before we start. First,
Sam is correct. I've been working on improving my tools to use
with the connection for two years, and I clearly haven't perfect-
ed them yet. Then again, I was training with other Tellers, who
aren't nearly as strong in their link with the connection as Sam
and the other Littles. What has proven to be sufficient to keep
other Tellers out obviously isn't enough to block Sam. That's
some valuable information that the other Tellers will want to
know."

Now it was Fiona's turn to react in a less than pleasant fashion. *"Two years! You Tellers have known about this for two years, and no one told the rest of us? The minders – the teachers, they all knew and they didn't warn us? Why didn't anyone bother to prepare us? They obviously went to the trouble of preparing you. Why not give the rest of us the same treatment? For that matter, why just up and leave us the way that they did?"*

Sam still dangled from Royce's angry grip. As intimidated as he was by the larger boy, he did not allow that to stop him from saying his peace. After all, the Control was only aware of part of the conversation. *"The Tellers weren't the only ones who were prepared – briefed on these Directives that Francis keeps talking about. The Controls were, too."*

"Sam, stop," Sarah warned meekly. *"Don't say too much. You're going to get Francis in trouble. You are going to get us all in trouble."*

Sam suspected she knew more now than he did. They would have to talk privately again later, if they got the chance.

He felt the boy who held him tense, becoming more aggravated as the discussion progressed without allowing him to listen in on everything. Sam could not actually observe Royce's reaction, but he could see Nathan's face reddening and his knuckles whitening.

"I said p-put him d-down. Now!" Nathan snarled.

"Nathan, calm yourself. Fiona, you settle down, too. Sam, Sarah, I don't want you speaking again until I ask you to, directly," Francis ordered, his thoughts weighing them down like a heavy blanket. Nathan relaxed immediately, allowing his hands to drop to his sides and his frown fading. Fiona stopped looking distressed and took a deep breath.

"This is messy enough as is, and I won't be able to stop Royce if it becomes necessary. This is part of why we are here. This is an example of what you have to learn to live with. You have to be tolerant of those who can't do what you can do. You have to learn some self-discipline, and some self-restraint."

Francis shook his head and rubbed at his temples, the strain of the moment fairly evident.

Sam craned his neck to look at the taller boy behind who still kept him suspended in mid-air. Royce was wearing a smug smile. He was well aware of what Francis could do – of what the Teller had just done. He was also aware of the advantage that being immune to Francis's influence gave him. With a forceful shake for good measure, he lowered Sam back to the floor. Then he stepped back and crossed his arms, his expression unchanged.

Francis sighed.

"The important thing right now isn't to argue about what led us to this point or why. What we have to focus on is the best way to handle it. We will all have to learn to get along, despite our differences. We all have to figure out how to make the best use of our talents, and those of us who are Connected have to start working on our controls. It's all in the Directives. Royce understands. If I have to, I'll make you understand, too. Do you get what I'm saying?"

Francis was hiding it well on the outside, but his attempts to shield the fact that he really did not want to have to make these kinds of statements was rather transparent within the connection, even to the less perceptive Fiona. Sam suspected that the display was to placate Royce, and for no other reason.

After Sarah had finished fixing Nathan, the small group joined the other forty-nine house-families closer to the front of the main hall. Nathan placed a firm hand on Sam's shoulder as they walked together, while making sure that Royce kept his distance.

"Stay here," Francis directed. *"I'll be back. I have to help with this."*

There was a stage at the front of the communal hall, and all of the Tellers were making their way there, leaving their groups for some unknown purpose. Sam realized he felt even more nervous with Francis gone, despite Nathan's reassuring presence. The blond boy had been with him since all of this had first started, and he was the only one in their house-family whom he trusted at all who had any real idea what was going on. Royce had some of that knowledge, but to Sam he was an unyielding and teetering brick wall, threatening to fall on him at any moment. Sam could not feel him there; he could not talk to him in any way, and for some reason the larger boy already hated him.

Sam was relieved that he had Nathan at his back, or he was fairly certain he would have been crying again at that moment. He wanted desperately to charge after Francis and as far away from Royce as he could get.

That was when things got even more interesting, as all fifty Tellers who had clustered on the stage began to speak, both inside and out, at the same time.

"The first purpose of this Gathering is to provide you with the Rules as set out by the Directives. You will listen, and you will obey them," they said in unison.

If Francis's commands had been a heavy blanket, this combined effort was like an avalanche, overwhelming and suffocating. This was the primary reason for the Gathering, Sam decided. They were here to have their wills properly subjugated, the rules so firmly embedded in their psyches that Francis would not have to struggle to enforce them. Of course, that would only apply to the Connected. The small boy glanced over at Royce. As if things weren't bad enough already, here was another problem presenting itself. Sam would be bound irrevocably to the rules, whereas Royce would not. Sam shuddered at this thought.

"Rule number one of the Directives is fairly simple. You will respect the order of things as set out by the Directives, including acceptance of your place within your talent-group and your house-family. Your responsibility as a talent supersedes your obligation to your house-family. If there is any question as to how you should respond to a particular situation based on the Directives, you are to ask your Teller, who will brief you on the matter," the Tellers instructed.

"What does that mean?" Sarah asked. A similar response from others echoed through the connection.

"It means that we have to do as we're told, that Francis is the boss, and that if we don't know how things work, we have to ask him," Fiona responded, not trying to hide her annoyance.

"It means that you're a Fixer first and a part of our family second," Nathan added. Sam had been planning to add his own response, but the growing buzz within the connection was starting to become debilitating and he leaned back against Nathan, his head spinning. There were multiple protests, expressions of fear and worry, some outbursts of anger and some lamentations. Not everyone within the connection was reacting to what they were being told in the same way, there was even some nonplussed acceptance and disinterested apathy in the mix, but while there was an extreme overall emotional response to the Tellers' words, there was one thing definitely not there. There was no actual resistance.

The Tellers waited for the chaos in the connection to settle before starting in on their next rule.

"Rule number two relates to the things that were left behind by the minders and the teachers, and all of the buildings that are not family-houses. The only people permitted to enter these buildings or handle those items that require magic that you have not been trained to use are the Keepers. That is part of their purpose, to maintain these things for possible future use."

Another wave of shock and confusion ran through the connection. Sam and Nathan had already broken this rule unwittingly, and Sam was startled at the realization that Francis had not corrected him – had even encouraged him at the time. Of course, he had entered the storehouse out of necessity, and Fiona had not been with him when he had gone in, in search of food. He suspected based on the general reaction out there, that they had not been the only ones.

"But what if I need to find things...?" Sam questioned.

"I think once you know where they are, you'll have to depend on Fiona to get them for us from now on. That is, if they're not out in the open," Sarah offered quietly.

"Great," Sam grumbled. He had been thinking he had a valuable gift, but now it seemed less significant. He didn't like the idea of enforced co-dependency, be it in the form of having Fiona play fetcher to his finding, or having to rely on Nathan for protection from Royce.

"Rule number three, once everyone has their controls for the connection in place, you will always knock before proceeding into someone else's space. You will only be permitted to push though without knocking if there is an emergency. The Directives outline what qualifies as an emergency. Your Teller will brief you on that. We know that this may seem difficult to believe, but we understand your need for privacy, and that need will be respected. All of these rules will apply to the Tellers just as they apply to everyone else," the Tellers continued.

The connection had now become uncomfortably quiet, and Sam could not help but wonder who had really organized all of this and why, especially if the Tellers had to live by the same rules as everyone else did. Who would steal away their normalcy and throw them into this bizarre, adult-less chaos, and why?

"And we feel it important to let you know that the laws of the island still apply. Just because the minders and the teachers are gone, doesn't mean that you can behave however you choose. Those laws will be enforced," the Tellers affirmed. They did not explain how, or by whom, but the children trusted enough in the truth of the connection that they did not doubt them.

"Your Tellers will now return to you. They will provide you with the basics on how to develop the tools that you will need to deal with the connection, and after you feel sufficiently prepared, you may fetch the keys and directions to your family-house and make your way there. When we are satisfied that you have the proper controls in place, other changes will come.

Until then, play the part of your designated role within your talent group, practice your controls, and try to live harmoniously with the other members of your house-family. Make your gifts and the connection work for you. If you want more information then that is the first step that you must take." That seemed to bring an end to their commands as a group.

Sam felt a rush of relief as he saw the Tellers begin to disperse, and then caught sight of Francis returning to them through the crowd. For some reason, he felt as though the blond boy were his only real link between the present and the past.

Francis led the five of them to a quieter spot at the back of the hall, and then proceeded to show them the basics of blocking others out of their thoughts – all of them but Royce, that is. The black haired boy watched them impatiently, wearing a disgruntled expression as he paced and fidgeted. More than once Sam turned to find Royce's eyes glued to him with an intensity and a bitterness that Sam just could not comprehend. It was distracting, and made a difficult task even more difficult.

By the end of Francis's little introductory session, Sam could manage walls that were as effective as tissue paper, when they would stay up at all, and the others were not faring any better. He could see why after two years of practice, with his more limited strength, Francis had only succeeded in reinforcing his walls to the equivalent of mental pressboard. It was going to take a lot of practice – a proper investment of time and effort. On the other hand, Sam suspected that the newly Connected would have more incentive than the Tellers had to put up their walls. If Sam had it figured correctly, with only fifty fairly weak Tellers making up the connection to begin with, all of whom having at least an inkling of what was going on, it would not have been nearly as noisy in their heads as it currently was in his. He figured if he could concentrate more than he was able to at the moment, it would have made things a lot easier.

"That's all that I can show you for now," Francis insisted. *"It's up to you to practice, and work at developing them more so that they really work. Once you can effectively block*

out the others, then I'll show you how to make a door to let them in again when you want to. You'll all have to learn how to knock, too, and push in emergencies, just like the Directives instruct."

"And you know how to do all of these things?" Fiona asked.

"In theory, and I have been practicing, but as you are all aware now, I'm still not perfect either. Now come on, let's go get our keys and head for home. We'll be right on the coast, so I'm afraid it's going to be a long trip. Until we get close enough, we have to look for it the old fashion way. There's no one waiting for us there to guide our Finder," the Teller advised.

The five others followed him to the designated area where the things that they needed to get them into their new home were located. Then they allowed their Teller to lead them away, feeling as lost as ever.

* _ * _ *

Sam awoke groggily to gentle shaking and a familiar whisper in his head. They had been forced to sleep outside, still days away from their house. It was a little cool out, but least it had not been raining.

"Wake up, Sam. Remember our promise – special friends? There's so much to talk about. I made sure the others were all asleep. Then I had to make sure that I found you and wasn't trying to shake someone else awake. I'm still not used to not being able to see. It's really difficult to tell the difference between people by touch alone. If you weren't smaller than everyone else, I'm not sure that I would have gotten it right."

"Sarah?"

Shrugging away his drowsiness, Sam glanced up at his small friend, who was kneeling next to him with her hand on his arm. He tentatively reached out through the connection to make sure that she wasn't mistaken. She was right – Nathan, Francis, and Fiona were all unavailable.

"What about Royce?"

"I'm not sure which one of the others is him, but even if he's awake, at least he won't be able to hear us. I'll lie down right here. If we keep our eyes closed, he won't be able to tell that we're awake," the wisp of a girl replied softly.

"He doesn't like me," Sam sighed inside as he lay back and shut his eyes again. *"In fact, I think he hates me. I don't know why. I haven't been able to talk to him. I don't know how I could have offended him."*

"I think that I know why," Sarah confessed. Sam enjoyed talking to her through the connection, all alone like this. Even though she had such strength, her thoughts were always so gentle. Sort of like an elephant tiptoeing through the jungle.

"You were distracted at the time, but I wasn't, and I could hear all of their inside thoughts – the deep ones that were supposed to be hidden. Even from Francis. He was thinking that Royce was jealous, that he blamed you for him being a Control, and not one of the Connected. Apparently, until they decided that they wanted the Controls, until they actually made the Littles to fill the gaps, Royce was supposed to be a Finder. Francis believes that Royce sees it as your fault that he is as deaf to the connection as you are to the rest of the world. Francis is worried that he's going to try and take that out on you somehow, especially after what happened at the Gathering today."

"Oh," was all that Sam could manage in response to this, as his stomach churned and his heart rate elevated.

This was nothing that he had actually done, nor was there anything that he could possibly change to mend fences with the black-haired boy. It was all a matter of perspective, Royce's perspective, and not even Francis had the ability to influence that. It wasn't even the case of Royce being a typical bully. The Control was under the impression that he had good reason to despise Sam, and perhaps all of the Littles. There was resentment there.   It was not some minor insecurity that could be erased with an offer of goodwill, and Sam wondered if all the Controls shared Royce's point of view.

"I'm sorry, Sam. I wish that I could fix this, but I can't," Sarah murmured in his mind. *"To be honest with you, I think that Francis is scared, even if he hides it well. He was expecting some irritation, but he didn't think that Royce would be this hostile about it. Francis knows that if Royce chooses to ignore the rules, there's nothing that he can do about it. The ones who left the Directives had a solution in case the Tellers abused their power, that's one of the reasons why they created the Controls in the first place, but who is there to handle the Controls if they don't stick to the plan?"*

"At least Nathan seems to be on my side," Sam mumbled.

"He won't always be able to watch out for you," Sarah warned. *"He has his own needs, just as we have. You need to find, I need to fix and he needs to watch, but it won't always be you that he's watching. I'm guessing, from what I got from Francis, that he has a specific area he has to cover. He's not just watching for our sake – he's watching for them, the ones who came up with the Directives, and the ones who set this all up. Francis was thinking that while you were looking for Nathan."*

"He said that it would be hard to test his gift. Maybe that's why. If it's something he just does, maybe there aren't a lot of ways to tell if he's actually doing it, just like with Fiona."

"She may be hiding it better, but she seems to be almost as angry as Royce is, and she blames Francis for her troubles. She wants everything back the way that it was, and I don't think anyone's going to be able to change her mind about that. She doesn't like either of us, but at least she doesn't hold us at fault. She doesn't actually hate us, but she believes that she's going to be expected to play the part of substitute minder for us, and she's not happy about that. She considers us a nuisance," Sarah

explained, trying to keep her thoughts quiet, and directed completely at Sam.

"You heard all of this through the connection – these things that I wasn't aware of, these things that they didn't want you to know?"

Sam was starting to understand how poor Royce felt. He had been convinced that the small glimpses he had gotten on occasion from the others, the ones that they had been hoping would remain secret, were something that had given him an edge, but he'd had to be particularly attentive and listen very carefully to pick up on those inner most thoughts. He also had to be extra careful when considering those thoughts, or others in turn would know that he had heard them. From the sounds of it, the other Little in his house-family could access these secreted ideas much more easily than he could. Then again, Sarah had always felt that much stronger than him.

"Like I said, you were distracted, either looking for Nathan and Fiona, or being interfered with by Royce," she assured him. *"I've noticed how it works. If you are panicky, or focussed on something that takes extra concentration, then you can't hear the mind whispers over your own louder thoughts. Once everyone has their walls set up properly, we probably won't be able to hear them at all anymore."*

Suddenly she went quiet. After a few seconds of feeling around in the connection to see if the others were awake, and finding nothing, Sam realised that something was wrong. He had felt a slight vibration in the ground upon which he lay.

Sam opened his eyes. Royce was standing over him, and was giving him a menacing glare. It intimidated Sam as much as Royce had intended it to and Sam reached out and mentally nudged Nathan, who stirred almost immediately. The Watcher sat up, rubbing at his eyes.

"G-go back to b-bed, Royce," the broad-shouldered boy muttered quietly. Sam saw the black-haired boy's lips move, but had no idea what he had said in response. He was grateful, however, to see Royce return to the place where he had been sleeping.

Sarah touched Sam's mind one last time before returning to sleep. It was a sad whisper.

"Royce said he thought he heard a rat."

Sam shuddered, and was ready to try to fight off his anxiety and attempt sleep again himself, when he noticed some movement. Nathan rose and shifted much closer to him, on the side opposite to Sarah. Sandwiched between the two of them, Sam felt surprisingly secure, despite the fact that Royce lay only a few feet away. Exhaling softly, and brushing both of their minds with the gentleness of a feather, he closed his eyes and went back to sleep.

NEW ROUTINES

The house was not anything special, in Sam's opinion. It was much like any other house on Fervor, dull-coloured and featureless, only three times bigger than what he was used to. There was no disputing who got what room, since nobody really cared. They all settled in, got used to their surroundings, and eventually, they all fell into a routine, as per Francis's directions.

Sarah tended to keep to the house, still unaccustomed to functioning with her blindness. If she wanted to go out she needed someone to accompany her, and mostly relied on Francis or Nathan to be her eyes. She would fix anything that was brought to her, for the most part items found by Sam or retrieved by Fiona, and she also fixed any injuries for the people in the house, more commonly Nathan than anyone else. His lack of sensory input from touch often led to small scrapes and cuts that he wasn't aware of. And every time he returned from his outings, Sarah would have to check him over carefully to make sure that he had not done himself any serious damage that might result in infection if not fixed.

Sometimes Sam would observe these little fixing sessions and felt envious of the attention Nathan was receiving. Maria had been a fairly affectionate minder, prone to hugs and cuddles, and he missed that human contact more than anything else. Of course, he realized that Nathan was not actually feeling Sarah's tiny hands brushing over his skin, so wishing that he could switch places was kind of pointless for Sam. The only thing that Nathan seemed to acknowledge was firm pressure. Besides, Sam had seen a couple of the more nasty gouges that Nathan had unwittingly come home with, and that much he did not want. Not being able to hear was not that bad in comparison.

Sometimes, Sarah would glance Sam's way, aware that he was there even though she could not see him. She'd had more time to practice her skills with the connection, and she had been stronger than everyone else to begin with. A couple of months in, and her walls were almost as strong as Francis's had been in the beginning. She was also getting much better at using other people's images projected through the connection as her eyes.

As her confidence grew, and her feeling of purpose as a Fixer developed, her sadness in response to all of the changes was fading, although her timidity did not. She had not been as close to her minder as Sam had been to his. She had also been growing stronger bonds with the Bigs in the house than Sam had managed. Fiona saw her skills as useful, and for the most part Sarah kept out of the older girl's hair, so the Keeper considered her more of a help than a hindrance. Francis was using Sarah's assistance to strengthen his own connection tools since she was the most capable of the five of them to get around any blocks that he put up. Seeing if she could get past them was the best test that he had to check on how well that they were working. All but Royce was invested in some way in their Fixer – since she could not help him.

Fiona was also a bit of a homebody, but for different reasons. She was the only one of them who could make any of the more complex appliances work, and as much as she had seemed reluctant to do so in the beginning, she settled into a role similar to that of the minders after only a couple of weeks. Sam was starting to relate to the older girl better as well. She was often a necessary component in his finding if his searches took him to one of the abandoned buildings on the island. They would often talk on those occasions, and Sam thought he was starting to grow on Fiona. He would even have guessed that she was starting to consider him a friend.

Fiona fussed over Nathan much more than she ever did anyone else, but Sam attributed this to the same issues that prompted Sarah's attentions, the fact that he often came home looking tattered around the edges. Nathan was fairly nonchalant about the whole thing. He was an easy going boy, and fairly pleasant natured. He tolerated her ministrations with his endearing lop-sided smile, despite the fact that if Royce were present he would tease Nathan about being "Keeper's pet", and if Francis were around he would give him a mocking stare.

Unlike her response to the Littles and Nathan, Fiona seemed to go out of her way to avoid Royce and Francis. Sam knew that it was because she still bore a grudge against the two older boys. They had known about the coming of the second exodus and the introduction of the remainder of the children of Fervor to the connection, and they had tolerated the fact that it would come as a traumatic surprise to everyone but the Tellers and the Controls.

Royce did not seem to care much that Fiona felt this way since he spent little time at the house and generally kept to himself when he was there. In fact, Royce did not seem to care much about anything at all. Francis, on the other hand, found her persistent disapproval disturbing. He spent as much time in their home as Fiona did and, much to his displeasure, he found himself resorting to having to order Fiona to do things more than he did with anyone else. Everything she did for Francis, she did begrudgingly, and Sam knew that this made the Teller very uncomfortable. In fact, the more she spurned him, the more Francis seemed to want to try to find some other way of pleasing her, like some forlorn puppy trying to please its master. Sam felt bad for the Teller. He knew that Francis always had good intentions, and felt trapped between a rock and a hard place. Sarah knew that, too, so they both tried to be extra nice to their Teller to make up for the way that Fiona treated him.

Francis was a secretive person, and while he did associate with the others much more than Royce did, he also spent a lot of his time avoiding them as well, particularly on those days when he came across as seeming more melancholic. He did occasionally leave the house for short stretches at a time, too, but he did not head out on daily outings like Sam, Nathan and Royce. Francis had meetings with the other Tellers once every few months.

Sam hated those times the most, because that left Royce in charge of the house. The smaller boy made a point of following Nathan on his rounds on those days, when he could. Sometimes it was difficult to do if his own obligations to the house-family took him in a completely different direction. After all, it was up to the Finder to make sure they had enough food, clothing, and any other supplies that they happened to need. If there were nothing specific that he was required to look for, he was expected to see if he could find something that would in some way improve their current lifestyle.

That was something that Sam actually liked about his gift. His life was now something of an adventure; his searches taking him to places he had never been before on Fervor. It let him lead a fairly solitary existence, and Sam was quite happy with that. If he had not been directed to find something specific, he would often spend his days scouring the beach or tracking through the backwoods, looking for anything new and spectacular that he might be able to bring home to his house-family. On those days, he often came home empty-handed and somewhat disappointed. But on other rare days, he would stumble upon something unanticipated, like a small cabin filled with canned goods that offered more variety than the storehouses' usual fare, and he would become the temporary hero, once Fiona had helped him retrieve his find and everyone was in the process of enjoying it.

He liked those days best, when they would be sitting around their kitchen happily and talking like a real family – not that Sam had ever known what a real family was like. Nathan would reach over and muss his hair, Sarah and Fiona would smile in his general direction, and Francis would give him the occasional approving look. Even Royce seemed to hate him a little less on those days.

Aside from that, the Control's antagonism towards him had not seemed to ease off at all as Sam hoped that it might with time. If anything, it appeared to get worse as the days passed. On a better note, Sam did not have to tolerate his cold hard stares and occasional, although no doubt purposeful, jostling as often as he used to. Royce made himself scarce on a regular basis, and Sam had to wonder why and where the black-haired boy was going. Then again, Sam was not clear on what the Control's full purpose was exactly. There had been no reason so far for him to step in and mediate between Francis and any of the others.

Francis was in no way heavy handed, and as far as Sam could tell, the Teller had not made any attempt to abuse his power. He seemed to respect everyone, and if anything, he appeared to dislike the sway that he had over the others. He certainly was loath to use it, and Sam could tell that Francis felt guilty, or perhaps ashamed, when he was forced to actually tell someone to do something because they were hesitant to stick to the Directives. Sam was thankful that he had not found himself in the Teller's shoes.

Of everyone in the house, Francis was the one who displayed the greatest sense of unhappiness because of his position. He had a natural charisma to him, which might have been why he had been chosen to be a Teller, if they had been selected partially based on personality, Sam surmised. But Francis also displayed the symptoms of a more fragile ego than his housemates – and a stronger tie to his conscience – which Sam assumed was why he seemed to sink into a quiet misery on a regular basis. Their situation appeared to be harder on Francis than on everyone else, when it should have perhaps been the easiest. He was missing almost nothing as far as sensory stimuli went, he had a link with the connection, unlike Royce, and he had an enviable gift. On top of it all, he had some idea of what exactly was going on, even though he could not share it.

By their third month together the six children had fallen into their new routines. There was no more school, but they had other obligations, and Francis spent part of the day teaching them what he could. On that particular morning, Royce and Nathan had already left. Sam was about to head out when Fiona informed him she needed supplies from the storehouse and that she wanted his help fetching them. With a shrug, the small boy agreed. They left Sarah with Francis and headed out together.

As they walked, Sam worked at his walls. He spent all of his free time trying to build on them, but they were still fairly weak and they fell easily to Sarah's most powerful pushes. Fiona still had the courtesy to push gently before speaking to him since Francis had not yet instructed them on doors and knocking, giving the smaller boy the opportunity to drop them rather than have her push her way through them.

"Are you getting used to all of this?" she asked him quietly.

"Starting to," he answered. *"I still miss Maria. I even miss school, and Royce scares me."*

"Nathan won't let him hurt you," Fiona assured him.

"He won't if he can help it. It feels like Nathan really is family, like he's my minder in some ways, but he isn't always around. Like right now, I could walk around the next corner and find Royce there. If he wanted to take his anger out on me, it's not like you could stop him."

"Why...because I'm a girl?" Fiona thought, with a hint of disgust. *"Nathan may be able to out-muscle Royce, but I have my own ways of dealing with him. You have a lot to learn, little boy. You only learned what the minders and teachers chose for you to know. They left out a lot, believe me. Like a real family? To you, a real family is a minder and one or more children. That's not a real family, Sam. You've never experienced one of those. Most of the children on this island either never did, or they don't remember what it's like. The only ones*

who could possibly recall what proper life was like are the Bigs, and for the most part, their mind doesn't allow them to go that far back. I'm one of the exceptions. We weren't supposed to remember, you know. We were too little ourselves at the time. They did that on purpose, I think, because they wanted us to be too young to remember. I was only two when they brought us over to Fervor. I remember anyway. The place that they brought us from, most children had parents, a mother and a father, and some children had siblings, brothers and sisters. I had parents, too, but something bad had happened to them. That's why I ended up with the people who brought us to Fervor. They did some testing on children like us, who had lost our family and who were young enough. The ones that had whatever it was that they were looking for ended up here. I still recall the very long hover trip that it took to get here."

"You remember? But that must have been more than ten years ago!" Sam exclaimed. *"How could you possibly remember?"*

"You have your gift, and I have mine, Sam. I remember things that I shouldn't. I always have. I've never forgotten anything that anyone ever told me, and I can leaf through my memories like paging through a book. Of course, it got even better after I became Connected. Now I can touch on other people's memories from time to time and add them to my own collection," she admitted.

"Wow. So that's what it means to be a Keeper. That explains why they chose you to maintain the buildings and to work the things that need magic. You remember any magic that the minders and teachers used in front of you. What about the hovers? Shouldn't you be able to use them?" he questioned. She firmed up her walls a little at this, becoming somewhat resistant to his prying. He had touched on something that she didn't like, another morsel of evidence suggesting that they had been manipulated towards this event from the very start.

"We lived within walking distance of the school. The few times that I ever rode in one, Martha, my minder, made sure that

I was distracted when she got it going. Not that it really matters. I couldn't use that magic even if I did remember it, Sam. Francis made it clear to me that using the hovers was forbidden by the Directives. Whoever did this to us, whoever brought us here, they don't want us leaving Fervor. At least, they intend on keeping us here as long as it suits their purposes, whatever those happen to be."

Fiona grimaced as she mentioned the Teller's name, her animosity towards him completely undisguised. It was not the same as Royce's anger towards Sam. It was more on the basis of the girl's perspective of an ethical stance on the Teller's part. She didn't fault Francis for her current circumstances, but she did see him as being cruel for withholding information.

"You can't keep blaming Francis for all of this, Fiona. He's just as stuck as we are. They've forced him to do the things that he does just as much as they have the rest of us. They just happened to have chosen the Tellers as their mouthpieces," Sam argued in Francis's defence. *"None of us volunteered for this, it was thrust upon him just as much as upon you and me. They didn't bring all of us here either. The Littles – they made us for this."*

"Made you? What do you mean, they made you? You can't make people...well you can, but you need two adults, and it's not like assembling a hover or stacking building blocks. You don't get to pick and choose what you get, and it doesn't always work."

She paused, giving him a funny look.

"I know that you seem smarter than you should for your age, and that you use words that I don't even understand sometimes, but it's not something someone your age would know. I'm not a woman yet, so while I do have an idea of how it's supposed to work from what the teachers told us, it's not something that I could ever do. It's not something that I've ever attempted either. The idea still seems kind of...icky. Maybe in a year or two, when I start changing into a woman, I might feel differently, but right now it wouldn't be something that I would want."

Sam tried to ignore these last comments. Even though he really didn't understand what Fiona was talking about, because of the connection he did know that it made her feel uncomfortable, and one side-effect of the connection was that you got to share in the feelings of the person that you were speaking with, so it was making him uncomfortable, too.

"Francis said that this last time wasn't the only time people had left Fervor," the smaller boy informed her, changing the subject. *"He claimed that there had been another exodus, but that I would have been too young to remember it. Do you have that one stored away in your memories?"*

Fiona nodded.

"It's not something that I'd forget, because in those days there were usually only one or two children for each minder. We were all very close in age. Then one day they said that we had to reorganize. For some reason, they decided that each of you Littles needed a minder of your own. You were special, more so than the rest of us. They pulled fifty minders out of their homes and redistributed the children that they had kept to other families. It was a great upheaval, and when it was done, that's when the others left, the other adults who weren't minders or teachers. They had already started preparing for this that long ago. I think...I'm not sure, but maybe they had planned to do this sooner. They had to wait until you Littles were old enough. I'm also not certain, but I think they might have even wanted to wait longer to see to it that you would be ready for what was going to happen, but they didn't want the Bigs getting too big. They used to test us regularly, weigh us, and even check our blood. Did they do that to you?"

Sam shook his head. All of this was news to him.

"I thought not," she murmured. *"Like I said, you Littles were special. They raised you differently. They treated you differently. Many of us were aware of that, whether they were trying to hide it from us or not. Then again, some of us knew more than the rest of us did. Some of us like Francis and Royce. And now the bastards won't tell us anything..."*

"Well, that just supports what Francis said. Maybe they really did make us just for this...whatever this is," Sam offered. *"Hating Francis and Royce isn't going to change anything, Fiona. It's just going to make life harder for everyone in the house. It's like Royce hating me because he was supposed to be the Finder in the house-family, if it weren't for me. It doesn't make any sense. It's not my fault."*

Fiona stopped walking in response to this declaration.

"Royce was supposed to be the Finder? How did you know that? Did Francis tell you that? Is that something else he decided that he couldn't share with the rest of us?"

"I didn't learn that from Francis – not firsthand anyway, and I don't think that I was supposed to know it anymore than you were. Sarah picked it up from him, back when his walls were much weaker. He let it slip, and she heard it through the connection. If she hadn't told me, I wouldn't have known," he confessed.

"See! That's exactly what I mean!" she pushed at him with greater enthusiasm, the connection carrying her feelings of frustration loud and clear. *"That's something that you should have had the right to know from the very beginning. There's so much that Francis is hiding from us. It's wrong, and I don't care what you think, he has some say in the matter."* She chewed absentmindedly at her lower lip like she always did when she was upset.

They walked in silence for a few moments, with Sam still reeling a bit from her last fierce push. Fiona didn't realize how much more receptive he and Sarah were to communication through the connection, and what felt like a firm mental statement to the older girl came across as a very loud shout to him. Eventually, when he had recovered from the experience, he started pressing her for more information.

"So do you have any ideas on why they did this to us – anything that you may have seen or heard, and remembered? Why do we suddenly have access to the connection? Where do these gifts come from, and why do we have them? Why did we

lose some of our senses? What's with these Directives and the way things have been organized here? Why won't they let us leave the island? Why do the Controls not share in all of this?"

Sam didn't mean to, but he bombarded the poor girl with one question after another, unable to control his curiosity. Since she seemed so bent on sharing anything that she did know, he was compelled to find any answers that might be hidden in the assortment of memories that she kept.

Despite being overwhelmed by the sudden influx of his forceful thoughts, Fiona grinned down at him. She reached over and tussled his hair.

"Ah, my funny little detective, I'm not sure exactly what treasures lie inside my head. I have to know what I'm looking for, or be lucky enough to stumble upon something by accident. I may have what you need, but it's going to be up to you to find it. That is what you do, after all."

She had a pretty smile, Sam contemplated. One that he had noticed the older boys sometimes found disarming. He often wondered if that was why Nathan and Royce tried to avoid her, and Francis tried so hard to please her.

Sam also suspected that she had invited him along on this errand for this very reason. She wanted to use him to ferret out any clues that her memories could offer, ones that she had not been able to recognize herself. He also knew that she, more than anyone else, felt cheated out of life the way that she believed that it should have been.

"How about we sit down for a moment?" Fiona gestured at a cluster of large rocks by the side of the path. *"Maybe we can address those questions one at a time."*

They each perched atop a large boulder, and Sam considered what she had told him so far.

"Do you recall anything about the adults that left the first time around? They weren't teachers or minders, you said. Can you remember anything about them?" he asked.

59

She sat back, staring off into space for a moment, and he could almost feel her delving back into her memories, looking for something – anything.

"Wait!" she finally said, her eyes widening. *"I do remember overhearing Martha say something to one of my teachers once. They were talking about scholars and technicians. I didn't know what they meant at the time, but I'm pretty sure they were talking about the people who were about to leave. Martha said something about what they would do if any of the hovers or appliances stopped working after they were gone. She complained that they didn't have to worry about having the magic to make them go, as long as they were in working order, but they would be in a fine mess if any of the parts wore out, or something just stopped working. She even made a point of mentioning that it wasn't like they had any functioning Fixers yet. The teacher said that there were enough teachers who had a generally knowledge of how those things worked. And if necessary, people could bring those items in to the schools for repairs. I was puzzled when I heard that. None of it made any sense to me, but Martha seemed satisfied with his answer."*

"That could prove to be useful knowledge," Sam suggested. *"At least it is one more piece to the puzzle."*

"There's probably more there, if we knew where to look for it. The problem is, I think Francis and Royce hold the keys, but they've made it clear that they won't share." Fiona frowned again, glancing back in the direction of their house. *"They might have something to offer that could trigger more useful memories."*

"That's why the fact that you hold such contempt for them could get in the way," Sam said, touching her mind with a little more focus and intensity than he had before.

She eyed him warily. She didn't like it when he talked like a teacher, especially considering how much younger he was than her, but Sam found that he couldn't help but look for the perfect words to try to describe what he was thinking, even if it made him sound far older than he was.

"If we want to get more out of them, then we have to pry it out of them, and you attract more flies with honey than with vinegar. You say that you have ways of dealing with them because you are a girl? Well maybe you should use that to your advantage. We don't have to get a lot out of them, just enough to point us in the right direction. Instead of pushing them away because you hold them at fault for this, use them instead. I can't get anything out of Royce. He hates me, and I can't even talk to him without someone's help, but I'll see what I can get out of Francis for you. That being said, I think you'll have better luck than I would, if you can somehow mask your true intentions. Better yet, when it comes to Francis, we might want to get Sarah on board, too. Sometimes, she can still manage to see past his walls, and catch things that he doesn't want the rest of us to know. That's how come I know as much as I already do."

"Be nicer to Royce and Francis you mean? I don't know if I can do that," she sighed. *"I've tried to, but I keep thinking about how they were a part of setting us up for this, and I get a bad taste in my mouth every time."*

Fiona laughed at this thought, realizing it wasn't a very good description in her case, considering that she couldn't taste anything anymore.

"Okay, so it's more like a bad smell, I guess, but you catch my drift. They make my skin crawl – especially Francis because he tries so hard to make me like him, and sometimes I almost do, when he gets really sad and quiet. I kind of feel sorry for him on those days."

"I would think he would be the most vulnerable when he gets like that, and now you have extra incentive," Sam pointed out. *"Maybe next time, you can act friendly towards him, show a little kindness, and then dig a little, but don't be obvious about it. If you can do that with Sarah around and listening in through the connection, maybe we'll get something really meaningful to work with."*

Fiona looked away, and was obviously going over the idea in her head, although Sam made no attempt to peer in past her walls and find out for sure.

"You sure are smart," she said, after thinking things over for a couple of minutes. She gave him another smile. *"You know Sam, I really like you. I'm sorry I was sort of mean to you when we first met, but I wasn't happy with the way things were, and I didn't know what to expect. I don't feel that way anymore. I'll try what you said, and maybe you can put a good word in for me with Sarah. If the three of us work together, we might even figure a way to get around these Directives and even get ourselves off of Fervor."*

With that thought, she got to her feet, and started heading for the storehouse again.

Sam watched her go, walking slowly along the hover path through the trees, and gave her some space before following after her. He was not sure if he actually wanted to leave Fervor, but he did want answers to all of the questions that he had asked her, and he was going to figure out a way to find them. After all, finding things was in his nature.

DEEPER

Sarah was happy to agree with Sam and Fiona's plans, and the three spent the next few months trying to draw out more information from Royce and Francis. Royce stonewalled Fiona's attempts to befriend him completely, making it clear that he did not trust her any more than he did any of the other Connected. In fact, he treated her approach with suspicion, and began avoiding her even more than he did everyone else.

Francis, on the other hand, appeared to be extremely grateful that Fiona was finally warming up to him. He gladly spoke with her at every opportunity, trying to encourage any positive feelings towards him. He would even break through his shell on the days when he was clearly feeling somewhat melancholic, and would open up to her when he was resistant to share with the others. She could not get anything out of him regarding the first or second exodus from Fervor, nor anything regarding his Teller training, but she did manage to drag a couple of interesting tidbits of information out of him, with Sarah's help.

The first item was something that Sarah had picked up on when Fiona had mentioned in passing about some of her memories of the adults other than the minders or teachers. Francis had seemed startled when she had spoken of the scholars and technicians, and had thought anxiously, *How much does she know? I know that Keepers are supposed to remember, but there are some things that they aren't supposed to be aware of in the first place. Does she know about the Trials? Does she know how this is going to work? Does she know what it is, exactly, that is expected of us? They'll never get the results that they need from this if she suspects too much.*

It was fairly obvious that Fiona's comments had caught him completely off guard that day, enough that he had let his walls slip a little, and enough that he had given away much more than he had intended.

There were only two other less significant incidents where a single thought had escaped past his walls, and had been picked up by Sarah. The first time was when Francis had been contemplating the fact that he had not been able to test Fiona and Nathan properly as of yet, but that he had something in mind for Nathan. Sam was fairly certain that he knew what this meant, having been tested himself, and having played the pawn in Sarah's test.

The second time was when Francis had been watching Fiona fuss over Nathan when he returned looking particularly ragged. Behind the Teller's green-eyed stare, Sarah had definitely picked up an unpleasant feeling and a thankfulness that the stasis was firmly in place and working, or that there would be problems.

The next time Francis went away for a meeting of the Tellers, and both Nathan and Royce had left the house, Fiona and the two Littles had gathered in their kitchen to discuss their findings. Fiona was the first to speak.

"What do you think he meant by Trials?" she asked the two smaller children.

"Well, he has already tested some of us," Sam offered. *"And all of this is new to us...the connection, and the gifts. Maybe the people who were here, the ones that left, set things up so that these 'abilities' or 'talents' would show themselves after they were gone."*

"You don't mean like some sort of experiment, do you? If they were going to do that wouldn't they stick around to watch what was going on? The whole point to an experiment is to rec-

ord observations, isn't it? And how could they compare things to normal people, if everyone else went away. Why would they do this to children?" Fiona demanded in frustration.

"Compare things?" Sarah piped up. *"That's why you have a control, when you do an experiment. To compare the changes and the results to something that hasn't been exposed to the same effects. You remember that from what the teachers showed us, right?"*

Fiona looked a little embarrassed. *"I always found experimental magic boring, so I didn't pay that much attention. I never realized how important it might be someday. They mostly talked about theory, and we rarely did anything hands on. That was what I found interesting."*

Sam was still lost in thought, considering what Fiona had said initially.

"Controls, like Royce," he finally said, sharing his thoughts with the two girls. *"They aren't Connected, and they have no talents. It would make sense. Maybe they thought that if we knew all of this, that it might skew their results. They had to let someone who was going to stay behind know what was going on, though, someone to police things in their stead, someone who could keep things on track if they started to slide. That's why they have the Tellers, and I think that's why they let the Controls in on it, too."*

"That's really creepy," Fiona moaned. *"Francis is keeping tabs on everything that we do, and making sure that we stick to the plan..."*

"Making sure that we follow the Directives," Sam corrected. *"But apparently, that's what they are for. I don't think that he is necessarily keeping track of us though. There are days that he purposefully avoids us, and times when he is gone for stretches. It would more likely be someone who is here regularly. Maybe, someone who didn't forget what they saw, so that information could be retrieved later."*

Fiona blinked at him, as it took a few moments for what he was suggesting to sink in. *"Me? I'm the creepy one? Oh that's not fair. I had no idea..."*

"Well, you can congratulate yourself then," Sarah interrupted. *"As soon as they find out what exactly it is that we've figured out, they may consider our part in their little experiment a failure. Francis might be in the middle of warning them of our suspicions right now, if he still reports to them somehow."*

She paused, looking somewhat puzzled.

"If he is still in touch with them, you would think that he would have given that away somehow, when all of this first started and his walls were fairly weak. I never got that feeling. In some ways, he was as disoriented as the rest of us. The connection had been small and fragile with just the Tellers. When the rest of us were added, many of us much stronger than the Tellers, it was as much a shock to them as it was to us. I got the feeling that in some ways it was worse for them. They had come to depend on a certain level of calm from the connection, and that had been yanked away. They had to get used to things all over again."

"So they aren't using Francis that way? He's just some sort of rules-monger, to make sure things don't go off course. You don't honestly think they would just leave us to sort ourselves out and hope that the Keepers' memories would capture everything that they needed know. What if they missed something?" Fiona protested. *"Or what if something went terribly wrong? We're just children after all."*

She sat back, staring at Sam and Sarah with a disconcerted look. *"In some cases exceptionally smart children, but children nonetheless. How irresponsible would that be?"*

"Well, maybe there is more to it than that," Sam stated. He was enjoying this. Every time they seemed to get a step closer to some answers, he felt a satisfying wave of accomplishment wash over him. *"It looks like we have our talents for a reason. There are Fixers to make sure we can handle injuries or any problems with any of our equipment, and they saw to it*

that we had Finders, to address our needs. The Tellers are to enforce the Directives, and the Keepers are to record things. That leaves the Watchers..."

"Of course," Sarah said quietly. *"The Watchers. And here I was thinking that Nathan was here to keep an eye out for our safety, to protect us, when all this time he has just been their eyes. That's why he patrols a circuit. That's why he never strays too far from home."*

"No, no, no," Fiona objected, jumping to the older boy's defence. *"He has no idea what's going on either. I'm sure of it. Don't blame him for any of this. If anything, he's the least guilty of the lot of us. Francis and Royce were in on it from the get go, and we haven't shared any of our findings with him. He is completely oblivious. He just follows that compulsion of his."*

"I wasn't suggesting that he knew, Fiona," the smaller girl explained. *"I was just saying that they are using him as their eyes, to observe without being here. They have been using all of us in some way, you included. That makes me think that the experiment isn't about our gifts necessarily, although they play a part in it. I think that it's all about the connection. That's the common factor, except for with the Controls."*

"That still doesn't explain why they would choose children for this, and just up and leave us. What happens as we grow up? What happens as we become adults?" Fiona demanded.

Sam hadn't considered that at all, but it was clear that it had the older girl worried. Then it hit Sam that he hadn't been thinking about it because he hadn't actually been growing. He hadn't experienced any physical changes, aside from his deafness, since he had woken up Connected. Normally that wouldn't have been something surprising for him. He often grew in spurts, and he had gone a few months at a time before with no signs of any change, but now that he thought about it, it had been the better part of a year, and none of them had changed physically in any way. That wasn't just unusual, it was clearly contrived.

"Stasis!" the small boy gasped, his grey eyes widening.

"What?" Fiona asked, but Sarah remained silent. She had been following Sam's thoughts as he had jumped from one conclusion to another, and she already knew what he meant by that.

"You don't have to worry about what happens when we grow up, Fiona, because we're not going to – at least, not until whoever has organized this decides otherwise. That's what Francis meant by stasis," Sam stated, a little shaken by this discovery.

"What? You're kidding. What would make you say that? Why would they do that to us, too?"

The older girl had seemed upset at the idea of an island filled with children growing up alone, but the notion that they wouldn't be aging physically at all made her frantic. Sam shrugged.

"None of us have gotten any bigger, and some of you Bigs should be starting to change in other ways. It's not happening. Haven't you noticed? Sarah and are the same size that we were when all of this started. You Bigs don't seem to have changed at all either. I have no idea why they would force this on us, as well as everything else. The older we get, the more complicated things are, and they want to keep things simple perhaps? Or maybe they see us as being easier to manipulate this way, easier to control. Francis probably knows why."

Fiona's face had reddened with anger, and her hands, that rested on the tabletop, were trembling.

"How can they do this to us? It's one thing to make us their experimental guinea pigs, play with our environment, and mess with our minds, but I don't want to stay this way forever!"

The push was completely random and out of control. Sam had not realized that Fiona could project her thoughts with such force, as weak as she was within the connection. He grabbed her hand and quickly threw his thoughts over her own, dissolving his walls and restoring them over Fiona, in order to try to restrain her.

"Shhh!" he hissed. *"Do you want everyone in the con-nection to hear you? You were shouting loud enough and erratically enough that even Francis might have heard you, wherever he is right now. You have to calm down. If they real-ize that we've figured some of these things out, there's no telling what they'll do to us."*

After she had settled down a little, Sam let go of her.

"Nobody said that they are going to keep us this way for-ever. Experiments usually come to an end eventually, and we have no idea if any of this is permanent. What we have to figure out now is exactly what they want from us, because the sooner we give it to them, the sooner they'll end this. That or we have to find a way to sabotage this without making it obvious that we were the ones who did it. Otherwise, we have no way of guess-ing how long this will last...it could be years."

Sam saw Sarah and Fiona start.

"The front door," Fiona told him. She hesitated, reach-ing out through the connection. *"It's Nathan. I think he heard some of that part, when I overreacted. I'll have to head him off and come up with something to distract him. He doesn't need to be involved in all this mess, and if they really are using him as a tool to observe us, letting him in on what we know might let them know, too. I'll handle this."*

Without wasting any more time, she disappeared through the kitchen door.

Sam had stood when she had mentioned that it was their Watcher returning. He dropped back into his seat, far too dis-turbed by the pieces of the puzzle that they were starting to uncover. After a couple of seconds, he glanced back over at Sa-rah. She was sitting quietly in her chair, small, thin, and pale. He could see that she was crying again, even though she had blocked this fact out in the connection.

"It'll be okay, Sarah. Nathan doesn't pry, and she'll find some way to divert his attention. We won't get caught."

"That's not what is bothering me. I don't want to stay this way. I'm blind and I'm one of the smallest of the Littles.

I'm completely helpless without the rest of you. Fiona thinks that this isn't fair, but she doesn't know the half of it. She's practically normal, and she's a Big," the waif-like girl lamented. *"She could get by without any of us if she had to. The only other person that could make that claim is Royce. This is cruel, Sam. What they've done to us is so cruel."*

"I'm sorry, Sarah," Sam replied soothingly, trying to keep his thoughts as gentle as he could manage. *"I'm sure they believe that they have good reason for what they've done, but I don't think that this was the right way to go about it. I promise you that I'll never let you down. If you ever need me, all you have to do is call, and I'll try to get to you, no matter where I am. You'll never have to knock with me. I mean that. Remember – special friends."* He reached out and put his hand on hers.

Sarah smiled at him through her tears, staring vacantly in his general direction.

"I won't forget…special friends."

* _ * _ *

Francis had been back for five days when there was a storm that struck Fervor. The six housemates had been holed up in their home for two days waiting for it to pass. Nathan was fidgety the entire time, pacing from one end of the house to the other, and everyone else mostly tried hard to stay out of each others' way.

Fiona was the exception. After her discussion with the Littles, she was more determined than ever to try to lure more information out of Francis. Despite her best efforts, he seemed distracted and aloof, sometimes ignoring her to watch Nathan pace, and to follow Royce and Sam with his eyes when either of them emerged from their rooms for any amount of time. It was clear that the brooding Teller had something else on his mind, and while disappointed that Francis refused to oblige her, Fiona went to great effort not to let this disappointment show.

Deeper

Sam was thrilled the following morning when the clouds rolled away and the sun came out. He had been starting to feel almost as antsy as Nathan, and while he had tried escaping the confines of his room more than once, Royce had always seemed to be there, making him feel as uncomfortable as ever.

Once Fiona had given up on pressing Francis for something to add to what they had already gotten from him, the blond boy had pulled their Control aside and had begun having a rather lengthy conversation with him. It was clear that none of the others in the house were welcome to participate in this discussion, and anytime anyone had even suggested that they might want to approach them, Royce had given that person a menacing stare and the person guilty of intruding had quickly backed off.

The first thing the young Finder did, once free to leave the house, was race down to the beach. Storms always left the potential of particularly good pickings on the shore, and Sam did not need Fiona's help when he was beach-combing. After days cooped up with a small crowd, he longed desperately for some time by himself.

Grateful for the warm weather, the fresh air, and the smell of the ocean as he inhaled deeply, he jogged happily along the damp sand, dodging the occasional rock and patches of slippery seaweed. Most of what he found on the way was junk, the odd empty bottle, an old buoy, or a tattered piece of rope, but he still had hope. Something inside him told him that he was going to find something completely unexpected that day.

Sam paused from time to time as he moved farther and farther along the beach, straying a fair distance away from their house. He had not intended to go as far as he did, but the compulsion to seek things out was very powerful in him that morning, to the point where it was impossible for him to resist. He dug up a couple of intriguing seashells that he thought Sarah might like, rinsing them off in the tidal pools that could be found sporadically along the long stretches of sand.

He finally arrived at a point where he was fairly certain he had gone farther than he should. He suspected he was about to move outside of the area that Nathan normally patrolled, and something about that felt wrong to him. He would have normally obeyed his instincts, too, if he had not noticed something that piqued his interest to a greater degree than he could willingly ignore. It was small and bright orange, and he could see it wedged between two rocks several feet from where he stood. Treading cautiously, he responded to impulse and made his way over to the small container.

Sam tried to pull the small wax-sealed box free, but the rocks that held it prisoner refused to yield their treasure. The small boy clawed at it, but the outer surface of the box was smooth, damp and slippery, and continuously slid out of his grasp. He spent a few frustrating moments worrying at his find, tugging at it and trying to wiggle it free. Pausing to see if he could come up with a better approach, Sam noticed some movement that he had not been aware of moments before. He peered over the boulders before him and spotted Royce, but the Control was not alone, and Sam did not recognize any of the Bigs gathered there with him.

The small boy ducked quickly back behind the rocks again, nervous that the black-haired Big might spot him and take issue with the fact that Sam was spying on him, even though that was not why the Finder was there. After crouching there for several seconds, his heart pounding and his breath coming in small gasps, he saw no sign of Royce. Sam assumed that he had not been seen, and began to relax again. Once his mind had cleared a little and he was no longer governed by fear, he set about trying to dislodge the orange box again. Much to his satisfaction, his find began to finally yield to all of his prying and a few moments later he clutched the small box in his hand. In fact, he was sitting in the sand staring at his prize, trying to figure out exactly how to open the sealed container when a shadow suddenly blocked out the sun.

Sam glanced up, puzzled, and was horrified to see not only Royce standing over him, but the group of Bigs that he had been consorting with hovering closely behind him.

Spurred by his own terror, Sam scrabbled backwards in the sand, almost dropping his newest find in the process. Before Royce had the chance to react, the small boy leapt to his feet, thrusting the small box deep into his pocket, he dashed away as fast as his short legs would allow. The Control sprinted after him, closely followed by the other strange Bigs. Sam could not help but think that he had stumbled upon something that nobody had been supposed to see, especially not him. He felt the thrum of feet pounding against the sand behind him, and a quick peek over his shoulder was enough to let him know that the black-haired boy was gaining on him. He would catch up to him soon, and if that happened, Sam was sure that the results would be less than pleasant.

It was at that point that Sam decided he had little choice but to call out for help in the connection. He did not have much time left to spare, which meant that there would not be any room for formalities. He figured that this situation might qualify as an emergency based on what Francis had told him about the Directives. He would not be knocking to make contact. In fact, when Sam did encounter Nathan, Fiona, and Sarah in the connection, those closest to him and yet still disturbingly far away, he pushed as hard as he possibly could, allowing fear to reinforce his thoughts.

"Help me!"

Nathan was the first to respond.

"On my way, little buddy. Hang in there." The thought was brief but firm, and Sam was thankful just to feel the larger boy's mind.

Fiona was the second to offer him some comforting words.

"We're coming, too. I'm bringing Sarah to you. We'll get there as fast as we can." She was not as close as Nathan, but her contact was just as temporary.

Sarah on the other hand, not only touched his mind, but seemed to hold on to him there.

"What do you see, Sam? Show me what you see."

The small boy whipped his head around and flashed the image of Royce and his cohorts bearing down on him to his Fixer. Nathan was still nowhere in sight. In fact, Sam was sure that his Watcher still had some distance to clear. If he didn't do something soon, Sam knew that Royce would reach him long before Nathan would arrive, and the black-haired boy looked like he had murder in his eyes.

"Can you swim, Sam? Can you swim? Francis told me once in passing that Royce couldn't swim. He won't follow you very far into the water. I don't know about the others, but you'll be safe from him there," she offered. He could tell that she was feeling just as desperate as he was.

Sam shuddered. The truth was that, while he could swim, he was a very weak swimmer. Given the choice of confronting Royce directly, and facing the chance that he might drown, however, the drowning sounded like the more pleasant way to go. Gritting his teeth, he veered towards the ocean and splashed his way into the water.

His charge into the waves did not deter the larger boy at first. Royce plunged in after him, until the water was waist deep for the Big. Sam struggled against the pull of the tide. The water was excruciatingly cold, and by the time Royce had stopped following him, the small boy was treading water. Sam felt his hands and feet going numb and he soon realized that he had no control over which direction he was heading. The choppy waves, still a little wild from the residual effects of the storm, lapped at his face and occasionally sloshed into his mouth and up his nose. As the taste of salt trickled into his windpipe, he began to gag and choke. Sam felt himself start to panic.

"Sam!" He heard Sarah loud and clear in his head. *"What's going on? Nathan's almost there and we won't be far behind him. Are you okay? Did you get away from Royce? You still seem so scared..."*

"I'm sorry, Sarah. I did what you suggested, but the water's so cold and I'm feeling so tired."

It was hard for him to concentrate as he struggled for breath. At the same time, he didn't want his last few thoughts to be shared with the rest of the connection. Anything he was going to tell her was to remain just between him and her. He stopped fighting the waves as fiercely, and steeled the link with Sarah.

"Royce was talking with others in secret – other Bigs that I didn't recognize. I don't think that they wanted anybody to see them, and that's why he came after me. I found something...a container. I know that it's something special. I think that it's still safe in my pocket. When they drag my body out, make sure you get that before they take me away."

"Your body? Sam – no!" Her push was so forceful that it gave Sam a headache. *"Nathan's just about there. Don't give up!"*

As much as he wanted to listen to her, it was at that very moment that a sizeable wave washed over his head and with little ability left to lift his face above water again, Sam began to sink.

"Sam! Sam!"

He could hear the cries faintly in his head as his vision blurred and the greyness fell over him. He wasn't sure who exactly it was calling to him, his ability to identify the person who spoke fading along with his consciousness. As the blackness overtook him, he thought that he felt something make contact with his forearm, and he could have sworn that he heard, just barely, *"Gotcha."*

* - * - *

"Sam? I think he's coming around."

The voice was a hazy one inside his head, but one that he would always recognize, and he knew it was attached to the small hand that rested on his chest, a chest that felt painfully constricted and water-logged. With a few coughing gags, Sam weakly turned onto his side and spewed saltwater onto the damp sand next to him. That was when he noticed that there was still a firm grip on his arm as well. Nathan was there, too.

"Dammit, little buddy, you scared us to death. Don't you ever do that again, you hear?" He felt the thick fingers by his elbow tighten their grasp a little – one brief and reassuring squeeze.

"What were you doing so far away from home?" Fiona demanded. She knelt beside Sarah, looking equally concerned. *"How do you expect Nathan to keep you safe if you don't stay where he can easily get to you?"*

"Fiona," Sarah protested. *"Give him a chance to recover before you start nagging at him. I'm sure that he didn't mean any harm."*

"Finding," Sam said shakily, as Nathan helped him to sit up. That was when the smaller boy noticed that Francis was on the beach as well. He stood a few feet away, his arms crossed and his expression grim. Royce has not that far away either, past the Teller. The other Bigs that had been with the black-haired boy were nowhere in sight. *"I was finding. I couldn't help it. There was something there, but then I saw Royce and..."*

Now it was Nathan's turn to respond unhappily. *"I heard Royce and Francis talking while Sarah was trying to revive you. Royce claimed that he was just doing what Francis had asked, giving you a bit of a scare so that I had to come help you. They said that it had something to do with testing my talent, whatever that meant. It sounds like they planned this, and Royce had suggested that he wasn't really going to hurt you,"* the broad-shouldered Big reported.

Sam reached out his mind and touched Sarah's. They both knew that Royce may have been telling the truth about Francis asking for his assistance in order to test Nathan's gift, but otherwise he was lying through his teeth. It was clear that he could in no way be trusted.

"Come on, little buddy," Nathan murmured, lifting Sam out of the sand. *"Let's get you home and rested. The finding can wait for another day."*

With that, he carried the smaller boy back to the house, Fiona and Sarah by his side. Francis, with his familiar melancholic expression, followed a few feet behind them, and Royce stood quietly watching them go, a self-satisfied smirk on his face.

MESSAGES

Sam spent more than a full day recuperating from his close call, with Sarah and Fiona checking in on him at regular intervals. Nathan stopped in a couple of times as well, but there was no sign of Francis at first. In fact, the Teller avoided the house altogether for a couple of days, realizing that he was in the proverbial doghouse for involving Royce in orchestrating the Watcher's test, and placing Sam at risk. The grazed knee while testing Sarah had been bad enough and Sam started to wonder if Francis had something that he kept hidden well behind his walls that would suggest that he were out to get the smaller boy as much as Royce was. He also didn't think that the strange Bigs that he had spotted with Royce had anything to do with Nathan's test, and that part still worried Sam.

When he was finally feeling a little more like his usual self, Sam pulled the small orange container out of his pocket and had Fiona and Sarah join him in his room. He displayed his find to them, placing it in the palm of his outstretched hand. He also offered a visual image for Sarah through the connection as she reached out to touch it.

"What is it?" Fiona asked, eying the strange box warily.

"Something special," Sam insisted. *"Something that I'm sure that I was supposed to find."*

"Okay, but what is it?" she repeated.

"I think that it's some sort of package," Sarah suggested. *"We need to get it open, to see what's inside."* She brushed her hand over its surface. *"It's smooth and slightly soft. Someone sealed it in wax, like they were trying to make sure that it was waterproof. I think that they did that because they intended it to pass through the water. What if someone sent it on purpose? What if someone actually used the storm to get it to us on Fervor?"*

"Why would anyone do that?" Fiona scoffed. *"It was probably something that was being stored somewhere by the shore, and they waterproofed it to protect it in case there were some sort of tidal surge. Although I must say, I am curious to see what's inside of it. How do you get it open?"*

Sam shrugged.

"We have to break the seal somehow," Sarah offered. *"But carefully. We don't know what's inside, and it could be breakable."*

"We could try heating it, and melting the wax away," Sam responded, watching Sarah run her fingers along its edges.

"We'd still have to be careful," the petite girl insisted. *"Whatever's in here might be flammable as well. We have no idea."*

Fiona disappeared into the kitchen, searching through the various magically fueled implements in order to find something that could help them safely break through the seal. She returned with a tool that generated a small flame and they set about carefully working their way into the container. When the casing finally yielded to their efforts, Sam gently pried it open. There was a roll of paper inside.

"Paper?" Fiona questioned.

"Like a message in a bottle," the smaller of the two girls laughed. *"Is there writing on it?"*

Sam both nodded and confirmed this through the connection, giving Sarah a visual flash of the note.

"Can I see?" Fiona requested. Sam passed her the paper

"Read it for me," Sarah asked.

"On the outside it says 'for Fiona.' It's for me..." the older girl looked startled and almost dropped Sam's unusual find.

"Go on, go on," Sarah stated excitedly. *"What else does it say?"*

"I hope that this makes its way to your Finder and then to you okay. I heard you recently and I know that you are aware of some of the things going on. I don't think any of the others suspect, not the others on Fervor, and not anyone here either." She hesitated. *"Here? Where's here?"*

"Maybe it says further along – keep reading," Sam said, eager to proceed..

"I intend on keeping your secret. I want you to know that I never agreed with the way that they decided to do this. The scholars insisted on it. I'm only a technician, but I know the difference between right and wrong – and this is wrong. You are people, not animals, and deserve compassion and fair treatment. I can't stop things at the moment, and it may be a while before I can come to your assistance, but I have a few ideas, and hopefully I'll be able to act on them. The Coming isn't planned for many years, and I warned them what sort of havoc that this might wreak on your systems, but they won't heed my advice. Thankfully, they don't suspect that I'm a latent, so they don't know that I'm trying to find a way to get around them. I'll keep you posted when I get the chance. I pray that this reaches the right hands. It will if your Finder is a strong one. Take care of each other and don't give up hope." Fiona paused, glancing over at Sam. *"It's only signed 'E'"*

"Maybe whoever sent this was worried that it might not end up where it was supposed to go, and if he or she gave us a full name, it would get traced back to them, and that would be an end to that," Sarah suggested. *"Whoever it is needed to protect themselves while they are trying to help us. It just makes me feel really happy, knowing that we have an ally out there, somewhere other than Fervor."*

"It makes me happy, too," the older girl agreed. *"You're right. This is like a message in a bottle, sent to inspire us, but it's still taboo. If we keep this, we have to make sure that it is somewhere safe, and well hidden. We might want to make sense of it first, if we decide that we have to destroy it – like, what did this E mean by 'a latent?' What is 'the Coming,' and why would it harm us?"*

"We don't need to destroy it," Sam claimed. *"There's an old hover behind the house, and you can hide it in there, Fiona. The rest of us aren't allowed to touch it, and certainly not allowed to go inside it. It will be safe there. I was thinking about the other things you mentioned. If E heard you the other day when you were shouting, and he knew your name, then that suggests that whoever it is has access to the connection. Maybe that's what this person means by being a latent. It is possible that someone other than the children on Fervor could be linked. I don't know what he or she means by 'the Coming" though, or why E would think that it will shake things up."*

He had also been thinking that he didn't like the fact that this 'E' had mentioned something about things going on for many years. However, he chose not to bring that up realizing how upset Fiona might become if he pointed that out.

"Francis had though something about 'the Coming' before. Remember. Sam? It was that time that we first found out about the stasis, too," Sarah added. *"If this E really is a latent user of the connection, maybe we can touch on him or her. Perhaps we could let our newest ally know that we got the message, and that we will keep hoping."*

"If you think that we should try that, then it should be you making the effort, Sarah. You are the strongest in the connection. You'll have the best chance of reaching this person," Sam insisted.

"But you'll have the best chance of finding him or her," she argued.

"So is there any way that you could look together?" Fiona asked. *"You find him, and then she speaks to him."*

Sam blinked, with his uncertainty showing in his expression. *"Can we do that? Use the connection together? What do you think, Sarah?"*

None of them had actually tried to combine their efforts within the connection. It was a strange idea, but it might work.

"It's worth a try," Sarah said softly.

They joined each other in the connection, and pushed their way past the many minds there together. Most of them were shielded to some extent anyway since the majority of the children had been practicing blocking with their walls since the day of the Gathering. Sam and Sarah moved carefully amongst them, Sam searching and Sarah following.

"E," they murmured softly as they went. *"Fiona sent us. E?"*

Sam felt a very faint presence at the far edge of the connection, and his finding instincts guided him that way. It seemed to be male.

"I think that I have him," he whispered to Sarah. *"This way. Come on."*

They proceeded with caution, skirting the occasional mind that still remained far more open than the others, until Sam had led her to the place where he believed that the person that they were seeking might be. He reached out and tried to brush at the faint contact there, but Sam realized that he had extended himself as far as he could go. Sarah was not equally limited. She inched past him, and barely touched that vague presence. Out of reach to Sam, he could not hear what they were saying. He was forced to relax and wait, hoping Sarah would be willing to pass along what E was telling her. After a few moments, she pulled back and they both restored their link with Fiona.

"His name is Elliot, and he is living on the mainland, on the closest coast to Fervor," Sarah informed them both. *"He used to be a technician here. He couldn't tell me much. The strongest Watchers patrol the connection as well, roaming a circuit, and if he's caught he'll be sent away. Then he'll never be able to help us. But he promised to keep sending messages, and*

to let us know what progress he is making. He's going to see if there is a way that he can either fix things for us here, or find us a way off of Fervor..."

She and Fiona tensed and they turned their heads towards the door. Fiona scrambled to shove the container and the message under Sam's blankets. At first the smaller boy thought that it was Nathan returning to the house again, interrupting them as he had before, but when he checked the connection, he found that it was Francis finally coming home. When their Teller stepped into the doorway, before Sarah or Sam could stop her, Fiona lit into him.

"How can you show your face here after what you encouraged Royce to do to Sam? I used to think that there was a part of you that was lost but salvageable. At times, I had believed that you felt cornered and had no choice in this, and that in some ways you were as much a victim as the rest of us." She moved towards him as she spoke, and with the way she was pushing on the inside, Sam suspected that she was at least speaking harshly at him, if not shouting, on the outside. *"But that's not it at all. I understand now that you have no soul. You may have had one once, but if that's the case, you let them take it from you, or maybe you handed it over willingly. Keeping secrets from us is only part of it, isn't it? I'd even wager that it's the least of it. Forcing us to do things against our wills, and deciding what's best for us, according to these silly Directives – that's even worse. But holding Sam out as bait for the sharks, and hoping Nathan would get to him in time? I don't care what sort of test that it was supposed to be, and I don't care what type of hold these people have over you. That's evil, Francis, pure evil."*

Once she had arrived within reach of the blond boy she began prodding him in the chest to accentuate her words. He had stepped back initially, but from that point onwards he had just stood there and taken it, looking at her with his green-grey eyes filled with pity. That only just seemed to spur her frustration, and Sam couldn't understand why the Teller didn't just order her to stop.

"Don't pretend that you want to be my friend anymore, and don't insist that this is a family. If you want me to believe that you would treat your family the way that you treat us, then I can only assume that it's because you enjoy tormenting others. In fact, unless you feel the need to order me around, I want you to leave me alone. I've had it with you, and from now on you aren't welcome in my room, you aren't welcome in my thoughts, and anything that I do for you, I do under protest," the older girl raged, and then stormed away to brood in the privacy of her own space.

Sam noted Francis's shoulders sag a little and his head droop.

"And here I was thinking that we had been finding some common ground," the Teller sighed. *"I guess that's over. I knew she wouldn't understand, but I wasn't given a choice. Nathan was the holdout. All of the other Watchers had been tested, and they said if I didn't resolve it before the next meeting, that one of the other house-families would get involved. I wanted to maintain some control of the situation, to try to assure your safety, but I never would have imagined that you would wander so far from home. Nathan should have been able to get to you much more quickly otherwise, and I'm certain that you would rather that I set this up with you than with one of the girls. What were you doing so far away from the house?"*

Sam couldn't lie, not through the connection, but he wasn't required to give specifics. *"I was finding, just like I'm supposed to do."*

The smaller boy knew that his find was still close at hand, hidden by his blankets. The fact that if Francis were aware, he could practically reach out and grab it, made Sam nervous. *"I have to follow the impulse, you know that. It happened to take me to a place not far from where Royce started chasing me. Maybe my finding brought me there in part to find him up to no good. He wasn't alone Francis. He was there talk-*

87

ing with other Bigs, ones I didn't know. I think that they had organized their own meeting, in secret, and didn't want to be found, least of all by me with the way that Royce reacted."

Francis frowned. This was clearly news to him.

"Other Bigs? What other Bigs? The family-houses were purposefully spaced apart so that our paths wouldn't cross to any extent, and so that we would have our own separate spaces to find in and watch over. How many of them were there?"

"I only caught a quick glimpse of them, with Royce chasing me and all, but it looked like there were four other than him, two boys and two girls. Obviously, I couldn't hear what they were talking about, but they didn't look happy," Sam revealed.

"Hmm," The Teller said, contemplatively. *"That might explain where Royce has been disappearing to on a regular basis. Aside from making sure that I don't bully you, he doesn't have much to do around here, and I thought he was just finding something at random to occupy himself with. Honestly, I don't think that he cares much what I do, Directives or no Directives. Thanks for telling me. I'll have to investigate."*

Sam shrugged, and shifted uncomfortably. He was hoping that Francis would leave and that Fiona would return to fetch the message so that she could hide it properly.

"You know that I'm telling the truth. I never intended for you to get hurt," Francis added, as he turned to go. *"I wouldn't want any harm to come to any of you. Whether Fiona is willing to see it this way or not, I was actually trying to protect you, not the other way around."*

Sam looked at his placid face, and knew that Francis could not lie to him through the connection. He only wished Francis did not have such a warped way of viewing things, or that he were more willing to share the burden imposed on him by the information he continuously kept from them. It was changing him. Fiona was right about that much.

Not only could Sam see it, he could feel it, too, whenever they made contact through the connection, and the Teller was not changing in a good way either. He was becoming numb to things in general, more or less a ghost of the quirky minded, pleasant boy that he had been at the beginning. Sam also worried that if this transformation kept up, soon he would not care about things any more than Royce did, and Fiona's outbursts weren't helping any.

"Don't worry, Francis," Sarah assured him gently. *"We believe you. Fiona just has a harder time accepting everything around here. She liked the way things used to be. It's going to take more convincing as far as she's concerned."*

Sam nodded in agreement, and could both see and feel the Teller's relief as he was walking away. When he was gone, Sarah reached out to connect with Sam alone.

"Why do things have to be this complicated?" she asked sadly.

While Sam shared this opinion he didn't like seeing her down. He gave her a mental pat on the shoulder and an inside smile.

"It will get better," he suggested. *"It has to."*

* _ * _ *

Fiona didn't get over her renewed dislike of Francis after a few weeks – or even a few months – the way that Sam and Sarah had hoped she would. She now lacked incentive, since the older girl was convinced that his walls were too strong for even Sarah to penetrate on occasion. They were all getting much better at blocking others out, to the point where Francis decided that it was time to instruct them on the methods of establishing a mental door, so that they could selectively allow others into their own inner space. Having a door let them do this without risking the chance that others might get to listen in if their presence was strong enough in the connection, or in some cases, allow some of their less controlled thoughts to get out. Nobody would be able to gently push their way past someone else's blocks any more. They would have to "knock", something else Francis was also able to teach them, or if the situation were sufficiently urgent, try to push their way in with much more force.

Sam would spend part of every day, once he had done his required chores, searching for some new sign that Elliot was trying to reach them, some sign of another message. But every day he seemed to come up empty handed. It soon became difficult for him and the girls to hide their disappointment, sometimes moving around the house in a bit of a funk. Royce and Francis both would watch them with some suspicion on those days, and Sam thought that he had detected Francis attempting to prod at him in some hope for answers to explain his moodiness.

Sam was pretty certain, however, that he and Fiona, thanks to Sarah's help, had fairly formidable walls, as they approached the halfway mark of their second year since being introduced to the connection. As long as Sam maintained his focus, Francis had no chance of stealing a glimpse at his innermost thoughts, and he would not allow any lingering doubts about Elliot to rise to the surface, including his worries that Elliot had gotten caught, and was no longer there to help them.

Nathan had a completely different approach when he noticed Fiona and the Littles appearing to be glum. He would find other means of trying to cheer them. He would tell them any interesting stories about his travels on the circuit, or he would tease at them in a playful way, often resorting to gentle roughhousing with Sam or Fiona. As much as Sarah might have enjoyed similar play, Nathan was clearly reluctant to include her. Sam suspected that Nathan was put off by her obvious frailty, concerned that he might prove to be more rough than she could handle, and particularly afraid that he might in some way harm their Fixer. After all, if someone broke their Fixer, who would fix her?

Sam put that question to Francis once, wondering what would become of their house-family, if Sarah became ill or injured, and could not fix herself, or worse yet, someone died and ended up beyond any hope of being fixed, leaving them shorthanded. Francis wouldn't answer his second question, although

Sam suspected that there was something to cover this possibility within the Directives, but he explained that if Sarah needed fixing, that they would have to seek out another family's Fixer for assistance. The other family wouldn't be able to refuse them, since the rules made it clear that their first obligation was to their talent group and not to their house-family. If someone else needed Sarah's fixing skills, for example, she would have to go with them, even if it meant her house-family would be short a Fixer temporarily.

As the end of their second year together approached, and Royce made himself more and more scarce on a daily basis, a second large storm struck, one as violent as the one that had carried Elliot's first message to them. After the storm had passed, and Sam and Nathan were allowed their freedom again, the antsy pair bounded out of the house as fast as their legs would carry them. Nathan disappeared into the woods, while the smaller boy made his way down to the beach.

Despite his excitement, he was much more cautious than he had been the time that his close call with Royce had occurred, and even though the finding itch burned within him like an overheating hover, he paced himself. Watching for the Control as much as looking for any potential signs from Elliot, he padded gently down the shore.

He had been searching for several minutes when Sam caught the glimpse of bright orange out of the corner of his eye at almost the same time as he also noticed Royce and his cohorts mingling in the same area. Feeling impatient, but not prepared to make the same mistake that he had last time, Sam backed away a little, crouching behind some seaweed covered rocks. Locating Sarah in the connection, the small boy reached out and knocked. After a few seconds, she opened her mental door to him.

"I'm pretty sure that I've found another message from Elliot," he informed her. *"Or, at least, it looks like it could be a similar container from here."*

91

"What are you waiting for then. Get it and bring it home. Fiona and I are as anxious to see it as you are. We've been waiting for this for so long," she exclaimed exuberantly.

"There's a problem with that," Sam explained. *"The same problem that there was the last time, and I don't want to find myself in the same sort of trouble."*

He wished at that point in time, more than he had in the last couple of years, that he could hear again, so that he could eavesdrop on the gathered Bigs' conversation. That was when it struck him that none of the five that he was trying to avoid were a part of the connection. That meant that they were all Controls. Francis had never mentioned the Controls having to meet the way that the Tellers did. Besides, when the Tellers met, they all travelled to the Hub to make it easier on them to communicate – all fifty Tellers on the island. But this? This was no convening of a talent group. There were only a handful of the Controls present.

"We need a way to distract them, to draw them away," Sarah sighed. *"I wish that we could bring Nathan on board. If we had his help, this would be so much easier."*

"You know we can't do that, Sarah," Sam reminded her. *"He's a Watcher. As much as he would never purposefully do anything to ruin our plans, if our theory is right, he would do it without meaning to."*

"I could try sending Fiona. Royce doesn't like her, but he has never done anything to threaten her. You could go together, and she could pretend that she was helping you to retrieve something. With the pair of you there, they are more likely to scatter than to confront you both," she offered.

"Is Francis there, too?" he asked.

"Yes. Why?" she responded.

"I don't want you there alone. Something's going on with the Controls. They aren't bound to follow the rules the way that we are, and you would never be able to tell that one of them was there if they decided to go after you, not until it was too late. The four that Royce has been meeting with are all Controls.

They're plotting something, and we don't know how many of them are involved. If Francis is there, though, I won't worry as much. Send Fiona. I really want to get that message." Sam peered over the top of the rocks. The Controls hadn't moved.

"I do, too," Sarah agreed. *"She'll be there in a few minutes. Do what you have to do to get it. This could be important."*

Sam tried to keep still and quiet while he waited for Fiona, desperate to get a hold of the message, but also filled with dread that he might be spotted. He traced Fiona's progress with his mind, just to remind himself why he should be patient, and to calm his racing heart and overall eagerness. The few minutes it took her to track him down felt like hours to the enthusiastic boy, and when he was certain that she was almost there, he turned and ran down the beach to join her.

Sarah had guessed right. The moment Fiona and Sam strolled into the area, Royce and the others dispersed, disappearing from view. Sam exhaled deeply, as he had been holding his breath almost the entire time that they had been walking the short stretch together, while anticipating the worst. Checking over his shoulder to make sure that they were not being watched, Sam crouched where the small orange box had been washed up onto the beach. It was not a matter of struggling to pull it free this time. It lay tangled in a mound of loose seaweed, and yielded easily to his small fingers.

Gleefully, Sam and Fiona rushed back with their new prize in hand, but they were so caught up in celebrating their success with Sarah, that they did not notice Nathan ahead of them until it was too late. They pulled up short, only several metres away from the house, as the larger boy approached them.

"Hey! Where are you going in such a hurry? What have you got there?" he asked, while wearing his friendly lop-sided smile.

Sam and Fiona froze. With a nervous look at her small companion, Fiona answered him. She couldn't lie, but she could limit what she told him. She would, however, have to make it convincing, or even someone as trusting as Nathan would start to wonder what exactly was going on.

"Just something that washed up on the beach. Sam thought that Sarah and I would like it."

Nathan laughed, with a glimmer in his eyes. He reached over and flicked the Little's chin.

"Spoiling the ladies now are we, little buddy? How am I supposed to compete with someone who's both cute and generous? What is it – some sort of jewellery box?"

Sam raised his eyebrows, unsure how to answer without giving too much away. Thankfully, Fiona could think faster on her feet.

"I'm not sure what type of box it is, but it is brightly coloured, and cute in its own way, just like Sam here. I'm sure it could have a variety of uses, if we think on it a bit. I would say we could count it as another one of his wondrous finds," she stated with a grin.

"Well then, I guess I best return to my circuit. Maybe I'll get lucky and stumble upon something that will impress our girls more than your gift did. Of course, you, Mister Finder, have a real advantage over me," Nathan chuckled on the inside. Then, after mussing Sam's hair the way that he often did, their Watcher strode off into the woods.

The two relaxed and Sam slid the box into his pocket. They didn't want to repeat a similar scene with Francis when they entered the house.

"He's gone," Fiona remarked. *"But that doesn't mean this is over. If Sarah's right, then they may know about this, and what does that mean for us?"*

"Your guess is as good as mine. If they are using him as their eyes, only time will tell what they intend on doing about this. At least he didn't get to see what was inside it."

With another glance in the direction that Nathan had headed off in, the two turned and walked into the house.

DISSIDENCE

Sarah, Fiona, and Sam gathered around the newest message in Fiona's room, counting on the fact that Francis was much less likely to interrupt them in there. He had taken to avoiding the older girl whenever he could after months of trying to re-establish any friendship that had been developing between them, but failing to meet this objective. He had not let her cold shoulder put him off at first, treading lightly around her, but remaining persistent. Eventually he had become discouraged and had given up any efforts at reconciliation.

The three used the same tactics at getting the small box open as they had the first time that they had received a message from Elliot. This time the note did not bear anyone's name. It was addressed to S, S, and F., but the hand-writing looked familiar, and the letter was much longer this time around. Fiona read it to the two Littles.

"I'm sorry for the length of time that it has taken me to get back to you, but it was necessary, I assure you. I had the opportunity to accept a transfer that took me temporarily away from the coast, but brought me much closer to an item that I hope will someday allow me to bring you your freedom. It is one that the scholars were having some of the technicians construct for them. This innovative magical device is something to help deal with some of the troublesome side-effects associated with the connection. It has other abilities, with the right magic to fuel

it, but I will have to do some more investigating before I will know the full extent of its many functions."

"A magical device? I wonder what he meant by trouble-some side effects," Sarah mused.

"There's more," Fiona told them, raising the paper before her. *"It also says that this has strengthened his belief that he will be able to assist us in righting the wrongs that have been done to us, but that he still has much more to uncover, and many more obstacles to overcome before he will be prepared to go the distance. He writes that the device is well guarded, and that he will have great difficulty coming up with a means of liberating it in order to bring it to us. He says that he has no one there that he is sure that he can trust, so he is forced to work alone, but he will keep working on our behalf. He goes on to mention that it may take him a fair amount of time, but he will continue to send us messages when he can, to keep us updated."* She paused, biting her lip in her typical nervous fashion.

"I'm just happy that nothing bad happened to him," Sam sighed. *"I was ready to give up on ever hearing from him again – to concede to this fate that has been thrust upon us."*

"That's not all of it," Fiona insisted. She took a deep breath.

"There is little that I can do for the moment, but I have a few leads, and I promise that I will do everything within my power to follow up on them. I know that I am asking a lot, but I need you to hang on, even if it seems to take longer than you might be willing to tolerate. I swear that I won't lose faith if you don't. There are solutions. I just have to strive for them. Until then, keep looking out for one another and be patient. E."

Sarah was grinning from ear to ear.

"He hasn't come to harm, and he hasn't deserted us. Right now I feel like the luckiest Fixer on Fervor."

"Why do you think that the scholars would be construct-ing this device?" Sam considered. *"Now that they have this experiment of theirs underway, what else is there for them to do?"*

"Maybe there were unexpected imperfections to their plans," the smaller girl hypothesized. *"Maybe they had to find a way to rectify them, or their experiment wouldn't work properly."*

"I don't know," Fiona responded, sounding doubtful. *"Why would they need to add more people on Fervor to the connection? You said they needed to keep the Controls for comparison, and they're the only ones on Fervor who aren't Connected. That doesn't make sense."*

"Maybe it isn't meant to be used now," Sam murmured. *"Maybe it is meant for whenever this experiment is done, and that could be many years from now. Of course, that's not something that we can really figure out without knowing what else it can do. Elliot seems to think that the things that he mentioned were only the tip of the iceberg."*

"I wish we could get Francis to tell us more," Sarah said quietly. *"I know that there's so much that he does know that he's withholding from us. He's scared that we'll find out eventually, and he continues to build his walls thicker and thicker to make sure that he can keep us out. It just gets worse every time he comes back from his meetings with the other Tellers. I'm worried. I know he says that it is important that we have our privacy, and that we can't have that without having strong walls to keep things in, and to block others out when we want to. But maybe, just maybe, there comes a point when you block too much out, and once you know what it's like to be Connected, I think that there is a danger to separating yourself too much. I've seen it in Francis. He's lonely, but it's all self-imposed. He's hurting himself, and he's doing it because he thinks that's what's best for us. Maybe we should tell him about all of this. Maybe if we shared with him, then he would share with us. Maybe..."*

"No," Fiona interrupted abruptly. *"This stays amongst the three of us. We can't trust Nathan because he is their eyes. It's nothing against him. You know how much we all like him, and he would never knowingly betray us, but the fact is, it*

wouldn't be a conscious choice on his part. The same should apply to Francis, all feelings aside and even if they conflict. Francis is as much their hands and mouth as Nathan is their eyes, and just like Nathan, because of his association with them, he can't be trusted."

Sam and Sarah were both fairly certain that the older girl did not see Francis as guiltless the way she perceived Nathan, but she did make a good point. As frustrating as it was to Sarah, who really believed that if they included the Teller and that if they showed him how much they already knew, he would stop fighting them and start working with them, she wasn't about to act on this belief if Sam and Fiona weren't in agreement.

When Fiona left to hide Elliot's message in the old hover along with the first one, Sarah pulled Sam inside her walls within the connection, and closed her door behind him.

"She's wrong about Francis," the smaller girl insisted, her thoughts noticeably forceful. Sam preferred her usual lighter approach, but he could sense that she was particularly anxious. *"Neither of you know him the way that I do. He doesn't like where he is. He feels trapped, like he's had to choose between two evils, and he's done his best to select the lesser one, but he would desperately like to have another option. He knows that the knowledge that he has been burdened with has damaged him, and he doesn't want to see that happen to us."*

"You aren't going to change her mind, Sarah. She was walking the line before Francis used me to test Nathan, and that pushed her the wrong way. She made her decision about him at that point, and I know that you don't agree with her, but I'm still undecided. There may be other options available to him, but he just can't see them because he won't stray from these Directives," Sam argued.

"Anymore than we can. That's not fair, Sam. Neither of you are being fair. You both expect more from him than you would expect from the rest of us. He's just as much a victim of this as we are. He's only a boy. You two are wrong about him.

I know you are – at the moment. If we don't make an effort to reach out to him however..."

She paused in mid-sentence and whipped her head around, listening attentively.

"Oh no," she mumbled getting to her feet and creeping towards the general direction of the door, her hands outstretched before her.

Sam clambered off the bed as well and joined her, taking her arm to guide her. *"What's the matter?"* he asked.

"Royce is home." The Control had been away for three days now. This was definitely outside of the Directives, and that meant that there was going to be trouble. *"He and Francis are arguing, and it sounds like it's going to be messy."*

The small boy didn't need any more prompting than that. He reached out for Nathan and knocked. A few moments later, the Watcher responded.

"What's up, little buddy?"

"I think you need to come home. Royce came back and he and Francis are at odds, according to Sarah. She thinks that it could get bad," Sam informed him.

"Hang on. I'll be there as soon as I can," Nathan said.

Sam led Sarah out of Fiona's bedroom to find a full-fledged stand-off between the two older boys by the front door. Fiona was already there, watching from just outside of the kitchen. The Teller and the Control were both leaning forward in a threatening manner, their expressions angry and their faces red. They both appeared to be shouting, or at least, that was what Sam would have guessed from their sharp intakes of breath and the way that they shook as they spoke.

"What are they saying?" he whispered to Sarah. Francis had his walls sealed up as solid as they could get during his dispute with the black-haired boy. For some reason, he did not want to allow the others into his thoughts while he and the Control screamed at each other.

"Francis was yelling about how leaving the house for several days without cause is against the Directives, and that

Royce can't be doing that," she reported. "And then Royce snapped that he had cause, so Francis could stuff it. After that, Francis said that if Royce had something that required him to be away for so long, then Francis would know about it. That was when Royce gave him that really mean look, and growled that Francis wouldn't know about it because it was a Control thing, and none of Francis's business. I think that made Francis really mad, because he shouted that anything that involves anyone in the house-family is his business, and he knows that there's nothing in the Directives that require the Controls to converge... converge? That means get together right? Like the Tellers having their meetings."

"Yeah, that's what it means," Sam told her. "Royce looks fit to be tied, and Francis doesn't look much better. I hope Nathan gets here soon. He may just have to play referee."

"You called Nathan?" Sarah questioned, a little startled. "Do you think that that's a good idea?"

"Better that he step in than see them come to blows," the smaller boy stated with a mental shrug. "Royce looks like he's ready to rip Francis's head off. I thought he had reserved that kind of hostility for me."

"I don't know if it is more out of ego or a fear of a loss of control, but Royce has decided to challenge whatever authority that Francis is supposed to have, and he's obviously stomping on Francis's toes in the process," the other Little sighed. "This is as much a battle of wills as anything else. Before Francis broadened his walls because of the argument, I got a sense of fear from him, but I don't know if he is worried that Royce will physically hurt him, or just concerned that he will beat him down with mind games. Royce has a huge advantage over the rest of us, when it comes to confronting Francis. He can resist Francis all he wants to and he can choose to ignore the Directives. Francis can predict how the rest of us would react to any given situation, but he can't predict what Royce will do. Maybe that's why he's scared."

Fiona had stepped forward, looking somewhat disconcerted by the escalating aggression between the two boys. She had dropped her walls, and Sam could tell that she was very upset. She would expect something like this from Royce, but definitely not from Francis.

"Calm down," she implored, speaking inside and out. *"You won't settle anything like this. You need to sort this out like civilized people. Maybe it's just a matter of a misunderstanding."*

Francis responded to her appeal. He hesitated, glancing her way. His pale greyish-green eyes revealed their customary need to please when dealing with Fiona, almost as though she had the same power over him as he had over everyone but Royce. The Control, on the other hand, ignored her. He made good use of the distraction to reach forward and grab Francis by the collar, yanking him forward with much more force than was necessary. Caught off guard, the blond boy stumbled to his knees, and Royce loomed over him menacingly, keeping a firm hold on him. Fiona, feeling somewhat responsible for Francis's current vulnerability, surged forward, waving her hands.

"Stop it! Stop it!" she exclaimed, shrieking it as well. *"Royce, let him go! Francis has a point. Aren't you supposed to be following the Directives, too? What good is fighting amongst ourselves going to serve?"* She latched onto one of the black-haired boy's arms and pulled.

Royce was not about to be swayed by simple words, not as riled up as he was at that moment. He turned and glared at her, trying to shake her off. When that didn't work, he released Francis's collar with his opposite hand, and gave her as harsh a shove as he could manage. Fiona's grasp had already been loosened by his first efforts, and she lost her hold on him when he pushed, stumbling backwards with little grace and then falling to the floor. Nothing was seriously hurt except her pride, but she stared at both boys with a pained expression from where she lay.

That was when the door opened and Nathan walked in. His eyes scanned the scene, and a frown settled upon his usually jovial face upon observing Royce and the position in which he held Francis. The crease in his brow deepened twice-fold as he spotted Fiona sprawled upon the floor. Sam was surprised at how the normally good-natured boy bristled. The Big's relaxed form tensed and seemed to almost double in size as he clenched his fists and gritted his teeth.

"This is over," he stated coolly, and with such finality. His typical stutter when he spoke aloud had vanished momentarily Royce looked over at him, contemplated the situation, and with a grimace, reluctantly released Francis. Sam felt Sarah's fingers tense and dig into his arm. She was not as convinced as Nathan was that the dispute had come to an end. There was still the possibility that this could get really ugly.

"If y-you can't p-play n-nice with one another, then I suggest y-you g-g-go your separate w-ways for n-now. Y-you have y-your own spaces. G-g-go there, and leave the rest of us in p-peace. We d-don't want to be a p-part of this b-b-battle."

His anger had faded a little, and as a result, his stutter had returned. Royce smirked at him. Giving Francis a solid elbow to the head, he marched past him and disappeared into his room.

"He said that that was all he wanted in the first place," Sarah reported. *"He said nothing would have happened if the ego-maniac hadn't gotten in his way. He claims that he wasn't planning to fight anyone until Francis stuck his nose into places where it doesn't belong."*

Francis did not go to his room. Instead, clutching at his cheek where Royce's elbow had made contact, he got to his feet and strode out into the kitchen. Nathan walked over to where Fiona lay and helped her up. It was clear to Sam that there was some conversation going on between the two Bigs, but just as Francis had been blocking him out during the friction with the Control, Nathan and Fiona weren't welcoming any intrusions either.

Sam was starting to think that he preferred things the old way, when he lacked some privacy, but other people couldn't hide things from him so easily either. Sarah gave his arm a quick squeeze and then released it.

"Do you think that's it then? No more fighting?" she asked hopefully.

"For now," Sam replied, relaxing a little. *"But as much as Nathan wants it to be, I don't think that this is over."*

That was when the smaller boy considered what really had just happened, and what sort of impact it had for him. He gazed at the Control's door. This had been an overt display of rebellion on Royce's part. Before now, Francis's instructions had been the only ones that he had been willing to listen to, and not because he was compelled to do so like the others, but for other unknown reasons. That had changed. Royce had made the decision that he wasn't going to follow the rules anymore if they didn't suit his purposes.

This revelation hit Sam like a brick to the side of the head. With the exception of any physical interference that Nathan had been able to offer, Francis had really been the only thing standing between the Finder and the older boy. What Royce had just done was essentially push Francis aside and now, if Nathan was not around, there would not be anything to help assure Sam's safety. Fiona had claimed that she could deal with Royce, but it seemed now that that was only talk, or at least, it didn't apply to any time when Royce was enraged over something, and lately that seemed more often than not.

The fear caused by these new circumstances gripped Sam violently, and hyperventilating slightly, he bolted for his room. Once inside, he locked the door behind him and leaped under his blankets. He huddled in the dark and shielding comfort that he found there, wishing that the sense of security they brought him was real, and not imagined. He also threw his walls up as thick as Francis normally did lately, and ignored all the knocking that came from the others. He wanted to feel like he was alone now, and safe as a result. If he could pretend that there were no threats to him, then he would not need anyone else.

* - * - *

On a day-to-day basis, things did not change much, but gradually, over the next two years, they got worse rather than better. Francis and Royce clashed on a regular basis, on the odd occasion that Royce bothered to come home at all, and the results involved some violence, usually on Royce's part, more often than not.

Royce's bullying of Sam worsened as well. He stopped making any artificial show of tolerance towards the smaller boy, and if Sam happened to be unfortunate enough to cross his path, he would usually have to run away in order to avoid any rough treatment. The Finder took to skulking through the backwoods when he had a choice, and as much as he liked the beach, he avoided it because of the lack of cover there.

Sarah, Fiona, and Nathan did not suffer to the same extent, but there was a general unease in their home, a sense of misery and hopelessness that hung over all of its inhabitants.

On the days following any storms, Fiona, Sam, and Sarah would all go out to scour the beach together, travelling in numbers in hopes that this might lend more security to their Finder. Sarah did not serve much purpose on these outings other than company, but Sam was still grateful to have her there. He was worried nonetheless. Running into Royce alone might not be a problem for the three of them, but if they encountered the five Controls that sometimes gathered there and the Unconnected Bigs decided to rid themselves of the perceived nuisance, there would be no contest. Two Littles and a female Big with only a moderate physical presence could never offer any real resistance to the threat that those five would pose.

They remained on edge while they searched, and they usually would not have to go far if there was nothing there to find. Sam could tell them within the first five minutes one way or the other, and on the days that there was nothing, they would return home both disappointed and relieved.

On five separate occasions, however, Sam was sure that he would find something there from Elliot, and they were forced to carefully make their way down the beach, keeping a constant lookout for danger. As if his own fear were not enough to deal with, Sam could feel Sarah's anxiety wash over him as well, and he gripped her small hand tightly, knowing it would not make any difference but finding the contact soothing despite this.

The first two times that they found the messages, there had been no sign of Royce whatsoever, and they recovered the little orange containers without incident. With the box happily tucked away in Sam's pocket, the three rushed back to the house to see what Elliot had to say. There were a few more details, but little in the way of progress suggested by the technician.

The first note had said that Elliot managed to obtain the name of the magical device that he was trying to steal and bring to them. He referred to it as the Languorite, and while knowing this would not help him gain access to the tool, it did let him know what to look for when scrounging for more information on the item. Elliot also said that he had managed to get a hold of a selection of the scholars' notes on the Languorite for a scant few moments and had scanned them as quickly as he could. The only new detail that he had picked up from them was that the device drew its magic from those around it passively, and that most of its effects were always active and persistent. There had been a couple of important exceptions, but Elliot had been forced to abandon his investigation at that point and flee in order to avoid getting caught. He had too much invested in making good on his promise to help the children of Fervor to risk being discovered.

The second note was somewhat apologetic. Elliot explained that he had not been as creative as he would have liked to have been, and had failed to get anymore information from the scholars. He did claim some success, however. As a technician, he had access to the blueprints of all the facilities on the mainland, and since he had assisted in the construction of the Languorite, he knew where it was being kept. He had gotten copies of the blueprints for that particular building in hopes that he could find a way in past security to gain access to the device. His note took on an air of despair from that point onwards, and he had obviously been discouraged by what he had found in those blueprints. He no longer seemed confident that he would achieve his objective, suggesting what needed to be done would surely require the efforts of more than a solitary man. He still asked them not to give up hope, and that he would definitely keep trying for their sake.

On their third venture to the beach that resulted in a find from Elliot, they did catch sight of Royce from a distance, and he them, but he was alone at the time. Much to their satisfaction, he chose to keep his distance from the threesome. They retrieved the orange box and made it back to the house safely with their treasure.

That message had been very brief, and Elliot had not offered anything new for them. He told them that he just wanted to let them know that he had not forgotten them, and that he was working on gathering equipment to help him break into the facility where the Languorite was being kept. He indicated that it was a very slow process. He did not have easy access to the resources that he needed, and he certainly did not have the manpower, but that would not stop him. He would find a way – somehow.

On their fourth successful trip to the beach, as they headed in the direction that Sam had guaranteed would lead them to the newest note from Elliot, Nathan had come across them just before they reached their prize. The day was quite grey and gloomy, and the Watcher approached them with a curious look.

"Hey! What are you all doing so far from home?" He wouldn't have been surprised to find Sam there on his own, looking for some good find. But he knew the small boy did not need Fiona's help to retrieve anything from the beach, and there was absolutely no call for Sarah to come along under any circumstances. It was also hardly the type of day that would prompt a casual stroll along the shore.

Sam shot Fiona a nervous look. She always seemed to be able to come up with a convincing reply, especially where Nathan was involved.

"Sam doesn't like to come to the beach on his own anymore. Ever since Royce started fighting with Francis and made it clear that he doesn't plan on taking orders from him, Sam doesn't feel safe," she suggested.

Sam nodded. Despite the inability to lie, it always amazed him how she managed to come up with answers that obscured a part of the truth. Neither he nor Sarah had mastered that skill.

"He asked me to come with him, but Francis wasn't at the house, and you know that I don't like to leave Sarah there by herself, so we brought her with us."

"Well that makes perfect sense. You happen to be right on the path of my circuit now. Do you mind if I walk with you? I like the company," the older boy stated.

This request actually presented Fiona with a bigger problem. She really did mind, but she did not want Nathan knowing that. How then to agree to his request without lying, or to dissuade him so that it would not be an issue? This time it was the older girl's turn to fidget uncomfortably. Sam came to her rescue.

"I'll be glad to have you with us," Sam told him.

He really meant it. Ever since Royce and Francis had started fighting, he was happy to have Nathan around whenever he could. It would delay things, and Sam would have to endure the horrible burning itch of passing the thing that he felt compelled to find, but it wasn't something that he would object to. Nathan had been quick to dismiss the first little orange container that he had seen as a meaningless trinket, but laying eyes upon a second one would surely generate some suspicion.

When his circuit finally drew the Watcher away from the beach again, they quickly made their way back to Elliot's message.

The fourth message said that the technician was finally making some advances on his plans, and that he was now in the process of hunting down a long-distance hover. He would need one in order to make the trek out to Fervor if and when he managed to get his hands on the Languorite. He still wasn't prepared to make any guarantees, but there was a renewed eagerness in Elliot's words, as if things had been going better than expected lately.

By the time they were done reading his letter, all three of them were twitching with excitement, so much so that when Francis arrived back at the house, he watched them for some time with suspicion. Since there did not seem to be any obvious reason for their buoyant mood on such a gloomy day, the Teller had good reason to wonder exactly what the three were up to.

The fifth and final message during that two year stretch came after a particularly violent storm shook Fervor with driving rain and fierce winds. When they headed out that day, before they had even reached the beach proper, Sam had been convinced that they would find something. Because he was so obsessed with finding the message that day, he had forgotten himself, thrown caution to the wind, and charged ahead of the girls. The box was half buried in the sand, and the small boy flung himself to his knees and started digging enthusiastically.

"Stop! Stop!" Sarah's familiar forceful push echoed urgently through his mind. *"Stop, Sam, please!"*

Sam knew that tone, and she had not bothered to knock. Something was wrong. He glanced up. Sarah and Fiona stood behind him and facing the opposite direction – in front of them stood Royce, and his four Control cohorts.

"He says they've seen us down here before, and that they know that something's going on," Sarah relayed. *"He says they want to know what we're up to, and that if we don't tell them what they want to know, they'll be forced to beat it out of us."*

Sam raised his gaze to where Royce loomed before them. The black-haired boy smirked down at him with malevolence gleaming in his brown eyes.

110

Dissidence

.

STORM

"Sam? Sam, what are we going to do? We can't tell him. It will ruin everything," Fiona demanded, expecting her Finder to offer a solution.

"Getting beaten to a bloody pulp will ruin everything, too," Sarah added, her thoughts panicky. *"We should call for Nathan."*

"Nathan may not get here in time, and if we involve him, he may find out what we're doing instead of Royce knowing," the older girl countered. *"I don't think that we should call him."*

Sam was thankful that they had the one advantage over Royce and his cohorts that allowed them to discuss their circumstances without the Controls listening in. That still left them with the current dilemma before them. This got Sam thinking. There were other differences with the Controls that could prove to be useful.

"I know we've gotten out of the habit, but we have to lie. Can either of you come up with a good story?" Sam asked.

At this point, Royce was growing impatient. He reached down and grabbed Sarah by the wrist, and then lifted her into the air. She squealed, kicking and flailing about.

"Just do something!" she thought desperately. The black-haired boy tightened his grip and she whimpered in pain as her struggling lessened.

"Don't hurt our Fixer!" Fiona protested. *"We need her!"*

"Sam, he said that you may need me, but that I can't fix him, so what does he care what he does to me. Then he said to answer his question or he'll break me so that I can't be fixed," the smaller girl whined internally. Sam knew that she was crying despite the fact that her face was mostly obscured by her dark hair, and he could tell that the larger boy's forceful grip was causing her a fair amount of pain. He had to come up with something convincing and fast.

"Fiona, tell him that we are trying to find a way around the Directives and that we come down here to discuss things away from Francis and Nathan. He doesn't like either of them, and I think at this point he hates Francis even more than he does me. Beg him not to tell Francis and say it like you mean it." Sam offered, hoping that, if nothing else, it would at least buy them some time.

The older girl did as he asked and the three waited anxiously for Royce's response. The Control turned to discuss the situation with his cohorts, and while they were distracted, Sam carefully felt around behind him until his fingers settled upon the shallowly-covered little box. With a few sharp tugs, he pulled it free and slipped it into his pocket.

Moments later, Royce turned back to face them again. He dropped Sarah into the sand in a careless manner. With exaggerated urgency, she crawled blindly towards Sam, not stopping until she had made contact with her small friend.

"Royce said that we can plot against the ego-maniac all we want, but not in his territory. He claims that from now on this part of the beach is reserved for him and his friends, and that he doesn't consider us his friends," she reported, her mind still frantic, but her fear beginning to lessen. She was still in pain however, and was rubbing at her wrist, wanting to heal the large bruises there, but not in the right mindset to concentrate properly.

"Tell him that we're going," Sam insisted. *"Tell him that we won't bother him here again."*

"But the message..." she thought plaintively.

"I've got it," he informed her. *"Let's just go, before he changes his mind."*

The three hurried away, thankful to have escaped Royce's clutches with minimal damage, and eager to see what Elliot had to say. Sarah did not even bother to ask the other two to stop long enough to allow her to repair her wrist. They scrambled back into the house, rushing past Francis towards Fiona's room.

"Wait!" the Teller commanded. They all lurched to an involuntary stop, as if someone had looped an invisible lasso over their heads and the rope had suddenly pulled taut.

"No, no, no, no, no," Sarah thought miserably. Sam and Fiona glanced tensely at Francis, wondering if somehow he knew about Elliot's message.

"What happened to you?" the Teller demanded, putting one hand on the petite girl's shoulder and reaching for her arm. *"How did you do this? And why haven't you fixed it yet?"*

"It was Royce," Sam admitted. He didn't see any harm in pitting the two Bigs against one another. There was already some conflict there. Why not use it to get them both out of their hair?

He felt a gentle knock from Sarah, and he let her in, blocking out Francis and Fiona.

"Don't do this, Sam," she begged. *"There are already enough problems between Royce and Francis. Don't make this worse."*

"What else do you want me to tell him," Sam snapped. *"It's not like we can lie to him."*

"I want to tell him the whole truth," Sarah stated. *"Please, I think it would work in our favour. He'll help us if he knows what's going on."*

"We don't have that much to gain by sharing this with him, and we have an awful lot to lose," Sam pointed out. *"Be-*

sides, Fiona would never agree to it, and we really do need her help."

"But Sam...." He didn't let her finish. He shook her free from his thoughts and focussed his own mind at Francis.

"Royce was meeting with those other Controls again. He told us that we weren't allowed on that part of the beach, that it was his territory. He picked Sarah up by her wrist and threatened to break her so that she couldn't be fixed."

No lies. All true. And just like that, they were off the hook. Francis frowned and covered his mouth with his hand, before turning silently and walking off into the kitchen.

"What have you done, Sam?" Sarah exclaimed angrily, pushing at him quite vehemently. *"He didn't need to know that. This is going to cause trouble beyond anything that would have happened if we had let Francis in on our secret. Why won't you trust him? Why won't you trust my instincts?"*

"You are too naive, Sarah. You are willing to believe that everyone deserves the benefit of the doubt," he retorted. *"We have to protect ourselves. We have to protect Elliot."*

Fiona knocked loudly, frowning at them from the doorway of her room. When they opened their minds to her, she chastised them.

"Quit bickering like preschoolers and get in here. I want to see that message. Don't you?"

Sam nodded and jogged past her into the room. Sarah followed with Fiona's guidance, somewhat reluctantly.

The message was different from the others. While they were sure that it had still come from Eliot, his handwriting was messier and less controlled than his prior notes. The scrawl seemed rushed and excited.

"This will be my last message for some time. I'm being relocated for my work, but it will bring me much closer to the Languorite. In addition to letting me study the facility where it is being kept firsthand, it will also allow me the possible opportunity to review more of the scholars' notes and get more answers on how exactly the Languorite works and what it can

do. I think that I have a lead on a long distance hover, one that can get me from the coast of the mainland to Fervor. I'll need one if I succeed in stealing the device so that I can bring it to you. It won't be soon. It could take me a year or more, but I believe more than ever that this can happen. Keep an eye out. If I fail, and I remain free, I will send another message. Then again, the next time that you hear from me, you may be encountering me in person. Keep your fingers crossed, and keep hopeful. E."

Fiona stared down at the crinkled paper, her eyes wide and her fingers now trembling. *"He said that he may be coming for us...finally, after all of this time."*

"If he comes here, we won't be able to hide this from Francis or Nathan. We need to tell Francis about this now, before Elliot gets here. Francis will know how to keep him from being discovered, and how we can let Nathan in on this safely," Sarah suggested.

"Let it go, Sarah," Sam sighed with a mental shake of the head. *"We're not including Francis in this. Besides, there's no guarantee that Elliot will make it here in the first place, and if he does it could be a long time in coming."*

"We can talk about this later. I just heard the door, and from the sounds of things out there, Royce may have followed us back here. Hide the message," Fiona said. Sam scrambled to bury the evidence under Fiona's bed as the two girls went over to the door.

"They're fighting again," Sarah admonished. *"And it sounds worse than last time. I told you, Sam. I told you."*

She blundered through the door and staggered blindly towards the arguing boys, worried at what might come of their newest dispute. Fiona and Sam followed after her.

When the smaller girl reached the Teller and the Control, she involuntarily drew Royce's attention away from the argument. Sam watched in horror as the black-haired boy's facial expression changed from that of hot-tempered anger to hateful resentment. He reached over and grabbed Sarah by the hair, yelling something at the waif-like girl.

"What's going on?" Sam pushed at Fiona, fearfully. *"Tell him to let her go."*

"I already called for Nathan. Royce is long past listening to us, and Francis can't make him do anything. He's really mad, Sam. Francis must have confronted him about our encounter on the beach. Royce said that Sarah ratted him out, and he called her a little bitch. I'm scared, Sam."

Sarah was screaming just as much on the inside as she was on the outside, and had grabbed the arm of the hand that clutched at her hair.

"You're in enough trouble as is, Royce," Francis stated sternly. He had dropped his walls completely, and Sam knew that this wasn't a good sign. *"If you do anything to purposefully damage our Fixer, they'll pull you off of Fervor. You'll be punished for the assault. You know how they feel about the Littles."*

Fiona continued to play the part of Sam's ears for the other half of the argument.

"Royce said that maybe that's what he wants, off of Fervor, and he doesn't care about the punishment. He says that he has been punished enough already. He claims that he was cheated out of the benefits that we have all had the opportunity to enjoy. He's bored, he's miserable, and we mean nothing to him. He says he won't let Francis try to intimidate him anymore and just to show that he means it – NO!"

Royce reached over and, getting a firm hold on Sarah with his other hand, he literally tossed her across the room and into the wall. The Fixer's link to the connection flickered and dimmed.

Fiona cried out the smaller girl's name and rushed over to her, while Francis grabbed the Control by the forearm. There was a pounding on the stairs outside and Nathan, near breathless, burst through the door. He lurched towards Royce and tackled him.

The two boys brawled without reservation beside the open door until the Watcher finally managed to overpower his opponent. Nathan shoved Royce away from him in order to gain enough space to pull in his legs and then thrust at the black-haired boy with his feet, with all his might. The aggressive gesture pushed the Control out through the open door and he rolled noisily down the front steps. There was a loud thud as Royce hit bottom, and he exhaled loudly, releasing a sound that was part grunt and part moan. Nathan then got to his feet, and stood in the doorway, shaking with rage and panting heavily.

"You hurt our Fixer, you hurt all of us. This is war, Royce. You hear me! War! Get out of here while you still can, before I change my mind. If I see you around here again, I'll kill you myself!" the Watcher roared.

No stutter… and he meant every word of it. Upon hearing this through the connection, Francis felt the need to step in.

"Calm yourself, Nathan," the Teller thought quietly at him. *"Nobody will be killing anybody."*

The distraught boy relaxed slightly, but not to the point of complete submission.

At the base of the stairs, Royce groaned softly, dragging himself painfully to a standing position. He wobbled a little and clutched at his left arm as if it might be injured. Then, with a dismissive grimace, he hobbled away. They all exhaled in unison.

Nathan did not wait to hear if anyone else had anything to say. He turned and strode over to where Sarah lay motionless on the floor, gathering her up in his arms as if she were a large rag doll. Her eyes were open, but she was clearly dazed.

"Can you hear me, sweetie?" he murmured through the connection, brushing a few strands of dark hair from her face. *"How bad are you hurt? I won't let him do anything like that to you again. I promise."*

She whimpered something incoherent, still stunned, and Nathan cradled her closer, while cupping her face in his hand. Sam prodded at her from within the connection, and he could

119

feel her faded presence growing stronger as each moment passed.

"I was worried something like this might happen," Francis admitted. *"It was obvious that he had no intention of respecting the Directives anymore, despite knowing the consequences of ignoring them. I wouldn't be surprised if they come to get him soon. Until then, I want all of you to keep your distance from him. He's much too unpredictable. He's dangerous. I had better go get one of the other Fixers. Sarah is in no shape to fix herself."*

As he stepped away, the smaller girl stirred.

"Don't go, Francis. I'll be okay," she assured him. A few seconds later, she seemed to have recovered even more of her senses. *"Just give me a few minutes to get my head together. I'll be able to fix myself then, I'm sure of it. I don't want you to go."*

"I'm sorry that he did that to you, Sarah," Francis apologized grimly. *"He knows better. He was just trying to get at me, and he knew that you would be the most effective way. He's gone rogue, and he's past the point of even trying to pretend that he cares about the Directives anymore. I saw it coming earlier, but I was hoping that we could change his mind. I don't know what they'll do to him. I don't know what they'll do to us either."*

This got Fiona's hackles up. She was always ready to find something negative in anything Francis had to say, and she was already in a foul mood because of what had just happened. She did not need another excuse to find him at fault.

"What do you mean, 'I don't know what they'll do to us.' Are you trying to rehash that old story that you were only letting him get away with all of his garbage because you were attempting to protect us? That tune's getting old pretty fast, Francis, and while you may believe it, I certainly don't. After what just happened to Sarah, you shouldn't believe it either. What's it going to take for you to stop playing these foolish games and start acting like something authentic? If you have any idea what

we might be expecting out of the ordinary, you should be telling us. You should have been telling us right from the start. Are you going to let us in on what's going on?"

With a disheartened expression, his face glum and his eyes sad, Francis looked away from her and did not answer.

"That's what I thought," Fiona thought with a sense of satisfaction. She crossed her arms before her chest. *"See, Sarah? I told you that he can't be trusted. Well, Royce may have been wrong about most things, but he was right about one, Mr. Teller, who thinks he is cleverer than the rest of us. You are an ego-maniac."*

She walked away, returning to her room.

Nathan had not paid much attention to their little altercation as he was still too busy worrying over Sarah. She was sitting up, and some of the colour had returned face, but she was still having trouble focussing. The Watcher glanced over his shoulder at Sam.

"I may not be able to kill that brute, but I'm going to break him the first chance that I get. What kind of monster would do this to someone like her?"

"Let this go for now, Nathan," Francis insisted. *"We can discuss this in greater detail later, when cooler heads prevail."* His gaze settled on Fiona's door as he said this. *"I still think I should go fetch another Fixer. Where Sarah's concerned, we can't take any chances."*

"No, please don't leave. If Royce went looking for those other Controls that he has been meeting with, it won't be safe out there – not while he's still as angry as he was when he left here." The smaller girl reached over and latched onto the hem of his shirt with her slender fingers. *"Look. I'll be fine."* She gestured towards the wrist of the hand that held his shirt. The bruises there were fading right before his eyes.

Francis seemed satisfied with that, but Sam could sense that the healing of those simple bruises was taking much more effort from the other Little than it normally would have. It was enough, however, to placate the Teller who gave a stifled sigh and a nod, and after freeing himself from Sarah's grasp, made his way to his own room.

Sam had a very uneasy feeling about how things had sorted themselves out. There had been a balance in the house before, a hostile one with plenty of tension, but a balance nonetheless. Now things felt completely off kilter, and there could be grave consequences for all of them as a result. As much as he hated and feared Royce, Sam was wondering if they hadn't all just leapt out of the frying pan and straight into the fire.

* - * - *

Under normal conditions, the elimination of Royce from the mix should have reduced the tensions in the house, but there were several problems that were aggravated by his loss. Over the next several months, things worsened in some ways instead of improving.

While the Control did not make any attempts to return to the house, he did not disappear completely from the area either. He left signs that he and his friends had been loitering within Nathan's circuit, sometimes vandalizing the structures that could be found there or carving rude messages into the trees on his usual path. Sam could not help but think that the black-haired boy would be very pleased to see that the five did not function perfectly without him.

For starters, Sarah, who had been fairly dependent on the others to begin with, became noticeably clingier. She would often go to great lengths to delay the departure of anyone leaving the house. At first, Sam thought that this behaviour might be some sort of reaction to the trauma that she had experienced just before Royce left for good. But that would have been easier to believe if she had concentrated most of her efforts on Nathan since he was obviously the one most capable of dealing with Royce should he try to force his way back into their home.

Instead, the majority of her stall tactics were directed at Francis and Sam. She hovered around Francis much more often than she used to, and while the Teller tolerated the smaller girl's presence, he didn't seem to be very comfortable with the persistent attention. She didn't moon over him like some sort of puppy-love crush, or suggest any interest that might be unnatural for a girl who was nearing thirteen but still looked seven or eight at best. Rather, she lingered around him with a sense of urgency or concern, and one that Sam could not really understand.

Her increased clinginess involving Sam was usually concurrent with the end of the latest storm. Her behaviour would become erratic at those times, and she would temporarily lose interest in Francis's activities and focus instead on Sam. He suspected it might have something to do with the fact that she knew that he would be making a trip to the beach, and possibly the fact that he now refused to take her with him on those days. If Francis was home, he would take Fiona, but after their scare on the beach when confronted by Royce and his cronies, Sam didn't dare put their Fixer at risk again. Not that it mattered. There had been no more messages from Elliot, just as he had warned.

Another change in attitude came from Francis. It was slow at first, but as it became more evident, Sam was wondering if perhaps Royce had served a greater purpose, keeping their Teller in check more than anyone had realized. Francis had never exhibited any real desire to exert his power over the others, except when the Directives deemed it necessary, but after Royce was gone, it was like an invisible barrier had dropped, and he had started overstepping whatever lines he had been willing to respect before.

On one of his less melancholic days, when he seemed irritable or generally moody, he would often order them around at whim, particularly Fiona. In fact, it seemed like there was a snowball effect when this would happen. The more the older girl resented Francis and the power that he had over them, the more he would lord it over her, and then, of course, the more she would resent it, and so on. He had stopped trying to please her as he had before, but Sam had noticed the Teller occasionally watching her when he was sure that she was not aware of it.

Fiona rarely spoke to the others in the house now, with the exception of the times that she would go out on a finding venture with Sam and the rare occasion that she would head out with Nathan on his circuit. In fact, Sam had noticed that, in a strange way, Royce had been a unifying factor, and now that he was gone, everyone other than Sarah seemed to go out of their way to isolate themselves.

They did not feel any safer without the Control in the house either. They now felt trapped there, never knowing what to expect if they dared to go outside. Would Royce consider Nathan's declaration of war a personal challenge? Would he be lurking behind a tree along the path trying to exact some sort of vengeance as a result of being exiled from their family? Was he plotting some sort of ambush or break-in with his friends, waiting for the moment that Nathan left before descending on the more vulnerable members of his family?

All of these ideas bothered Nathan the most, and the Watcher became edgy and sullen. He always seemed reluctant to leave in the morning, and would run himself to near exhaustion every day trying to complete his circuit as quickly as possible in order to get back to the house before anything undesirable could happen. There was now a quiet misery to the boy who had always been smiling, an air of helplessness that was completely out of place in someone like Nathan.

The Watcher, who had been blissfully ignorant of the lack of change in his cohorts in the past, now began questioning Francis, too, who would shrug his shoulders in response and otherwise refuse to answer. It had been easy for someone who was overly trusting, and who had been the size of a fifteen-year-old when he was almost thirteen, to dismiss the lack of growth in himself and even his smaller companions in the first few years. Now that almost five years had passed since they had been abandoned on Fervor, he could no longer pretend that nothing was wrong. He should have been practically an adult by this point, as well as Fiona and Francis, and Sam and Sarah should have been entering adolescence. It was clear that they had not physically aged a day, let alone five years.

As the stresses on the five grew, they found themselves facing the worst storm that had ever hit Fervor, at least as far back as they could remember, even Fiona. The house creaked and rocked under the strain of the gale force winds and torrential rains, and the children huddled together in the kitchen after Nathan and Francis had covered the windows with blankets.

Despite being there together, Sam felt more alone than ever. No one spoke, with their walls raised high and thick. Sarah even sat away from the table in a corner, rocking a little to soothe herself and hugging at her arms. When Sam could tolerate the silence no longer, he slunk away from the kitchen, seeking solace in his room.

Sam had not missed his life before the connection in a long time, but that night he could not help but feel miserable and longed for Maria and the old ways things were done. He had not bothered to cover the windows and lay on his bed watching the lightning flare outside, feeling sad and drowsy.

Then, there was a sudden movement out of the corner of his eye, along with a chilling draft, and he realized that the door to his room had blown open. Curious, Sam rose and wandered out to see what was going on. The front door was open, too, but he was the only one there to investigate. Sam dropped his walls and felt about the connection to see why no one else was around, and much to his horror, he could not find them there. How was that possible? He was a Finder. If they were there, he should be able to find them. Had Royce and the other Controls been to the house? Had they done something to the rest of his family?

Sam felt a faint and brief push from somewhere outside. The contact was such a weak brush from the other mind that Sam was not able to identify it, although he could tell that the other person was in trouble. Sam tried to latch on, but the thought dimmed and the link slipped away and was lost to him again. He had to get closer if he would hope to re-establish it.

Braving the storm, he staggered his way down the steps and headed for the beach.

The rain was so heavy that Sam was practically blinded by it, and there was only the vaguest hint of moonlight that managed to trickle down through a small parting of the dark clouds. The only time he could really see anything was when the sky would light up with a flash of lightning. He struggled down to the shore, trying to follow his finding instincts despite being mostly blind and completely deaf, blown about by the harsh winds and soaked to the bone.

When his foot finally sank into the sand, Sam paused. Another brilliant flash exposed a figure prone on the beach before him, too large to be Sarah, Fiona or Francis. Was it Nathan? Sam was about to move forward when he noticed the taller silhouettes around him, barely visible in the dimness. It was the Controls – he was sure of it. His heart lurched and his pulsed quickened.

Before he could react, a hand grasped his arm and started shaking him. It had to be Royce. The lightning flared a third time, and the dark-haired boy loomed over him, but instead of his usual malicious smirk, his face was that of a gruesome monster.

Sam shrieked in terror, but he realized that he had heard his own screams outside as well as inside, and he knew that that just wasn't right…not only that, but the hand that was holding him and shaking him was much smaller than Royce's should be. His subconscious made him deny what he was experiencing, and moments later he woke up with Sarah at his side.

"Wake up. Sam, please wake up," she begged. *"It's Elliot. I felt him, only for a split second, but he's here, on Fervor. I had him, and then he was gone."*

Sam sat up in bed, startled by what she had just told him. Part of his dream had been real. Even sleep was not enough to suppress his finding instincts.

"I know where he is," Sam insisted. *"We have to go get him, but you and I won't be able to do that alone, even with Fio-*

126

*na's help. It looks like you are about to get your wish. We are
going to have to let Francis in on this."*

9

FOUND

"Tell Francis?" Sarah exclaimed. *"What?"*

Sam stumbled out of bed and hurried through the door. *"We have to go get Elliot and we may have to carry him back. You can't come with me, you'll just get in the way, and he looked bigger than Nathan even. Fiona and I won't be able to fetch him on our own, and even with Francis, it will be a stretch. We really should have Nathan's help, but I don't see how we can make that work."*

As Sam threw his rain gear on, a bleary-eyed Fiona and a yawning Francis emerged from their rooms, responding to a summons by the Finder. The smaller boy reached out through the connection towards the general area where he expected Elliot would be. He found the vaguely familiar mind, but it was dim, dimmer than Sarah's had been immediately after her encounter with the wall, and it was completely non-responsive to Sam's gentle prodding.

"We need to hurry," he suggested, pushing with some urgency at Sarah. *"I think something may have happened to him. I don't even know if he's conscious."*

"What are you doing?" Fiona demanded unhappily. *"It's the middle of the night, Sam. There's a terrible storm out there. You can't go out there like this."*

"We have to go, Fiona. We have to go get Elliot, before it's too late." Sam thought this openly to all three in the room,

129

not making any attempt to block Francis out. The older girl's eyes widened at the mention of the technician, but then she realized what Sam had just done. Her expression fell, horrified at the fact that Sam had just exposed them to the Teller.

"Elliot? Who is Elliot?" the blond boy asked, with the question as open as Sam's statement had been.

"Sam! How could you? I thought we had agreed..." Fiona began, her thoughts a whirlwind of emotion.

"So this is something that you are aware of, too," Francis interrupted. *"Well then, I want the most concise answer that I can get, and that is, after all, what Keepers are for. Tell me everything that you know about this Elliot, Fiona."*

Clearly disgusted with what she was being forced into, the older girl did just that. The words spilled out of her like Francis had just released the magical restraints holding back the waters in a reservoir. She spared no detail as she described from the first message that had come into Sam's possession to the last one that the Little had found on the day that Royce had been exiled from the house. Francis had thrown up his walls the moment Fiona's revelations had begun, allowing only her to see his reaction to her response in the face of his command. When she was done, she turned away from him trembling with anger, ashamed at what she had done and viewing the Teller as more despicable than ever.

At first, Sam watched all of this with curiosity, and Sarah stood behind him, wishing she had a better idea of what was going on. Then, wary of the delay, he hunted through the connection for Elliot again. When he did find him, he could see why Sarah had lost contact with him. His presence there was now so dim even Sam could barely sense him. Sam took the opportunity to redirect Sarah to Elliot, suggesting that she hold fast to him until he had been retrieved. A push from Fiona drew the Finder back to the house again.

"Why, Sam? Why?" Fiona murmured tearfully, her cheeks flushed from her shame.

"I told you, Fiona. We have to go out there and get him. You and I can't do that alone. We need Francis's help. I'd rather we go through this here and now, than find ourselves arguing about this while standing out there in the storm. He was going to find out eventually, once we actually get to Elliot," he thought in his own defence. *"Now that that's out of the way, we had better go, before it's too late for him. His presence in the connection is very dim. I think that he is hurt worse than Sarah was when Royce attacked her."*

"Close to what Sam was like when Nathan pulled him out of the water. Sam's right," Sarah agreed.

"But what about Nathan?" Fiona disputed, with her thoughts poignant and shrill. *"Better Nathan than Francis!"*

The Teller cocked an eyebrow at her with this comment. He dropped his walls again.

"I would hazard to say that you are wrong there. It would be a bad idea to bring him along, unless you really want to get this Elliot of yours into trouble."

"See, I told you," Sam mumbled, the thought directed at the Keeper. *"He is their eyes."*

The smaller boy's comment drew a startled reaction from Francis. Before he could say anything, however, Sarah began physically pushing the Teller in the direction of the door.

"Enough talking and more doing," she insisted. *"He needs you. I can feel him fading. No more delays."*

Throwing on their own rain gear, Francis and Fiona followed Sam out into the storm. It was just like his dream. Once away from the house, the pathway was barely visible with the exception of when the lightning flashed overhead. The notion that Royce and the other Controls might be out there was enough to bring goose-bumps to the smaller boy's sodden flesh, remembering the monstrous face that Royce had been wearing in his nightmare. Sam refocused his efforts on finding Elliot as a means of escaping these frightening ideas.

The beach proper was not as agreeable as it had been in Sam's dream, however. The clouds did not part to allow any

moonlight through, and the lightning flares were even more sporadic. Sam sloshed forward into the wet sand using the
connection to search for Elliot more than anything that he was
using in the physical world. Fiona and Francis followed closely
behind him, and fortunately were using more caution than he
was or they would have fallen with him when he actually tripped
over Elliot's prone body. Sam tumbled into the sand next to him
and momentarily lost his bearings. When he sat up, the sky lit
up briefly, and Sam, Francis, and Fiona all grabbed for Elliot's
sprawled form.

"*How are we going to manage this,*" Fiona moaned internally. "*We need Nathan for this.*"

"*We'll manage,*" Francis assured her calmly. "*Fiona,
you take his feet and I'll grab him at the shoulders. Sam can
help bear some of his weight and brace him at the middle. Pay
close attention. I'll direct you both to the best of my ability.*"

The girl obeyed, as she had to. They felt around in the
dark in order to get into position, and following the Teller's instruction, they all hoisted Elliot from the ground. Then they
began the treacherous trek back to the house.

They had to stop to rest and restore a proper hold on their
heavy burden three times before reaching the house. The third
time, they were close enough to the house that the outside light
that Fiona had illuminated on their way out gave them the
chance to see Elliot properly for the very first time. He was
dressed in a simple and strangely slick navy cover-all, looked
like he was about a head taller than Nathan with a similar build,
and had coarse, shoulder-length hair the same light brown colour
as Sam's. He also had facial hair, something that none of the
children had ever remembered seeing. The other thing that Sam
noticed was the patch of blood on the side of Elliot's face.

"*I wonder what happened to him,*" Fiona thought, reaching over and touching his beard with some trepidation.

"*I wonder what happened to his hover,*" Francis added,
trying to catch his breath as the rain ran in thick rivulets across
his face.

He was not built for this kind of work the way that Nathan was. The blond boy was of average build and not particularly athletic. Despite this, he had been bearing the lion's share of Elliot's weight, but had not complained about it once, unlike Fiona.

"Without it, he'll be just as stuck on Fervor as the rest of us. He was crazy to think that he would make it here without getting caught. They had everything all calculated out before this all started. They didn't want anyone interfering with their plans, especially not someone from the mainland. Things were supposed to go as scheduled. They won't be pleased about this. The punishment will be harsh."

Sam was surprised. This was more than they had gotten out of Francis in the last year. Perhaps Sarah had been right after all. Perhaps by showing their hand, he would be willing to show them more of his.

"Is that what you are afraid of, Francis?" the smaller boy asked. *"Are you afraid that if you don't follow the Directives, that if you tell us too much, they'll punish you, too?"*

Before the Teller could answer, Fiona spoke up within the connection.

"What is that, around his neck?"

The two boys looked to see what she was referring to. There was a black case suspended on a strap that rested on Elliot's chest. The strap had been knotted so that the loop was too small to fit over the man's head. It was something that he had secured purposefully so that he would not lose it.

"The Languorite," Sam guessed. *"Maybe that's the Languorite."*

Francis went to reach for the case, but then hesitated. After displaying an unexplained twitchiness, he withdrew his hand again.

"No, it would be silly to look at it out here. Besides, it's only short stretch more to the house, and Sarah is waiting for him. I think I'm rested enough to make it now," the Teller suggested.

They positioned themselves around the unconscious man again, and struggled through the remainder of the journey to their door. Once inside, they hastened to get Elliot into Sarah's room and lay him on their Fixer's bed.

Francis's twitching was now rather pronounced. He chocked it up to physical exertion and stumbled his way back to his own room. Had Sarah not been so preoccupied with Elliot, she likely would have followed him, just to make sure that he actually was okay. Instead, she leaned over their technician friend, trying to make the connection that she would need to start healing him.

"It's so faint," Sarah lamented to Sam. *"I don't know if I can make this work."*

"You have to at least try," Sam pointed out. *"This is Elliot that we are talking about. We need him."*

"It wouldn't matter who it was, Sam. I'm a Fixer; I would have to try anyway. I'm just saying that this is going to be really difficult. I need you to prepare yourself for the fact that I might not succeed. That certainly doesn't mean I won't try, it just means that there is a possibility that I'll fail."

Sarah pushed Sam away after that. She threw up her walls as solidly as she could manage so there would be little to disrupt her concentration on Elliot. Resting her small head on his chest, with one hand perched atop his ribs, and the other gripping Elliot's shoulder, she closed her eyes and went to work.

Sam cautiously opened the case that they suspected contained the Languorite. It had slid to the side opposite of Sarah, resting on the bed. Sam could not unknot the strap and lift it over Elliot's head without disturbing the Fixer, so he resorted to sliding the case's contents out into his hand. He and Fiona moved away from Sarah's bed to examine it.

"It looks a little like a glow torch," Sam observed, shifting closer to Fiona.

The casing was made out of some non-descript metal, a darker coloured material with a silvery sheen. Instead of the flat lens covering the colourless crystals that illuminated in response to the user's magic that you would find in a glow torch, there was a small, many-faceted sphere affixed at one end. It shone with a myriad of colours without any fuel from an outside force. Sam wondered if it had its own internal fuel source, or if it automatically drew magic in from those around it. Elliot had mentioned, after all, that the Languorite functioned on a passive level, and for the most part, did not need activation from those who were using it.

That was when a notion struck him. If what Elliot had said was true, the Languorite was likely working right now, and they still did not know exactly what it could do yet. This idea startled the smaller boy so much that he almost dropped it. Without any hesitation, he raced back over to the bed and hurriedly slipped it back into its case.

"What are you doing?" Fiona protested. *"We weren't finished looking at that."*

There seemed to be something odd about her. Sam looked at her more closely. There was a tremor to her limbs as well, reminiscent to Francis's twitchiness, but to a lesser extent. She had not been willing to carry her share of Elliot's weight, and therefore was likely less fatigued than the Teller, but apparently, the effort had taken its toll on her as well.

"I had a good enough look at it to know that we likely shouldn't be handling it again until Elliot is awake," Sam explained.

"If he wakes up at all," the older girl sighed.

"We don't know everything that it does, and some of its functions are passive and persistent, remember? Who knows what it is doing right now?" Sam stated, watching Sarah adjust her position as she moved on to healing some of Elliot's other injuries. While still very dim compared to Sam, Fiona, and especially Sarah, the man's presence in the connection was actually strengthening as a result of her efforts. That boded well for Elliot and the youths that he had vowed to help.

"Of course I remember," Fiona grumbled internally. *"I am a Keeper after all. Aren't you curious? He assured us that*

the Languorite would help us, not hurt us. That's why he was bringing it to us. How could it do any harm to examine it? The passive functions would already be having their effects on us anyway, and there's no chance that we could use any of the ones that need to be activated without knowing how to do it. I'm sure that it's safe."

"Well you can look at it all you want – I'm not going near it," Sam declared. "I'll stick around until Sarah's done, though; in case she needs anything, or in case Elliot wakes up."

"I wouldn't hold my breath," Fiona murmured, admiring the thing that they had been waiting for, for so long. The faceted sphere seemed to glimmer in strange ways at unexpected moments. "It's so pretty, and holding it makes my skin tingle, like the nice kind of goose-bumps you get when something makes you feel really good."

"What?" Sam hadn't really noticed anything like that when he had held it, but now that she mentioned it, there was a prickly pleasantness to his own skin. She held it out to him.

"Hold it again, and see for yourself," she offered.

He shook his head, and took a step back, just to make it clear that he still wasn't willing to handle it again. Beside him, Sarah muttered something incomprehensible from her bed and had now moved up to Elliot's head wound, but her gestures had become sluggish, and it was obvious that this fixing was taking a lot out of the small girl She was barely able to hold her head up. Sam was pretty sure that she was going to crash soon, and not necessarily when she had finished all the fixing on Elliot that she had had to do. It was bad enough that they had been forced awake during the middle of the night. He knew that the weaker the link to the connection the person that she was fixing had, the greater the toll her fixing efforts took on her.

Fiona shrugged and went back to fiddling with the device while Sam focussed his attention on Sarah. She lasted about twenty more minutes before she started moving towards Elliot's feet and then slumped forward across his lower legs, too exhausted to move any farther. Sam walked over and gently eased her off of Elliot and onto the end of the bed. He pulled one of the blankets over her, checking in on Elliot through the connection as he did so.

"That's enough for now, Sarah. You've done what you can, and from what I can tell, he ought to pull through. You get some sleep, and prepare yourself to see what more you can do for him tomorrow. Maybe then we can get some answers from him, like what happened to him and his hover, how he managed to get his hands on the Languorite, anything new that he discovered about what it can do, and anything else that he knows that can prove useful to us. It's a true miracle that he's here. Let's just hope that it wasn't all in vain." He thought this quietly at her, as he felt her slipping into slumber, remarking on the situation more for his own benefit than for hers.

Sam glanced over at Elliot. Sarah's handiwork was evident. The wound on his head was gone, and his breathing was now more fluid and regular – not shallow like it had been when they had finally managed to get him up the front steps. He had lost some of his pallor and the blueness to his lips.

Sam moved a little closer, looking intently at the sleeping man's face. He allowed his gaze to linger there, not having seen an adult in almost five years. He wondered if he would ever have the opportunity to grow, and to look like this. It was frustrating being trapped in the body of a small child, no matter what the benefits, when his maturing mind had now overstepped the capabilities of his immature body, and being as small as he was made him so vulnerable to outside threats.

As these thoughts rose to the surface, movement caught Sam's eye. Fiona was returning what they had assumed to be the Languorite to its case, a grimace on her usually placid face.

"Is there something wrong with it?" Sam asked. She shook her head.

"No it's fine. It's me. I'm tired and feeling a little off, and I think I pulled something when we carried Elliot up from the beach. There must have been some way that we could have included Nathan. He's so much stronger than we are. With his

help, we would have gotten Elliot back here in half the time and with half the effort from the rest of us," she replied, some of the strain that she had mentioned showing in her face.

"We can talk to Francis about it tomorrow, when there's more time to discuss things like this, once Nathan has left for his circuit. Maybe he'll have some ideas on how we can tell Nathan about this without exposing Elliot to the people who Nathan is on watch for," the smaller boy stated.

Fiona made a face at the suggestion of discussing anything with the Teller, still holding a grudge. She sighed.

"I suppose you're right, and maybe I should have been more willing to listen to Sarah in the first place. Francis seems to be more interested in going along with all of this than I would have expected, even to the point of starting to share some of the information that he had been hiding from us. I still don't like him though, and I doubt you'll ever convince me that I should. He goes on about doing things in order to protect us, but after our conversation, I'm certain that everything he ever did was primarily to protect himself," she griped.

"You know he couldn't lie about that. He really did think that he was protecting us," Sam countered. *"That's why Sarah trusts him so much. That's why she thinks that you are being unfair."*

"Maybe he talked himself into believing it, while he made up excuses for his own behaviour. Did you ever consider that?" She grimaced a little again, and yawned. *"I'm going back to bed. There's nothing more that we can do here right now. Like you said, we'll talk about it again in the morning."*

Looking somewhat uncomfortable, she headed off for her own room.

Sam stared for a few moments at the sleeping man and the small girl curled motionlessly at his feet. Elliot's arrival was going to change things for them one way or another. Either they would have the opportunity to let the Languorite work its magic, and perhaps not even Elliot knew what all of those changes would bring, or they would get caught by those who had thrown them all into this mess to begin with, and none of them knew exactly what those consequences would be, although Francis had suggested he had some idea. As if that was not enough, there was still the possibility that Royce and his friends could somehow get wind of this, and that could easily be another disaster waiting in the wings.

Sam shuddered, and not just because these thoughts had him worried. He could still see the goose-bumps on his arms, as the tingle continued there, as well as on his cheeks and along the back of his neck. It wasn't uncomfortable in anyway, but it was distracting enough that despite being desperately tired, Sam wondered if would actually be able to fall asleep. He decided that he had better try. After seeing Sarah stir a little, and then settle again, he headed for his own room, planning on returning as soon as he awoke the next morning.

He had just stepped out of Sarah's room, and was closing the door when Nathan appeared at his own doorway.

"Sam? What are you doing up. I thought maybe that last bit of thunder had woken Sarah. I felt a little distress from her through the connection when the crash nearly shook me out of bed. Why would you be awake? There's no way that you would have heard that. I figured you were down for the night when you wandered off to your room earlier."

Sam froze. He could not let Nathan know about Elliot because then the Watcher would want to see him, but he could not tell the larger boy that he had been checking on Sarah because of the thunder either. Sam knew that it was not Nathan's fault that he wanted to know why Sam was creeping around at night. It was that protective urge that was part of being a Watcher, the one that had brought him out here in response to the last loud crash in the first place, and if any of the house-family was acting out of the ordinary Nathan would be compelled to find out why. He just wanted them to be safe.

"I-I had a bad dream, and then I couldn't go back to sleep." That was, after all, how the situation with Elliot had

started, and he couldn't have gone back to sleep because it was necessary to fetch the injured technician.

Nathan drew closer.

"You're soaked! Were you out in the storm? What were you doing going out there, in that mess, in the middle of the night? It's dangerous!"

"It was because of what I dreamed. In my dream, I was finding something, out on the beach. I ran into Royce and his friends there, and Royce turned into a monster. It was one of the worst nightmares that I've ever had."

Sam didn't know what else to say. His venture into the rain had been caused by what he had seen in the dream, but there had been so much more involved, and if he gave away any more, Nathan would find out about Elliot.

"Are you trying to tell me you were sleepwalking? You've never done that before..." Nathan began.

"I was with him. He wasn't alone. He was fine," Fiona thought at the older boy, emerging from her room. She had been almost asleep when she had picked up on their awkward conversation in the connection. She could tell that Sam was struggling, and while she didn't have any ideas on how to distract or deter Nathan from his line of questioning either, she at least could lessen the burden on Sam.

"If there was a problem, why didn't you wake me?" the Watcher demanded.

"Someone needed to stay behind with Sarah. Besides, Francis told me not to," Fiona thought matter-of-factly. Both comments were true, although incomplete.

Nathan was aware that Francis had taken to ordering Fiona around on a whim, with preference to her over all others. This made what she was telling him easier to swallow. Sam could tell that trying to deceive Nathan, even if only by omission, was something that she found really distasteful, and he was grateful that she was willing to go to such lengths to protect Elliot.

The next thing that happened however, took him a little by surprise. Standing in the same room as him, Nathan and Fiona threw up their walls and had a very lengthy conversation with one another, behind closed doors.

Sam felt a little like the unwanted playmate shoved to one side at the playground while the other children whispered in secret. He had seen them do this before, but they had not been quite so blatant about it, usually doing so when several people were present, but otherwise preoccupied. He recognized that, as Bigs, they might want to discuss things that they felt he would not understand. He still didn't enjoy being left out, especially when one slip from Fiona could expose Elliot.

In the end, their private discussion concluded sooner than expected. After they had been like that for a few minutes, Francis also made an appearance looking very tired and still somewhat twitchy. He gazed upon Fiona and Nathan with an expression that Sam could not interpret, and continued to stare at them for a little while before he actually intervened.

"The storm's settling and everyone should be fine. There's no need for people to be loitering about. We should all get back to bed. That includes you Nathan – go back to bed. I have a feeling that we're going to have a very busy morning," the Teller stated.

Sam was surprised to hear Francis give Nathan a direct order. It was something that he was rarely inclined to do, even when he was being moody. Fiona gave him a harsh stare, and Sam got the feeling that he was missing something. There was certainly something unspoken going on amongst those three.

Without a choice, Nathan returned to his room, and Fiona begrudgingly went back to hers as well. Sam looked at the Teller, wondering why he had felt the need to interfere. Francis sighed and shook his head.

"You too, Sam. I meant what I said. If Sarah manages to bring your Elliot around tomorrow, we are going to be facing a lot of big changes around here. We'll need to be well-rested and clear-headed to make sure that we handle the situation

properly. This would have been a lot simpler if you had made me privy to all of this information much sooner. I don't under-stand why you felt you had to hide this from me. I could have helped you with all of this. I wouldn't have betrayed you."

"Fiona doesn't trust you and I'm not sure that I do ei-ther, Francis. Whatever your reasons for it, you've kept too much from us for us to be willing to openly discuss our finds with you, not without sufficient motivation...and now we are all keeping things from Nathan. This won't work. We're going to have to find a way to let him in on what we are doing. He'll fig-ure out that we are hiding something from him eventually. He almost did tonight," Sam suggested.

"You don't trust me, eh? Well, I can't say that I blame you. I can't say that I would trust me either, if I were in your shoes. The other Tellers warned me that it would be this way... they encountered it before I did. They all claimed that they felt isolated because they weren't allowed to pass what they knew along to the others. I told them that my house-family was differ-ent. I guess it just took longer for me to see it." He closed his eyes and breathed in deeply. *"I don't feel like talking anymore. Go to bed, Sam. We'll handle this tomorrow."*

Sam did as he was told, unable to resist, but he did not go to sleep right away. He sat up wondering and worrying. He wondered what Elliot would do for them, and he worried that he had just broken Francis in a way that Sarah would never be able to fix.

10

EFFECTS OF THE LANGUORITE

Sam had not yet opened his eyes when he awoke the following morning, but he lay in his bed wondering where the terrible pains in his lower legs had come from. The sensation was like a severe migraine, only in his ankles and calves instead of in his head. It was that ache that had actually roused him from sleep, along with the soft singing coming from somewhere within his room. He was still only half-conscious, and not wary that something had changed drastically for him, in order for him to be hearing something that wasn't coming from inside of his head. Also, he had not registered the fact yet that he had not heard music in years since music did not transmit through the connection.

As he eventually regained a little more of his senses, the novelty of the situation finally struck him. He slowly opened his eyes. Sarah was sitting in a chair across the room humming and singing happily to herself as she waited for him to awaken. When she saw Sam looking her way, she grinned at him. She looked bigger than Sam remembered her.

"Hey sleepy-head," she said. "I was the first one up, and I did some more fixing on Elliot. I think I've done as much as I can for him. It should be enough. He's still resting, and it might be a while yet before we can talk to him, but..."

He could hear her. He could actually hear her. And she was staring right at him.

"You can see me," Sam remarked, both outside and in.

It was his first time attempting to use his own voice since he had become deaf, and it was raspy from disuse, but he heard himself loud and clear.

Sarah nodded and smiled broadly again. "I think I figured out what Elliot meant by troublesome side-effects. Oh, Sam, you don't know how wonderful it is to finally see you first-hand, and not skewed by someone else's perception. All of the others saw you a little differently, and I don't think any of them did you justice. Of course, right at this moment, you might want to brush your hair," she laughed.

Her laughter was contagious. She didn't realize how much he had wanted to hear her voice, listen to her giggles, or even just find out what she sounded like when she sneezed. He had missed so much over the years, even things as simple as the roar of the waves, the cry of the gulls, or the whistling of the wind. They had seemed like nothing to him once, but when they were gone, they had left a noticeable void behind.

"How?" Sam breathed in amazement.

"Elliot must have brought us that Languorite that he had talked about, and it's already working. I have no idea how it could do this, but I'm sure Elliot will be able to explain. He is a technician, after all. I think that he'll have a lot to tell us about, things that he couldn't put into his messages. Maybe he can tell us why they did this to us. Maybe he can give us some idea of how they made all of this happen."

He had not seen Sarah this happy in the entire time that he had known her. That timidity that seemed to be a natural part of her personality was not there anymore either.

"I'm not helpless now," she thought with a warmth that he could feel run right through him. *"I can take care of myself from this point on."*

As almost a complete juxtaposition to her joyful and soothing thoughts, the connection was suddenly blasted by panic, and they heard a half-shriek, half-moan, coming from the

Watcher's room. Sarah's eyes widened in response and she turned to look at the door.

"Ah! Nathan's awake. He wasn't expecting any of this. Oh no! Who knows what he will think is happening. This will be a horrible shock to him," she gasped.

"But I thought you said that this was happening because of the Languorite," Sam protested. "We didn't let Nathan get anywhere near Elliot. The closest he got was a few feet from your room. Why would it be affecting him?"

Sarah rose and headed for the door.

"I'm just guessing, Sam. Besides, we have no idea how close you need to be to the device for it to work. I'm assuming that if it has affected Nathan, it isn't a matter of close contact."

"Then it ought to have some sort of impact on Francis and Fiona, too," Sam concluded, moving to climb out of bed and follow her. The pains were still throbbing through his calves and ankles. When he went to stand, his legs did not function the way that they used to, and he almost fell over. He stared down at his feet. They were farther away than he remembered. Confused, Sam looked over at Sarah, who had paused at the door, and then he glanced at his arms and hands. They were bigger, too.

"Yes – there's that as well," she acknowledged. "I have a theory that maybe the Languorite somehow impedes the stasis, or eliminates it altogether, Sam. We seem to be growing again, and at an accelerated pace."

There were more plaintive moans from Nathan in the other room, and Sam saw a potential problem in the sudden removal of the stasis for the Bigs in their house-family. For him and Sarah, it would be an unpleasant adjustment, trying to adapt to their limbs changing in length, apparently with some pain involved because of the rapid growth. But the changes involved with the Bigs suddenly becoming adults would have much more serious consequences. He remembered something than Elliot had once said.

"Hard on their systems," Sam muttered as he stumbled clumsily to the door alongside Sarah, trying to get his arms and legs to behave the way that they were supposed to. Sarah seemed to be moving with much more ease than he was, having had more time to learn how to cope with the changes.

When they both stepped through the doorway, they found Nathan crouched on his hands and knees on the floor, obviously in a great deal of pain. He glanced up pitifully at the pair. He was ashen, and his cheeks and chin were splotched with dark stubble.

"Hey, Sarah sweetie. I need your help. My skin feels like it's on fire. I don't understand it. I haven't felt anything like this is ages – I'm not supposed to feel anything at all. I need you to fix me," he begged.

She knelt by Nathan, but looked back at Sam with doubt. He knew that she was not sure if she could fix the Watcher. He wasn't exactly broken. He was just going through a series of transformations much faster than he was meant to, and he had grown so accustomed to not experiencing pain that the combination of the restoration of his sense of touch and the removal of the stasis was proving to be excruciating to him.

"I'll try, Nathan," she murmured, placing her not so small hands on him. She was hoping, if nothing else, that the gesture might have some sort of placebo effect – that he would draw an element of comfort from the attempt. She found there were some minor repairs she could make, some damage to his skin from the rapid growth that she could fix, but it brought with it minimal relief.

Nathan forced himself into a sitting position, still cringing and doing his best to suppress the vocalization of his discomfort. His muscles appeared to ripple under his skin in places, and he was so tense that Sam would not have been surprised if the young man had started frothing at the mouth and climbing the walls.

"Is that all you can do?" he asked desperately. *"What's happening to me, Sarah? Why does it hurt like this? Why am I feeling things again, and why can't you fix me?"*

"She can't fix you because there's nothing to fix," Francis replied, joining the conversation. He clung to his own doorframe with gritted teeth, fighting his own agony. *"You were right, Sam. We're going to have to explain a few things to Nathan, carefully. Your friend's device appears to have had some of the effects that we discussed earlier, without anything in the way of a warning. Nathan, you and I are going to have a very private little-one-on-one. This is extremely important. I'm telling you to let only me in, once you have put your walls up with as much strength as possible. I want you to do that right away."*

The two young men seemed to go off into a world of their own making, their thoughts vigorously protected against any intrusion. Under the circumstances, Nathan normally would have not been able to achieve the level of concentration required for such effective walls, but the compulsion from Francis's orders made it much easier, despite his pain.

Sarah rose from the floor and backed away until she was standing beside Sam again. She reached for his hand for some sort of reassurance. They could feel what their friends were going through, by means of the connection, but they were not living it themselves. It made them both feel sad and a little guilty that the discomfort from their transformations was mild in comparison.

The conversation between Nathan and Francis was a lengthy one. When they were done, Nathan rose silently and shakily to his feet. He staggered back to his room to get dressed, averting his eyes away from the others as much as possible.

"What did you say to him?" Sarah inquired.

"I'll tell you in a moment," Francis thought at her. *"Give him the time to set off on his circuit and I'll explain everything. I don't want to block him out until he is out of the house. Right now, I can't predict what could happen around here, and I may need to preserve what I have left of my focus in order to*

149

deal with anything unusual that crops up. Once Nathan is gone, I can relax a little, and I'll tell you what I told him."

Although it was not showing as much as it did with the Watcher, Sam and Sarah knew that the Teller was going through some of the same torment as what Nathan had been experiencing. His stance was shaky and his face was drawn.

"His circuit?" Sam objected. *"He can barely walk. How do you expect him to complete his circuit?"*

"It will definitely take him longer than usual, but he'll manage. The compulsion will help him force his way through any pain or discomfort, and I reinforced it when we were talking," Francis countered.

"Did you want me to see what I can do to help you," Sarah offered. *"It won't be much, but it may improve things a little for you."*

"I don't think that there will be time for that, Sarah, but I appreciate the offer," Francis stated. The three of them watched as Nathan returned, moving with great difficulty, and made his way out of the front door. He did not look at any of them as he passed through the room, grimacing as he went.

After a few moments had passed, Sam turned to face Francis.

*"So what **did** you tell him?"* he asked.

"Well, to sum it up, I shared with him something that maybe I should have shared with you sooner, but I was afraid of the consequences. Now that this Elliot of yours is here, there's no avoiding it anymore. I told Nathan that he was being used by the people that abandoned us here – that they wanted to keep tabs on all of us on Fervor, but for their own safety, they decided it was best to observe from afar. As long as he is a Watcher, anytime he talks to us without the proper walls, and anytime he looks at us, with the way that we are changing, or looks at Elliot, there's the risk that one of the scholars will learn what's going on here. For our sake, he's going to have to keep his walls up the best that he can when he talks to us – no more open conversations with him anymore, and he will try to avoid looking at us

if at all possible. He should even avoid looking at his own reflection, if he can."

"Oh, poor Nathan," Sarah murmured, distressed at his plight. *"It will be like he is blind by choice and isolated, too. He'll be miserable."*

"No, he won't," Francis insisted, allowing himself to sink to the floor as sweat beaded across his face. *"He'll be doing that to protect us, and as a Watcher, protecting us is as much a compulsion as following his circuit. He might feel a little lonely, but as long as we all make an effort to keep in touch with him behind closed doors, and make sure that he is kept abreast of everything that is going on in a way that the scholars can't see, he'll get by. It will only be temporary, I hope, until we sort things out with your technician friend."*

Sarah could not resist the urge to help their Teller any longer. She darted forward in a slightly clumsy manner and began looking for any relief that she might be able to bring him.

"You don't have to be so stoic," she chided.

Sam recognized that Francis did welcome her soothing touch, and that it was his own reaction to the contact that he was worried about. The responses from the Teller's body were unpredictable at the moment because of the withdrawal of the stasis, and far beyond his control. If there was one thing that Sam could define as a solid trait when describing Francis, it would be the fact that he felt the need to maintain a certain level of control. He was not displaying it as outwardly as Nathan had been, but these changes were proving to be as hard on Francis, in a different way, as they were on the Watcher.

"What did you mean when you said that they chose to observe us from afar for their own safety?" Sam demanded.

"Understand, I don't know that much more than you do, Sam," Francis remarked. *"They only told us things that they thought were relevant to us as Tellers. They did want us to watch out for some dangerous behaviour. Apparently, one of the reasons they chose to try this with children in the first place is because when they had attempted this on a smaller scale in the*

past, with both children and adults on separate occasions, the children responded much better, and there were fewer problems. With the adults...supposedly, they could not adapt to being introduced abruptly to the connection properly. Some of them went insane, and the situation became violent. I was instructed to watch for that in all of you. They rarely saw similar effects in the children, and only the older ones, but they had been working with very small samples. It was still a possibility."

"And that was the reason for the stasis then. They were worried what would happen when we became adults," Sarah interjected, glancing up from her attempts to fix Francis. She had done what she could for the moment, and it had not helped the Teller anymore than it had Nathan. Sam noticed she seemed to be persisting with Francis, however, reaching for something more, when she had been willing to concede defeat fairly quickly with Nathan.

"But Elliot was worried about what would happen when the stasis came down, and I got the impression that they wouldn't be able to maintain it forever," Sam added. *"Like the longer that it was up, the harder it would be on us when they finally removed it. It has only been five years, and look at what Nathan was going through. They didn't really think things through, did they, Francis? We were just lab rats to them. They wanted to see if they could make this work, but they didn't really care what the implications would be for us afterwards. How long were they planning to keep this going? What were they intending to do with us when all of this was over?"*

"I don't know," the Teller admitted reluctantly. *"I told you, they didn't share as much with me as you all seem to think that they did. I really have no idea why they were doing this, other than they wanted to test the connection on a larger scale. Maybe your Elliot can tell us more. He seems to have more clues about what exactly is going on."*

Francis paused and looked at Sarah, who was still fussing over him, with a frown. He pushed her away gently. *"That's enough of that. Time's the only thing that's going to sort the rest of this out. Save your efforts for Fiona. I'm sure that she will need your help soon enough."*

Sam was not sure why, but he could see that Sarah was not satisfied with leaving things at that. She had been prepared to admit defeat with Nathan after limited success, but there was something else bothering her as far as Francis was concerned. Of course, now that the Teller had actually directed her to stop, there was nothing that she could do about it other than obey.

Deciding that he had more pressing matters to deal with, Sam instead decided to take advantage of the fact that Francis was being forthcoming, and ask him more questions.

"What about the problems that we had with our senses, the ones that are gone now thanks to the Languorite? Can you explain those?"

Francis was in the process of shrugging, and claiming ignorance in this, too, when there was a terrible shriek that rang through both the house and their heads, filled with fear and pain. Fiona had always been the worst of them all when it came to controlling her thoughts and restricting her responses. She was the most likely of the five to push without focus or concern as to who would be hearing what she was saying or how loud and disruptive she was being within the connection. That had worked in their favour as far as attracting Elliot's attention was concerned, but it was seriously threatening to expose them all at the moment. Francis leapt on this immediately.

"Quiet!" he commanded her harshly. *"Get a hold of yourself! Do you want to give us away?"* Fiona's frantic cries instantly changed to subdued whimpers.

"Francis...please," Sarah pleaded. *"Go a little easier on her. She's going through something similar to what you and Nathan are, and we've all seen how she has a lower pain threshold than you two."* She stood and was headed for Fiona's door when there was a second disturbance as a now familiar figure appeared in Sarah's doorway.

"Loud...it's so loud... make it stop...make it stop."

Elliot stood swaying at the entrance to Sarah's room, clutching at his head. His discomfort was even greater than Fiona's, if that were possible. Sam realized what was happening. Until Elliot had made the trip to Fervor, he had only been exposed to the connection from a great distance where he could hear those who were strongest, such as Sarah, or the occasional outburst from those who gave exaggerated pushes without any control, like Fiona. Even though the connection was much quieter than it was when Sam had first been introduced to it, it was still proving to be very troublesome for the man. Francis had already explained the kind of risks such exposure could pose to mature adults, even a weak latent such as Elliot.

Sam knew that he had to act fast. He remembered how he had put up blocks for Fiona, the time that her extreme reaction had led Elliot to them. He wondered if he could do that again, but for Elliot instead of Fiona this time. It was worth a try if it would allow their technician friend to preserve his sanity. They still needed him in more ways than one, if they ever hoped to escape from Fervor and from the scrutiny of the scholars.

Sam threw up his walls around Elliot, giving the man a sense of reprieve. It was only a temporary measure, but Sam was depending on Francis to be able to give Elliot enough instruction for him to erect walls of his own in the interim, even if they would be a little flimsy. How strong they were would not matter that much as long as no one tried to push through them, and even if someone did, if they used sufficient restraint then they would not overpower the technician in the process.

Elliot gazed at Sam with his eyes filled with gratitude. The man had been exposed to a much smaller, much weaker version of the connection before, but he had never been taught to block others out, and had been completely unprepared for the overwhelming rush and chaos when he had first come into range of Fervor's connection. That was what had caused him to crash his hover, and not the storm. Sam could pick this up from all of Elliot's surface thoughts while he was sheltered within Sam's walls.

The Finder's rescue efforts had come just in time. Elliot's thoughts were horribly tangled, like he had been trapped in some terrifying nightmare that he could not escape. There was an inflexibility to the technician's mind that hadn't allowed Elliot to adapt when confronted with something that seemed far beyond his comprehension. Children's minds were more like uncongealed gelatin, willing to shift and flow as necessary. It was already assumed that there were things that they might not understand and that they might have to accept at face value. Elliot's mature mind, on the other hand, was searching for something concrete, something well-defined within the connection, and he had not been able to find it. That was the primary cause of his psychological distress.

While Sam and Francis struggled with Elliot, trying to bring his walls up to minimal standards, Sarah stood in front of Fiona's locked door, begging the young woman to let her in. Sam could follow their conversation on a basic level, although most of his attention was required to keep his walls up around Elliot.

"Maybe I can help. I helped Nathan and Francis a little. It's not as bad as it seems, Fiona. The stasis is down, and your body is just trying to catch up to where it should be," the Fixer said, trying to reassure her. *"Let me in, please. We're all going through our own issues at the moment."*

"You have no idea," Fiona moaned quietly. "I'm not coming out of here ever. It's awful. I'm a complete mess. I don't want Nathan seeing me like this."

"Fiona, be reasonable. You know that we can't make anything work around here without you," Sarah sighed, not sure why the Keeper was so reluctant to let her in. She didn't want to resort to having Francis order Fiona to unlock her door. That would just aggravate an already unhealthy situation. *"Besides, Nathan more than likely won't be seeing anything. He's under strict orders from Francis to try to avoid looking at any of us, and he's not supposed to make contact with us without keeping solid walls up."*

"What?" Fiona protested. She wanted to voice her annoyance loudly, but she was still subject to Francis's earlier command. "Now he's messing with Nathan's head? Why that weasely, good-for-nothing, pain in the..."

"Don't be like that, Fiona," the Fixer chastised. *"It was necessary, for Elliot's sake – and therefore for our sake, too. Just open the door. Let me come in. Sam and Francis won't see anything, I promise. They are too busy with Elliot."*

"Elliot?" the Keeper sniffled. "Did you finish fixing him? Is he okay? Can we talk to him?"

Sarah welcomed the distraction as far as negating Fiona's outcry against the Teller, but it still had not assisted her any at getting through the locked door.

"I finished doing what I can for him, but he's not okay – not yet, anyway. Sam and Francis are helping him to set up walls. There's a problem with introducing adults to the connection. Elliot found that out the hard way. Francis said that that was why the stasis was in place to begin with. He says..." But Fiona didn't allow her to finish the thought.

"Oh, so now he's finally talking, now that we are buried up to our necks in steaming manure. First Royce, and now this. This knowledge would have been much more useful to us ahead of time. He thinks he's going to win my favour by offering us information that we were in the process of learning anyway? How does that prove anything?"

"That's not fair," Sarah contested. *"I told you we needed to let him in on what was going on sooner, but you wouldn't listen. You claimed he wasn't trustworthy."*

"He isn't," Fiona stated bluntly.

The argument between the Fixer and the Keeper was proving to be a greater distraction than Sam had anticipated, and he felt his walls slipping. He glanced over at Francis with concern. The Teller was also having trouble concentrating with the two girls bickering in the background.

"Enough!" Francis barked, and everything went silent. It stayed that way until Francis had made sufficient progress that he felt comfortable testing Elliot's ability with what he had just been taught. Sam lowered his walls, and everything seemed to be functioning well enough that Elliot appeared to be no longer at risk.

"Let me talk to Fiona," he thought softly at Sam and Francis, who had maintained their link with him in case they had needed to jump in for him again. *"This would be a lot simpler if I was a woman. While I know what she is faced with in theory, I haven't experienced it myself. Still, I think I can offer her some solace if she's willing to hear me out."*

Sam was amazed at how faint Elliot still was in the connection, even though he had been properly fixed by Sarah and he was sitting there in front of them in person. It was almost as though he were a ghost instead of a real being. Sam felt like reaching out and touching the man just to make sure that he was actually there and not some sort of illusion sent by the scholars to trick them.

Francis hunched his shoulders and shot a quick look at her door.

"You are free to do as you please if you can get her to listen. I think they gave us the most stubborn Keeper on all of Fervor."

"She's frightened. That much I can understand. What they did to you is so wrong. And what they did to your parents..." Elliot hesitated, and Sam could tell that this statement was directed at Francis and not himself. *"We have an awful lot to discuss, and I'll tell you everything that I know, I promise you that, but this will be a lot for all of you to digest, probably best handled in smaller doses. And then there's the issue of my hover, not to mention the fact that if they picked up on anything unusual from your Watcher, this could be over before it has barely had a chance to begin."*

"What about my parents?" Sam asked.

Elliot gave him a look that the boy knew could only mean that he was treading in places where the technician was not prepared to go just yet.

"That will have to wait," Elliot sighed, looking very uncomfortable. *"I will have an awful lot to explain before we get to that. It could get – awkward."* Sam wasn't sure that he wanted to know what Elliot meant by that.

"It's worst than that," Francis confessed. *"We had problems with our Control. I had to report him. I would have refrained if I had had any idea what these three were up to, but they left me in the dark. I don't know what the scholars will be doing to respond to that. It wasn't a problem that they had been anticipating."*

"But you told Royce that they might be sending someone to get him. You didn't know?" Sam said, surprised.

"It was a possibility. It still is, and if they send someone to replace him, or come in to investigate our house-family as a result...well, let's just say that if Elliot here has any specific plans, we can't allow for any delays. The longer we let things go, the more likely we could be facing another kind of trouble," the Teller replied.

Sam had a feeling that when Francis was saying "we", the emphasis was more on himself. He was the one who was supposed to uphold the Directives in intent as well as in what was written. If they were caught, Francis would be the one taking the fall and bearing the brunt of any punishment, along with Elliot.

"Well, I can't accomplish what I need to if Fiona won't come out of her room," the technician assured them. *"Let me see what I can do."*

He approached her door, standing next to Sarah and spoke to her quietly, not making use of the connection. That in itself seemed to encourage the young woman, and moments later Fiona allowed entry to Elliot and Sarah, locking the door once more after them.

Sam watched Francis stare at the door for a few moments before he wandered away again, hissing in pain. He wished the Teller were not such an enigma, and he would have traded his greatest find to know what Francis was thinking at that moment.

Effects of the Langurite

11

CHALLENGES

Fiona did spend a fair amount of time speaking with Elliot and Sarah in her room, but she continued to refuse to come out and put her walls up to everyone else. She agreed that she would come out eventually, when she was feeling more at ease with everything that had happened, but at the moment she was still in shock and in pain, and would rather suffer alone than face her insecurities.

Sam did feel bad for the Keeper. She had never handled any changes well, and this one added insult to injury. Nevertheless, he could not imagine that things were as bad as Fiona was making them out to be. Not that he would know for sure. Sarah would not talk about it to Sam, respecting Fiona's wishes.

By that point, Sam was starting to feel a little isolated. Elliot had returned to Sarah's room, in need of more rest, and the Fixer sat outside of Francis's room waiting for him to come out again. The whole house-family seemed to be in an unnatural state of disorder, and Sam didn't like it at all.

Realizing that everyone had forgotten about Nathan, dealing with their own problems, Sam decided that he had better check in on their Watcher. Francis seemed fairly convinced that Nathan would manage just fine, but the Finder wanted to make sure of that himself.

Sam suspected that, where Francis was concerned, there was a little bit of bias when it came to Nathan. He didn't understand this, because Nathan had always respected Francis's authority, had never resisted the Teller's instructions, and hadn't held him at fault the way that Fiona had. The only suggestion of defiance from Nathan that Sam had ever seen had been a matter of compulsion, when the Watcher felt that the safety of one of his family members had been somehow placed in jeopardy. In fact, of anyone one in the house, Nathan had always been the most carefree, the most kind, and the most forgiving. Any tension between the two of them clearly originated from Francis, and without any obvious explanation.

Sam could sense that Nathan's walls were unusually thick that day when he reached for him through the connection. Francis had indeed succeeded in helping the Watcher compensate for any distraction caused by his painful transformation. Sam knocked really hard, and after a few moments Nathan let him in.

"How are things going, Nathan? You looked pretty bad when you headed out this morning. I'm sorry about all of this, especially the lack of warning. We wanted to tell you what was going on, but under the circumstances, we couldn't."

"It's okay, little buddy – I guess I can still call you that can't I? You're not so little anymore, but you are still smaller than me." Nathan chuckled a little internally, with a bit of a mental groan. *"It still hurts, a lot, but I'll get by. And I understand you not telling me anything about your 'new friend'. It only makes sense considering everything that Francis told me. How are the rest of you handling all of this? Are you and Sarah okay? What about Fiona? I know that she was still asleep when I left. The last couple of times I took a break, when it got to be too much, I tried to talk to her but she wouldn't answer me. Did I do something to make her angry with me?"* There was a hint of anxiety in the Watcher's question.

"No, Nathan – it's nothing like that. She's shutting everyone out right now. She spoke for a little while with Sarah and Elliot but..." Sam began.

"Don't use his name when you speak to me, Sam," Nathan interrupted. *"Francis warned me not to. You never know when they might be listening in."*

"They won't be able to hear anything. Your walls are rock solid. I tested them myself," Sam assured him.

"That may be so right now, but you never know when I might let them slip, especially with all of this pain. It's like someone's trying to stretch me from the inside out. And places are itching too – places that shouldn't be itching. I never missed any of the pain or itching over the last few years. I didn't mind giving that up," the young man admitted.

Sam counted himself fortunate. The discomfort that he was enduring was much less severe than Nathan's.

"So why is she shutting everyone out?" Nathan demanded, returning to the original topic at hand. *"That's not like Fiona. She has always been willing to talk to me in the past. Going through this would be a lot easier if she would just let me in. She usually knows what to say to make me feel better."*

Sam shrugged mentally. *"She doesn't seem to be all that happy with the way things are changing for her. I don't know if this has anything to do with it, but she spent quite a bit of time in direct contact with the Languorite last night..."*

"Don't mention that by name either," the Watcher insisted, interrupting for a second time. *"Just call it the 'new find,' just like you have your 'new friend.' I'll know what you mean."*

"Fine," Sam sighed. *"Anyway, until we get a chance to discuss all of this with my 'new friend' we'll have no idea how fast everything is happening. We know why, but we don't know all of the 'what' and we don't know exactly how. Sarah finished fixing him, but he's still resting – recovering. He'll probably be up to talking this evening, although I'm not sure that we can get Fiona to participate. Maybe then we can get some answers."*

"You can count me out too, little buddy," Nathan responded. *"I'm already exhausted, and I'm only about half way through my circuit. It will take everything I have just to drag my sorry butt the rest of the way through this thing and collapse into my bed when I'm done. Besides, I would have to drop my walls to have a conversation with the lot of you, and I can't do that right now. Francis made sure of that. I'm surprised he left me with the ability to talk to anyone but him."*

"I'll admit Francis is a bit of a control freak," the Finder conceded. *"But he's not outright cruel. I'm sure he wouldn't have done this if he didn't think that it was necessary. The rest of us didn't know what to do."*

"I realize that. I just wish that there were some other way. Sam, you said that Fiona let Sarah talk to her. If she lets Sarah in again, can you ask our Fixer friend to put in a good word for me?" Nathan asked. *"I'd really like to talk to Fiona. It would make me feel a whole lot better about all of this if I could. I'm not used to her blocking me out like this."*

"Sure thing, Nathan," Sam agreed. *"And I'll brief you on whatever Eh—um…my 'new friend' has to say. I'll be in touch again tomorrow."*

"I really hope that you guys can make this work, Sam. I don't know how much longer that I can keep this up. I'm not as good with my walls as you and Sarah are. But I understand what this means for us if you can make it happen. I'm sure that I want it as much as you do. Like what's going on right now. I may have to suffer for a little while, but in the end, it will be worth it. I'll put up with whatever I have to, if it means more freedom and a normal life for us all in the end." Sam could feel Nathan's excitement as their minds made contact, and the Watcher was not usually an excitable fellow. It gave Sam some renewed hope.

Satisfied that Nathan was coping reasonably well, Sam broke their link. Glancing around the room, he saw Sarah getting to her feet.

"I talked to Nathan," he informed her. *"Francis was right. He's managing okay. He'd like to talk to Fiona, if you can convince her to let him in."*

Sarah gave him a dubious look.

"She was reluctant enough to talk to me and Elliot. And I don't know if we'll hear or see her again until she's good and ready. She won't stay in there forever. She can't. She still has the compulsions of a Keeper and eventually they'll override whatever sense of self-consciousness she has that is keeping her in there, but it may be a couple of days, you know. I think, for the moment, this business with Elliot and the Languorite will have to fall on yours, mine, and Francis's shoulders. We can't wait for Fiona, and we can't include Nathan."

"Self-consciousness? It can't be all that bad, can it?" Sam laughed.

Sarah chose not to answer that question.

"She's still changing, Sam. We'll have to wait and see when she's actually done. I don't think that I should say anything more than that. She wouldn't want me to."

Sam tried to quell his imagination, but he could not seem to prevent the series of grotesque images of potential mutations of the pretty girl from flitting through his mind. He threw up his walls before Sarah could get a glimpse and, with a quick good-bye, set off to do some finding for the day.

Sam still felt the constant throbbing ache in his bones, joints, and muscles, but it wasn't enough to reduce his compulsion to go looking for something useful, nor dampen his thrill at actually being able to hear things en route. He paused briefly at points to reorient himself and to pinpoint where his finding was directing him. It gave him a chance to just listen and enjoy the sounds of the birds singing and the wind blowing through the trees. He was sure that he would never take that for granted again.

His finding drew him to the beach, not a big surprise considering the severity of the storm that they had been through the last couple of days. Sam knelt by the place where he had found Elliot and glanced up and down the shoreline. The urge to head towards Royce's "territory" on the beach was overwhelming. Sam had not had a single run-in with their Control since he had been exiled from the house, but he had also avoided that section of the beach completely. He fought with himself at that moment, struggling to resist the desire to search for the thing that he knew lay somewhere in that area. He couldn't even be sure that Royce still spent any amount of time in the house-family terrain, but he did not want to risk a confrontation, not with the Bigs all functioning at minimal capacity. Sam did not even consider the fact that, as things stood, Royce would no longer have the same size advantage over him as he had had in the past.

Sam resisted the pull, but could not avoid it altogether. He started to drift unwittingly towards the place where he feared to tread, and was thankful when, in addition to not actually encountering their Control along that stretch, he also caught sight of what had attracted him. The urge to continue farther down the beach began to subside, as one compulsion countered the other. The object that had captured Sam's attention was a very unusual looking hover, badly damaged and lying upside-down on a series of seaweed covered rocks. Most likely, he assumed, Elliot's hover.

The average hover was shorter and stouter, not meant for high speeds or travelling great distances. The island hovers were also fabricated from fairly light-weight and flexible metal, meant for ease of use, for regular outings, where as the one perched haphazardly on the rocks appeared to be a much sturdier construct, intended for longer journeys over greater distances and to be made at higher speeds. He wondered how fast Elliot had been able to make that hover go, when it was in proper working condition.

The other thing that Sam noticed about the magical device, even from a distance, was that it was much larger than the regular hovers on Fervor. The snub nosed vehicles that he had ridden in, in what now felt like ages past, were designed to carry four people, at most, and that had been the maximum combination of minder and children per household before the second exodus. This beast of a hover, on the other hand, looked like it could carry at least twice that. It could easily hold Elliot as well as the five young people remaining in Sam's house-family, with room to spare.

Sam wanted to get closer to the hover, and he knew that there were supplies somewhere within its metallic shell. It was those supplies that had attracted him and not the hover itself. The magical device actually repulsed him, because of the embedding of the Directives during the Gathering at the Hub. Hovers were strictly off limits for Finders. That worried Sam. Elliot had talked about offering them solutions to their shackled existence, including, possibly, a way off of Fervor. If they could not get close to a hover, let alone enter one, how were they ever supposed to make their way to proper civilization? He hoped Elliot would be able to offer an answer to this dilemma as well.

Of course, all of that might be a moot point to begin with. In its current condition, Sam was quite certain Elliot's hover would be going nowhere. It would need some extensive repairs, and considering that they had no parts available to them, such repairs might prove impossible. Elliot was a technician, however. It was possible that some of the standard hovers could offer something that could be adapted for use in the special one, and if that were the case, Elliot might be able to find a way to fix it. In fact, if Sarah could manage to get close enough to the flying device, she might even be able to offer him some assistance in doing so.

Sam peered at it a little longer. At some point, they would need to get the hover right-side up, and it looked exceptionally heavy. Even if Elliot could somehow offer them a way of overcoming the compulsion to avoid the hover, Sam doubted the six of them could flip it on their own. The only ones with any real physical strength were Elliot and Nathan, and Nathan wasn't in a position where he would want to look at it. His effort would be an awkward one at best. For the first time since

Royce had left their house, Sam actually wished the black-haired boy were still around. Better yet, he wished he were around and free of the stasis, in order to lend a helping hand.

Sam's other finds were not all that rewarding that day, once he had pulled himself away from the sight of the hover. He returned home mostly empty-handed, having only gathered some slightly frayed heavy rope after scouring the friendlier parts of the beach. Still, just being able to report finding the strange hover, even in its less than favourable state, seemed like a prize to the Finder.

When he trundled through the door, dropping the rope on the floor beside it, Sam noticed that Sarah had returned to her spot in front of Francis's room.

"Elliot's up," she reported. *"He's in the kitchen waiting to talk to us, and Nathan made it back a few minutes ago, but he's already in his room, asleep. Fiona is still refusing to come out of her room, and Francis was just waiting for you to get home so we could join Elliot."*

"Why aren't you both with him then? You knew that I would be home soon," Sam asked, curious.

"Elliot makes Francis nervous. So does the Languorite. I can't blame him exactly. We've had time to get used to the idea that Elliot might be coming, and that he might be bringing changes with him. We dumped this all in Francis's lap pretty abruptly. Considering how Fiona reacted, I think he's taking all of this quite well," she replied.

"Then why are you still planted outside his door? You could be in the kitchen, waiting with Elliot yourself," Sam demanded.

"I was hoping I might get to fix Francis some more, but he wouldn't let me."

There was an edginess to Sarah's response, and that intrigued the Finder even more. Sam had watched her do as much for the Teller as she had for Nathan earlier. He wondered what more there could be for her to do. That was when Francis opened his door.

"Come on," he said to his two younger house-mates. *"Let's see what Elliot has to say about all of this."*

Sam noted that, while Francis was still moving like someone who was in pain, he was standing straighter and more upright than he had been earlier in the day. Whatever stress there was on his system appeared to be starting to ease a little. Francis was nowhere near as tall as Elliot, but he was definitely several inches taller than he had been. The Teller glanced towards Fiona's closed door. He shook his head.

"I don't want to order her to come out," he sighed. *"But she is our Keeper. How are we supposed to keep things functioning around here without her? If it's necessary..."*

"It's not necessary," Elliot interrupted, standing in the entranceway to the kitchen.

His presence in the connection was still a mere shadow, but his physical stature made up for it. He was similar to Nathan in that aspect. None of the minders or teachers had been imposing in any way, and Sam could see why Elliot made Francis nervous. With his shaggy light brown hair and beard, he reminded Sam of pictures that he had seen in school of lions.

"If she needs more time to adjust, let her have it. I can work anything that can be found in this house and then some. You don't need her for that while I'm here. She can listen in on what I have to say from her room. Why don't you three join me, and I'll do my best to answer your questions with the information that I managed to gather for you. I won't have all the answers, mind you, but I'll do my best."

They walked into the kitchen where the Languorite was sitting atop the table. Francis frowned somewhat, and then glanced at Sam and Sarah with his familiar slightly melancholic expression, a hint of fear in his pale green eyes. He did not advance any closer.

"I guess that we start with that," the Teller said, gesturing towards the magical device. *"It can bring down the stasis, as we've seen firsthand. What more can you tell us about that?"*

"As a passive function, it can bring down any magic in effect that is in place for the purpose of suppression of natural influences. That would include the stasis, which the scholars had put in place to suppress natural aging. If any of you were not Connected, it would change that, too. The Bigs were all chosen because you were telepathically stronger than the latents. Your parents were all first generation offspring of purposefully inter-bred latents. The scholars considered you the next step in the evolution of our race. Magic runs strong in you, too," Elliot explained.

"The Bigs? Do you mean the Controls as well?" Sam asked. He knew that Francis had unintentionally suggested Royce had been slated to be a Finder, until the Littles had been introduced into the mix. The gifts of the Talent Groups were seemingly interwoven with the connection – such as the Tellers only being able to influence other Connected. Was Royce deaf to the connection because this had been suppressed in him? If that were the case, all of the Controls had a legitimate reason to be angry.

"There wasn't a child on Fervor that began life without the potential to be linked to the connection," Elliot admitted, turning to face the Finder. *"You should have all had that from day one. They suppressed it until they were prepared to commence their experiment, and then lifted the magic on all of you but the Controls. They didn't realize that suppressing it for so long would cause damage."*

"The sensory damage?" Sarah concluded.

"Not in the way that you might think, based on what happened to you. It damaged the nerves actually used for the connection, so the scholars had that newest sense rerouted through another existing channel, one that best matched your potential strength. You had already been organized into groups using the diversity of your potential strength, your house-families, which is why you had had the mixture of resulting loss of senses. The restoration of your senses was another function of the Languorite that works on a passive level. It repaired that

damage and returned the senses to their appropriate channels," the technician acknowledged.

"And that's why I can see again," Sarah murmured, her dark eyes glistened with fascination.

"Hmmm. I'd thought that'd had something to do with our gifts," Sam said.

Elliot smiled at him. Sam got the impression that the technician considered him to be clever.

"Not directly, although yours gifts were provided to you based on your anticipated ability with the connection, as well as certain personality traits."

"But Royce, our Control, was originally supposed to be a Finder, instead of Sam," Sarah retorted. *"Explain that."*

Francis scowled a little upon this revelation, and Elliot shifted uncomfortably in his seat. Sam thought it was interesting. Despite being here to help them, there were things that the technician was just as reluctant as Francis had been to share with them. The situation was a little different, however. While the temptation was there to push through or peek around Elliot's paper thin walls, the way that he and Sarah had once done with Francis's sturdier walls when they had first met, Sam couldn't bring himself to do it. Unlike with Francis, Sam had faith in the fact that there was good reason for Elliot to hold things back, and Sam was sure it would come out eventually if he didn't pry now. That was not the case with the Teller.

"I'm not going into detail today about what happened there. I'm already giving you a lot to absorb, and I think there are some things that you need to be ready for before I share them with you. You can trust me when I say that I don't think that you are ready for that. The scholars never looked at you as people. They should have, but they didn't. They have done things, many things that I think the majority of people in society at large would consider highly unethical, no matter what the ends or the objectives in all of this," Elliot stated.

He paused, facing a dissatisfied stare from the Fixer. She was convinced that she could handle whatever he might have to tell them. The technician shifted in his chair again, and thumped his boots on the floor a little, in a nervous and unconscious attempt at a distraction. Sam decided to throw him a life line, and come to his rescue.

"Speaking of Finders, I believe that I found your hover today," Sam mentioned. Elliot's face brightened and he sat up, visibly relieved.

"Well – that is good news. I was more than a little concerned that we might be stuck here," the technician exclaimed happily.

"Don't get your hopes up just yet," the boy warned. *"It looks quite severely damaged and it's resting on the rocks upside-down. To make matters worse, it's located in the section of the beach that Royce and his Control friends have deemed 'their' territory."*

"Damage is repairable," Elliot insisted. *"As long as we can locate the proper tools, materials and other supplies, I'm quite certain that I can fix it. We may have to jury-rig a few things from some of the standard hovers on the island, but I can probably make it work. Righting it won't be a problem either, with enough hands."*

"But that is a problem," Sarah countered, pushing herself back from the table in frustration. She appeared to be attempting to avoid Francis's gaze in the process, as if he would find what she was about to say offensive. *"None of us can get close to the hover, other than Fiona, and running it is off limits, even for her, because of the Directives. You and Fiona won't be able to flip something like that alone. You might be able to set up some sort of hoist, with pulleys, or maybe use some of the regular hovers for leverage, but it will be really awkward on those rocks."* Sarah was not sure where her ideas had come from, but they at least offered a partial solution.

"You leave that to me," Elliot said. *"If there's a way of sorting this out, I'll come up with it."*

Sam got the impression from the dishevelled man that he was not used to speaking with children, and that he was not sure how or if he should adjust his approach when dealing with them, compared to interacting with other adults.

Francis, who had remained silent since the beginning of the conversation, finally spoke up.

"All of this won't matter if you can't override the instructions embedded during the Gathering. You fix the hover, and Elliot and Fiona get to ride off without the rest of us. I really don't think that was what you intended when you came here in the first place."

"Not at all, Francis," Elliot replied, with a wry smile. He pointed at the Languorite. *"Our solution to that dilemma lies in its other functions, the ones that require activation."*

"What other functions?" Sam questioned, always the curious one.

"The gifts that you have aren't exactly talents as the Directives would have you believe. They are tools as much for the scholars use as for your own benefit. They are not natural, unlike your ability with the connection. They are magical enhancements, used to highly exaggerate inherent traits that you possess and to warp them in order to simplify the scholars' work." Elliot placed his elbows on the table and leaned forward, hunching his shoulders as he did so.

"Like Nathan being their eyes," Sam observed. *"And Fiona their means of recording what happens for later use."*

"And Francis being their mouthpiece," Sarah piped in.

The Teller had fallen silent again and watched the pair of not-so-little Littles with heightening suspicion. It was clear that he did not like the way that this conversation was going.

"Exactly," the technician affirmed. *"Sam here was intended to assure that you did not go without the necessities. I can guarantee you that there is enough food here on Fervor in stasis to keep you going for many years. I was never able to find out what end date they had planned for this experiment, the supposed Coming that was mentioned in their documentation, but my guess would be not for several more years in the future, if not longer."*

Sam did not want to imagine what sort of torture emerging from stasis would have been for them if their aging had been delayed to that extent.

"I was here to make sure that things remained in working order, including the subjects of the experiment themselves," Sarah added, not trying to hide her disappointment. This knowledge, now verified, seemed to tarnish what she had once considered her silver lining, when everything else had seemed dark and gloomy.

"It's not a bad thing, Sarah," Elliot suggested. *"You still have very useful abilities – it's the compulsions associated with them that can prove to be problematic. I'm afraid I can't remove one without the other, but the Languorite can strip you of those 'talents' if used properly, in theory. I'd like to guarantee success, if I was to try, but I've never had the opportunity to use it in practice. I wouldn't want to make the attempt unless you deemed it necessary. You would lose some benefit if all went well, and if I got it wrong, the repercussions could be horrific."*

Sam did not want to give up his gift, even if it involved some compulsion. As far as he was concerned, the benefits far outweighed any deficit.

"I may be able to use it to eliminate any compulsions imposed on you by the Tellers as well," the technician continued. *"That much wasn't clear. But when the time comes, it may be worth a try, despite the possible risks."*

Sam and Sarah agreed, but Francis said nothing. That was when Nathan appeared in the kitchen, bringing all conversation to an immediate end. He kept his eyes averted from them as required. He was still flinching from time to time in pain, and he looked dead tired.

"I'm s-sorry t-t-to interrupt, b-but I'm st-st-starving," he spoke aloud only, not willing to drop his walls in order to speak through the connection openly. "F-Fiona hasn't c-c-come out y-yet, has she?"

"No," Francis replied, in a subdued manner.

"Allow me," Elliot offered quietly. "It won't be fancy, but it will be something." He got to his feet and set about preparing a simple but edible meal, filling in for the Keeper. The rest of the conversation would have to wait for another time.

12

HOVER

After Nathan had left the next morning, Sam tracked him down through the connection and briefed him, to the best of his recollection, on everything that Elliot told them the evening before.

"Fiona should really be the one telling you all of this. She's the one with the picture perfect memory," Sam insisted. *"I don't know if she even listened in last night. It's almost like she doesn't want anything to do with us right now."*

"She still won't talk to me," the Watcher admitted sadly. *"Are you sure that I haven't done anything to upset her?"*

"I can't see what you could have possibly done. Our 'new friend' claims that she just needs time, and Sarah said that her compulsions will force her out soon enough. Just have a little patience, Nathan. She'll come around and start acting like her old self again before you know it." Sam hoped that what he was saying was right, and that he was not just riding on Sarah's hopefulness.

"So this 'new friend' of yours says that he can take away our gifts with that thing? I can understand why you or Sarah or Francis might object to this, but look at what I have to put up with, and what do I really have to show for it? Why can't he just take it away so that I don't have to run my circuit anymore, or put up my walls like this? Do you know how frustrating it is, not being allowed to look at all of you? What if something goes

177

wrong? How am I supposed to be there for you if I can't even see what's going on?" Nathan asked.

"Francis and I talked about this, because I suggested the same thing, but he said that that would be a terrible idea. It might make things easier on you, but the scholars will definitely send someone to investigate if they stop being able to see through you. They'll assume that you're dead, and they'll want to know what happened to you," Sam replied.

After their talk with Elliot, he had been as quick to come to the same conclusion as Nathan had, but the Teller had been equally quick to naysay his idea.

"Besides, our 'new friend' has to activate that function, and he has never actually used it on anyone before. You would be playing guinea pig, and where would it leave us if things went wrong?"

Sam did not mean to prey on Nathan's protective impulse to dissuade him from this line of thought, but the Finder didn't like the notion of the young man being the test subject for the Languorite's untried functions, not until they were all ready to commit to the same thing.

"I'm not worried about me. I'd rather play guinea pig than let one of you suffer that fate. I can handle whatever he throws at me, but I don't want to get us all in trouble. On the other hand, Francis said that they would be coming because of Royce. It has been almost a year since I threw him out of the house, Sam, and Francis reported the incident at the next Teller meeting. Where are they? I still see signs that Royce and his friends are out there. While we may have been the only house-family to exile our Control, the fact that Royce has allies suggests that we were not the only ones to have problems with our Control. What about their house-families? The scholars never came. I doubt they even care that we sent him packing. Francis can't be sure that they'd come if I did this either," Nathan remarked forcefully.

Sam had been thinking the same thing, too, at one point. When Royce had first left, Sam had been constantly watching over his shoulder, prepared to make himself scarce should the scholars make an appearance. After a while, the threat had become decidedly less likely, and until just recently it had been mostly forgotten.

"When Royce left the house, Francis said that they **might** *come. He wasn't sure,"* Sam argued. *"The scholars only valued the Controls so much, and it was possible that Royce had already served the better part of his function. But if you stop watching for them, if you get Elliot to take your gift away, Francis is sure that they will come. They'll be blind without you. They'll have no choice but to come and observe us first hand. What you do is much more important than anything Royce had to offer."*

Sam believed that for the most part, at least as far as the scholars were concerned. He was not so sure, on the other hand, that this was as true for their house-family's situation in general. He was becoming more and more convinced that Francis required boundaries – boundaries that he no longer had with Royce gone.

Nathan went silent. Sam knew that he was frustrated and not quite himself. Things were chaotic enough in Nathan's head to make Sam uncomfortable, and that had never happened before. The Watcher, for the most part, had a peaceful mind, and even when he was upset, his thoughts tended to be focussed on the particular thing that was bothering him. Sam was almost regretting that Elliot had come in some ways.

Eventually, the Watcher did think at him again.

"What about that hover? Did you need me to come down to that section of the beach, after I'm done my circuit? I don't know how much good I can do you like this, but I'll help in any way that I can," he offered quietly.

"Not yet. We'll be heading down to the shore with him, Sarah and me. We need to figure out what exactly has to be done first—what I may need to find and what Sarah might have to do to help him fix it. We'll need your help only when it is time to right it, and we'll let you know when that time comes. He may

as well make the repairs that need to be made on the bottom of it, before we turn it over. It only makes sense," Sam replied.

There was another pause from Nathan.

"Do you think that this is going to work, Sam, or are we crazy for even trying? What happens if we pull this off and get away from here? We've never known any other life, and if we do get away, will we always be running from them? What will we be running to? Maybe we should just forget this and stick with what we know. It hasn't really been that bad has it? Aside from what happened with Royce, I liked the way that things were. I was happy. I thought we made a good family, and at least then Fiona would talk to me," Nathan sighed.

"We've set things in motion that can't be reversed, Nathan. You were happy, but the rest of us weren't. I haven't had a day without fear since Maria left, Sarah's been in the dark until our 'new friend' came, and you can't pretend that Fiona liked the way that things were. Francis had his off days, and even Royce had good reason for feeling cheated. He shouldn't have taken it out on the rest of us, but they did rob him of something that they should have given back. If you would prefer to stay on Fervor, you don't have to come with us when we go, but I want off this island, and I can almost guarantee that Sarah and Fiona will be coming with us."

Sam was watching Sarah readying herself to go out with him and Elliot while he spoke with Nathan, and he could see Fiona's closed door as well. She would be coming with them when they left, he thought, if she would ever come out of her room.

"I suppose there's no way to go back to the way that things were. I don't want to stay behind by myself, Sam. You all are my family now. I can't imagine going on without you." He hesitated. *"I had better get back to my circuit now. When I'm done, I'll keep working on trying to get some response out of Fiona,"* the Watcher murmured. *"Maybe if I'm persistent, she'll finally let me in. Thanks for keeping me in the loop, little buddy. I really appreciate it."*

Sam broke away from his link with Nathan, and he joined Sarah and Elliot who were making their way towards the door. The three trudged down to the beach without a single word passing amongst them. Sam found himself staring at the hulking figure of Elliot as they walked, wondering what exactly had possessed a man like him to help them, aside from the fact that he was a latent himself. It might have been some sort of attempt at self-preservation, perhaps anxious at what might happen to him if he were discovered. But the scholars didn't know his secret, and doing what he was doing now was much more likely to expose him than just keeping mum. Sam also wondered how exactly the large man had managed to get around the security systems he had told them about in his messages. At one point he had seemed convinced that it would be something beyond his ability. The curiosity was eating away at Sam, but he felt almost as intimidated by the technician as Francis did, and he did not dare to start asking those kinds of questions.

Sarah gasped aloud as they reached the stretch of rocks and sand where Sam had found the hover. Nothing had changed— its silvery bullet-like form still upended precariously atop the rocks—but the dark-haired girl had not expected that it would look quite as mangled as it did. When Elliot saw it, his own expression fell as well. Viewing his reaction, Sam felt immediately disheartened.

"You can't fix it then? It's that bad?" the Finder mumbled.

Elliot advanced on the hover, leaving Sarah and Sam lingering at a distance. The pair wanted to follow him, but there was a greater discomfort in doing so than there was in hanging back and observing from afar. The technician knelt beside the damaged craft and started running his hands over its buckled sides, scrutinizing it intently. He groaned a little and frowned.

"That's not a good sign," Sarah whispered.

After a few moments, Elliot rose again and returned to them. He looked unhappy, but not completely forlorn.

"Should we forget leaving Fervor?" Sam demanded.

"Not yet, not without putting in a good attempt at repairing it," Elliot stated gruffly. *"It's not impossible, just difficult without the proper tools or materials. A lot of the damage is cosmetic. That's a good thing. As long as I can come up with a reasonable substitute for the siding, and find some basic tools, then I'm fairly certain that I can fix that. It's the few areas where it has been damaged internally that worry me the most. Those will be harder to repair without the appropriate replacement parts. I might be able to alter standard hover parts to work, but these things can be finicky. This will probably take longer than I had originally anticipated. That is, if I can make it happen at all. I'm definitely going to need your help. Sarah, I know if we can make this work it will be because of your gift. We'll have to get you close enough to the hover so that you can assist me in identifying everything that we need to fix this. Then we can make a list, and Sam and I can go out hunting for the parts, materials, and tools we need. If they are available, I know Sam will be able to help me find them."*

Sarah glanced over at Sam warily. His role in this would be simple. He did not have to get close to any of the hovers to help the technician. He would just have to guide Elliot to the places where the things he sought were contained, and then leave it up to the man to retrieve them, the same way that he had with Fiona. Finding everything they needed might take them a fair amount of time, and they might have to venture into the spaces of the other house-families, but it would not be that great of a challenge. Sam did not mind the notion in the slightest. He was not even afraid of running into Royce or the other Controls as long as Elliot was present. Royce would not dare try anything that the hulking man might consider a threat. It was like travelling with his own personal bodyguard.

Poor Sarah, however, was expected to approach the hover immediately. This was no simple feat. Unless they returned to the house and they tried using the Languorite on her, which Sam figured Elliot would be reluctant to do at this point, then she would have to fight the compulsion to avoid the hover for the entire time that she would be assisting him.

Elliot gestured for the Fixer to follow him back to the hover, and she tried to obey. She gritted her teeth and took a few trembling steps towards it before her will failed her. Then she stood there looking helpless until the technician returned for her. His massive form, larger than that of the average man, dwarfed her petite one, small for a girl her age even with the additional growth that the Languorite had provided. He reached down, hoisted her up and carried her over. Once there, he kept an iron grip on her delicate wrist to prevent her from attempting to put greater distance between her and the hover. Sam was thankful that physical forces could still prove to overpower some of the psychological ones.

It was soon obvious that this process was going to take some time, and his own urges to do some finding started to become unbearable. After several minutes of fidgeting where he stood and watched his two companions discussing exactly what needed to be done, Sam gave in and headed down the beach in the other direction. He was surprised to come across Francis there. He figured that maybe the young man had followed them down to the ocean, wanting to steal a glimpse at the wreck himself. He was not looking in the direction that Sam was approaching from, however. Instead, he was sitting on a rock and staring out at the water, running the fingers of one hand through the sand.

"Elliot says that the repairs on the hover will likely take longer than he had anticipated," Sam informed him.

"That's a shame," Francis stated, his face looking rather vacant. *"The longer it takes him, the more likely it will be that your friend will be caught. If you hope to get off of Fervor, you'll have to try and speed things up. Nathan won't be able to hide all of this forever. They'll figure things out eventually."*

Sam noticed that the Teller had said "you" instead of "we." He recognized what that implied.

"You're not coming with us?" he remarked with some surprise.

Francis shook his head.

"I belong on Fervor. Besides, you said yourself that you don't trust me. It wouldn't make any sense to take me with you. I'll stay here and take whatever punishment they decide that I deserve for hiding this from them. I'd rather face a situation with a known outcome then blunder off into the unknown future that you are creating for yourselves."

"Sarah won't be happy about that," Sam suggested. *"She has always trusted you. She won't want to leave you behind."* Even though she knows just how much you were hiding from us, Sam considered, blocking this thought from the Teller. *"And Nathan considers you family."*

Francis gave a small smirk, the first offering of any sentiment that the young man had made since Sam had found him on the beach. However, the blank stare in his pale green eyes did not change any.

"She'll cope without me, and Nathan won't miss me, no matter what he has been telling you. Believe me, it is best this way."

He paused, twisting and stretching, still tormented by aching muscles, tender skin and painful joints. He closed his eyes and shrugged.

"Fiona has always viewed me as the bad guy. Maybe she's right. Maybe I was a coward. Well, I won't be one anymore. I'll keep helping you to see this through to its conclusion, and then I'll take whatever's coming to me."

Sam was disappointed, and he knew Sarah would be even more so. Perhaps trust was lacking for the Teller, and perhaps there were unresolved personality issues, but Sam did not want Francis playing the part of the sacrificial lamb. His outlook seemed much more defeatist than it had been before Elliot had come, and Sam could not help but wonder what exactly had caused this change. There was an element of shame to his attitude, a hint of guilt, one that did not seem to have anything to do with the scholars and their despicable experiment.

Leaving Francis to his thoughts, Sam scoped out the remainder of the other end of his beach, but found nothing of interest other than a water-proofed sealed package of wafers, that might have been washed free from Elliot's hover, and a small wooden puzzle involving cups, balls, and string. Tucking his find under one arm, he headed back for the house. Francis had already left his perch, and Sarah and Elliot were nowhere in sight.

Everyone was seated in the kitchen when he arrived at the house, while Elliot was making supper yet again. Nathan had already made his way home and was sitting in a corner of the kitchen staring up at the ceiling, apparently lost in thought, his walls as thick as ever.

"He has finally gotten Fiona to talk to him again," Sarah said quietly, gesturing for Sam to sit, too. "He's been like that since he got back. She still won't come out, but if she's letting Nathan in, that's progress. I doubt we'll hear from him until she stops talking. They have a lot to catch up on."

Francis was equally silent, although much more present than Nathan. He was leaning over the table with his hands clasped together, examining the Languorite closely, although occasionally shooting a glance over his shoulder at Nathan.

The meal prepared, Elliot ungracefully thrust plates on the table in front of his young companions and sat with a grunt. Sarah stared at him as they ate, her dark eyes displaying more appetite than her stomach. Without warning, she paused in mid-bite and spoke.

"What happened to the Bigs' parents? You said that they were the first generation from interbred latents. I'm assuming they did that in an attempt to strengthen their abilities with the connection. How come they weren't here with their children?"

Elliot halted almost as abruptly as she had, and nearly choked on his current mouthful. He gazed at her for a moment without answering, his eyebrows raised.

"I suppose I did promise you more answers," he finally conceded. "I'll answer a few of your questions, but I get to decide when enough is enough – and there will be no protests when I say that we're done. I also get to save anything for a later date if I feel it's something that you aren't ready to know just yet."

Sarah smiled and nodded, satisfied with the fact that he would yield a little more to their curiosity.

"Fiona remembered something about that," Sam offered. "She said her parents were victims of some sort of accident."

Now Elliot looked extremely startled. "How could she possibly...?"

"Keeper," Francis mumbled. Sam noted that he looked even more dejected than he had on the beach.

"Oh – I suppose," the technician acknowledged, scratching at his beard. "Well, she was probably only repeating what she had heard said around her at the time. I'm sure the scholars considered it an accident. As I mentioned before, they had tested the connection on a smaller scale with adults, and there were problems with grave consequences. It wouldn't have been so bad, had they managed to keep the damage contained to the location where they were performing the experiment. The main complication was that, when a greater portion of those adults did lose all reason and sanity, they became either terribly despondent, which resulted in them taking their own lives, or very aggressively violent. After killing those who had resisted the psychological strain of the connection, the violent ones broke free from that area and ran rampant through the entire facility, killing anyone that they could find before security was able to take them down. The nursery where the next generation was located was preserved, and the Bigs protected as a result. The entire tragedy was horrific, and I would hope that you won't dwell on it and that you will try to put the idea out of your mind."

"I don't understand. These people were stronger telepaths than the latents, and you said that they never suffered damage from suppression of access to the connection," Sam commented. "Why weren't they Connected from birth, like the Bigs would have been? Why was it an abrupt exposure to the connection?"

"They were stronger than latents, but weaker than the Bigs, Sam," Elliot explained. He shuffled his feet under the table and fiddled with his fork, convinced that, by him telling these young people the terrible truth, he would be somehow scarring them for life. "They would have had a weak connection of sorts had they been raised in close proximity to one another. For testing purposes, the scholars wanted to keep them 'pure', so they raised them scattered about the mainland. There were a few smaller groups of some of the stronger telepaths in the bunch that had made contact with one another as children. They may have been some of the ones that did not react violently – that wasn't clear from the scholars' notes. Anyway, the scholars did suppress their ability to connect briefly, when they did bring them together as adults, after they had already made sure that there would be an even stronger second generation. They wanted everything prepared for monitoring when they lifted the magic that suppressed their telepathic skills. They weren't prepared for what happened, however."

Sam took everything in stride, not shaken by Elliot's revelations, but the same could not be said for everyone. Sarah had put her fork down and had pushed herself away from the table. She had not been expecting Elliot's brutal honesty, reinforced by his faint echo in the connection, and she had to block him out briefly to keep from losing everything she had just eaten. Perhaps, at first, the scholars had not realized just how much they would be playing with the lives of their subjects, but once they were aware of the possible side-effects, they had made a conscious decision to ignore the potential impact and do what they wanted despite it.

"So what about us?" Sam questioned. "What about the Littles?"

Elliot hesitated with the look of a deer caught in the headlights. Sam had brought up this topic before, and the technician had balked then as well. The large man dropped his gaze, staring into his food, and shook his head.

"No, not ready," he stated without any real sentiment.

"That's why they put us on Fervor," Sarah concluded. "In case things got out of hand – it was damage control. That's why they decided to observe from afar. That's why everyone else left before they removed the suppression."

"Not exactly," Francis murmured, not offering to expand on this further.

"That's right," Sam agreed. "They introduced the Tellers to the connection long before the rest of us, so they would be ready when the time came to bring in the others. That's when they discovered the sensory damage, right? Is that why the Tellers aren't amongst the strongest of us? Is that why none of the Tellers are Littles?"

Francis got up quickly, his chair scraping noisily across the floor, and left the kitchen. He was not pleased where the line of questioning was going. Sarah rushed after him. Elliot watched them go, a flicker of concern briefly altering his expression.

"None of you chose this," the technician sighed. "Although the weakness of the Tellers is, to some extent, of their own making. As I mentioned before, your gifts were assigned to you based on personality traits that happened to coincide with your strength within the connection. The Tellers tend to have a desire to try and control their environment, including the people that surround them. It makes them a prime candidate for their gift, but it limits their strength in the connection. You can't control what goes on there, and it is the freer spirits that do much better as one of the Connected."

Sam's eyes lit up. "Oh! I understand now. Before they even had their gifts, the Tellers yearned for control, the Fixers didn't like seeing people hurt, or things broken, the Watchers felt the need to protect others and keep a close eye on things, just like Nathan."

Elliot nodded. "Like I said, you were selected based on your personality profile. If your Control was originally slated to be a Finder, then he must be the curious sort, just like you – he just didn't happen to have the potential strength as a telepath that the scholars decided that they needed in a Finder. If there hadn't been the antagonism between the two of you, as Sarah described to me, you likely would have gotten along swimmingly."

Sam flinched a little at the burly man's choice of words. There seemed to be some irony there considering past events.

"And of course, that's why your Keeper is still holed up in her room. She clings to the past, and always will, I suspect. This has been just another in a long line of changes that she has tried unsuccessfully to resist," Elliot said, fidgeting and eying the exit.

Sam suspected these kinds of discussions were easier for him when he was dealing with the entire house-family. One-on-one conversations seemed to make the man excessively self-conscious. It was time to give him an out.

"You probably shouldn't say much more without the others listening in." Nathan and Fiona were walled up solid, as was Francis, and while Sarah had left herself open, she appeared to be quite distracted. "One of us would just have to repeat it to the others, so no point in wasting the effort. Besides, I may be dragging you halfway across the island tomorrow to find some of the things that you need. You may want to get some rest. I'll clear away supper, and then I'll be headed that way myself."

Elliot was not about to argue. He was not normally a domestic person and jumped at the opportunity to make his escape.

As Sam stacked the plates away in the cleansing device for future activation, he glanced over at Nathan still seated silently in the corner. He had closed his eyes now, and wore a huge grin, his cheeks occasionally flushing. He looked more relaxed than he had in days. The Finder wished he were a fly on the inside of one of Nathan's mental walls, so that he could listen in on his conversation with Fiona. Since Elliot had arrived and she had isolated herself, she had not spoken to Sam anymore than she had to Francis, and Sam actually missed her. He could understand why the Watcher had been anxious to speak with her after all this time.

Sarah returned to the kitchen dragging her feet and looking morose. Sam put the last dish into the base of the device and turned to face her.

"Why so glum?" he asked her.

"Have you ever seen a chip in a hover windshield?" she countered, answering his question with one of her own.

"Sure," Sam replied. *"It happened to our hover once. Maria took it to the school for one of the teachers to repair it. She told me that if you didn't get it early, the strain on it would eventually make it grow. She also said that if you let that happen, the chip would become a small crack, or perhaps a series of small cracks. At that point, it would be even harder to fix, but if you didn't, chances were, the crack or cracks would continue to spread until you had something that ran right across the entire windshield – some kind of divide or a network resembling a spider's web. When that happened, it would be so weak that the slightest jolt or the smallest impact could make it shatter. Something that started as a minor blemish could turn into something ultimately dangerous."*

Sarah nodded as he spoke, not meeting his gaze. There was almost a haunted look to her eyes.

"We have a chip," she insisted. *"And it's spreading."*

At first he thought she was talking about Elliot's hover, but with some prodding at her through the connection, he soon realized that she was not. She would not elaborate further, however. Sam tried various tactics to cheer her up, including offering her his latest find, but nothing seemed to work. It was so unlike Sarah. Then he came up with an idea.

"Will you come with me and Elliot finding tomorrow? You've been cooped up in this house for years. You must have

enjoyed getting out today. How about we try that again? It will help you get your mind off things, not to mention who knows where we will be going. It'll be an adventure, the kind that should be shared by special friends," Sam said with a smile. Sarah's expression softened a little and she responded with a half-smile of her own.

"Sure, Sam. Maybe that would be best. I can't fix what I can't access. Maybe if I just leave it alone for a little while..."

That was as much as Sam could hope for, and it was getting late. Leaving Nathan in the kitchen in his mirthful state, they both wandered off to bed.

13

FINDING

When Sam came out of his room the next morning, he watched Nathan bound around the house with a level of enthusiasm that the young man had not displayed since Elliot had arrived. The last time that the Finder had seen him with this kind of energy, he had still been the size of a large boy. Now there was no denying that Nathan was an adult.

It had been a few days since they had started their rapid growth, and from all appearances, it was finally coming to an end. The pain and irritation was subsiding, they were all noticeably taller, and the Bigs had lost anything childish to their look. If anyone outside of their house-family had caught a glimpse of Sarah or Sam, they would have just assumed that they were Bigs. But if anyone spotted Nathan or Francis, the change would have been undeniable and their reaction would be unpredictable.

As Nathan rushed past Sam, breakfast in hand, Sam noticed a problem that he had not paid any attention to before. Sarah and Sam had been borrowing some of the Bigs clothing, which fit comfortably, but the Bigs had been forced to continue to wear their own clothing, since Elliot had not been able to get into the hover to offer any spare garb that he had brought along. Nathan's looser fitting tunics and pants were just barely sufficient to accommodate Francis, fitting snugly on the average-sized man. Nathan on the other hand was wearing odd-fitting items that Sarah had cut and re-sewn. She was a Fixer, but this was more a case of fabrication rather than repair, and in this respect, the petite girl was not as skilled. As a result, the Watcher looked like a patch-work quilt of neutral tones and varying textures. And then there was the issue of footwear.

Cobbling larger boots from smaller ones was not a feasible option without the proper equipment, and Nathan had resorted to slicing open his boots towards the toe and taping over the ends with heavy duty work tape where his feet protruded. It was definitely only a temporary solution, and Nathan had been forced to carry the tape with him, replenishing what had been applied to his footwear en route, as it occasionally failed him. Sam offered to keep an eye out, in case any of the minders or teachers had left something behind that would prove to be a better fit.

Nathan gave Sam an exhilarated smile, without actually looking at him. He opened the front door. *"I think I've convinced Fiona to finally join us for supper tonight,"* he remarked happily. *"We'll be all together, like a real family again. She knows all about the hover. She's anxious to see it fixed so that we can leave here. She's really excited."*

Sarah had been accommodating Fiona's wishes to avoid the others and had been bringing the young woman her meals in her room. She did not need to join them for supper. If she had agreed to do so, it suggested that she was finally coming to terms with her transformation and was willing, perhaps, to adjust to it.

His feet barely touching the stairs, Nathan skipped down the front steps and loped joyfully off on his circuit. Sam closed the door behind him and turned back to see Francis standing there wearing a perplexed expression. Before Sam could say anything, he shrugged and made for the kitchen from which Sarah and Elliot were emerging.

"Time to do some finding, Sam," the technician stated, gesturing towards the door with paper in hand.

Sarah did not look ready to go anywhere. Sam frowned. *"I thought you were coming with us?"*

She glanced back towards the kitchen before answering.

Finding

"I helped Elliot write up the list. You don't really need me with you, and I don't want to get in the way."

There was a nervous tremor to her thoughts. Sam could tell that she was anxious again, and still yearning to fix something that she felt was beyond her reach.

"You can't say that for sure. Who knows what I'll find, and what state I'll find it in. We could very well need your help. Besides, you agreed to come with us last night. You agreed that there isn't much that you can do here right now. You know how important getting this hover fixed is to us. Please, Sarah," Sam thought plaintively.

"I..." she began, hesitating as some internal struggle ensued. She clenched her eyes shut, and then moments later seemed to give in. *"Alright, give me a couple of seconds."*

The petite girl dashed over to her room and disappeared from view. Elliot watched her go with a hint of interest as Sam took the paper from him and scanned the list written upon it.

"What's bothering her?" the large man asked the Finder.

"Something about chips and cracks in windshields," Sam replied evasively. "I think she's worried that Fiona is not the only one who isn't handling the transition well. This isn't a new thing for Sarah, Elliot. She started behaving this way after Royce left – it's just that it has gotten a little worse, that's all. I think she just needs to get out of the house more. It's making her a little stir-crazy."

The technician looked a little relieved at this. "She started acting like this before I got here, and it has only gotten a little worse? That's okay then. If you see any drastic changes in anyone, you'll let me know, right? I wasn't sure what effect the Languorite was going to have on all of you, and I don't want any repetition of what happened with the Bigs' parents. I was worried about Fiona at first until I had the chance to get in and talk to her. Her problems didn't run that deep, and she let Sarah do what she could for her. At that point I was fairly certain that Fiona's situation wasn't all that serious. Some disabling insecurities and a bit of drama, but for the most part harmless. Not that

195

I would expect there to be any show of trouble at this point if it hadn't manifested yet."

"To be honest with you, I wouldn't recognize anything like that in the others with all the chaos that has been going on around here," Sam conceded. "Nathan is all tangled up in the directions that Francis has placed in his head, and Francis is upset with Fiona and the way that she has been treating him from the start. Not that he seems to be holding it against her, really. I think that if we can just get that hover repaired and get going, everything will sort itself out."

This was when Sarah reappeared from her room, dressed and ready to go. Sam seized on the opportunity and, grabbing her by the hand before she had the chance to change her mind, he pulled her out of the house after him.

"Come on, Elliot!" he called over his shoulder. "I think that I may have a lead on something!"

Sam followed his instincts with Sarah closely in tow, circling around first of all to the old hover where Fiona had once hidden the burly man's messages. Elliot crouched by the abandoned vehicle and started stripping away anything that was potentially useful. Sam and Sarah sat back a short distance, watching him as he worked.

"I won't be able to get everything I need that's salvageable from this. We will have to come back here after we have found some of those tools on our list. I need them in order to actually retrieve some of those items. I managed to gather a few all purpose tools from the house, but anything specific to working on the hovers, if they were left behind, would likely be found in the garages," the technician grunted as he leaned awkwardly around the edge of the hover.

"No – none of the minders had any clue about maintaining or repairing the hovers," Sam corrected. *"If there's any hope of finding those tools, we'll have to go to one of the schools. It had been left up to the teachers to keep them in operational condition."*

"What?" Sarah said with a hint of fear. *"We'll have to go through the spaces of at least three of the other house-families. What if they see us? And we won't be able to follow you in. It's against the Directives."*

Elliot paused and glanced over at her sternly. *"If you want me to repair that hover, I need those tools. I'll be having to make enough compromises with regards to parts and materials. It will be impossible if you are expecting me to work empty-handed. We'll have to take our chances with the other house-families, and I guess it's time to test out the other functions of the Languorite...see if we can override those Directives. I'll be back."*

He clambered to his feet, and headed into the house.

"You and I are okay," Sam assured her, once they were alone. "Although they may start asking questions about why we have strayed from our designated space – we just have to make sure that they don't see Elliot. We won't be able to explain him away, no matter what story we come up with as to why you and I happen to be there. They'll assume we're Bigs, and we'll have to run with that."

Sam actually liked the idea of leaving the space that they had been practically imprisoned in for the last five years. He looked forward to the idea of having the opportunity to scavenge at a school. Sarah did not appear to be nearly as pleased with the idea.

Elliot returned a few moments later with the Languorite in hand.

"Pray that I can make this work," he murmured, pointing the device first at Sam. "I'm going to try to limit it to the compulsions from the Tellers, but I can't make any guarantees. I certainly don't want to strip you of your gifts right now. We still need them."

There was painful flash of multi-coloured light, and Sam felt a slight tingle to his skin and a temporary fogging of his thoughts, but those were the only signs to suggest that it had worked. Elliot then repeated the process with Sarah. Once again, from all outward appearances, nothing had changed. The success of the technician's efforts would be tested soon enough. He returned the Languorite to the house, and then set his sights on the old hover once again.

The pair observed Elliot's tinkering in silence for a while, considering possible cover stories to offer other children if they happened to have any encounters, before Sam found himself lost in other thoughts. The talk of them passing themselves off as Bigs brought his focus around to the idea of the Littles versus the Bigs again, and the missing information that Elliot had denied him twice already. It niggled at him, like a fly buzzing about his head. He hoped that this was a sign that his gift had remained untouched, his curiosity burning in the pit of his stomach as fiercely as ever.

"Why don't you think that we're ready, Elliot?" he pushed very lightly at the technician. *"What is it about our parentage that you find disturbing? If it makes a difference as to how much you'll tell us, Francis already suggested that we were somehow made to be what we are, even though Fiona tried to suggest that this wouldn't have been possible. I think we deserve a straight answer."*

Sarah gave him a nudge, and shook her head disapprovingly as Elliot lifted his head to centre on the Finder with a disconcerted stare.

"I don't think you would really want to hear the truth, and I can't predict how you or the Bigs will react. I will say that Francis is right, and Fiona is wrong. You were designed to be what you are. The scholars tailored you to fill perceived gaps – the ones that the Controls could not fill properly," he admitted, directing his attention back to his work, specifically so that he would not have to make eye contact with the two children as he spoke.

"You mean the way that we were raised and our education?" Sarah asked.

"No," Elliot mumbled. "More than just that."

He was growing tense and as he tried to remove a part with one of the household tools that he had brought with him it slipped, twisting in his hand and the sudden movement resulted in the technician gashing his thumb open against a sharper edge. He cursed and he shook the offending digit, which immediately began to drip blood. Sarah moved quickly forward to help him, her Fixer compulsion kicking in.

"Our parents, then? They were selected more carefully than they were for the Bigs?" Sam demanded.

Elliot hissed in pain, allowing Sarah to take the injured hand. She set about fixing it right away.

"I don't want to talk about this right now. Just let me do my work. You'll get your answers when I'm good and ready to give them," the technician protested, relaxing slightly as Sarah's efforts drew some of the pain away.

Sarah and Sam talked quietly between themselves as Elliot continued to pull pieces of the old hover. They decided that if they encountered anyone in the other house-family spaces that they would have to traverse, their story would be that they were searching for a necessary part required to repair a needed device. They would be referring to Elliot's hover, but they would be hoping that anyone asking might jump to some other conclusion. If they were lucky, the questioner might assume that they meant a part for some kitchen appliance, such as the cooking implement. This would not be a find that they would be able to locate in their own space, and ought to be explanation enough as to why they would need to stray outside of their boundaries. This plan was far from fool-proof, leaving a lot to chance and to the interpretation of the person with whom they would be speaking.

When Elliot had accomplished what he could, they set off toward the closest school. In addition to the necessary tools for the hover, Sam hoped that they might find some adult-sized clothing there, left behind by their teachers, particularly footwear. Anything even somewhat snug would be better than what Nathan was making do with at the moment.

Just as they feared, on their way trespassing through the second house-family's space, Sam felt the familiar mental prodding that suggested someone recognized that they were there. Giving Elliot an abrupt shove into the bushes, Sam threw his walls up around the ill-prepared adult. The Finder knew that anyone searching would push through the man's paper-thin walls with little effort. Throwing up his guard to protect Elliot from scrutiny might draw some suspicion from anyone that they happened to encounter, but it was their only option.

Within seconds, a wiry Little, with strawberry blond hair and freckles, rounded the corner along the pathway that they had been crossing. He looked up at them with some surprise, his pale blue eyes also displaying some excitement.

"Who are you?" the thin boy demanded. He did not bother with any pleasantries. *"Or better yet, what are you, and why are you here?"*

"I'm Sam, and this is Sarah. I'm a Finder," Sam said. *"We're sorry for the trespass, but it was unavoidable. We needed parts for one of our devices that made leaving our space necessary. We're only passing through, and we won't disturb anything here."*

The strange Little's eyes narrowed for a moment as he looked them both up and down.

"She must be your Keeper then, eh? My name's Julius and I'm a Finder, too. I heard that there were some Big Finders out there, but you are the only one that I've met. Don't worry about crossing over. I've had to do it a few times myself. That's how I met Cynthia and Jerome. They're Finders near here, too, but they are both Littles like me."

Sam was trying to do the math in his head. There were only fifty Littles, from what he had learned, and three hundred children altogether. That meant that if the Littles were evenly distributed amongst the house-families, there would be one per group. Since he and Sarah had both been Littles, it was clear that this had not been the case. That meant that some groups would not have any Littles whatsoever, perhaps in the case where their Big Finders and/or Fixers had proven to be sufficiently strong. Then again, it was hard to predict the scholars' rationale behind any of this. Perhaps the Littles had been purposefully concentrated in an area. There was no way of knowing for sure, not unless Elliot's information gathering had offered some insight that he just had not gotten around to sharing yet.

"Well, we're still sorry for the intrusion, Julius," Sam offered. *"It was nice to meet you, and we'll try not to make it a habit."*

"Just promise me you'll be as forgiving if the tables are ever turned, and if so, then we're good. It's nice to meet a Big outside of my house-family as friendly as you. Some of the Bigs around here are pretty surly," the smaller Finder chuckled. Sam couldn't help but wonder if Julius had had a run-in with Royce or any of his friends. He also wondered if the boy might be referring to his own Control.

"If it's up to me, you'll always be welcome in our space."

Sam had meant it when he had said it, but realized a few seconds later that Julius wandering freely through their space could quickly prove to be problematic, particularly if he laid eyes on Elliot, any of the Bigs, or Elliot's hover.

"I wouldn't go at the moment, however," Sarah chimed in, giving Sam a chastising nudge. *"Some members of our house-family are not feeling their regular selves. It would probably be best to keep your distance for now."*

There had been no signs of illness in the children since they had been abandoned on Fervor, and it was likely that the Fixer would be able to resolve any health issues that arose, but for the moment that theory remained untested. Her words seemed to be enough of a deterrence.

"I'll keep that in mind, and consider myself warned," Julius assured her. *"I don't foresee the need happening soon, but in the future I may take you up on your offer. I'll see you*

both around. I've got some errands to run. I'm sure you under-stand."

Sam nodded, and the Little set off down the path again. They waited until he was out of sight, and his walls seemed to be quite solid again. Sam kept his walls up around Elliot, letting Sarah in instead.

"Well that proves one thing – the stasis is still up around here," Sam remarked. *"Obviously, that effect of the Languorite doesn't extend beyond the limits of our space. If it had, there would be nobody like Julius around here."*

"You have to be more careful, Sam. We can't be inviting others into our space. It's too dangerous," Sarah chided.

"What else was I supposed to do? He had just caught us in his space and he was being gracious about it. I couldn't ex-actly refuse him, now, could I," the Finder retorted. The two had rarely argued, but the tension of the moment had been weighing heavily on both of them.

"No harm done," Elliot intervened. *"The crisis was averted and we don't have time to spare for bickering. Point me the way to that school."*

The remainder of the trek was uneventful, although Sam kept his walls up around the ghostly presence of the technician in the connection, just to be on the safe side, until they had ar-rived.

The school looked much the worse for the wear, the re-sult of years of disuse. It had been a very plain building to begin with, just like the majority of the buildings on Fervor. Now it looked ragged around the edges, where the storms had dislodged siding and roof shingles, and on one occasion, had forced a large broken tree branch into one of the windows, shattering it in the process. There were no signs of life, and certainly no evidence of upkeep. It disheartened Sam to see it that way, remembering the productive, and sometimes joyful, days that he had spent there. Elliot pushed his way past some of the overgrown shrub-bery to the front door.

"I was expecting to have to disable the lock, but someone has seen to that for us," he observed. "Of course, my method would have left it intact. Whoever did this didn't much care."

Sam and Sarah joined him by the entrance. Someone had wedged something solid into the door crack and had worried at the edges until they had worked the door free of the lock. As a result, it now hung loosely on its hinges, unable to be closed properly. It creaked loudly as Elliot pulled it back.

"Well, if there's a welcoming committee, that may have just let them know that we're here," the technician muttered. He peered into the dark corridor and activated the magic to illuminate the lights there. There was a soft hiss, a flicker and then a warm glow that lit up the space before them.

Sam held his breath. Looking at the empty hallway brought back memories that made him heartsick for the days when he had lived an innocent and uncomplicated life. He wished that he were still ignorant to what he really was and why they were on Fervor. He wished that he were still his minder's charge and not responsible for anything more than a few small chores around the house and his performance at school. He missed that life. Now he was facing a very ambiguous future that might be spent perpetually on the run. If he had had the ability to go back in time and freeze things as they had been at that moment, that day before he woke up to the screams in his head and to Francis in his room, he would have.

"This was your school."

Sarah didn't phrase it as a question. She could see from the expression on his face. She had come from another part of Fervor, with different classrooms and teachers. Sam hunched his shoulders and shrugged, trying to pretend as if it held no greater meaning for him.

"Where would your teachers make any repairs?" Elliot asked gruffly.

Sam's misery in the face of his old school made the technician horribly uncomfortable. He wanted to rush in, get the tools, and make a fast exit again, as quickly and as painlessly as possible. He did not want to seem heartless, but he did not have the patience to tolerate a dejected boy dragging his feet. Sam gestured further down the hallway.

He led the technician through the maze of corridors that brought them, eventually, to the place where the teachers were known to store and repair various equipment, including hovers. As the dim lights came up in response to Elliot working their magic, the technician's eyes lit up as well. He jogged into the centre of the room, and snatching up a heavy duty bag obviously intended for transporting tools, he began to scan the room for any of the items on his list. A conscientious Sarah joined him, but she began rooting through the lockers there and pulling out adult-sized work boots, and coveralls similar to Elliot's. Distracted as they were, they did not pick up on the shifting shadows at the far end of the room. But Sam did.

Sam guessed that the boy crouching there and watching the search had heard them come through the squeaky door and had fled ahead of them, seeking possible escape in here. He had not anticipated anyone having the ability to bring up the lights and had started when it had happened. Now his dark eyes were glued to the pair who clambered around the floor, gathering what they had come looking for, and Sam would recognize that face, framed by black hair, anywhere. It was Royce.

The Finder froze, not knowing what to do. Their Control had clearly sought shelter here after his exile from the house. There had been some supplies to scrounge up within the school proper and when those had run out, Sam assumed that Royce had turned to scavenging the surrounding area, avoiding the house-families in the process. He would still meet with his Control friends, but in many ways he was very much alone.

The Control observed Sarah and Elliot for a little while, awe-stricken at the sight of an adult, and then he noticed Sam. There was a gleam of recognition in his eye, and his jaw dropped. He strode immediately towards the Finder, and Sam started backing away, but he had soon edged himself right into a corner, with nowhere left to go. He stood his ground nervously at that point, until Royce was upon him.

"How?" Royce demanded, staring Sam practically eye-to-eye.

Royce was only a little taller than Sam was now, but at this point, not by much. The Finder was unsure if he should give an answer to the question, nor was Royce actually expecting him to, still believing him deaf. Sarah had now noticed the Control and had approached Elliot, grabbing his arm at the elbow and giving it a vigorous shake. The technician paused in mid-reach, looking up.

Sam wondered what it had been like for the Control to live here for the past year, but it made sense that he had come. The place would give him more room than one of the abandoned smaller houses, as well as more access to potential pickings while scrounging. Royce had, after all, been originally expected to be a Finder. He had good instincts for this sort of thing.

Faced down by the slightly larger boy, Sam felt as intimidated as ever, but the Control's expression held far more surprise than anger or bitterness.

"Things have changed," Sam finally managed to splutter. "It's difficult to explain."

Elliot had moved up to them by this point, his hulking form casting a shadow over Royce. The black-haired boy glanced over his shoulder nervously.

"Is this the Control that you spoke of? The one that your Watcher ran out of the house?" the man inquired, his eyes fixed on Royce's. The awe that Sam had noted earlier returned to Royce's expression. Sarah looked on from a distance, rubbing unconsciously at her wrist and appearing prepared to sprint at the slightest sign of trouble. Royce turned back to Sam.

"We're not here to bother you, or to be bothered, Royce. We just need a few things that we can't get anywhere else, and then we'll go," the Finder insisted. "We don't want to cause you any problems."

"You've changed," Royce blurted, his confusion reflected in his voice – a voice unfamiliar to Sam. The Control's gaze drifted over to Sarah. "She's changed, too. You shouldn't be here, either of you. How can you be here? Did they come for us? Did they lift the stasis?" The Control backed away as he spoke, eying Elliot warily. "Is it over?"

"It's not over," Elliot stated bluntly. "You don't honestly expect the scholars to abandon all of their work that easily do you?" Royce was still moving backwards, and had almost reached the door.

"They were quick enough to throw some of us away," he spat bitterly. "I saw some of the ones that didn't come out quite right. They were monsters...horrible mutants. How do you know that they all aren't like that inside?" The Control gestured at Sam and Sarah as he spoke. This wasn't going well.

Royce's hostile words had clearly disturbed the technician, and he gazed at the boy sympathetically, his gray eyes filled with pity. He slouched a little, not really prepared to contend with the issues that the Control was attempting to stir up.

"The scholars wouldn't have kept them if that were the case," Elliot murmured. "They probably thought it necessary to study them."

Sarah watched Royce, wide-eyed, completely bewildered by what he was saying. The Control had never mentioned such things before.

"They're not right, that's all I'm saying." Royce added quietly. His hand reached for the door frame behind him.

"None of this is right," Elliot replied. In response to this, the black-haired boy made a scoffing noise before he turned and fled into some of the unlit areas of the school.

"What did he mean by that?" Sam demanded after Royce had left. "What was it that he saw exactly, the ones who didn't come out quite right?"

"Not ready," the burly man grunted, averting his gaze. He returned to his search, refusing from that point onwards to answer anymore of Sam's questions. Sam and Sarah looked at each other and sighed.

14

EMERGENCE

Sam, Sarah, and Elliot were heavily laden when they returned to the house. It was already twilight, and too dark to do any fixing. They had found about two-thirds of the items on their list, and they had decided that the rest could wait until the following day.

Sam was famished, and his mind was awhirl with many thoughts. He was still stunned by their encounter with Royce and confused by the tidbits of information that they had gained from their Control, as well as from the occasional slip by Elliot. They would finish the finding tomorrow, and if all went smoothly, they might even begin fixing the hover before the day would be through. Sam could not help thinking about the fact that, once his assistance was no longer needed, he would have the freedom to go wherever he wanted and do whatever he felt like doing. He was no longer bound by the Directives, and that would allow him to hunt down answers on his own.

After storing their finds in one of the closets in the house, they all wandered into the kitchen. Francis and Nathan were already there, both fidgeting anxiously. Nathan stared at the floor, glancing up as they entered for a brief moment before quickly averting his gaze again.

"I was hoping you might be Fiona," he sighed, shuffling his ill-clad feet. Francis said nothing, leaning back in his chair,

but Sam suspected that his feelings were the same. *"She should be out soon."*

With a stifled laugh, Sarah darted out of the kitchen. Elliot began rummaging through the cupboards, and Sam took a seat at the table with the young men.

"Sorry to disappoint you," Sam commented with a chuckle.

"Don't get me wrong, little buddy. I'm happy to see you. I'd just be even happier if you were Fiona," Nathan confessed. *"It's about time that she comes out of her room. If she stays in there much longer, she's bound to grow roots and meld with the furniture."*

An excited Sarah stumbled back into the kitchen, her arms filled with some of that day's finds. In particular, she had the boots and coveralls that they had foraged out of the school lockers.

"A gift," she laughed triumphantly as she slid them into Nathan's averted line of sight. His smile broadened.

"You are forever my angel of mercy, aren't you, Sarah? I thank you for remembering me, and my poor mangled toes thank you, too. Where did these come from?" he inquired.

"We got them from the school," Sam informed him. *"We had to go there to get some of the tools that Elliot needed."*

"You mean Elliot went there to get them," Francis said pointedly, *"While you waited."*

"No," Sarah admitted. *"We went in with him. He needed our help."*

The Teller sat up in his chair, looking irritable. *"But the Directives...they should have stopped you."*

Sam and Sarah glanced at each other, unsure how they should respond. That was answer enough for Francis. He glared at Elliot.

"You used the active features of the Languorite on them, without discussing it with the rest of us? What if it didn't work the way that it was supposed to? What if there were side-effects? Wouldn't it have been better to test it first on me, or

Nathan? All the knowledge that you had was theoretical. What if you failed to apply it properly? We need Sam and Sarah far more than the rest of us. What you did was dumb and put us all at risk," he spat.

Nathan did not outwardly support Francis on this, but Sam suspected that behind the Watcher's reinforced walls, he was in agreement. He had mentioned the desire to be the one to play guinea pig for the Languorite before.

"We had a problem, and that was the most obvious solution. You may consider yourself the ruler of this roost, but you don't get to dictate my actions, Teller. I refuse to be a part of your power trip," the technician growled, standing to his full height to add impact to his words.

A strange look settled upon Francis's face, and he stared at Elliot intently.

"It's not that simple anymore," he murmured. The push was gentle, but with such focus that it almost overwhelmed Elliot immediately. *"You are part of the connection now. The old rules don't apply. You do **not** do anything to any member of my house-family without my express permission. I dictate what I choose, and like it or not, you **will** oblige me. Don't test me, or I'll show you exactly what I'm capable of. You are in our world while you are on Fervor. Any power that you had you left behind on the mainland."*

"You don't speak for everyone here, Teller," Elliot retorted, trying to maintain his composure despite the mental assault from Francis. *"I was doing what we deemed best for repairing my hover, and Sam and Sarah were agreeable to it. There was no harm done."*

"You are wrong," Francis insisted, his jaw set. *"I **do** speak for everyone here as long as I am Teller. If I decide that you won't be going anywhere in that hover, your work on it is done. If I decide that I don't want you using the Languorite on them again, and that it is mine to possess, then that is how it will be. If I decide that you aren't according me the respect that I*

deserve and want you out of this house, you will be gathering your things and walking out that door."

Sam was shaken, a ball of despair building in his stomach. He could understand why Elliot would want to challenge Francis, but they really were dependent on the Teller going along with their plan. Even if Francis was not in control of their situation, they had to make him feel that he was or he might seize that control. He could shut them down with a few words, and Elliot had not had the opportunity to see Francis demonstrate that ability to the extent that the rest of the house-family had. He had to offer a distraction, to end their dispute before they all regretted it.

"Royce was there," he piped up, hoping this would catch Francis's attention. *"He has been living at the school. He saw us."*

Sam's tactic worked like a charm. Francis abandoned his confrontation with the technician instantly and jumped on the fact that they had stumbled upon their errant Control. The Teller bombarded Sam with questions.

"Royce? Really? Were his friends there, too? How did he look? What did he say?"

"We got to see him up close, and we spoke with him as well, so I'm sure that it was him, and he doesn't seem to be in bad shape. I think he's surviving quite well there," the boy answered. *"I don't know about his friends. He was the only one that was there...but he saw Elliot. He got a good look at me and Sarah, too. He could see something strange was going on. He asked a lot of questions."*

"The school...hmm. That would make sense. He didn't try anything, did he?" the Teller inquired.

Elliot had already let the earlier issue slide, since Francis was no longer interested in pursuing it. The technician had chosen instead to ignore them and began rummaging through the cupboards.

"No," Sarah replied. *"But he said something...something that made us think that the Controls, and maybe the Tell-*

ers, knew more about us Littles than we did. It sounded like he knew some of the things we have been trying to get Elliot to tell us, but that he has refused to share with us so far. I was almost tempted to follow Royce when he ran off and see if he would give me more answers."

Elliot paused in his shuffling, but did not turn to look at her.

"Royce wouldn't pull any punches," Sam agreed. *"If he was willing to tell us, he wouldn't worry about whether or not we were 'ready'. He wouldn't consider whether or not we would find it too shocking. He would just tell us the truth. That's all we're asking for. That's all we ever asked for, and that includes from you too, Francis."*

The Teller scowled at this comment and Elliot hung his head, sighing.

"If it's that important to you, then why don't you just pry into his thoughts the same way that you clearly did with mine when we first met. It's not like he can stop you. His walls are much weaker than mine were at the time. No? The notion hadn't crossed your minds?" Francis's thoughts dripped with sarcasm. *"Maybe you just respect him and his privacy more than you ever respected me and mine. Or you just happen to believe that he is withholding information to protect you, but that obviously wasn't the case with me? Somehow I managed to master the unknown skill of lying through the connection."*

Sam gave him a sheepish look and Sarah blushed a bright red, entwining her fingers nervously. Francis was about to proceed with a second tirade when the kitchen door opened. Fiona stepped in.

Everything that had been happening ceased to happen immediately. Elliot glanced over his shoulder at the sudden silence and gave Fiona a broad smile. Sam was wondering what all the fuss had been about. It was still Fiona, only she looked much more like Maria. She was taller than his minder had been, and perhaps a little curvier with paler skin, but she certainly was not the vile creature that he had been imagining. He could not understand then why Francis and Nathan's reaction to her seemed much more extreme.

Nathan normally would not have looked at her at all, but he was already on edge because of all the arguing and posturing that had been going on in the kitchen, not to mention the discussion of Royce, and she had entered with no warning. His protective compulsion overrode Francis's directions and he leapt to his feet with his gaze quickly focussed on the intruder. As soon as he recognized that it was Fiona, he averted his eyes, but not before his breath caught in his throat and his cheeks flushed in response to the sight of her. All she noticed, however, was how quickly that he had looked away. Her expression fell, and she tried to cover herself with her arms in a very self-conscious gesture. She also moved to step out of the kitchen until Francis spoke up. He had gotten to his feet as well, and was staring at her, his mouth slightly open.

"No! Don't go back in your room!"

She came to an abrupt halt.

"He only turned away because he's following orders. For our own safety, he's not supposed to look at any of us. He's not even allowed to look at his own reflection. He didn't turn away because of you specifically, Fiona. From what I can see, you look wonderful. The change suits you, I promise."

"He's right, Fiona." Nathan said quietly, allowing those gathered in the room into his thick and otherwise unyielding walls. *"I'd gaze at you all night if I could. You look incredible. The change does suit you."*

He beamed a wide grin in her general direction, keeping his eyes on the opposite wall. Sam rolled his eyes at this, and Sarah muffled a giggle with her hand

The Keeper still appeared to be feeling somewhat self-conscious, her arms locked around her torso, but she did relax a little.

"See? You know that we wouldn't be lying to you, even to preserve your feelings." Francis assured her. *"Now come closer and let me get a better look at you, then tell me why exact-*

ly you felt it necessary to hole yourself up in your room for days."

Sarah stopped laughing.

Fiona grimaced and reluctantly approached him. She slowly dropped her arms as she went, and twisted away from him as much as she could will herself to. When she was standing directly in front of him, she followed his second command.

"I didn't want anyone to see me. Everything was happening so fast, but some things seemed to be changing faster than others. It wasn't pretty. It was downright disgusting at times, and there were even moments where I was...lop-sided."

A flicker of pain flashed across her features, and she did not try to hide that she despised Francis for getting her to tell him this. Sam had to bite his tongue not to laugh at the dramatics over something he thought was ridiculously silly. Sarah noticed his expression of restrained mirth and elbowed him hard in the ribs. He quickly lost any suggestion that he had been tempted to laugh as he groaned inwardly and clutched at his side.

"Any more of that, and I stomp on your foot, too," she warned, under her breath. "That part wasn't funny. Many girls are very sensitive about those kinds of things, and Fiona happens to be one of them."

"Oh come on Sarah," he whispered to her mentally, temporarily pulling her outside of Nathan's walls. *"We're all family here. Whatever she was going through, we could have helped her through it. We weren't about to judge her. Nobody would have cared if her transformation wasn't...balanced."* He wanted to laugh again, but the ache in his side was enough to convince him otherwise.

"Don't be cruel, Sam," Sarah hissed inside his head. *"You may not judge her, but you can't speak for everyone. Plus, I don't think it's your opinion that she was all that worried about. Francis made enough fuss about all of this on his own. He embarrassed her, and she already hates him. He doesn't care about her feelings, especially when he decides he knows*

215

better than she does. He won't even give her the opportunity to do what he would like her to do of her own accord. He doesn't even bother asking anymore. He just tells."

"Now Sarah, she does overreact at times, and when was the last time that she obliged him when he was asking, hunh? I don't like the way he orders her around anymore than you do, and he may abuse the situation at times, but she hasn't left him any choice when it comes to the important things."

Francis and Nathan had returned to their seats and Fiona had used the excuse of helping Elliot to prepare a meal as a means of escaping Francis's direct and discomforting scrutiny. That did not stop him from watching her as she worked, and Sam wondered if she could feel the young man's pale eyes on her. If it was making Sam half as uncomfortable as it was probably making her, she more than likely wanted desperately to return to her room – only, thanks to Francis, she could not.

It was a horribly awkward evening. The underlying tension between Elliot and Francis still remained, the Teller viewing the technician as a threat to what he believed to be his rightful authority within the house, and the technician seeing the young man as trying to wrest more power than his years and his knowledge should merit, merely because he possessed the unnatural ability to do so. Sam was starting to actually think that it was a good idea for Francis not to leave Fervor with them, if only to avoid more of this kind of conflict once they were on the run.

There was also a second tension because of Fiona's presence. Fiona spent her first time out of her room in days completely on edge. As long as she was forced to remain in the kitchen with them— listening to Sam, Sarah, and Elliot discuss repairs to the hover for the most part—then she had to endure Francis's predatory eyes and occasional orders. Sam felt bad for her, but he knew that he was not capable of dissuading the Teller, who had seemed possessed by various impulses since Fiona had emerged from her room.

Emergence

As an offshoot of that uncomfortable situation, Nathan, who had appeared to be quite joyous at Fiona's return to mixing with the rest of the family, eventually picked up on the overall sense of discord in the kitchen that night, even though he only got a subtle glimpse of it when he let more than just Fiona in past his reinforced walls. As the evening progressed, he did this less and less often, since he found the upkeep of those walls while including multiple minds inside greatly fatiguing. As a result, he mostly reserved that privilege to just sharing with Fiona, especially since he did not really feel like he was a part of anything that was happening with the hover. When he did finally become aware of the unease involving Elliot, Francis, and Fiona, he became disturbed as well.

Sam was happy to finally excuse himself and head for his bed, but he was the first to leave. Sarah had been flitting about the kitchen like a nervous little animal when he had made his exit, trying, and failing, to play mediator and to bring a better sense of peace to those there. Being an adult seemed to be a very complicated affair, and Sam was grateful that he was not there yet. On the other hand, he was starting to see some of what was bothering Sarah so much about Francis lately. There had been times after Fiona had joined them that the Teller had definitely not seemed himself. Instead there had been something disjointed about Francis, something out of place. Sam tried to remember the friendly boy who had helped him counter the fears caused by the connection, and found the memory shallow and short-lived, since none of that person appeared to remain in the transformed Francis. Tossed around by these thoughts, sleep did not come easy for Sam that night.

In the morning, he, Sarah, and Elliot gathered the remainder of the items on Elliot's list, much simpler now that they had the appropriate tools, and then they set off for the beach so that Elliot and Sarah could start work on the hover. Sam sat and watched as the two stripped off the siding in places, planning on repairing any internal damage first. He tried to observe quietly, but his curiosity continued to get the best of him, and he found himself asking one question after another about what they were doing. After the first few minutes of this, Elliot sat up with a grunt, bristling with annoyance.

"Why don't you make yourself useful and go find something," he grumbled. "This is going to take us days to finish. I'm sure that you'll be bored beyond belief."

"We did enough finding this morning to fulfil that urge," Sam assured him. "And this is plenty interesting. I didn't really know anything about hovers when we started. I'm learning a lot. Of course, if you are getting tired of my questions, I can change the subject. We could talk about the argument that you had with Francis last night. You really shouldn't be challenging him like that. He's right, you know. You are part of the connection now, and you are a weak part at that. Our Teller's showing quite a bit of restraint presently, and he could pin you down like a little bug if he chose to subvert your will. At the moment he views you as floundering and ignorant, so he excuses any missteps on your part, but if you fight him too much, that will change. We've had years to get used to the idea that we only get to refuse Francis's wishes if he is willing to let us. As long as we don't resist him on a regular basis, he doesn't tend to push us around."

"Unlike Fiona," Sarah muttered, trying to reshape a standard hover part slightly so that it could be used to replace a damaged one in Elliot's vehicle.

"So...what?" Elliot growled as he rummaged through the grouping of tools that he had laid out on the sand. "Am I supposed to be grateful that the tyrant has spared me?"

"You don't understand," Sarah sighed. "He was better when Royce was around. Nobody realizes how hard this is on Francis. He's all alone in this."

She paused.

"I think this is done."

She held the part that she had been working on out to him. He took it from her and started to examine it carefully, turning it over in his hand.

"Is it true, what he said about you two messing in his thoughts, and being able to sift through mine?" the technician said, without looking up.

"We only did it with Francis in the beginning, and only because we had no clue what was going on since he wouldn't give us any proper answers," Sam remarked defensively. "It wasn't personal, it was survival."

Sarah nodded in agreement.

"We won't do that to you. You've done nothing but help us. I'm sure you'll tell us everything eventually. Francis wasn't about to do that. He figured the less that we knew, the better...at the time. I don't know if he feels that way now. He's never shared much with us, and that much hasn't changed."

Elliot looked at Sam contemplatively.

"Maybe I judged you wrong then," he murmured. "Maybe you are more mature than I originally thought. Maybe you are ready."

"You're going to tell us about our parents then? Are they still alive? Will you be able to return us to them when we leave Fervor?" Sarah suggested hopefully.

The technician glanced at her with a pained expression.

"Don't...don't think like that. If I'm going to tell you this, I want you to keep an open mind and try not to see everything that I have to say in a negative light. I don't think you'll be able to predict what I have to say, so don't try. It will just make things worse. And yes, you could say that your parents are still alive."

He hesitated, scratching at the back of his neck and searching for words. "Did they teach you anything in school about genetic manipulation?"

"You mean the scholars using magic for selective breeding like you said they did with the Bigs' parents? Not much. We did talk a little about genetics and how various traits are determined by your genetic make-up, but nobody said anything about purposefully trying to influence the outcome," Sam replied.

"And cloning," Sarah added. "Don't forget about that. They talked about identical twins and how it is possible to duplicate a living thing if you know its genetic coding. There are no identical twins on Fervor, however."

"With good cause," Elliot stated, playing absentmindedly with the tool he held loosely in his hand. "The scholars did manipulate the genetics of the Bigs, selecting a variety of traits in their parents to see how they would combine. Theirs was not a natural conception, guided by magic so there were no natural anomalies like identical twins. But...but that wasn't enough for the scholars. They decided that the traits hadn't been combined appropriately, and that their Fixers and Finders needed to be stronger. They would replace the hundred children that they had slated for the positions, keep half of them as Controls, and send the other half back to the mainland with the minders and teachers."

"But the Bigs' parents were dead. Where would they find the people with the right traits to produce that kind of telepathic strength in their children?" Sarah admonished. Her words triggered a response from Sam, who was suddenly starting to see where Elliot was possibly going with this.

"The Bigs," the Finder answered coolly. "It was the only stock that they had left to work with. But there are only fifty Littles, not a hundred. There were no children who left with the minders and the teachers. This has something to do with what Royce told us, doesn't it?"

"The Bigs can't be our parents. They were only around five years old when we were born," Sarah protested, unhappy with where this was going.

Elliot shook his head.

"The scholars used genetic material from the Bigs and surrogates, Sarah, but they didn't use a simple method of merely two donors. They wanted as much strength as possible, a predominance of ability with the connection. They wanted to cheat evolution, so they pulled genetic coding from multiple Bigs. You don't have two parents, you have many, and they happened to be scattered around Fervor. You could have genes from any of them, even from Fiona, or Nathan, or Francis. Even from Royce. The Controls did carry some of the traits they were looking for, just in a less concentrated way. So you see, I can't take you to your parents, because in a way, you are already with them."

Sarah's face grew ashen, and she looked like she was going to be ill. Sam, on the other hand, was not satisfied with this alone. He felt the need to dig deeper.

"Why were there only fifty Littles, instead of a hundred, Elliot? What happened?" he demanded. "And why did Royce think that there was something wrong with us on the inside?"

"The scholars had never tried to splice while manipulating genetics before. They used questionable methods, and this yielded inconsistent results. Half the children were viable, resembling the Bigs that they were built from. The other half..." Elliot grimaced, unwilling to meet their stares.

"They died?" Sarah breathed, clutching at Sam's hand.

"Some of them didn't survive birth," the technician conceded.

"But some did, didn't they?" Sam pressed. "And some survived long enough that Royce got a look at one of them. They didn't look human, that's why he called them monsters. They must have had them hidden somewhere on Fervor, because none of the rest of us ever saw one. Royce did have those Finder instincts though. He probably saw something that stirred his curiosity, and followed those instincts until it led him there. What happened? Did they leave with the first exodus or the second? Or are they still hidden here somewhere? Would they have been able to be part of the connection like us, and that ability was magically suppressed in them too?"

"I don't know, Sam," Elliot insisted. "They considered that part of their experiment a failure, and while I'm sure that they had the details recorded somewhere, it wasn't with their active research notes. That was all that I could get my hands on, and only because I was actually working on the Languorite for them."

"So what you are saying," Sarah summarized in a tremulous voice, "Is that our parents are not really our parents – that they are only five years older than we are, and that all of the Littles are siblings, in a way, only we aren't? Royce was right. We are monsters."

"Sarah, no," Sam said with a frown. "Elliot's right. You can't think like that. This doesn't change anything. This just gives us more insight as to what exactly those scholars are willing to do, in the name of their research. It doesn't have any bearing on us."

But Sarah wasn't that easily consoled. She lurched to her feet looking horribly distraught and ran off down the beach. Elliot watched her go, and then hung his head and sighed.

"Not ready," he mumbled with an edge of misery to his voice. "Should have gone with my first inclination, trusted my intuition."

He threw the tool he held into the pile, with a 'clank'.

"I need her if you want me to finish this."

"I'll fetch her back," Sam offered, knowing he would have no problem finding her. "Do what you can without her for now. I won't be long."

He traced Sarah back to the house and found her sitting with Francis, clinging to him in her misery, and sniffling quietly. He was stroking her hair trying to soothe her, and eyed Sam with some distaste as the Finder entered.

"I told you that this was a bad idea. There were some things that you didn't need to know – things that would only be hurtful. Elliot doesn't really understand what life has been like for us, or how we think. I do. Take advantage of him and his hover if that is what you want, but stop digging," the Teller stated.

Sam gritted his teeth as the sudden wave of compulsion hit him with the command. It did not have to be permanent. Elliot could easily remove it with the Languorite. It was the principal of it. Francis threw it out as casually as regular speech. He had never done that to Sam before.

"How about we discuss that later? We need to work on the hover while it is still light out. Elliot needs Sarah's help." Sam did not try to make excuses. There was no time for that.

Francis's pale green eyes held the Finder for a few moments, a small crease in his brow. Then he took Sarah by the shoulders and forced her to sit up.

"Fine. Sarah, go help Elliot with the hover. Forget about what he last told you for a little while, and focus on your fixing," he murmured. She nodded, and got to her feet, making for the door.

That was two orders in the last few minutes, and Francis almost never told the Littles what to do.

A worried Sam returned to the beach, trailing after Sarah. She was right about Francis. Something, Sam feared, was wrong.

15

ABUSE OF POWER

When they arrived back at the house that evening, Fiona had already prepared a meal and was sitting mutely across from Francis at the kitchen table. Sam could tell that she did not want to be there, and he suspected that Francis had not given her a choice. They were waiting there in silence for the others to return, with Fiona fidgeting and watching out the window trying to ignore the Teller. Francis, on the other hand, was just staring at her while wearing a contemplative expression.

That evening was even more tense than the one prior, but was thankfully much more short-lived. There was little conversation. Sarah, who had initiated talk on many of the occasions that the house-family had gathered in the past, was silent and moping. Francis seemed equally unyielding, his eyes glued to Fiona and rarely affording a glance for anyone else, clenching and unclenching his jaw from time to time. Elliot seemed to be imitating Nathan during most of the meal, averting his eyes and refraining from commenting on anything that had happened during the day. Fiona and Nathan basically kept to themselves, returning to the way things had been before Elliot's arrival and shutting the others out in the process.

Sam found the quiet stifling, but it was decidedly better than yesterday's heated debate. There would be no winners in the dispute between Francis and Elliot, and Sam was sure that if the technician pushed the Teller too much, the losers would include him, Sarah, Nathan, and Fiona. After he finished eating, Sam concluded that he had nothing to contribute to the situation that would help improve dampened spirits or mend broken fences, so he excused himself and went to his bedroom.

For the second night in a row, finding sleep proved to be a challenge to Sam as he fretted over all of the trouble surrounding his house-family. If they could only hold out until the hover was ready before someone collided with their breaking point, they could make it off of Fervor and leave all of their cares behind them. He worried what would become of Francis once they were gone, but he also realized that taking him along would cause any existing problems to persist. They could bring him along if he would willingly submit to having his gift removed by the Languorite and pass over any authority that he possessed to Elliot, something that the Teller would surely refuse to do. Francis had not wanted to go with them in the first place. He certainly would not agree to it if it involved such stipulations. As Elliot had mentioned, Francis needed to feel like he was in control, and as things were getting more stressful, that need seemed to be intensifying.

There were also no guarantees that leaving Fervor would help Sarah cope with what they had just learned. Sam admitted that it was unusual, and a little shocking, but he was quite certain that he could live with the fact that where they had come from was not quite normal. He was more curious about what had become of the odd ones that had managed to survive – the ones that Royce had discussed discovering. He had planned on hunting the Control out the next day and trying to drill him for information, but in addition to overcoming enduring fears of the black-haired boy, Sam now found himself plagued by the restrictions placed upon him by Francis. He could go to the school the next morning on the basis of doing more finding, but he would not be able to prompt Royce with questions. If Royce were going to provide him with anymore answers, it would have to be at the Control's choosing and not Sam's request.

When Sam arose sleepily the next morning, a disgruntled-looking Elliot and a chagrined Sarah were preparing to set out for the beach. Nathan had left, and Francis and Fiona were up. The Keeper was milling about, having already started on her household chores for the day, and she was trying to give Francis as much of a cold shoulder as she could muster. This did not seem to put the Teller off. He was watching her as much as he had been since she had emerged from her room, but Sam thought there was something off in Francis's mannerisms that day, something different. There was heightened interest and intensity to his pale green eyes that had not been there before, as well as a nervousness to his movements that seemed out of place for Francis. Sam did not like it, and he was tempted to stay behind to reassure himself that there was nothing unusual in the works, especially since his Teller had been acting somewhat out of the ordinary in general lately.

Unfortunately, his finding urges eventually overcame any reluctance he had to leave, and when he saw that Sarah and Elliot were finally ready to go, he beat them to the exit.

When Sam opened the door, he found the morning to be less than pleasant. The air was damp and cold and the sky was gray, but there was no sign of actual rain. The weather cast an additional air of gloom over the house, but it did not deter any of them from attempting to achieve their objectives for the day. As the three reached the bottom of the front steps, Sam started out on a separate pathway while Sarah and Elliot headed towards the shore. When Sarah noticed that the Finder was not joining them, she stopped abruptly.

"Where are you going?" she called out to him.

"To do some finding," he called back. "I've helped you as much as I can. You don't need me anymore for anything associated with the hover. Right now I'll only get in the way, and you know that I still have to find. I'll come to check back on you later, when I'm done."

Elliot was visibly relieved, pleased that he would be able to work in peace and not be assuaged with questions, but Sarah drooped in response to Sam's words, her eyes sad. She understood, nevertheless, and did not suggest that Sam shouldn't go.

Rushing through the trees without worries reminded Sam of the days before Royce had left the house, earlier on when the Control's hostility still remained fairly minimal. That was when Sam had enjoyed finding the most. Dashing across the other house-families' spaces was so much easier without Sarah and Elliot, and he liked being alone. He had not had much opportunity to do things this way lately and had almost completely put the thought out of his head that he was about to confront the Control on his own terrain. There would be no Nathan to rush to his rescue if things went wrong. Then again, Sam and Royce were now on much more even ground. It was possible that Sam could even hold his own against him.

As he approached the school, a shudder went up his spine, still haunted by the vision of bleakness that did not correspond with his memories. He wanted to see the school as it had once been, and not the way that he was seeing it now. He paused before entering, reconsidering the choice that he had made to come in the first place. It was an all out battle between fear and curiosity, and in the end, curiosity won.

Sam crept up towards the door. Elliot had not extinguished the lights when they had departed, but his magic had expired once he had left the general area, so there was only darkness in the corridor past the entrance. Sam had been expecting that, and reached into the bag that he had brought with him, pulling out the glow torch within. It had been some time since he had last used it, but the method of activation still remained fresh in his mind, probably because it was some of the very limited magic that he could actually use. The Finder cautiously reached for the door and swung it open rapidly with an exaggerated jerk. He illuminated the device clutched fervently in his fist and stepped forward.

He followed his finding instincts that led him to what once was the school cafeteria. There were things in the kitchen that were prime scavenging items, but which had been left untouched by Royce. Sam noted the likely reason why. They were all items that required the use of a cooking implement, and while Royce had unlimited access to one, he no doubt had no idea how to make it work. There was always the option of cooking over an open fire, but that required knowing how to work one of the fire-making devices, and Sam doubted that the Control could do that either. That made those particular food items useless to Royce, but a perfect find for Sam. He started dropping some of the packages into his bag.

"Stealing from me now?"

Sam was so startled by the sudden sound that he almost dropped both the bag and his glow torch.

"You can't make claim on this, Royce. The school is fair game for finding. You know that. Besides, if you could use this, you would have used it by now. Don't play dog in the manger."

Sam felt his breath quicken, and he couldn't bring himself to turn around and face the Control.

"Fair game for finding, yes. Fair game for a Finder, no. I would have no cause for protest if you were a Keeper, Sam, but your being here goes against the Directives. Where's Fiona? How did you and Sarah manage to get in here in the first place?" Royce sneered.

While there was still a bitterness to his words, the underlying threat that Sam used to detect was not there anymore. Tensing his shoulders, the Finder finally got up the courage to turn around.

"We aren't bound by the Directives anymore," Sam acknowledged.

"And how is that possible? How did you escape the stasis as well? Does it have anything to do with that man who was here?" the Control snorted, hands on hips.

Sam nodded. He did not see any harm in revealing any of what was going on to the boy who had already chosen to go against the Directives and would be on the outs with the scholars. If he answered Royce's questions and kept the conversation going, who knew where it would go.

"That was Elliot, a technician from the mainland. He has been helping us. He's providing us with a way to leave Fervor," Sam admitted.

"You're going to leave Fervor?" Royce murmured in disbelief. His eyes brightened in the soft light from the glow torch. "You have a hover? I'm surprised you're willing to tell me all of this. What if I told the scholars?"

"That would mean exposing yourself when you hadn't followed the Directives. I don't think that it would be worth it to you. You'll find yourself with just as much trouble on your hands as Francis will have when we leave."

"You managed to hide this from Francis? You're leaving him behind?" Royce said.

"No, he knows. And as far as staying behind is concerned, that's his choice. He doesn't want to leave Fervor," Sam suggested.

"Hmph," the Control scoffed. "And you trust him on that? I would wager that he'll turn you all in the first chance that he gets. I'm surprised he has let you get this far, but maybe he's just playing with you. He can do anything he wants, now that I'm not there. If he hasn't abused his power yet, it's just a matter of time. That control freak will eventually tire of the games and start showing his true hand. Then you will all just become hapless slaves to his whims. I'd rather be here alone than in your shoes when that happens."

"He wouldn't turn us in," Sam retorted. This conversation was not going the way that he wanted it to with Royce questioning him and not offering anything in return. "He said he wouldn't, through the connection, and you can't lie that way."

Royce smirked at this.

"He would find a way around that if he really wanted to. Do you know why he was chosen to be a Teller? They picked him because he was smarter than the rest of us. All of the Tellers were like that. For some reason they decided that intelligence was somehow a factor in good judgement, and they wanted their appointed leaders to play their role as directed. They didn't account for things like ambition, jealousy, or power-lust. They didn't figure that those of us with more common sense might outwit their brainy figureheads."

Sam frowned slightly. He hardly considered Royce's current position a measure of how well he had outwitted Francis. This was just another form of posturing on the part of the Control, attempting to tear others down in an effort to build himself up.

Royce eyed him warily.

"So if everyone is aware of what is going on, why are you here alone? I would have expected you to bring a buddy to back you up. My friends are going to be arriving any minute. Not that I have to warn you, I don't owe you anything, but I thought you might like to know that they won't take kindly to you stealing from me either, or nosing around here for any other reason. You should have known that you wouldn't be welcome here. Do you honestly think I believe that you came back here just for the purpose of finding?"

Sam didn't answer. He couldn't explain why he was there, other than for the finding, because that would be making his intentions of wanting to retrieve more information clear, and Francis's instructions would not allow him to dig. The fact that he could be there at all was a technicality, and one used to Sam's advantage.

"Speechless, eh? That is so not like you from what I had gathered from the others." Royce's eyes narrowed. "Francis gave you some sort of order, something that prevents you from asking too many questions, didn't he? You must have been getting too close to something he didn't want you to know."

"Not exactly," the Finder confessed. "Francis was concerned because Elliot told us a few things that really upset Sarah – things related to the stuff you mentioned yesterday. He didn't want me making things worse."

"That explains it," Royce chuckled cruelly. "She always was a touchy little bitch, wasn't she? Couldn't hack the truth that you Littles are a bunch of freaks...even more than us Bigs. I was surprised to see her with you yesterday, traipsing around on your Finder trip. Does this mean she's your girlfriend? She's no Fiona, but she's not that bad to look at."

"We're just friends, and I don't want you calling her that. She doesn't deserve to be called that, and *she* never did anything to hurt *you*. I was the one who ratted you out to Francis," Sam murmured, his face reddening. "She's helping Elliot fix the hover, and she had come to help find the tools and parts that we needed."

He felt his muscles tensing, quietly fighting the rage that brewed within him in response to the Control's callousness.

Royce rolled his eyes. "Relax, twerp. I'm kind of grateful about all of that now. I'm glad to be out of that house, and I wouldn't be interested in a flaky little thing like that. Although, if all of you have aged properly, I wouldn't mind getting an eyeful of Fiona. I can just imagine the mess back at that house. She must be fighting the other boys off at every turn."

"No. Things haven't changed that much. She wouldn't come out of her room at first, and when she did they were nice about it," Sam replied.

He did not mention anything about the latest tensions in the house. He did not want to add any fuel to the fires of Royce's mean-spiritedness.

"For now maybe, but you mark my words. They won't stay that way. I may not be book smart, but I know people. You and your house-family are staring down the barrel of a loaded gun. You may have thought I was bad, but at least I couldn't control your thoughts. Get on the wrong side of Francis and you won't be able to run and hide. I'm much better off how and where I am. It may be rough, but at least I'm free," the larger boy mumbled.

"Are you telling me if you did have the chance, you wouldn't want to be Connected?" Sam questioned.

"I'm telling you I'm glad that I never had the option. Now get out of here. I'm not going to say it again. The other Controls will welcome you even less than I do. They are angry at you lot for throwing me out of the house. They think I've been done an injustice...so beat it." Royce tossed Sam one last package of food, one that had been slightly out of the Finder's reach, and gestured towards the door.

Sam stooped to gather it into his bag and then headed for the door. He was a little intimidated by the fact that the other Controls would soon be making an appearance, but what had really motivated Sam to go was what Royce had said about Francis. The Control had been convinced that there would be trouble, and Francis's behaviour lately had been more than a little disturbing. Considering how at odds the Teller and Elliot had been lately, that was Sam's first concern. As he began jogging back towards the house, he reached out towards the beach and specifically the technician, through the connection. He was interrupted in his efforts, encountering Fiona in the connection part way there. She was searching frantically for a familiar mind, her walls thrown wide open.

"I don't hate you, Francis," he heard her think at the Teller. *"I hate the fact that you hid so much from us for years before all of this started. I don't understand how you could justify doing that. It was wrong. We should have known what they were doing to us. We should have known what they were planning. And I don't like the power that you have over us."*

Sam was surprised to hear Francis respond. The Teller should have noticed how open Fiona was and that a second presence lingered nearby. There was something to Francis that was terribly distracted, however. Something disjointed even. It was almost as if he were focussed so single-mindedly on Fiona that he was blind and deaf to everything else. It was like tunnel-vision within the connection, something that Sam had never encountered before. There was an abnormality about it that seemed completely out of place.

"You always knew that I wanted you to like me," he said. *"I tried so hard, but nothing ever seemed to be enough for you – to make up for the mistakes that I had made. The more time that passed, the more I wanted you to like me. Well, now I want you to love me, Fiona. Tell me that you love me."*

Sam's stomach lurched. It was one thing for Francis to tell people what to do, when he needed things done specifically for the benefit of the house-family, and Sam had even been willing to overlook the times that he had ordered people to do negligible things on a whim, but the Teller had no right messing with Fiona's emotions.

"I love you," she obeyed, in a mental whisper.

"Say it like you mean it," Francis insisted.

"I love you," she repeated, sounding much more committed to the statement this time. *"What else are you going to make me do Francis? Haven't you tortured me enough? Please stop before you ask for something you'll regret."*

Before he answered, he finally noticed that Sam had been observing.

"Put up your walls, Fiona," Francis directed quietly.

She did as she was told and that left Sam without access to what was going on. He could have tried pushing through, but then Francis would likely give some command that would limit what he could do, and he didn't want that. Still, the Finder was not about to leave things as they were. Instead, he located Sarah and Elliot at the beach through the connection and quickly pushed through Elliot's fragile walls, knowing it was the quickest means of getting his point across. The technician recoiled instantly at the sudden intrusion, but could not avoid Sam's abrupt message.

"Elliot, you told me to tell you if anyone was acting drastically different? Something's wrong at the house. Francis is acting very strange, and I think Fiona might be in trouble. I'm sure that you and Sarah can make it back there before I can. Go! I'll meet you there."

He did not wait for an answer, now galloping breathlessly towards the house while searching desperately through the connection for Nathan. The Watcher was farther away than Sarah and Elliot, halfway through his circuit, and his walls were rock solid, just as Francis had instructed that they should be. Sam threw himself mentally at those walls—both pushing and knocking in one go with all of his might. It took three exhausting goes before the walls finally yielded and Sam burst in upon a very surprised Nathan.

"Sam?" he said, astonished.

"Go back to the house," Sam begged. *"You have to go back."*

"Sure, little buddy, I'm turning back right now. What? Why? Is it Royce?"

"No, it's worse. It's Francis. I'm not sure how we're going to stop him, but Fiona needs your help. Hurry, Nathan!"

The Watcher did not need to be prompted twice. Sam could tell he had understood the urgency of his message and was now moving as fast as was physically possible. Sam had sped up as well, almost stumbling over several small anomalies in the path as a result. When the house finally came into view, he found his second wind and sprinted for the door. He scrambled up the steps, missing half of them in the process, and then charged in. Elliot and Sarah were both standing there looking helpless, but neither Fiona nor Francis was present. Sam knew they were in the house though. He could detect their walls there. Sam started towards Fiona's room, fairly certain that he would find them within.

"Wait, Sam," Sarah whispered aloud, keeping her thoughts very quiet. "He stopped us. He told us to stay here until he gave us leave to move. If you go in after him, he'll just do the same to you."

It did not take a solid link in the connection to know how miserable she was at the moment, but Sam got the impression that more of her sympathy lay with Francis rather than with Fiona. That aspect of Sarah had never made sense to him.

235

Sam hesitated and looked at the pair expectantly, hoping that they might offer some alternate solution.

"I was worried something like this could happen," Elliot muttered softly. "Especially with the Tellers. They were all practically little control-hungry adults to begin with, and the scholars' research that I saw suggested that because of their personality type they didn't cope well with stress. Francis has been through plenty: the conflict with your Control, Fiona's intolerance, and then my arrival with all the complications associated, particularly the removal of the stasis. It was probably just a matter of time. I need you to fetch the Languorite from my room. I can't do it myself."

Elliot had been staying in Royce's old room, and it was now considered his by the house-family.

"What are you going to do with it, Elliot," the Finder asked warily.

"Please, Sam. Just get it." The technician sighed softly.

Sam obliged him, but anxiety attacked his stomach as he did so, and it churned uneasily. He bit his lip as he passed the device to Elliot. Since Elliot did not move to take it from him, Sam pressed it into his hand.

"I never would have thought I would be attempting to use this on myself," he mumbled unhappily. There was the temporarily blinding multi-colour flash, and then Elliot could move freely again. He then turned the device on Sarah, who sagged and almost fell when she found herself liberated from Francis's command.

Sam released a ragged breath. He'd been convinced that Elliot had other intentions for the Languorite.

"Now, to finally test its other use," Elliot announced, his words barely audible.

"Other use?" Sarah squeaked piteously. "You're not going to strip him of his gift? As far as he is concerned, it's the only thing that he has left."

"It's not like he has left us with any other option. He's the one who chose to abuse that power. He made a conscious decision to use it as he pleases now. I'm sorry, Sarah. I have to do this quickly, before he suspects what I'm up to."

Sarah hid her face as the technician stepped towards the room. Seconds after he had gazed past the open door, there was a brilliant rainbow flare, many times brighter than the one that had accompanied the erasing of the Teller-induced compulsions.

With a yelp of pain, Sam turned his eyes away as well. But he did not need to see to know that Nathan had arrived. There was a floor shaking crash as the front door exploded open and a slight breeze as the Watcher rushed swiftly past them. Sam's sight began to clear as the large young man shoved Elliot out of the path to the entrance to Fiona's room and then he surged out of view. He returned to line of sight two seconds later, half dragging and half throwing a partially dressed Francis from the room, before dropping him violently to the floor. Francis glanced around the room, disoriented.

"Get up!" Nathan barked, barely able to contain himself, and fighting with himself to keep his eyes averted. "Get on your feet!"

He was panting raggedly, holding back the urge to tear Francis limb to limb, as Fiona could be heard sobbing in the next room.

Francis scrambled to his feet and reached out at Nathan with his disjointed mind.

"Go away," he instructed. *"Stop interfering."*

He had not yet grasped what Elliot had done to him, and much to his dismay, the Watcher went nowhere.

"How could you do that!" Nathan railed, the hurt echoing through all of their heads.

He had never pushed so forcefully and so openly before, like Fiona's rare uncontrolled outburst, only more prolonged. It was enough to bring Elliot to his knees.

"I trusted you, Francis! I trusted you! I thought that we were on the same page. You know she loved me! How could you betray me like that?"

237

Francis did not answer, and Sam doubted that he was actually capable of doing so. The blond man's mind, normally so orderly, was jumbled and chaotic. There was shame, anger, frustration, and disappointment there, but not much else that made sense.

"Answer me!" Nathan bellowed, and Sam found it difficult to concentrate. He had never seen Nathan this angry or unrestrained, even when he had tossed Royce out of the house. Elliot had put his hands on his head, crouched on the floor, and Sarah stood nearby and watched, with a stunned expression.

Francis hung his head and looked away. He was lost, in more ways than one, and unwilling to face the Watcher's accusations and interrogation. He still had not come to terms with the fact that he was no longer a Teller.

Everyone was so distracted by the physical conflict and Nathan's outrage that they did not notice the quiet thought that pulsed beneath the surface. Everyone, that is, but Sam.

"I'll kill him. I'll kill him," the thought repeated quietly, and this made Sam panic. He had picked it up through the connection, which meant that it was not an exaggeration.

As Nathan raised his fist to swing at Francis, which no one else was prepared for, Sam lunged forward, planting himself squarely between the two men. The only problem with this plan was that he did not allow for the momentum in the attack, and the fact that Nathan would not be able to abort the strike to avoid the Finder – that was if he had even been able to see him in the first place. His eyes remained averted, and he was lashing out blindly in Francis's general direction.

The last thing that Sam saw before things went black was the shocked look on the Watcher's face as Nathan's fist collided with the side of Sam's head. The last thing that he felt was an explosion of pain and the crunch of bone as Nathan struck him with a full-forced blow that had been entirely intended for Francis, who stood cringing a couple of feet past him.

16

UNFIXABLE

Sam was not sure if it had been seconds, minutes, hours, or days. There was blackness and there was excruciating pain. Sam did not dare open his eyes once he became conscious of his existence again for fear that any exposure to light might add to his agony. As a fresh wave of hurt rushed through him, he tensed his muscles and clenched his teeth. He could not hold back a moan.

"Sam! Sam!" The voice was muffled and distant, like he was listening to it underneath water, but he was sure that it was Sarah's, and it was definitely excited.

"I'm so sorry, little buddy. I'm really, really sorry. I shouldn't have been trying to hit him. I'm sorry that I lost my head and that you were the one to pay for it."

Sam was sure that that was Nathan, and from the proximity of his presence in the connection, the Finder could tell that Nathan was crouching over him. Sam noted that the young man was not trying to make any excuses, which meant that he was back to his usual self. The average person would try to suggest that Sam should not have gotten in the way, but not the Watcher. He was prepared to shoulder all the blame for the incident himself, not pointing a finger at Francis for instigating his outburst, and not chastising Sam for interfering where he was not welcome.

Sam opened his eyes and tried to sit up…both bad ideas. The world seemed too bright and blurry, and the movement triggered a searing pain that started in his jaw and ran up the side of his head.

"Lie still," Sarah demanded. *"I only just began to fix you, you silly boy. Nathan packs quite a punch when he's as angry as he was at Francis. What were you thinking? He could have killed you."*

"I was thinking he was going to try to kill Francis, and I didn't want him to do something that everyone would regret," Sam mumbled groggily. *"I know how furious he was. I thought if I got in the way that it would stop him."*

"He wasn't even looking at Francis properly when he threw the punch, Sam. It was mostly a wild swing. Why would you have thought that he would see you in time?"

Her fingers brushed the sorest part of his face at that moment, and Sam flinched reflexively and whimpered.

"Is he going to be okay?" Nathan said. His thoughts were filled with concern. *"Is there anything I can do to help? Anything at all?"*

Sam shook his head very carefully, knowing that sudden movements would send that jarring pain through his skull again, and feeling bad for his large friend. The Watcher hung his head in his hands and pulled at his hair in frustration.

"How could I let this happen? How?"

"I'm pretty sure that I can fix him," Sarah offered soothingly. *"It'll be okay, Nathan. We'll figure things out. We'll repair the damage."*

"No, it won't be okay, not as long as I'm cursed with this ridiculous 'gift.'" He stood up and faced Elliot with great conviction, struggling to look at the technician but failing. *"Get them out of my head. Do to me what you did to Francis. I don't want them there anymore."*

"But chances are that the scholars will notice something is wrong if I do that. Francis was right about that much. Is it really worth the risk?" Elliot argued. *"Not to mention that*

you'll lose that heightened protective instinct, and it has clearly come in handy in the past."

"I don't care!" Nathan yelled, his ire rising again. *"I'm fed up with not being able to look at anybody. I can't stand constantly watching what I think, but at the same time having to run that stupid circuit. And I'm going to feel protective towards Fiona, Sam, and Sarah no matter what you do to me. They really are my family after all this time. Getting this out of my head won't change that. I have to be free to be there for Fiona right now. She needs me, especially after what he may have done to her..."*

Sam had not thought that there was a connection equivalent to getting choked up, but Nathan appeared to have stumbled upon it. The possibilities were so difficult for the Watcher to consider that he could not bring himself to properly contemplate them. Sam also noted that he had not included Francis in that list of those that he considered his real family. The sense of betrayal that he felt due to the young man who had been their Teller was so strong that it was enough for Nathan to have essentially 'disowned' him.

"Well I suppose that it's possible, if Sarah and I really buckle down and work during every moment available, that we can get that hover up and running in a couple more days. That won't give them much time to respond to the loss of your feedback. It may give us the chance to get away before they get here," the technician reflected, bringing his hand up to his chin.

He glanced at Nathan, who displayed conflicting body language, his stance bold and determined, but his head bowed.

"If I do this," he continued, gesturing with the Languorite, *"Then I want to have a commitment from Sam and Sarah that they are agreeable to this, and that they will do whatever they have to in order to get the repairs on the hover completed in the most expeditious manner possible. If I don't have that, I won't do it – it would be too dangerous."*

"Sarah?" Nathan stated plaintively, hoping she would say what he desperately wanted her to say.

Fervor

"I'll do whatever is necessary, Elliot," she responded quietly. *"Nathan's right. Fiona needs him right now, and he's not much good to her the way that he is at the moment. We have enough of a mess on our hands not to make the best use of all of our resources, including what Nathan has to offer."*

Sam was having difficulty grasping what everyone was saying, his mind still muddled as Sarah continued to work on him. The damage had been extreme and, without Sarah there, might have proven to be very serious, if not fatal. Even Nathan had not survived the mishap unblemished. He had struck without any regard for his own well being, driven only to hurt Francis as badly as he could possibly manage, and he had split open his knuckles in the process, a result of the level of force with which he had made contact. Sam's injury had taken priority, however, so Nathan now stood with his hand dripping with blood as he waited expectantly for Sam to consent as well.

"This wouldn't have happened if I had been here, Sam. You know it. Tell him to let me go. That way I'll be able to help Sarah and Elliot with the hover, and maybe speed things up a little," he urged.

"Nathan will be a better Watcher without his 'gift'. Use the Languorite on him. Let's deal with this and be done with it," Sam muttered, finally able to sit up with a tolerable amount of pain if he supported himself on Sarah. She slid an arm around him to anchor him in place, the fixing less burdensome as well if he were sitting up.

"Okay, I just wanted to make sure that you are all in agreement," Elliot conceded. *"There are still threats out there. Your Control and his friends know about me, and since they have already demonstrated a willingness to break the rules, they may see you as more vulnerable now that I'm here. Then there are the scholars themselves. If we don't work fast enough, who can predict what will happen if we are still here when they come to investigate what has happened to Nathan. I'll take him outside to do this. Sam seems to be faring well enough that I would imagine that you can handle him on your own, Sarah?"*

Unfixable

The Fixer nodded. Sam was no longer in agony, the pain having lessened to a dull, throbbing ache as long as he remained fairly still. They were both fairly certain that she could finish the job within the next several minutes.

Elliot placed a hand on Nathan's shoulder and guided him toward the door. When they were gone, Sam finally noticed something that hadn't come to his attention while they had been there.

"Where's Francis?" he asked.

Without giving Sarah the opportunity to answer, he started searching the connection for the young man. Sam found him a fair distance from the house and moving away from them quickly. His walls were up, and for the most part solid, but dotted with holes in some areas, like Swiss cheese. Sam ventured close enough to glimpse at Francis's mind through those holes. It was frantic and chaotic, nothing like the Francis Sam had known for years. Sam had never seen anything like it. He frowned glancing at Sarah.

"Where's he going?"

"I don't know," Sarah replied glumly, pausing a moment at the mention of his name and hanging her head a little. *"He lit out of here as soon as you presented Nathan with a distraction. He didn't take anything with him. In fact, he didn't even bother to grab his boots."*

That was startling news to Sam. Considering the pace at which Francis was moving, he clearly was choosing to ignore any discomfort or damage that it would be causing to his feet. There might have been feelings of pain intermingled with the other thoughts Sam had sensed through those holes, but he had not been able to tell – they had been so jumbled.

"What happened to him, Sarah?" Sam demanded.

"I told you. We had a chip. Now our windshield is cracked straight through," she replied with a ragged sigh. *"And what happened here today might just have been enough of a jolt to cause it to shatter. I knew he was in trouble, Sam, but he wouldn't let me fix him. If it had been one of the rest of you, I*

would have done it anyway, but with Francis, I couldn't do it, not as long as he didn't want me to." A single tear rolled down her cheek and she brushed it away hurriedly. "*I failed him.*"

"*Don't say things like that. You can fix him now; he won't be able to stop you anymore. Maybe when we get the hover fixed, we can track him down before we leave Fervor.*"

She looked at Sam with dismay.

"*I'm pretty sure that will be too late for him,*" she murmured. "*I know that I promised Elliot that I would focus on the hover, but if there's any way I can help Francis, then I need to.*"

"*The damage isn't physical, right? Can you possibly fix it through the connection? After it's too dark to work on the hover tonight, I can help you locate him. You could try it.*"

Sam was not sure if he could concentrate well enough at the moment to guide her to him, a trick much more difficult than just tracking Francis on his own. His mind was still too foggy from the blow, and by the time Sarah had him fixed to the point that he would be fully functioning, Elliot would likely be done with Nathan and want to get started on the hover right away. With that thought the windows flashed with brilliant light. It was too late for anyone to change their mind now.

"*I don't know if we can afford to wait that long, and I don't know if I can do it that way. I've never tried anything like that before,*" Sarah protested.

"*You'd never catch up to him on foot,*" Sam thought. "*He has a good head start on us.*"

Sam was also tempted to add "and he's running like a madman", but he somehow felt that this would upset Sarah even more, and chose to restrain the thought.

"*If you can't fix him through the connection, you would probably have to wait until the hover is repaired anyway, just to be able to reach him.*"

Sarah never got the opportunity to answer this, interrupted by a new distraction.

"What just happened to Nathan?"

It was Fiona. She stood trembling in the doorway to her room, her face tear-stained. "There's something different about him. Did Francis do something to him, too?"

Sarah released Sam, who could now support himself on his own, and scrambled to her feet. Then she cautiously approached the distraught young woman.

"Francis is gone, Fiona. It's okay. You're safe now. He can't hurt you anymore. If you need me to fix..."

"You didn't answer my question!" Fiona barked angrily. "What just happened to Nathan!"

The front door opened and the young man in question walked in. He looked over at Fiona and locked eyes with her, his face suddenly apologetic.

"I'm so sorry. I should have been here. He should have never been able to lay a finger on you."

He never had the chance to finish his thoughts on the matter. Fiona ran over to him and wrapped her arms around him, burying her face in his neck. He silently returned the embrace, trying to avoid getting any blood on her from his wounded hand.

"Can you walk? I can finish fixing you down on the beach between stretches of working on the hover," Sarah whispered.

Sam nodded. He was not as concerned about himself now, feeling much more like his usual self other than the fuzzy thoughts and mild ache. Sarah was already looking exhausted from her efforts with his injury. He hoped that Elliot would recognize that and give her plenty of opportunities to rest once they started work on the hover again.

Sam rose shakily to his feet. Weaving their way around the older couple, who no longer seemed to really notice them anyway, they joined Elliot outside. The technician was staring up at the dark clouds overhead.

"It's going to rain. We had better hurry. If we work fast, we may be able to finish up the bottom of the hover before the weather worsens. We won't be able to do anymore than that until Nathan helps us flip it, and we're going to have to set up that hoist that Sarah suggested first. Then it will just be a matter of some few final touches and we can finally leave this cursed island," he muttered.

The tide was high and the waves choppy when they reached the shore. Sam was surprised at how much progress that they had already made since he last laid eyes upon the hover. The sleek, bullet-like shape was gradually being restored; and although it was discoloured in places and its surface slightly marred in others, Sam could get a good idea of what it had originally looked like before the accident. If Sarah had invested as much effort in mending the vehicle that morning as it would appear, followed by having to fix him, Sam was amazed that she was even still able to stand. Nevertheless, she joined Elliot unwavering, a determined look in her eye and desperation in her expression.

Sam wished he could be more useful while sitting around waiting for Sarah to have a moment to spare. She flitted back and forth between him and the hover, and just watching her do this made him tired, but her energy seemed limitless despite her fatigue. Sam gained a new respect for her that day, deciding that perhaps it made sense that she was the Fixer with the strongest presence in the connection out of everyone in the house-family, since she seemed to have the strongest spirit. He knew that it was because she was so anxious to find Francis, and that the sooner the remainder of the repairs for the day had been made, the sooner they would be able to try and hunt him down and possibly fix him.

From time to time, Sam did check on the young man by means of the connection. Francis was still on the go, and getting steadily farther away. There was purpose to his travels, but Sam could not figure out what that was. He did not dare peer in through one of those Swiss cheese holes, for fear he might get lost in the turmoil and chaos that he saw within and never escape.

Unfixable

Sarah and Elliot did manage to finish the repairs before the rain began, with time to spare. Elliot called Nathan down from the house to help set up the hoist, but the Watcher would not agree to leave Fiona alone in the house no matter how far away Sam claimed that Francis was. Sarah had fixed the Finder to her satisfaction, so he volunteered to return from the beach.

Fiona and Nathan met him at the door. She was reluctant to let the young man go, but she understood the importance of completing the restoration of the hover as quickly as possible. As he departed, she dragged herself over to a chair and stared forlornly out of the window. Sam sat nearby and fidgeted for a while, not knowing quite how to deal with Fiona anymore.

"Are you going to be alright, Fiona?" he finally asked, the stillness in the room getting to him.

"I wasn't sure at first," she answered, still gazing out through the window. "I had my problems with Francis, but I never expected him to try anything like this. I was worried about the memories this would leave. You know what it's like for me. Once it's there, it's there for good. It isn't a matter of time making the experience fade for me."

She hesitated, shuddering.

"It was awful, Sam. The things that he made me say...the things that he made me do. He was merciless. I didn't want any of it, but I had to do it."

"I'm sorry. Sarah said that he was broken, and I don't think that she was mistaken," he offered quietly. "Elliot has been right all along. What they've done to us – the changes that they made to us and the changes that they prevented – the enforcement of the Directives, the making us act like little adults, but stealing the capability from us to actually grow up. How can they justify any of it?"

"I'd probably be just as broken if it weren't for Nathan," Fiona admitted. "He's giving me memories that overshadow the ones Francis left with me. Any time that I'm haunted by the bad things that have happened over the years, all I need to do is hold on to the ones of Nathan and they can't hurt me anymore."

"Whatever helps you to cope, Fiona. Hopefully all of this will just be a bad memory soon for all of us. We'll find something new – something better. Elliot has a plan for us."

Sam saw her smile, still watching outside.

"It's raining," she announced. "That means that they'll be back soon."

Fiona relaxed into her chair, her relief almost tangible.

She was not wrong, several minutes later the threesome piled into the house. Nathan was tired and grimy, smeared with oil in places. Fiona greeted him joyfully and dragged him off to the kitchen to clean him up. Elliot, who entered behind him, was carrying Sarah, who was curled into him, exhausted. She was so tired that she had actually dozed off on the way back despite the awkward position in which he was forced to hold her. She was petite for a girl approaching thirteen, but Elliot was as fatigued as Nathan was, and Sarah was no longer a little child. He lay her down the first chance that he got, and headed off to shower. She stirred immediately.

"Sam?"

Groggily, she searched for the Finder first thing, wanting a resolution to the situation involving Francis.

"Sam, we're done. Now you have to help me find Francis so that I can fix him. You promised."

"How are you going to manage that, Sarah? You can barely keep your eyes open. Even if we do reach him, what good to him will you be," Sam objected.

"Sam, please," she begged, leaning forward and clutching at his tunic. *"I have to find him. I have to fix him. If you won't help me do this, then I had better go pack my things and set off in the direction that I think he might have gone."*

"Don't be ridiculous," Sam scoffed. *"It's pouring out there, and you won't have any chance of catching up to him let alone finding him. You'd be better off waiting until morning when you're well rested."*

"And when I'll be expected to go back out there and finish working on the hover. I'm dead serious, Sam. I need this

like you need to breathe. I have to know where he is, I have to know that he's okay, and I have to try and fix him, right now."

Sam already knew that the errant young man was far from okay, and he was not so sure that Sarah was capable of fixing him even when she was well rested and at her full strength. Still, he decided it was better to humour her rather than have to fight with her and restrain her to keep her from wandering off into the rainy night. He heard Nathan and Fiona laughing in the kitchen — a sound that still persisted despite communicating through the connection — and knew that they would not approve of this. Nathan saw Francis as a despicable traitor at the moment – worse than Royce — and Fiona would be happy to see Francis rot in hell. They certainly did not share Sarah's dedication to the man who had been their Teller, unwarranted or not.

"Alright. I'll do this, but not here. Let's go to your room. It's quieter there, and more comfortable." Not the reasons he wanted to go there, but truthful nonetheless. *"I'll do my best, but I can't make any guarantees. Even if I do find him, he may still insist on blocking you out."*

The pair crept stealthily into her room and settled into place side by side on Sarah's bed. With an apprehensive expression, she grasped his hand and waited. Releasing a soft sigh, Sam began his search.

He knew where to begin, having followed Francis sporadically during the day. There was something familiar to Sam about the path that Francis was taking, but he was not sure why. Their ex-Teller had long left the general area and was not headed towards the Hub. It was somewhere else – somewhere accompanied by an uneasy feeling. He tried to remember where that was, but Sam was no Keeper, so it did not come to him immediately. Sarah was following behind him in the connection and experienced the same awareness.

"Where is he going?" she demanded fretfully. *"We're not supposed to be here. Why would he be going somewhere where we are not supposed to go?"*

Sam shrugged mentally.

"Sarah, I can't explain why he's doing anything that he's doing right now. He's not acting rationally. He's not acting like Francis. I wish I could give you some answers, but I can't."

As they neared the ex-Teller, Sarah seemed to cringe.

"What's wrong with his walls? He's gotten worse, hasn't he? He's much more broken than he used to be. It's not just because of what happened with Fiona, is it? It's because Elliot took his gift away."

Her words were frantic as she struggled to get near Francis. Then suddenly, he was gone.

"Where did he go?" she gasped.

Sam had no idea. He had never lost anyone in the connection before. They had grown faint, and sometimes had been beyond his reach, but never just disappeared.

"Go back," Sam insisted. *"Leave me alone to look for him. He must have slipped away from us somehow. I'll be able to focus better on finding him if I'm alone. I'll come back for you when I find him."* He had done that with Elliot when he had first appeared on the beach, and he hoped that he could do it again with Francis.

Sarah obeyed, distancing herself from Sam and returning closer to home. Sam began searching. He started in the area where he had last seen Francis and then moved away from there, looking desperately for the young man, but he could not find him. In fact, after a short while, when his panic subsided a little, Sam had to acknowledge that he was not going to find him no matter how hard he tried. His instincts told him loud and clear that Francis was no longer there in the connection to be found.

Sam paused before rejoining Sarah, returning to the location where they had lost Francis in the first place. He wracked his brains to figure out where he was and why it bothered him so much. Finally it came to him – Francis had gone to the High Barrens.

There was a part of Fervor that did not have sandy beaches and rocky shores and it was called the High Barrens. Instead, along that stretch of the island there were sheer cliffs that dropped off into the ocean. It had always been off limits to the children because it was considered to be too dangerous a place to venture. Sam suddenly felt queasy.

If Francis really were no longer part of the connection, there were two possible reasons why. He may have found some way to subvert his access to the connection again, something like the Languorite, or whatever devices the scholars had been using to begin with. Of course, Sam was sure that the ex-Teller did not have the Languorite with him because he had seen Elliot use it on Nathan. As far as Sam knew, there was nothing else like it on Fervor.

The other possibility was that Francis was no longer part of the connection because Francis was no longer part of anything.

Sam rushed back to Sarah, almost in an attempt to escape everything that had just come to light. When he reached her, however, his heart filled with dread as he realized that it now fell upon his shoulders to share his impressions with his Fixer friend, and she would not react well to what he would have to tell her.

"Did you find him? Can you take me to him again?" she asked excitedly.

"No, Sarah," Sam confessed. *"I can't take you to him again. He's gone."*

She froze up a little, confused.

"Gone? Do you mean he left Fervor?"

"No, not in the usual sense anyway. I mean he's simply not there anymore, Sarah. If he had somehow managed to leave Fervor, I still should have been able to find him – he couldn't have gotten far enough away to avoid me. Like with Elliot. He was on the Mainland, but I still managed to guide you to him the first time that we went looking for him," he thought at her, trying to be kind about it. It was difficult, because Sam had already fought through his panic and was now starting to feel numb.

"If he didn't leave Fervor, then how can he not be there anymore?" Sarah questioned, bewildered. She had not considered the possibilities that Sam had.

"He was at the High Barrens, Sarah," Sam explained as delicately as possible. *"He's gone."*

There was an instant backlash of denial from the petite girl.

"No, no, no! You just didn't look hard enough. You have to go back! You have to look longer. You have to find him for me," she pleaded tearfully.

"I'm sure," he sighed. *"He's not part of the connection anymore."*

"You're wrong," Sarah sobbed. *"You have to be wrong. I never had the chance to fix him. Please, Sam. Tell me that you're wrong."*

Sam looped his arm around her sympathetically. He felt badly about this, and he knew that Sarah would be feeling much, much worse. She still cared about Francis, no matter what he had done. It saddened Sam as well that Francis would likely not be missed by the others

"I'm sorry, Sarah," was all the solace that he could offer her. He had never lost anyone this way before. It was a very strange feeling.

"Why?" she wailed. "Why wouldn't he let me fix him before all of this happened? He was special. It should never have ended this way. Why wouldn't he let me fix him?"

She dropped her head into Sam's lap, weeping loudly. A few moments later there was a knock at the door.

"Sarah? Are you okay?"

It was Elliot.

"I'm here with her," Sam replied. "I have this handled." *Not well,* he thought, *but handled.*

"Oh – alright. That's good."

The technician was relieved at not having to sort out some emotional outburst from the girl. He still felt very awkward around the children, and Elliot figured that it was some delayed response to what had happened earlier in the day. The Finder had already decided that telling Elliot, Fiona, and Nathan about Francis could wait until morning. Sam had Sarah to deal with for now, and he would have to try and comfort her himself. Fiona wouldn't understand, and Nathan had always been wary about how he should behave around Sarah, viewing her as more fragile than the others.

Sam spent the rest of the evening just letting her cling to him for consolation as she cried. He stroked her hair the way that Francis used to, and continuously reassured her that it was not her fault. Eventually, she cried herself to sleep, still lying in his lap.

17

THE HIGH BARRENS

Sam woke before Sarah did the next morning, which was not a big surprise considering how exhausted she had been when she had finally fallen asleep. He was glad. He had somewhere to go and something to do, and it would be easier for him to leave with her asleep. Leaving as quietly as he could manage so as not to disturb her, he headed out of her room and into his own. He gathered up several of his things in his backpack and crept into the kitchen.

He collected supplies for his trip from the cupboards, since he could not necessarily guarantee that he would find what he would need en route, and he guessed that he would be gone for at least two days. He would not be able to match the outrageous pace Francis had maintained as he had made his way barefoot to the forbidden grounds. Sam realized that this meant that the others might take the hover and leave without him, but he needed answers and it was a pull that he could not resist.

He tried to be stealthy as he moved to slip out of the kitchen again, and to sneak over to the front door, but Fiona was there as he opened the kitchen door.

"What are you doing up this early, Sam?" she asked casually. Then she took note of the backpack. Her expression darkened. "Where are you going?"

"I have a special finding trip that I have to make." He wasn't planning to elaborate. He wanted to make his escape before Nathan and Elliot got up as well.

"What kind of special finding trip? Why would you need your backpack to go there?"

Sam hesitated, reluctant to tell her anything. Then, to make matters worse, Nathan appeared as well. Sam sighed.

"I'm going to look for Francis," he admitted.

"So you can bring him back here?" Fiona exclaimed. "No!"

"How far away is he, that you need your backpack?" Nathan added.

"I wasn't intending on bringing him back here. I just want to figure out exactly what happened to him, and why he went there," Sam replied.

"Went where?"

Sam could see Nathan was growing concerned over the direction of this conversation.

"The High Barrens," the Finder confessed, shifting the backpack up onto his shoulders and reaching for the doorknob. Fiona immediately looked horrified.

"You can't go there," she insisted. *"It's off-limits."*

"Why would Francis go there?" Nathan questioned. *"It's dangerous."*

"That's what I want to find out," Sam explained.

"Why don't you just ask him then?" Fiona grumbled, rolling her eyes. *"Following him all the way out there is crazy. He's not worth the risk."*

"I can't just ask him." Sam just wanted to go. He had been hoping to avoid this kind of interrogation. He dropped his gaze. *"He's not part of the connection anymore."*

Fiona frowned.

"What do you mean, 'he's not part of the connection anymore'? You can't just leave it when you feel like it."

Sam did not answer. If she did not understand, then he was happy to leave it at that. He did not need to explain to Nathan, however. The young man put his hands on the Keeper's shoulders.

"Let him go, Fiona," he thought quietly.

As Sam opened the door, Nathan asked, *"Does Sarah know?"*

Sam nodded.

"She was very upset, to say the least. She likely won't be any better when she wakes up. I did my best to comfort her, but that was Francis's thing, not mine. You have to convince her that she needs to pull herself together in order to fix the hover. Remind her that she made a promise to Elliot. That might be enough."

"I'll take care of her," Nathan assured him.

"If you can keep her on track, she'll likely have the fixing done before I get back. If you feel the need to leave without me, I'll understand."

"We'd never leave without you, Sam. I meant what I said yesterday, you are still family, gift or not. If Elliot wants to leave without you, he'll have to leave without me, too," Nathan murmured.

"That's not going to happen either," Fiona stated forcefully, gripping Nathan's arm tightly. *"Nobody gets left behind. You do what you have to do, Sam. We'll be waiting here for you when you get back."*

Sam gave her another acknowledging nod, and then started out on what would no doubt be a long and lonely trip. Or at least, that's what he thought it would be. Within a couple of hours after taking his leave, when he actually found himself wallowing in grief in the silence that surrounded him, Sarah made contact.

"You should have woken me, Sam. It wasn't fair of you to leave without saying goodbye."

She had followed Sam through the connection the evening before as he had tracked Francis and had remembered the route well enough to locate Sam there now.

"You have your business to take care of, and I have mine. You should get back to working on the hover."

"We haven't started yet," she thought. *"I'm waiting for Elliot. Besides, with you gone, there's no rush now. Elliot's fit to be tied. He said what you are doing is irresponsible and inconsiderate."*

"I didn't expect him to understand. He's never felt the Finder itch. Francis left me with a lot of unanswered questions."

Sam also believed that he personally was partially at fault for his current circumstances. He wondered if he had been less of a coward and had been willing to peek into Francis's tormented mind, he might have been able to prevent this. At least he might have had a better idea as to why the ex-Teller had chosen to head for the High Barrens, of all places. He could not allow himself to be weighed down by feelings of guilt at the moment, however, and the compulsions that drove him would not let this rest.

"I'll be checking in on you, Sam. You're the only real friend that I have left. I can't afford to lose you, too."

Her sadness was heavy and stifling. As much as Sam wanted to offer her more solace, he also wanted to avoid getting caught up in her emotion.

"Sure, Sarah. You can let the others know how I'm faring. I still have quite a distance to cover, though, and it's easier to follow his path if I don't have any other distractions. You pay attention to helping Elliot, and we can get in touch again when you're done."

As much as he wanted to spare himself from her emotion, he also wanted to keep her distanced from his. He still had no idea what he would find at the High Barrens, and if it was disturbing enough, when she linked with him in the connection, he would not be able to hide that from her.

"Promise me you'll be careful," she whispered. *"Stay away from the cliffs."*

"*I'll be careful,*" he thought softly in return. "*I promise.*"

While he did not regret encouraging her to let him be, for both their sakes, he did miss the company. Sam liked solitude in smaller doses, but after several hours by himself it started to close in on him. He longed for his house-family, and even though there were several walled minds within easy reach because of the connection, he had not felt this alone in years. He was grateful when Sarah eventually touched his mind a second time, in the early afternoon.

"*Are you still there, Sam? You haven't actually reached the High Barrens yet, have you?*"

"*Not yet. I'm guessing it won't be until dusk. I stopped mid-morning to do a little finding at a school, and there's no way that I can match Francis's pace.*"

Sam still found it hard to believe how much ground that the young man had covered over a shorter interval with no boots. He had been moving like a man possessed.

"*Did you finish the hover?*"

"*Not yet. It was too damp for some of the final touches. Elliot says that they will have to wait until tomorrow,*" she replied. Sam wondered if that was an exaggeration on Elliot's part, to justify waiting the extra day for Sam. "*So will you be back tomorrow?*"

"*I'll try, but no guarantees, Sarah. I don't dare search the High Barrens at twilight, so I'll start at break of day. It depends on how long it takes me to find what I'm looking for, whatever that is,*" Sam offered.

"*Hurry back,*" Sarah pleaded. "*Elliot is grouchy and Fiona and Nathan aren't interested in anything but each other right now. I really miss Francis and I'm lonely without you.*"

"*I know. I'm sorry that I have to do this. Hang tight,*" he said. "*I'll talk to you when I'm done with my finding tomorrow. It will probably be safest if I do it without distractions.*"

She sighed, and broke off the link.

Fervor

Sam had calculated correctly, and as the sun was setting, he finally reached the fence that marked the perimeter of the area that was considered off-limits. Someone had bashed through the wire mesh with a large rock, no doubt Francis. There was still enough light to venture in and do some exploring, but he likely would not make it back while there was an appropriate amount of visibility and Sam had promised Sarah that he would be careful, so it would have to wait. To make matters worse, a fog was starting to roll in off of the water, a common phenomenon on Fervor. That was yet another reason to stay put for the moment, on the safer side of the fence.

The night was a chill one, and Sam had nothing in the way of shelter. While he was fully capable of entering any building on Fervor that he wanted to now, nothing had been built within close proximity of the High Barrens, with good reason. There was no point in having any of the children living in tempting view of something that was supposed to be taboo, not considering the sparse population of the island, and the large quantity of space available to them.

From what Sam had seen through the fence, the area had offered little in the way of scenery. The ground was rocky with meagre foliage. It was bare of trees, exposing it to harsh winds and salt spray from the ocean, allowing for little to actually succeed in growing there.

Sam spent the night huddled in some long grass not far from the fence. He slept very lightly since he was frightened at having to endure the night and the howling wind all alone. Every time he awoke, shivering and tense, he cursed the compulsion in him to see this through. He even found himself brushing away tears a few times from the corners of his eyes, an embarrassment to him even if there was nobody around to see them. He curled in on himself a little more, and blamed the wind for making his eyes water.

When dawn finally lit up the horizon past the cliffs, coloring it with warm hues of pink and orange, Sam shook himself free from the grass that now had him entangled and approached the hole in the fence. He examined it carefully in the growing sunlight, noting that some of the sharper out-juts bore several strands of bloody fibres similar in texture and colour to the neutral-coloured tunics the children all wore. He wondered if this were possibly evidence of Francis's passing into the forbidden zone. If this had come from him, he had made his way through the fence in a great hurry, and not bothered to bash and bend back any of the more hazardous protrusions. Sam was much more cautious. Grasping the rock that had likely been the ex-Teller's tool, he slammed at the pointy wire bits until they were rounded nubs that no longer posed any threat to anyone. Dropping the rock to one side, he took a deep breath, and stepped through.

Merely being on the other side of the fence made Sam uncomfortable. Not because of any residual effects from the Directives, but just a matter of general conditioning. Since as long as he could remember having Maria in his life, she had driven home the fact that certain places were not to be entered without the accompaniment of a minder or teacher and a select few places, like the High Barrens, were completely forbidden. He had often wondered why. And had he lived much closer to the boundary of the area, his curiosity might just have propelled him past any need that he had to obey the rules.

Maybe, he considered, that was what had happened with Royce. Perhaps he had dared to venture into one of those forbidden locations and found something that he wished he had not.

Sam glanced down at the ground. It had been muddy that night, the rain pouring down as Francis had plunged through the hole in the fence and run along the edge of the cliffs. Sam could still make out some of his footprints. The young man's bare feet had left toe indentations that were fairly deep and the impressions had not completely washed away. In fact, they had dried that way, allowing the Finder to track Francis's path exactly.

Sam paused, and crouched, brushing his fingertips along the caked and crusty earth. He had a good idea what Francis had been running from. His brief glimpse through the holes in his walls had allowed him to see that the turmoil beyond included an intense feeling of shame and sense of mourning. He had realized that there would be no returning to the house for him. But there had also been some purpose there as well. He had not been just running from something, he had also been running to something as well.

He neared the edge of the cliffs with great trepidation. He had promised Sarah that he would be careful, and the soil was loose and dusty in places, making it somewhat slippery. There were also several rocks that wobbled dangerously when they were trod upon, enough of a warning to Sam to keep him from venturing too close to the brink. Following Francis's tracks, however, made keeping a safe distance difficult. It was clear that the ex-Teller had cared little about the risks involved, despite being here in the dark and the rain.

Sam was contemplating this thought when he came to the point where the footprints suddenly stopped. There was a break in the soil at the cliff's edge...there...an indentation. Sam had two theories about this. The cliff-side may have given way to Francis's weight, weakened by erosion from the weather, and collapsed beneath him. That would explain why the footprints had come to an abrupt end, and why Francis had just disappeared from the connection without any forewarning.

Lowering himself to his hands and knees, Sam crawled cautiously towards the slight gap. His second theory as to why it existed was that Francis might have actually seated himself here for a moment, staring off into the rain or the ocean. Sam ran his hand over it. There was a roughness to it that suggested it was not formed from one man's weight compacting the mud there. If he had sat there, then the loose soil suggested that he had slid off of it, and the only place to go from there was down.

Sam leaned forward, his stomach tightening, as he prepared to peer over the edge. He braced himself carefully, making sure that none of his weight was centred in the dip. If that happened, and part of the cliff had given way beneath Francis, Sam would be placing himself in jeopardy of succumbing to the same fate. He did not want to look, but his finding instincts would not let him have it any other way. He held his breath, and then he stared at the water far below.

Sam scrabbled backwards as quickly as he had inched forward slowly. He had spotted exactly what he had been hoping not to see. He wished that he could convince himself that the bloated and mangled body that he had seen bobbing amongst the rocks and seaweed could somehow be someone else. He sat for a moment, staring up at the sky, his breath coming in small gasps as his heart pounded in his chest and his stomach threatened to rebel against him. He had been hoping that he would be able to give Sarah different news, and finding Francis like this did not provide him with the answers that he had been searching for, and now presented him with a newer question – one that he likely would not be able to answer. Had Francis's fatal fall from the cliffs been accidental or intentional? There was little chance that Sam would ever know.

Sam sat for a few more moments seeking calm. He struggled with his own feelings of guilt and shame before the most prominent question rose to the surface of his thoughts. Why had Francis come here in the first place?

Sam's eyes searched his surroundings. Francis had left no signs, no clues for Sam to find. Had the tormented man come for one very simple purpose, or had there been some other reason? Sam shrugged, gave a slight shiver, and glanced over his shoulder farther along the High Barrens. He wasn't sure of anything anymore.

And then there was the glint.

Sam blinked, rubbed his eyes, and blinked again. A few more seconds passed, and a second glint followed. His Finder instincts went wild. Driven by a fierce curiosity, Sam got to his feet.

He did not see the glint a third time, but he was fairly certain that he could target the spot that it had come from. He could not resist. He started forward.

When Sam arrived at the point where the glint had originated, he could see that the soil there was cracked and that some
had collapsed in a little, leaving a slight hole. Without concern
for the consequences, Sam shoved his fingers into the hole.
Within, he felt a cold hard metal edge. Sam began to dig.

A few minutes later, he had cleared the area of dirt and
was staring at a metal lever. He hesitated a little, a million ideas
of what it could be for racing through his head.

"Sam?"

It was Sarah again.

*"We're at the beach. We should be able to finish the
hover today."*

*"I'll try to be back by tonight, but I can't guarantee it. I
found something unusual here, and I'm not sure how long it will
take me to investigate it, or where exactly it might lead me,"* he
informed her. He was not able to hide his excitement.

*"No hurry, Sam. Elliot decided that since you were gone
and nobody was willing to leave without you, he plans on teaching Fiona and Nathan how to activate the hover when it is ready.
He said there was no point in wasting good time, and that it's
best to have more than one person around who can run the hover anyway."*

Sarah paused, her mind growing still.

"Sam," she thought quietly. *"Did you find Francis?"*

He could not bring himself to reply, but that was answer
enough for the girl.

"I'll check back with you later," she murmured. *"Hopefully, by then, you'll be on your way home."*

Sam suspected that this little exchange may have set off
another round of tears from the Fixer, but he would be little consolation to her with such a distance between them and he had
other things to deal with. He broke the link and turned back to
the lever.

After examining it from every direction possible, Sam's
curiosity overcame good sense and he reach over and pulled on
it. There was a rumble and a shake, and Sam almost fell over as

the ground began to shift beneath his feet. Startled, he leapt away from the space upon which he had been standing, and tumbled even farther out of reach. The earth fell away and Sam realized that he was now looking at a stairway that descended below ground. Was this what Francis had come for?

Sam wondered why this thing had been hidden so well from view, and then it struck him that it had not likely been accessed in years since the children had all been purposefully warned away from this place. Sam suspected, however, that Francis and the other Tellers had been in the know. Francis had never been one to break the rules, not until his house-family had required it of him.

This notion brought the first solid wave of sorrow over Francis's loss to the surface for the Finder. He had to concede that Francis was gone now that he had seen the evidence of this first hand. And, while the Teller had mistreated Fiona, he had never, from all appearances, exposed the house-family's transgressions to the scholars. Perhaps, he had even come here as a means of leading Sam to some of the answers that he had known the Finder had been looking for.

Sam found that he was tearing up a little now and struggled to choke it back. He was not Sarah. He would not fall victim to his emotions as quickly and as easily as she normally did.

Pulling his glow torch from his pack, Sam started down the stairway. He could see a door at the bottom of the steps. He hoped it was not locked, since he had no tools available to him to pick or break a lock, or to force the door open despite the lock. Much to Sam's relief, the handle yielded to his touch and he found himself staring down a dark corridor. His glow torch revealed the spaces within, piece by piece. There were four glass doors. Without opening them, he lit up the rooms beyond them, scanning them one by one.

The first looked like a strange classroom, much larger than the small and intimate rooms at the school. Those rooms were only meant to accommodate a couple of dozen children. This one looked like it could easily hold a hundred.

The second room appeared to be a laboratory of some kind, approximately the same size as the giant classroom. It also was very different from the much smaller and sparsely equipped labs that were used by the teachers at the schools. Sam could not recognize half of the items that his glow torch illuminated beyond that glass door, but he suspected that Elliot would know what they were.

Sam began to realize just how isolated and sheltered that the children of Fervor had been — and still were. The scholars had orchestrated their education with the help of the minders and the teachers. Anything that they had learned had been deemed appropriate, or in some cases necessary, by the scholars, and everything else had been simply withheld from them — like learning how to activate most of the devices on Fervor to those who weren't Keepers, or learning how to run and drive a hover.

All of that was about to change. Once they actually left the island, they would be able to learn anything that others would be willing to teach them. Someday, Sam promised himself, he would know what every single item in that laboratory was for.

There was nothing more in either of those rooms to tell Sam succinctly what this place was, but Sam had already formulated his theories. Since it seemed to him that Francis had known about this place, Sam concluded that this might be the location where the minders and teachers had brought the Tellers and Controls to instruct them on the Directives, and where the Tellers had trained for two years with the connection prior to the second exodus. It would make sense that they would choose a secluded place where other children on Fervor would not stray. That way, there was little chance that the truth of their existence would be discovered. That explained why no one but the Tellers and the Controls had had any idea what was going on. This was all part of their secret.

Before Sam could approach the third door, Sarah was with him again.

"We're done, Sam. The hover is ready. I have all the time in the world to talk to you now. Elliot will be preoccupied with showing Fiona and Nathan how it works, but there isn't enough room there for me to see what he is doing, too. I wish you were home so I didn't feel so left out. If we had a Finder with us, we could take the hover out to fetch you."

She seemed a little more like her regular self. Not that she had recovered entirely from the loss of Francis, but her excitement at reaching one of their objectives softened the blow a little for the moment.

"That's okay, Sarah. I can make my own way home, and then it won't be long before we can finally leave Fervor," he assured her.

"Did you figure out what it was that you found?"

He shone the light on the glass of the third door. There was a familiarity to the room beyond, too. It looked like the garage in the school where they had fetched the tools for Elliot, only much bigger. Aside from tools, it appeared, at first, to be empty. Then he saw something gleaming at the far end of the room. He turned his torch on it and could make out a surprising bullet-like form—partially disassembled—with its pieces scattered about on the floor. Sam gasped.

"What? What is it?" Sarah demanded.

"I found a hover here – a long distance one like Elliot's. It looks like they had been in the process of repairing it and they must have had to leave it behind. I can't believe it. It has been here this entire time, and none of us knew."

Not that they could have taken it and fled Fervor any sooner, he considered. Only Fiona could have gotten anywhere near it until Elliot had arrived with the Languorite, and none of them would have known how to operate it.

"Where's here?" Sarah asked. *"I thought you had gone to the High Barrens?"*

"That's where I am, only inside," he answered.

269

"Inside?"

It was hard to explain with words. It had been several days since he had tried the trick, but he realized that the easiest way was to show her…just the way he used to do when she was blind. He scrambled back where he had started outside, and then gave her a brief tour, projecting images to her from each area, as he went. He could sense her bewilderment.

"That was there," she thought with an edge of awe. *"That was there and none of us had a clue."*

"I think Francis knew," Sam suggested, *"And possibly Royce. I'm not positive, but I suspect that this is where they trained the Tellers in the use of the connection. I think this might be where they instructed them on the Directives as well."*

"Do you think…do you think Francis wanted you to find it?"

"I don't know. You were right about Francis being broken, Sarah. I don't believe that you could have fixed him by the time Elliot took away his gift. I think he was beyond saving. You can't blame yourself for that. You know that, right?"

This time, it was Sarah's turn not to answer. Sam decided that he needed a distraction. He was not in the right frame of mind to deal with this.

"There's one more door, Sarah — one that I haven't investigated yet. Did you want me to take a look and show you what's there?"

Sam could not imagine what he would find. Maybe this was where the technicians and scholars once lived, out of sight of the rest of Fervor, except when they went out to test the Bigs.

"Okay, Sam. I can't believe that they kept all of this underground. It must have been built right into the cliffs," she hypothesized.

Sam did not doubt that they had the capability. These were the same people, after all, who had built the Hub. Anyone who had the wherewithal to build that monstrosity likely had the knowledge and resources to construct an underground training and research facility.

He took a few steps forward and shone the glow torch on the last door. Beyond the glass, there was a network of hallways and doors, like some sort of residential area. Perhaps he had guessed right, he thought triumphantly. Perhaps this had been where the other adults had lived. That was when he caught a glimpse of movement and heard a sudden noise. Sarah got a taste of his anxiety.

"What's the matter?" she questioned.

"There's someone else here. There's someone in the building."

Sam practically jumped out of his skin as that same something slammed up abruptly against the door. Sam actually heard the glass crack. There was a figure on the other side, but he was not so sure that he would call it a "someone". The misshapen form looked like it had been intended to be human, but its legs were gnarled and tree-like, and its skin didn't seem to be properly conformed to its body, hanging loose in some places and stretched taut in others. One arm seemed to end in a proper hand, albeit a somewhat talon-like one, but the other ended in a lumpy nub.

The worst part for Sam, however, was the face, or more like the lack of one. It was like someone had pressed a person's face against the glass and smeared it out of shape: the eyes awkwardly placed at odd angles, no ears to speak of, the nose squashed flat and pointed upwards towards the right, and a gaping maw with a sprinkling of crooked teeth jutting out in all directions. But this face was not actually pressed against the glass.

Sam could not help himself. He screamed.

That was when the second figure appeared next to the first, slamming up against the door with equal gusto. Sam could not bear to stay there long enough to get a good look at this one. He turned and ran as fast as his legs would carry him.

UNCONTROLLED

18

UNCONTROLLED

Sam finally came to a stop quite a distance from the High Barrens, curling over and gagging as he tried to catch his breath. He felt like he had been running full tilt for hours, driven by fear and disgust. Sarah had been calling to him the entire time that he had been barrelling away from his latest find, trying to get him to slow down and share with her what had upset him so much. He had not taken the time to project the images from the final door to her in his panic, so all Sarah knew was that Sam had left in a hurry, and that he had been running scared.

When he had calmed himself enough to finally respond to her, she was starting to become anxious that maybe he had been physically hurt in some way. He assured the fretful girl that he had not been harmed, just frightened out of his wits.

"I think it was them," he thought, trying to shake the memory of their misshapen forms from his head. *"Why did I have to see that?"*

"Them? Who, Sam?"

"The ones Royce talked about – the Littles that didn't turn out quite right. Elliot was right. Some of them did survive. I saw two of them, but there could have been more. They left them here, Sarah. The scholars just left them, like they did with the rest of us. They were holed up down there, underneath the High Barrens, and who knows what those villains left them with?"

Fervor

Sam wondered if the scholars had provided the odd ones with a proper supply of food and access to water. They clearly had some resources, or they would not have survived the years since the second exodus. Sam was also sure that they did not have access to the connection, but he was still unsure if that was because they lacked the capability, or because that capability still remained suppressed for them. The odd ones had not tried to open the door that had stood between him and them using traditional means, so he had to conclude that it was barred in some way to prevent their escape. They were prisoners on Fervor, too, with even less freedom than the other Littles.

"You're positive it was them?" Sarah asked, finding all of this difficult to accept.

"If what Royce and Elliot suggested is true – I have no doubt. Sarah, I want to get off this island, now more than ever. I don't want to be a pawn in the scholars' games anymore. I want to know what it means to be a real person, not manipulated by outside forces."

Sam felt really tired all of a sudden, and there was so far for him to travel to get home. It seemed like it would take him forever to get back.

"Hurry home then. We'll be leaving soon. We'll be free, and we can find somewhere to start over," Sarah offered soothingly.

But Sam knew better. They would not be free just because they left Fervor. They might always be on the run. On the positive side, though, they would no longer be under the scholars' thumbs. In fact, with Francis gone and Nathan's gift eliminated, they were already almost there.

"I'll get back as quickly as I can," he responded. *"Be watchful – they may come looking to see what happened to Nathan soon. If it comes down to it, Sarah, and it's leave without me or be caught, don't let Nathan or Fiona be stubborn about it. Just go."*

He broke off the link with her, as anxious as ever to get home and wanting to concentrate on making his way back there.

UNCONTROLLED

They made contact a few more times during the day, mainly just so that Sarah could check in on Sam and could confirm that all was well. As twilight was approaching, Sam arrived in the area by his old school where Royce was hiding out. He was relieved that this was a sign that he did not have much farther to go. He was less than comfortable, however, with the fact that he had to pass through these parts at near dark. The woods that surrounded him were frighteningly shadowed, making his imagination run wild, and the memory of his encounter with the odd ones was still very fresh in his mind. He found himself glancing over his shoulder every few moments, and he had that prickly sensation a person gets on the back of their neck when they suspect that they are being watched or followed.

Sam told himself that there was no way that they would have succeeded in forcing their way through the door in as little time as they would have needed to take in order to pursue him. Still, that did not stop the less rational part of him from conjuring up various scenarios of how they might ambush him. The thoughts did manage to spur him onward more quickly.

As Sam finally neared his own home territory, he detected something unusual in the connection, faint at first, but growing gradually in intensity. It reminded him of a wounded animal languishing in pain. He tried to remember the last time he had encountered anything like it. The closest thing that he could recall was when Elliot had first come to them. There was a similar sense of disorientation, confusion, and panic, but there was an odd agony to this presence. Also, Elliot had started and stayed faint, never becoming more than a shadow within the connection. What Sam felt now was different. Like someone waking up, achieving new awareness of the connection... and screaming. He remembered that feeling. What astounded the Finder even more was that there was something eerily familiar to this presence.

Sam could not help himself. His curiosity stirred, he had to find this thing – this person – wherever or whoever they were. He plunged through the brush, searching, and soon the shrill

277

screams that he heard with his ears were as loud as the ones in his head. He could also hear the swish and crackle of foliage as the person in question thrashed about on the forest floor, rolling about in obvious pain. Sam approached, still skittish because of the morning's encounter, and cautiously crouched by the dimly lit figure, unable to make out the person's features in the near-darkness.

Suddenly, the person lurched forward, clutching at Sam's shoulders. The startled Finder fell backwards into a layer of dried leaves, the other person falling somewhat on top of him. Sam looked up into Royce's face, the other boy's eyes filled with terror and agony. Then there was a flicker of emotion there that surprised Sam even more. He thought he had seen relief.

"What's happening to me? What's happening to me?" Royce pleaded, still gripping Sam's shoulders with an unshakable grip. Despite the strength in his hands, the Control's fingers were trembling violently. Sam could feel Royce clawing at him internally almost as vigorously as he was physically.

Fortunately, Sam had some experience at dealing with this before. He cloaked Royce with his walls, shielding him from the rest of the connection. Royce relaxed somewhat in an instant, but he did not let Sam go, and the Finder knew that the remainder of the black-haired boy's tenseness was due to the fact that he was still in terrible pain. He recognized that pain. He had seen it before in Nathan and in Francis.

"I'll help you to get back to Sarah. It would seem that you aren't subject to the stasis anymore, and this is how we get to pay for delaying the aging process for several years. One of the good parts to all of this is that Sarah will be able to fix you now. It won't cure everything that ails you, but it will help a little," Sam told him, trying to keep his thoughts subdued in order to limit their impact on the Control. "I need you to tell me something. Did you go anywhere near the house?"

Royce shook his head in denial, but there was no response through the connection. Sam was sure that he was not being truthful.

"You can't lie to me anymore. It won't work. You are part of the connection now. You may be able to lie with your mouth, but not with your thoughts, Royce."

Sam had experienced the attempt once from Fiona. She had tried to convince him that she was feeling sick when she had decided that she was not interested in going with him to retrieve a find that he could not access. This had been before they had become proper friends. Her mouth had made the claim, and there was a veil of thought containing the deception that bordered the truth – the truth which reverberated more loudly beneath that veil. He had called her on it, explaining how transparent her thoughts actually were, and that was when she had confessed the fact that she had been trying to mislead him. In a way, it had been that incident, as well as Sam's willingness to forgive the lie, that had helped initiate their friendship to begin with.

Royce clenched his eyes shut as he cringed and whimpered. He released Sam, dropping back down to the ground, where he writhed in discomfort.

"The truth, Royce," Sam requested softly.

"I-I wanted to see what Fiona looked like after what you had told me at the school. My curiosity got the best of me, and I snuck over here. I was scared…I was scared that Nathan would catch me, and I figured he must be really big now. He must look like a proper man."

Royce paused as he was gripped by a particularly severe wave of pain. Sam nodded.

"I waited until it was starting to get dark, so that he'd be finished his circuit and it would be easier to hide. I was nearing the bottom of the front steps when…when…ahhh! Why does it hurt like this?"

"Nathan doesn't run his circuit anymore, and this hurt even worse for him because he hadn't felt pain in years when it happened. What came next?"

Sam reached over and started to hook his shoulder underneath the larger boy's arm. Considering how tired he was from his travels over the last couple of days, Sam hoped that Royce could support his own weight to some degree once he was standing again. Otherwise, getting him back to the house and Sarah was going to be an extreme struggle.

That was when it struck him. The effects of the Languorite had taken several hours to completely kick in when he, Sarah, Francis, and Fiona had been exposed directly to it. The changes in Royce would not have been immediate either.

"Wait. You came out here more than one night running, didn't you? Was this your second night out here?"

"Third," the Control admitted, before biting his lip. Tears of pain streamed down his cheeks. "How did Nathan get out of his circuit? I thought that he couldn't avoid it?"

Sam hoisted him up from the ground. The larger boy was trying to brace himself and not force Sam to lift him on his own, but Royce was extremely unsteady. Sam thought back to the positions that they had been in about a year ago. He never would have imagined that they would end up like this someday. Sam felt his own muscles begin to shake a little from the strain and fatigue.

"He was exposed to the Languorite just like you, and Elliot used it to strip his 'gift' away so that the scholars couldn't use him as their eyes anymore. We expect they'll come looking for him at any time now," Sam explained.

Royce's eyes widened.

"You've got to be kidding! Francis must have blown a gasket!"

"It's complicated," was all that Sam was willing to say. He took a few very wobbly steps with Royce in tow, and then hesitated.

"You have to put a little more into this, or I'm going to have to call Nathan out to help us. Maybe if I was fresh I could do this on my own, but I just travelled all the way to the High Barrens and back."

"No...no, not Nathan. He said he would kill me, and he meant it. Besides, as soon as Francis sees me, he'll just be all over me for ditching you and abandoning the Directives." He cocked an eyebrow, trying to ignore the pain and bear some more of his own weight. "Did you say the High Barrens?"

"I don't think Nathan will kill you, especially once he understands what you're going through. He'll probably be pissed that you were creeping over to sneak a peek at Fiona, but he'll get over it. And as for Francis, that won't be an issue. Francis is gone," Sam muttered, already panting from the effort.

"Gone? Where did he go? Is that why you went to the High Barrens? Did you follow him there?" Royce sputtered incredulously. Sam sighed.

"You could say that. Never mind Francis. He's not coming back," the Finder replied solemnly.

Royce frowned a little, puzzled at first, but then the look in his eyes changed to that of sudden comprehension.

"How did it happen?" he asked, his customary sneer having long vanished.

"I'm not sure exactly, but Sarah claimed that he was broken and that he wouldn't let her fix him. There was an incident, involving Fiona, and Nathan would have throttled the life out of him if he'd had the chance, but Francis left instead. I would suggest that you not bring up Francis at all once we get back to the house. He's a sore point with everyone right now."

They were getting closer to the house and Sam was just hoping that his strength would hold out until they got there. Royce struggled to make things easier on him, but he was not being very successful. The larger boy went quiet for a few moments; all that could be heard was their laboured breathing and peeper frogs.

"Were you trying to tell me that all this is happening because I got too close to the house?" he inquired.

Sam nodded.

"Not the house *per se*, but the device Elliot brought with him from the mainland, the Languorite, which happens to be inside the house right now."

"Then there's a possibility that I won't be alone in this," Royce suggested with dejection.

"What do you mean?" Sam grunted, the sweat trickling down his face.

"I told you, I was scared of Nathan. I brought back-up with me in case he did decide that he wanted me dead. They were waiting in the woods, but they got fairly close to the house. They ran off when I started freaking out. We have to track them down. They could be going through this, too."

There was legitimate concern in the Control's voice. He may not have gotten along with his house-family, but he clearly cared about the other Control rebels.

"We have to help them," Royce said.

"What we have to do is get you to Sarah. We have enough to handle with your situation for the moment, and I don't know how many people I can shield from the connection at one time anyway. I've only ever blocked for one other person at a time before. You have what, four friends? I don't think that I can do it. We'll go after them, but not until Sarah's helped you deal with some of the pain, and we've shown you how to set up your walls. Then she and I can go find the others one at a time," Sam thought.

They were now in view of the silhouette of the house and he was anxious to get there, finding it difficult to half drag the larger boy through the woods with what little light that still remained for them.

"Maybe you can tell me their names and describe them for me a little while she fixes you. It will help me to find them."

The front steps were not that far away now, but before they could reach them, Royce suddenly jerked and stumbled to his knees, his arm locking solidly around Sam's neck as he was wracked by a rather intense pain. Sam was not able to escape the choking grip, and he realised that part of the problem was that his walls were not being as effective to shield the Control as they had been initially. That was partially because Royce's presence in the connection kept shifting and growing slightly, like trying

282

to wrap a handkerchief around a balloon that someone was still in the process of inflating. Sam was worried, in addition to the pain from the physical changes that Royce was going through, he had the psychological strain of being introduced to the connection for the first time. Experiencing one was shock enough to a person's system, but both at the same time? Sam grabbed at Royce's tensed and trembling arm, trying to free himself from its strangling hold in order to breathe again. Unsuccessful, he called out for Sarah through the connection.

Sarah picked up on his discomfort immediately and came rushing out of the house, concerned that Sam was injured in some way. When she saw Royce there, she immediately jumped to the faulty conclusion that for some reason the Control had chosen to assault Sam, despite months of avoiding one another. She cried out Sam's name and rushed forward.

"No, Sarah, no!" Sam insisted, as she grabbed Royce's arm and tried to pull him off the Finder. *"He needs your help."*

Sam also needed to breathe, but thankfully, Royce's choking grip had started to ease off as the spasm from the sudden pain subsided.

The three sat on the steps and Sarah worked at bringing the Control some relief while Sam re-established the walls that shielded Royce from the rest of the connection. Sam was a little worried at first, wondering if Royce was at risk of the same devastating results as the Bigs' parents because of the combined effects of the Languorite, but Royce was a fighter and seemed to be holding his own. Sam was also aware that there was gratitude there, and a display of trust that the Control had never demonstrated towards Sam or Sarah before. Any resentment that Royce had ever held towards them was gone.

Sam heard the door open.

"What's he doing here? He knows that he's not welcome here."

It was Nathan, and his reaction to the Control's presence was instantly a hostile one.

"I brought him here," Sam admitted, facing the Watcher. *"I found him in the woods. He had been exposed to the Languorite, and he was having twice the problems that any of the rest of us had. The stasis has dropped for him and he's part of the connection now."*

"Part of the connection?"

Nathan was surprised at that revelation, and Sam could feel him prodding at his walls tentatively, wanting to sense Royce there for himself to confirm the fact.

"So Elliot was right. The Languorite removed that suppression as well. That still doesn't answer my question though. He wouldn't have been exposed to the Languorite if he hadn't been hanging around here. What was he doing here?"

Sam could already see the irritation in Nathan's face in the light shining through the open door. He did not want to aggravate the situation, so he recognized that he had to choose his words carefully. It was true that Royce had specifically come to spy on Fiona, something that would surely rile Nathan, but Sam was aware that part of that could be attributed to something that he and Royce had in common.

"He knew what was going on, because he had run into me, Sarah, and Elliot at the school. He was curious to know more. He was supposed to be a Finder, and he has Finder instincts just like me, Nathan – not the same compulsions with the same strengths as having the gift, but a driving force nonetheless. He wanted to see more, to see some of the changes for himself. I know what that's like. I can't fault him for it," Sam pointed out.

"You seem pretty forgiving, considering how badly he treated you in the past," the young man retorted, crossing his arms over his chest. *"I would have expected you to be the least willing to see him come back here."*

Nathan apparently was not going to be as quick to accept the explanations and excuse past behaviours. Sarah looked up at him with sad eyes.

"It hasn't been that long since you went through this, Nathan. Have a heart. He's suffering, and it's worse in some ways because he has two things to contend with, not just the rapid aging. We're all victims here. He just didn't handle it as well as the rest of us. It will be different now that he's a part of the connection. He won't be able to hide behind some tough exterior or some false bravado. I think that he probably knows that, too, or he wouldn't have been willing to let Sam help him, to let the person he considered his biggest rival see him at his most vulnerable. I'm willing to give him a second chance. We've lost enough already – they've beaten us down and stolen something from each of us. Why throw away the opportunity to gain something for a change?"

The two Littles stared at the Watcher expectantly, but Nathan did not offer any sort of response, still contemplating their circumstances. Royce groaned, trying to follow the conversation, but unpleasantly distracted.

"There's more," Sam added. *"Royce wasn't sure how safe he would be, so he didn't come alone. Others have been exposed to the Languorite as well, the Controls that he always hung around with. When we're done helping Royce to whatever extent we can, Sarah and I have to go find them, too. It would probably be best if we bring them back here when we find them."*

"So what you are telling me is that not only are you asking me to let him back into the house, you want me to make allowances for the other trouble-makers in his little band. Are you both out of your minds?" Nathan exclaimed, never having anticipated these kinds of demands from Sam and Sarah.

Elliot appeared in the doorway beside him. He had picked up on the conversation and glanced down at the three on the steps with a slight frown. He recognized Royce from their encounter at the school.

"So your wayward Control's come home, has he? In more ways than one, too, I see. Perhaps the latest events have not been a complete loss then."

Sam suspected the technician was referring to what had happened with Francis. Did Elliot actually feel bad about that? Perhaps even partially to blame by showing up in the first place?

"Bringing in his friends is not exactly a bad idea. They've proven their willingness to rebel against the Directives. I would think that we can recruit them safely to our cause. I wouldn't pass up the opportunity. The more we have willing to join us, the more we can uproot what the scholars have put in place. I had thought I would just have to satisfy myself with assisting your house-family, but if I have others who are willing, and more resources than I was expecting..."

Sarah did not allow the burly man to finish his thought.

"I'm going with Sam to find them, with or without your approval, Nathan. I have to fix what I can. It will be less risky for all of us if we can bring them back here. They've probably all headed back to their own spaces by this point, and if the effects have set in, they may be sprawled somewhere in the dark, just like Royce was. We need to find them as quickly as possible, or who knows what will happen to them. Royce and his friends are the first ones to go through both things at the same time. It could be bad."

Royce was huddled against her at this point, relishing the relief her touch was bringing, no matter how insignificant. He was also listening as attentively as he could to Sam's instructions on constructing his own walls. The Control would need something in place before Sam and Sarah could set off to retrieve the others, and he wanted to facilitate that as quickly as possible, worried about how his companions were faring in the face of their agony and their chaos.

Nathan relaxed a little and his look softened, his resistance beginning to subside.

"Well, if you are going, I insist that you take me with you. Poor Sam here has endured enough, trekking out to the High Barrens and back, and then dragging that great lout back here when he was probably exhausted. Sam can find them, you can start fixing them, and I'll bring them back. My only problem

is leaving him here in the house without me being here." He gestured towards Royce. *"Fiona still hasn't gotten over what happened with Francis yet. She'll probably get upset and lock herself in her room again, and we can't afford to spend several days trying to convince her to come out. We've wasted enough time already. We should be long gone from this wretched island by now."*

"Get him up into my room...his room. I guess it doesn't really matter whose it is now," Elliot muttered. "I'll keep an eye on him, keep him away from Fiona, and it will give us a chance to chat. Your old Control here suggested he knew more than I might have suspected when we ran into him at the school, I think we have a great deal to discuss."

Sam was not sure, but from this statement alone, he got the hunch that Elliot had been more annoyed with the Finder heading off to the High Barrens, not because it had delayed their departure, but more because Elliot hadn't been invited to accompany him. He was searching for something, Sam guessed, and not just a means of getting some of the children of Fervor off of the island; he was already in the process of doing that.

"Besides," Elliot continued, "it's not like he'll be going anywhere fast, or be able to cause us any real trouble in his current condition."

Nathan seemed agreeable to that. He jogged down the stairs and grasped Royce by the shoulders. Yanking him gracelessly to his feet, the Watcher manoeuvred into a position of support and helped Royce hobble up into the house. The others followed the pair into Elliot's room.

"I never thought I'd come back here," Royce said, as Nathan lowered him to the bed. He stared at Sam as he thought this, and the Finder figured that this was as close to an apology or a thank you as he would ever be getting from the Control. Sam was fairly certain that that had been Royce's intention, and that was good enough to settle things. It wouldn't make up for what had happened – Sam wasn't sure anything would – but it

would allow them a truce for whatever length of time one would be needed.

Sam spent a few more moments making sure Royce's walls were secure. They were stronger than Elliot's were from the very beginning. In fact Royce was stronger overall in the connection at this point, possibly rivalling Nathan. There was not that much of a difference in telepathic ability between Sam and the Control, but apparently it had been enough to justify the scholars' efforts in creating the Littles.

"You can rest now. We'll go fetch your friends, but we need names and descriptions...something to help Sam locate them," Nathan stated.

Still cringing and trembling from time to time, despite the fixing that Sarah had provided, Royce started going through the list of the other four Controls. There were the two other boys, Paul and Anthony, who had both been intended to be Finders like Royce. He related their physical descriptions and the location of their House-Families. Paul, from the sounds of things, was the Control of the boy, Julius, whom they had met on their first trip to the school.

Royce followed with the description of the two girls, Angela and Katrina, both slated originally to be Fixers. Sam noticed that Royce lingered on the description of Katrina, offering greater detail than he had with the others.

"Can you find her first, Sam?" he asked softly. "Please?"

Sam glanced at him with some curiosity. It made no difference to him which of the four that they looked for first, but if it would further increase Royce's gratitude, then he could see some benefit in complying with his wishes.

"Sure, Katrina first," Sam agreed.

And with that, Sam, Sarah and Nathan departed to retrieve the other Controls, leaving Royce and Elliot to their discussions.

INSURRECTION

19

INSURRECTION

Sam, Sarah, and Nathan did manage to recover the other four Controls before any real damage appeared to have been done. Sam gave up his room to the two girls, bunking in with Sarah instead, and the two boys took Francis's room, which was now vacant. Royce remained with Elliot, and the two seemed to be very friendly, spending a lot of time in exclusive conversation. It made Sam a little nervous, and he desperately wanted to know what they were saying. He had learned his lesson with Francis, however, and he did not pry. It would have been easy for him, but it certainly would not have felt right.

They spent the next day further dealing with their transitions with Sarah's assistance. They seemed to be coping sufficiently, and Sam stopped worrying about consequences similar to what had happened with the Bigs' parents. The Finder wondered if the Bigs' parents had had someone who could understand how to shield them and to help them construct their walls, could that tragedy have been avoided — or would there still have been those who would have ended up like Francis? They would never know. The theory was long past testing.

Elliot, Nathan, and Fiona went out for another round of lessons on how to activate and guide the hover. Elliot felt that with one more day of instruction, and a quick outing the following day, they would be ready to go. They were all excited by this notion, looking forward to the opportunity to escape the island and discover the real world of the mainland. In the meantime, the technician was also hopeful that the Controls would start adapting better to their changes.

As usual, Sam could not fend off the compulsion to find, but Sarah and Royce asked him if he could make proper use of the inclination and go to gather a list of items that Royce and the Controls had left behind at the school. That told him that Royce and the Controls had no intention of returning there – they had come back to the house to stay. Not that it made any difference. Sam's house-family would be leaving soon enough anyway, and abandoning the house to disuse if no one else were to live in it. It meant that Royce and the others would have to handle any scholars or their lackeys who happened to come snooping around because of the loss of Nathan as their eyes, or because Francis failed to report in to the next Teller meeting. Chaos would be erupting soon enough on this part of Fervor. It likely did not matter where the Controls chose to call home.

Sam made it to the school without interruption and scrambled about gathering everything on the list. It was a lengthy one, and in a way, Sam felt as though he were salvaging the last year of Royce's life. In amongst the requested items were things that had obviously not come from the school, including items of clothing that Royce had not left his old home with. There were even a couple of items Sam was fairly certain had come from their own house, even though Nathan had tossed the Control out empty handed. It made Sam feel justified that he had never believed himself safe after Royce had left, but now...

Sam paused in his finding, shaken by how much things had changed in the last couple of weeks. The thought hung heavy in his heart and he found himself sitting down quickly. First there was Elliot's arrival, and then all of the changes, followed by the hope of eventual escape, and then the loss of Francis. And now there was the entire affair with the Controls. He sat for a moment with his head on his knees, breathing deeply and trying to wish everything away. It did not work, and gradually he managed to steady himself again, returning to his list.

Sam plodded his way back to the house once he was done while keeping off all the established paths and making sure that nobody spotted him. He thought it possible that there might be someone out looking for one of the missing Controls, although, if their relationships with their house-families bore any resemblance to that of Royce's with his, they would not be worrying about their disappearance just yet. They may have headed out for more than a day at a time in the past just as Royce used to do, and their Tellers had possibly dissuaded their house-family's interference with their Control, just as Francis once had as well.

Nathan, Fiona, and Elliot had already returned when Sam arrived home, since he had been gone the better part of the day.

"Elliot says we leave tomorrow," Nathan announced, as Sam strolled through the door. *"You should pack your things and be ready. We'll be making one more run in the morning, just to be sure Fiona and I are ready, and then we finally get to head for the mainland."*

The Watcher grinned broadly as he thought these words. He had probably felt the burden of their precarious position due to the threat of investigating scholars more than anyone else, still having a natural protective streak despite the departure of his gift. He was all too aware that if they did not leave soon, it could be disastrous.

Sam knocked on Royce and Elliot's door, and found the pair of them in there again deep in discussion. Sam was almost offended that Elliot was spending so much time with the mean-spirited boy – although he was not exactly a boy anymore. Royce's transformation was almost complete, and once again, he out-sized Sam by a fair margin. He actually made a strikingly handsome young man, with sharp-cut features, a lean but muscular build, and a maturity that now matched his challenging stare. Nonetheless, Elliot had heard many of the tales regarding the various conflicts between Royce and the different members of the house-family, Sam in particular. The Finder could not comprehend why the technician had taken such an interest in Royce, knowing what he knew.

Without saying anything, Sam placed the bag of requested items on the bed and turned to go.

"Sam – wait," Elliot said. As usual, the technician tended to speak aloud whenever he communicated through the connection, because his presence there was so faint. "I was hoping you could give us some details about your little excursion to the High Barrens. Royce here has already shared with me everything that he remembered from the time that he spent there."

"I'll tell you, but I don't see why it would matter. We're leaving tomorrow," Sam replied, a little wary at the inquiry.

"It matters to me, believe me. Did you see any documentation, any records perhaps?" Elliot demanded.

Sam shook his head.

"I didn't see much, honestly. I didn't go through any of the doors below. I just looked through them. There was a large classroom there, but I'm sure Royce told you about that already. And there was a sizeable laboratory of some type. There may have been records in there. I have no idea. I would have thought they would have brought any paperwork with them, wouldn't they?"

"You didn't go in? But you are a Finder. I would have expected the compulsion to be overwhelming," Elliot said with dismay.

"There are some things stronger than the compulsion to find. Like fear, the powerful kind, for one. I saw those odd ones, the other Littles. I was scared to death, and no curiosity was going to keep me there. I'm sorry, Elliot. I guess I can't help you," Sam sighed.

"No — no. You've helped me enough already, Sam. Don't feel bad. Knowing what to look for there, knowing that they have another hover there, even if it is in disrepair, well that means something. As far as the documentation goes, I was just grasping at straws. They probably took everything with them when they left. I was being hopeful."

Sam found the technician's comments strange. Did he plan on making a stop at the High Barrens before they left Fervor? Sam could not bear the idea. He didn't want to go anywhere near that place ever again. The terrifying encounter with the odd ones aside, he didn't want to risk getting another glimpse at Francis either. Even considering the fact that the tide had been coming in and going out, with the way the body had been tangled in the seaweed, chances were it would still be there. Sam shivered reflexively. He left the room before the conversation could trigger any more unpleasant memories.

When Sam entered the room that he was now sharing with Sarah he found that she was already sprawled on the bed, lost in slumber. Curling up in his chair, he watched her sleep for a little while and was glad that she did not look as distressed as she would have been, had it not been for the distraction afforded by the Controls. They had replaced the hover in occupying her time, keeping her from dwelling on the latest events, and giving her something more positive to focus on. Trying to focus on the positive himself, the fact that they would be finding freedom tomorrow, Sam dozed off.

In the morning, Elliot, Nathan, and Fiona climbed into the hover and set off on one final test ride. Sam noted the hover had a different sound than the ones that he was accustomed to. The standard hovers on Fervor were almost silent, with only a slight low rumbling drone as they travelled from one location to another, but Elliot's hover was different. It had a high-pitched whine to it as it moved — a sound that was almost painful to hear. Perhaps because it had been reassembled from ill-fitting bits and pieces. It also gave off a sporadic popping sound, almost like a little hiccup, every few seconds. Sam hoped that it was no indication of how well the vehicle would function.

"They're taking it out along the beach, to avoid being spotted by any of the others," Sarah informed him. *"We're to*

*bring our things, and meet them there, after we eat. They al-
ready have their stuff with them."*

Sam felt almost too excited to stomach any food, but he
knew it was going to be a lengthy trip, so he forced himself to
swallow his breakfast. He and Sarah were both seated at the table when they heard a somewhat familiar whine outside.

"I thought they were going to meet us at the beach?"
Sam remarked. Curious, that the hover had lost the popping
noise that had made it seem distinctive earlier. He mentioned
that to Sarah as well, who was glancing out the window with a
startled look on her face. Her eyes remained glued to the scene
outside, her face blanching.

"That's not Elliot's hover," she murmured.

As Sam joined her by the window, he could see the bullet-like form outside, but there were no dark patches, no marring
of its surface anywhere. Sarah was right. It was not Elliot's
hover. The Finder's heart dropped, and he immediately felt nau-
seous.

"It's them...it's the scholars. They sent someone. What
are we going to do?" Sam breathed.

Sarah sent out a panicked warning to the others still in
the house, and then she gestured towards the window behind
them.

*"Let's go out the back. We push at Nathan, Fiona, and
Elliot – tell them to stay away, and that there is trouble. We'll
let them know that we'll meet them at the beach just as we
planned, and that if we don't show, that they should leave without us. I hope the Controls can save themselves."*

The pair scrambled through the window and dropped
down to the ground below, tossing their packs out before them.
Sarah squealed as she landed funny on her ankle, grimacing in
pain, and Sam grabbed her and dragged her into the bushes.
They lay there panting, and stayed hidden there when they heard
voices several feet from where they had come to a stop.

"Can you fix your ankle?" Sam asked.

Sarah nodded. She was already clutching at her leg, attempting to mend the damage. Sam knew there would be delays, even if she was successful, since it always took more time for her to concentrate and fix her own injuries.

"I'll contact the others. You just focus on repairing that," Sam suggested. He started searching, trying to ignore the voices that sounded much too close for comfort.

Nathan was the strongest of the Bigs in the connection, and therefore had always been the easiest to find, so Sam went looking for him. It took longer than it would have if Sam had known their intended path and timing, but with a mind as familiar as the Watcher's, Sam did manage to root him out eventually. The Finder pushed frantically at Nathan's walls, which were not as thick as they had been prior to Elliot removing his gift. He forced his way through on the first attempt.

"They're here, Nathan! They're here! Don't come back to the house, whatever you do," Sam exclaimed, relieved to be making contact.

"Whoa – calm down, little buddy. What are you talking about?" the young man asked.

"The scholars, they sent somebody to investigate. They're here at the house!"

Sam tensed up as the voices came worryingly close. He was thankful that they were not part of the connection. He could shout at Nathan through their link without any fear of being detected.

"They're at the house? You sit tight and we'll come back for you..." Nathan began.

"No! Stick to the plan! We made it out of the house and we're hiding in the woods. We'll meet you on the beach, but you should turn back now. There isn't much time, and they may find us if we don't hurry," Sam insisted. There was a pause and a faint and garbled whisper that Sam could not make out.

"Elliot wants to know if the Controls are with you," Nathan imparted. Sam realized that they were far enough away, that with Nathan's walls and the distance involved, Elliot's weak

presence in the connection had become distorted so that he was not able to hear him properly. That left Nathan playing messenger.

"No, they aren't. What does it matter? They can fend for themselves, and the scholars would be sending someone to locate you, and maybe the rest of our family, not them. Royce might have something to be concerned about, but the others should be fine."

Sam relaxed a little, noticing that the voices were moving away again.

"Elliot says that it's important. We'll hurry back," the Watcher assured him.

"We should be there shortly, as soon as Sarah finishes fixing her leg. She sprained her ankle when we dropped from the window but she's mending it right now." Sam hesitated, reluctant to think what he wanted to say next. *"Nathan, don't wait for us long. They may catch us, and we don't want them catching you, too. If we aren't there when you get to the meeting point, or we don't arrive soon after, be prepared to leave without us. If nothing else, you and Fiona can make it to the mainland, and serve as a voice for the rest of us on Fervor."*

"Nonsense, Sam. Get a move on. We'll see you there."

Nathan was firm on this, much to Sam's dismay. He broke the link and glanced over at Sarah. She had apparently finished with her leg, and was peering through the bushes.

"They went around to the other side of the house," she remarked anxiously. *"Royce let me know that he and the other Controls made it out of the house. I told him that you were warning Nathan to keep away, and that we were still planning to meet the hover at the beach. He actually seemed happy that we got out safely."*

"We better go," Sam responded. *"The sooner we get off the island the better. They're not going to like the fact that we screwed up their experiment, and I think that Elliot will be in even more trouble for sabotage."*

INSURRECTION

The pair got to their feet and began to sprint through the woods towards the planned meeting point on the beach, ignoring the branches and thorns that caught at their clothing and occasionally snagged their hair. They had to slow in order to cross a boggy patch, and that was when Sam noticed the disturbing whine, and a bullet-like shadow pass overhead. They both froze, and he looked at Sarah with wide eyes.

"Do you think they saw us?" he thought fearfully.

"I hope not. Maybe it won't matter. We're almost there."

She was right. Seconds later, they stumbled out of the brush and into the clearing where the trees gave way to the shore. It was only a quick run from there to where they would be meeting the others, but a stretch that offered no cover. Sam took the lead, dashing for the rocks that lined the beach. He was half way there when he heard an odd buzzing noise, saw a flicker of bright light, and then found himself unable to move, as if something were restraining him. He twisted his head as far as his new limitations would allow. It looked like he was wrapped in some bizarre netting, but instead of being knotted from rope or twine it was instead woven from thin crackling strands of light. Sarah screamed through the connection, diving back into cover, but her loud mental cry carried, likely echoing through most of the minds in the general area.

"Sam! What was that? What's happening?"

It was Nathan again, but he was much closer now. He had readily picked up on Sarah's expression of alarm, but the girl was in a full panic and her thoughts were somewhat incoherent. The Watcher had chosen to turn to Sam for answers as a result.

"I'm caught, Nathan, and I expect they'll get Sarah momentarily," Sam admitted. *"Don't stop for us – it's too late. Just go. They likely won't be that harsh on us. If we're lucky they'll see us as less to blame than you, Elliot, Royce, and Francis. Maybe they'll even go easy on us."*

299

It was a hope, but not a likely one. Nathan did not reply, quickly breaking their link.

Sam strained to see the two figures that were also standing in the clearing, and caught the gleam of sunlight flashing off of their hover. They were both dressed in plain gray tunics and pants, and they were both similar in build to what Francis had been. They also both appeared to be carrying some sort of unusual device, and not one that Sam could identify.

One of them, a fair haired man, approached him. The stranger shifted his grip on the unwieldy device to hold it single-handed, and pulled a much smaller device from his pocket. He passed it over Sam, as if he were scanning him for something.

"Is it him?" the man farther back demanded.

"No," the closer man replied, with some disappointment. "This one's a Finder. It's not him."

"I thought their Finder was a Little," the first man remarked.

The one with the scanning device looked at it attentively.

"He was...he is. That settles it, doesn't it? Masterson has obviously been through here. Farrell was right. You're going to have to pay up when we get back." The two men chuckled at this light-heartedly.

"So what do we do with this one then? We can't just leave him, can we? Who knows what Masterson told them?"

The man next to Sam eyed him with a hint of disgust.

"Farrell's going to be pissed. Leave it to some of these little fuckers to screw things up thanks to Masterson's interference. We'll have to round up the whole house-family and pull them from the experiment so that they don't skew the results. We're going to have to hunt down Masterson, too. Who knows where the bastard's hiding. Of course, Farrell's going to want to study them. Test them to see the full effects of the Languorite, and what it has done to them. He might even want to dissect them."

The two men laughed at this as well, but this time it was more brusque and mean-spirited. Sam suspected that they were just taunting him, but he could not be sure.

"This one wasn't alone. I saw a girl with him," the more distant stranger commented. "Dark hair, younger-looking. She disappeared back into the woods when we caught this one."

"Probably their Fixer," his companion concluded, sliding his scanning device back into his pocket. "If Masterson exposed them all, the Bigs would be adults by this point. We're going to have to watch out for them."

He paused, examining Sam with a perturbed expression.

"We should probably get this one into the hover and then start tracking the others. I'd hate to be their Teller at this point. He should have been able to prevent all of this, and the fact that he didn't doesn't bode well for him. He's going to be in deep, deep trouble. Farrell's going to want to string him up and let him rot. That, or toss him in some dark hole somewhere, lock him up and throw away the key. That boy had to be insane or just plain stupid. He would have known the consequences."

The more they spoke, the more Sam despaired at his predicament. They continually referred to him as if he were an object, oblivious to their words. He did not like that feeling, and he was worried that they would catch Sarah and the others, just like they claimed they would. He was wishing that she would run, but he knew that she was still hiding nearby, lost in panic. To top it off, everything that they were saying about Francis was making him even more miserable. From the sounds of it, he really had been trying to protect them all along.

The man beside him released the large device he was holding so that it hung from a shoulder strap and shifted it to his back, out of the way. Then he reached for Sam.

That was when a small clump of bushes along the rocks exploded as Nathan charged from them, a large piece of driftwood held menacingly over his head. He took a well-aimed and forceful swing at the stranger's head and made contact without difficulty, catching the man completely by surprise. He teetered for a second after taking the blow, his mouth open but making no sound, and then his eyes glazed over and he dropped limply into the dirt. That was when Sam realized two things: Nathan had been far enough away that he may not have heard the casual exchange between the two intruders, especially with the roar of the waves masking the sound, and Nathan's position had kept the second man out of his line of sight.

"Nathan, watch out! There's another one!"

Sam was too late however. There was a brilliant flash and the Watcher was suddenly stranded in a similarly energized netting, the criss-crossing of light suspending him in place. The second man in gray jogged over to them, a horrified look on his face and his device clutched firmly in both hands.

"Shit! Shit! You better not have killed him! Oh, you're going to pay for this, you brute. If Farrell would have been pissed before, he's bound to have a conniption now. I warned Norm that you guys were going to be nothing better than wild animals, but he didn't take me seriously." He looked at the fallen man and heaved a heavy sigh. "You stupid shit, you should have listened and kept on your guard."

The man in gray grabbed Sam by the collar, and dragged him carelessly over to the hover. He dropped the trapped Finder roughly in the dirt at the base of the vehicle and disappeared inside it. He emerged again a few moments later with a third device, and hurried over to where his companion still lay prone on the ground beside Nathan. It was likely some sort of fixing device, Sam guessed, to heal the damage that the Watcher had caused. From all appearances, Sam and Nathan were doomed.

But the man in gray never got the opportunity to use the device to rouse his cohort. The sudden flurry of activity that followed caught Sam as much by surprise as it did the unsuspecting stranger. While his view was somewhat obscured, Sam was fairly certain that Elliot had not come rushing into the clearing, nor would the burly man necessarily be that effective on his own since the intruder in gray had been wary after the first attack and had been watching for a second. He had perhaps been anticipating that the technician might interfere again, or perhaps there would be trouble from the rogue Teller or Control from Sam and Nathan's house-family, but he was not ready to take on a group of five full-grown adults. He managed to stop one of them with his device before he was swarmed and overwhelmed by the four others.

Sam wanted to know what exactly was going on but found himself closing his eyes and cowering away from the scene as much as his restricted position would allow, trying desperately to bring up his walls as quickly as possible in order to block out the assault of anger, resentment, and even hatred that flared from the four Controls still able to act. In a fury, they wrenched the entrapment device from the man's hands while forcing him to the ground. The events that happened next left Sam with nightmares and was something he wished that he had never had to live through. The enraged mob of Controls, with Royce in the lead, beat the man savagely, bashing at the man with the otherwise non-injurious weapon that they had torn from his hands. The man's screams were blood-curdling, and Sam would have willingly submitted to being deaf again if he could have avoided hearing them, but he wasn't even able to cover his ears. He could sense Nathan's discomfort as well, horrified by the violence going on inches away from where he was forced to stand.

Sam shivered as the beating continued, until the man finally went silent. The Controls had used the opportunity to take vengeance on the scholars for everything that had been done to them, losing a piece of their humanity while they exhausted their frustrations and outrage on this symbol of their oppressors. The others had stopped when it was clear that the man had been overpowered and had no fight left in him, but Royce had been especially driven, mercilessly dealing the man blow after blow despite the intruder's pleas for him to stop. The stranger had not been that far off when he had suggested that they little more than wild animals. Sam wondered what would have happened if Royce had had free reign to take out his frustrations on him when the Control had attributed him with the blame for his circumstances.

Things went very quiet after the man's screams had stopped, and Sam lay there helplessly, wondering what to expect next. He heard Sarah emerge from the bushes, sniffling and dazed.

"I can't fix them," she murmured over and over again, staring at the fallen men. "I can't fix them."

Nathan was struggling futilely to escape his binds, but none of his efforts proved successful.

That was when Elliot and Fiona arrived. Elliot gathered up the devices that the men had been using and activated them to release Angela, Nathan, and Sam from their restraints. He then took the fixing tool that was now lying in the dirt and examined the men.

"I can help this one," he said quietly, gesturing at the man that had succumbed to Nathan's attack. "But the other one is beyond saving. We'll have to dispose of the body."

He did not ask for an explanation or some recounting of the grim details. The blood spatter and the drawn faces spoke volumes.

Elliot first entrapped the unconscious man in one of the stranger's own energy nets, and then the technician set about using the healing device on him. While he was doing this, Nathan and Fiona had shuffled Sarah away, leading her from the frightful scene and taking her back to Elliot's hover.

Sam sat at the base of the hover in the clearing, still trying to make sense of it all. It was just another case of everything going wrong, and as per usual, the scholars had been at the root of it. He was worried that this would change things and make it worse for them while they were on the run. What did this mean for Royce? What did this mean for Elliot?

After he finally managed to motivate himself briefly out of the stupor that he found himself in, Sam got to his feet and followed in the same direction as Nathan, Fiona, and Sarah, willing himself not to look behind him. He would have to put all of this behind him, as they all would. He only hoped that when he left Fervor, he could somehow leave all of this, too.

20

NEW BEGINNINGS

Sam stumbled across the beach toward the marred-looking hover, his mind dazed and his heart numb. He stared at the vehicle with some reservation as he approached it. Getting into the hover and leaving Fervor represented an end to everything Sam had ever known – his only reality – and a leap into something frighteningly new. His feet felt like lead weights with each step. Sam was beginning to understand why Francis would have rather faced punishment than go with them. He wanted his freedom but was definitely afraid of the unknown.

Nathan met Sam at the door, looking him over carefully, the Watcher's face demonstrating great concern.

"Are you okay? Did they hurt you, little buddy?"

Sam shook his head as Nathan checked him for a second time. The Finder felt like he was somehow lagging a few seconds behind the rest of the world. He had a few scrapes and bruises from being tossed into the dirt, but they seemed meaningless after what had happened to the investigators. The sounds of their cries seemed to be repetitively echoing through his mind.

Sam was tired and cold, even though the sun was shining brightly and he and Sarah had barely just risen for the day. He wanted to curl up in a corner and go to sleep, pretending that none of this had ever happened. It certainly was not what Sam had been expecting when he had awoken that morning. He wondered where he would be waking up the next day.

Nathan ushered Sam into the hover and guided him into the seat next to Sarah's. She trembled like a leaf and was slouching in the chair, staring wordlessly at the chair back in front of her. Her dark eyes had a glassy and vacant look to them. Sam edged closer to her, trying ineffectively to get her attention and put his hand on hers, both offering and seeking comfort. She did not respond, neither flinching away nor accepting the gesture. She did, however sigh very quietly.

Nathan joined Fiona at the front of the hover, sitting next to her and draping his arm across her shoulders. She leaned into him, and Sam wondered why he had not really noticed their attachment before the incident with Francis. The two thought quietly to one another through the connection, but not behind closed walls as they usually tended to do. Sam did not pay much attention to what they were saying, still lost in a bit of a mental fog, but he did pick up the occasional words like 'fugitive', 'safe-house', and 'coordinates.'

Nathan glanced back at the Littles every now and then as they sat talking and waiting for Elliot to rejoin them. He also gave Sam an encouraging smile from time to time, even though the Watcher's eyes were sad. Sam could tell that Fiona was anxious to leave by the way she twitched in her chair and eyed the exit, but they did not want to leave without Elliot.

There was a fair delay before the technician appeared at the door of the hover, but he did not enter. Instead, he stood back and allowed four of the Controls to start clambering into the seats at the rear of the vehicle – all of them but Royce. They were going to the mainland too, apparently, Sam considered in his fog. He hadn't been expecting that since there had been no discussion of the Controls joining them at all. In fact, Sam had just assumed that they were going to be staying behind on Fervor when Elliot and his house-family left.

Eight seats, Sam thought numbly. Eight seats. Even as muddled as his thoughts were, he could still do basic arithmetic. With the five Controls, Nathan, Fiona, Sarah, Elliot, and himself, there were ten. That was two people too many. He stared at Elliot without voicing the question, as Paul, Anthony, Angela, and Katrina each took a seat. Nathan and Fiona looked equally confused, and no longer fairly at ease.

"What's going on?" Nathan demanded. *"What are they doing here? We won't all fit in here."*

Elliot did not respond to this at first. He slid in between the seats, the fixing device in hand, and drew up next to the unresponsive Sarah. He took her small chin in his large hand and searched her face with worried eyes, then activated the device. Within a few moments she stopped shuddering and relaxed, leaning forward into him and gradually dozing off into a light sleep.

"Shock," the technician explained, his comments mostly directed at Nathan. "She'll be okay now, physically, but you'll still have to watch her. From what I understand from the research notes, Fixers don't handle death well, especially not if they witness it firsthand. Francis gave her enough to deal with, with his trip to the High Barrens, and this pushed her far past her proper peace of mind. She shouldn't have had to see that confrontation with the investigators. You make sure she doesn't see any more of it once you get to the mainland. Shelter her. Keep her safe."

Repeating an earlier sequence of events, Sam's eager mind fought through the fuzziness to grasp what Elliot had just said. "Once *you* get to the mainland," he had said, not: "Once *we* get to the mainland." That could not be right. Sam recognized what that implied. He started shaking his head.

"N-no, he's not coming with us. He's saying that he's not coming with us. You can't let him do that, Nathan. No, he can't do that. Make him come with us," Sam stammered. Elliot hushed him.

"I think you may need a taste of this medicine too there, boy," the technician said with a gentle laugh, and he targeted Sam next with the fixing device. The fog started to lift from his weary mind and the numbness in the rest of his body began to ease off as well. It did not change his awareness that Elliot had suggested he would not be accompanying them and it certainly did not change his resistance to the idea. If anything it prompted Sam to be even more defiant when faced with that truth.

"How are we supposed to manage without you? Why aren't you going with us? When Sarah wakes up and you aren't with us, she'll be even more devastated. Why?" Sam demanded. *"You can't just throw us out there. We aren't sure how things work on the mainland. We need you to help us adapt."*

Elliot leaned back with a sigh, looking tired and unhappy.

"Well, first of all, as your Watcher so perceptively observed, we won't all fit in this hover, and secondly, I have friends on the mainland that will be ready to take you in and help you to figure things out. I briefed Nathan and Fiona on what to expect when you got there."

"But you didn't tell us that you wouldn't be coming back with us," Nathan objected. Sam already knew that. If the technician had suggested such a thing to the Watcher, he certainly would have let the Littles know. This was news to him as well.

Elliot shrugged.

"Your Control and I discussed this in great detail. He wanted to be able to get his friends off the island, and I wanted to see as many of you liberated as our resources would afford. *This* hover shouldn't be leaving here with any empty seats, and I'm the best person to make sure that the others don't either. I know that you've had your differences in the past, but Royce's companions have a right to their freedom just as much as you do. I'm sure you can manage to get along for the time it takes to get from here to the mainland. Once you get there, you'll be free to part ways, although personally, I think you would all be better off sticking together. No one else there will quite understand where you're coming from and what you've been through."

"But we don't even know where we're headed," Sam protested. *"Where will we be going, and how do we get there without you? We were depending on you."*

"I'm not leaving you high and dry, Sam. Give me more credit than that. You are going to a safe-house that was set up for latents on the mainland, the ones who were avoiding recruitment into the scholars' experiments. The scholars have government support which meant that any known latent telepaths were being conscripted, like it or not. We won't let anything like that happen to you. You'll get new identities once you are there, and enough resources to start a new life, somewhere where they will be very unlikely to track you down. You don't need me to get there, Sam, or to keep you safe. There will be many hands there to protect you, mostly people who lost family or friends to the scholars. They couldn't help me when I was trying to get at the Languorite, it was too risky, but they can help you now. Besides, Nathan and Fiona know what to look for, and the coordinates are pre-programmed into the hover. They'll make sure that you arrive safely," the technician advised.

Now it was Fiona's turn to object.

"You never told us that you wouldn't be coming with us. It doesn't make sense, Elliot. Helping us to escape Fervor, only to stay behind yourself? If it's a question of space, why not leave one of us behind instead?"

She glanced at the Controls as she said this, and Sam realized that she actually meant one of them. From their expressions, they did not appreciate the suggestion.

"Who said anything about staying behind? I'll just be delaying my departure." Elliot chuckled. "I have every intention of returning to the mainland at some point. I have access to not only one long distance hover but two, other than this one, now that the investigators have delivered me another one and one in perfect working condition at that. Between that hover, and the one at the High Barrens, that's fifteen more children I can take with me – fifteen more children who would have been trapped on Fervor. I had planned on completing repairs on the hover that Sam had uncovered and seeking out another house-family to bring back to the mainland, but now that the scholars have kindly donated a second one, why stop there? Would you deny the others the same opportunity that I've helped you to obtain?"

Fiona turned away from him again, facing the front of the hover with a glum expression. Being a tad on the selfish side, Fiona would have been willing to deny others the opportunity to allay her fears. On the other hand, she could not argue with him and his decision based on that rationale, but she still did not like it.

Nathan gave her shoulder a squeeze in consolation. His eyes were warmer now, and less disappointed.

"They are bound to send more people after you when the first two don't return," the Watcher observed. *"What then? They may send more next time, and if they figure out what happened to the first two investigators, they might not just stop at taking you prisoner. They'll probably send an entire small ar-*

my, and I would expect them to be better armed, with something other than those net devices."

"If they want to send us more hovers, all the power to them – it may just prove to our advantage. I'll be fine. By the time they realize that their investigators aren't returning, I expect to be arranging a small army of my own. Royce says he has other contacts amongst the Controls, ones who are just as unhappy with their circumstances as he was. We'll be going into hiding on the island, somewhere near the High Barrens most likely, and we'll start organizing. Eventually, we should find ourselves with fifteen others who also want to leave Fervor, even if it happens to just be other Controls. I'm actually hoping to find at least one other house-family or two that are something like yours, and looking for answers."

"We? Royce?" Nathan murmured.

Now Sam understood why Elliot had been spending so much time in conversation with the Control. They had been plotting this ever since Royce had returned to the house, aware of the existence of the second long distance hover at the High Barrens by that point. Sam suspected that Royce had approached Elliot about sending the Controls back to the mainland as well, and the plot had spawned from there. That was why they had been excluding the others from their talks.

"He's willing to assist me, and as you mentioned before," Elliot stated, glancing around the hover. "We won't all fit in here. Royce volunteered to stay behind with me. He thinks that the scholars should not be allowed to benefit from what they've done on Fervor, and that my plans will help to prevent that, or at least, will allow us to reduce the effectiveness of what they are doing here. It may take several days before the departure of the Controls is even noticed, and our main obstacle will be the Tellers, rather than the scholars or their lackeys. Your Francis...he was an exception. The other Tellers won't allow me to intercede so easily. Many of them are completely on board with what the scholars are doing. We'll have the Languorite to help us fight back, but that doesn't guarantee our success. It will be a matter of timing, and our ability to infiltrate. I'd hate to have to strip anyone else of their gifts, but with the Watchers, I don't see how it could be avoided, and with the Tellers, well – if we don't then we leave ourselves vulnerable to their whims, don't we?"

"But Royce?" Nathan questioned, more than a hint of doubt in the tone of his voice.

Sam could hear the other Controls shifting uncomfortably in the back of the hover. This was an area of discord between his house-family and Royce's friends, the appropriateness of this situation because of Royce's involvement in particular. They had always supported Royce in his efforts. In a way, they had appointed him their unofficial leader. They were losing something in this arrangement as well by leaving him behind, and they weren't particularly pleased about it.

"He and I have more in common than you would think, Nathan. Royce may have had a bad start, but that doesn't guarantee him a bad future. I know that display back there may have you wondering how safe I am allying myself with him, but I can assure you that none of that animosity is directed at me – and it won't be. He and I are on the same side, I would bet the Languorite on that. While I don't condone what he did back there, I'm willing to turn a blind eye. I've been at the point where he is myself. I know exactly how he is feeling and how it can affect you responses," the technician admitted.

"Why?" Sam demanded. *"Why have you been at that point? I know why Royce is the way that he is, and it all has to do with being excluded from the connection and being denied the opportunity to be a Finder. How can you possibly suggest that you know what someone like Royce is feeling? You said that you were helping us because you knew what the scholars were doing was wrong. That wasn't the only reason, was it, Elliot? There was something more, another thing that you haven't been willing to share with us."*

Elliot stared at him, scratching at his forehead a little, and then rubbing at his chin.

"You didn't believe that my finding you and offering to help you was merely a happy accident, did you Sam?"

Sam shook his head. He had always suspected that there was more to Elliot's story than he had been telling them, and now he was also puzzled by the fact that the technician felt he could identify with Royce and his anger. Sam found that difficult to believe. He had never seen the kind of hatred in Elliot's eyes that was perpetually threatening to boil over in Royce's, even when Francis had knocked heads with him.

"No surprises there. You always were the clever one," Elliot said with a smile.

He reached over and mussed Sam's hair, a friendly gesture much more appropriate for a younger child, but Elliot had never seemed all that clear on how he should treat the Bigs or the Littles.

"Truthfully? I was looking for you and the rest of Fervor long before I stumbled upon Fiona's impressive and impulsive outburst. Because of my work with the scholars, I knew that Fervor existed, but I didn't know where, and as I've told you before, I had no one else to assist me, not with that anyway. I actually had constructed a locater, so that I could find you – not you specifically, but Fervor as a whole. I just needed a reading, only a brief one, and your Keeper thankfully obliged. It allowed me to gain the coordinates to the island that I so desperately needed. That's how I managed to guide my messages to you. Once I had those coordinates, I had hope."

It was Fiona's turn to speak.

"Hope for what? What were you looking for exactly? Why were you looking for Fervor in the first place, since you weren't looking specifically for us?"

"Whatever it was, he hasn't found it yet. Have you, Elliot? That's another reason why you are willing to stay behind," Sam added. The pieces were finally starting to come together. *"Did they take something from you, just like they did with Royce? Is that why you feel like you understand him? Is that why you were so angry with them? That would explain why you feel the need to do this."*

The technician leaned away from Sam, not meeting the boy's inquisitive gaze.

"You could say that, yes. I think I fought through the worst of my frustration long before I made contact with you. It had been years since I had suffered my loss, or felt the worst of it, anyway. I had chosen by the time I found you to channel my anger into purpose. You may not believe it based on what you recently saw, but it's not too late for Royce to do that as well, with the right guidance – the right influence. Once he acknowledges that he can fight the scholars by trying to make a positive difference, I trust that he'll stop lashing out, and that he'll see that he can thwart them strategically rather than just trying to wound them with brute force. If he sets his mind to it, he can work wonders. He's almost as clever as you are, Sam."

There were some derisive snorts and giggles from the Controls in the back, implying that they thought that the suggestion that Sam could be smarter than Royce was absurd. Elliot cocked an eyebrow, and shot a look of disapproval at them over his shoulder. The gesture silenced them fairly quickly; they weren't as cocky or as confident without their ringleader.

Dealing with their continuing presence would be awkward, but Sam was willing to adapt, for Elliot's sake, just as they had at the house. He doubted that Royce would be making an appearance to say goodbye and he was thankful for that. The Control would not deem it necessary, and considering the way that he probably still looked after his brutal run-in with the investigators, it was no doubt for the best. Sam did not need any reminders of the trouble that they had just faced, and he had no great urge to see Royce one last time.

"What did they take from you?" Fiona asked quietly, breaking the uncomfortable silence. "Tell me. I want to know, Elliot, and I think this is important to you. I want to be able to remember everything about you, in case we never see you again. Why does all of this matter so much to you?"

"I'm a latent...as I've discussed with Sam and Sarah before, it's a genetic trait. That fact is knowledge that the scholars have used to arrive at all of you. You wouldn't be who you are without their careful..." He paused and eyed the Littles. "Or in some cases, not so careful, manipulation. I was fortunate that I wasn't strong enough for them to notice me and conscript me. Otherwise, I would have been amongst those who parented you and paid for the experimentation with my life as your parents did. I wasn't strong enough for them to weed me out because that kind of strength wasn't in my genes – not to the extent that they were looking for, fortunately for me. But I got my weak telepathic ability from my mother, and I wasn't alone in that. I was her first child, but she chose not to stay with my father. She chose not to stay with me either, leaving me with him, which turned out to be a blessing in disguise. She found someone more suited to who she was. Latents tend to be attracted to one another. It's easier to trust someone when you know what your partner is thinking."

Elliot's gaze drifted over to Nathan and Fiona, and Sam thought he detected some envy in the man's expression. Sam wondered if this had anything to do with why Elliot had neither a mate of his own, nor any children.

"My mother left with another man who happened to also be a latent, and they had a child, my half-sister, Amelia. She wasn't as strong as any of you telepathically, but she was definitely stronger than me."

"They conscripted her. They conscripted Amelia," Nathan deduced, starting to see where this was going.

"She was one of them – one of the Bigs' parents," Sam exclaimed.

"Amelia...I don't think my mother's name was Amelia. That's not what I remember," Fiona declared. "She was somebody's mother, though. It wasn't somebody here, one of us, was it?"

Elliot shook his head and grimaced. "I couldn't be that lucky, that while grasping wildly at straws, I would draw the one that I wanted? No, but I did manage to find out his name. It's Malcolm, and I know that he's a Watcher somewhere on Fervor. That's as much information as the records on the mainland provided. I was hoping I might find something here, maybe what house number my nephew had, so that I would know where to look for him..."

"That's why you wanted to know if there were any documents left at the High Barrens," Sam interrupted. It normally was difficult to interrupt in the connection. The thoughts would just blend together and become incoherent, but because Elliot's presence was so faint in the connection, it was easy to overpower him, and for Sam to make his own thoughts heard over the technician's. Sam didn't mean to be rude, he was just excited that things were finally starting to make sense for him. *"You were hoping that I had found something that might point you in*

the right direction. You were anticipating that I could give you more answers."

This tidbit of information actually generated some interest from the Controls, who had stayed out of the conversation for the most part until that point.

"The Hub," Paul, the most out-spoken of the Controls offered. The other three nodded in agreement. "If you're going to look for that kind of information, that's where you'll find it. The Tellers needed those kinds of details for the Gathering so they could make sure that we were organized into the proper house-families, and I doubt that they would have destroyed the records. They still meet there every three months, and they tend to be a little excessive when it comes to organization and control of affairs. You should be able to find lists that outline all of the house-families there."

Sam, Fiona, and Nathan agreed with this as well.

"Your timing would be okay for that," Nathan thought. *"Francis wasn't due to go back for more than a month. You and Royce could avoid the Teller meeting if you go now. You ought to be safe."*

"No, not necessarily," Fiona objected. "Francis mentioned once that a couple of the Tellers visited the Hub regularly. The ones that lived nearby…that Bryan fellow for example… might be there. You don't want him catching you off-guard. He wasn't one of the more forgiving Tellers, and Sam won't be able to come to your rescue with the Languorite if Bryan catches you and orders you to stop. Not once we're gone."

"We'll take all of that under advisement before Royce and I come up with plans of our own," Elliot replied with a half-grin, albeit a slightly melancholic one. "I want promises from all of you. No more worrying about us, and no attempts to make contact with us either. That would just make things all the more dangerous for everyone involved. Royce and I, we'll make things work, and I'm sure we'll meet up with you again some-day. What I need for you to do is to focus your energies on re-establishing, and perhaps even laying the groundwork for the others to follow. You'll be able to create your own connection somewhere on the mainland, preferably far away from prying minds"

Fiona crossed her arms and scowled, pivoting away from him. This was just another unpleasant deviation from the anticipated that she was unwilling to accept. Nathan gave Elliot a sympathetic look. He had gotten used to Fiona's way of looking at things.

"I expect you to take good care of these three," Elliot stated firmly to the Watcher, his eyes dancing good-naturedly. "You promised if I took away your gift, that it wouldn't change anything with regards to them. I'm going to hold you to that."

"Don't worry," Nathan laughed. *"Now that I can actually look at them again, I'm not going to let them out of my sight."*

"I'm depending on that. You need to remember that you'll be each other's best means of protection. As I said before, you'd do best to stick together." The technician shot a look at the Controls. "All of you."

With that Elliot slid back out through the open door.

"Time to go," he concluded. "It's not a short trip, but I suspect it will go better for you than it did for me my first time across. Nobody will suddenly come barrelling through your heads – a few quiet whispers, maybe, but nothing that your walls can't handle. The first person you will likely see is called Elaine. Say hello for me, and tell her that I'll see her soon."

He moved to step away, but then his eyes settled upon Sarah, who made quiet sleepy sounds, but otherwise did not stir.

"Tell her the same." He gestured at Sarah. "And tell her I still owe her one for fixing me, so I'll have to make sure that I track her down again to make good on that."

With that, Elliot closed the hover door.

At first it was as quiet as death in the hover. The Control that had been introduced to them as Katrina stared at the door, looking almost as upset as Fiona did. The others looked away, trying to find something to serve as a distraction.

"You heard the man," Paul said, finally breaking the silence and directing the remark at Nathan authoritatively. "Time to go."

The Watcher took one last look at the door and then turned back to the hover console. Giving Fiona's hand a squeeze…that she returned encouragingly…he focused on the device. Everyone held their breath as they waited, hoping that Elliot's tutelage had been successful. Nathan broke into his usual broad grin as the vehicle relented to his efforts and began to hum slightly. The sound intensified to a higher pitched whine, occasionally disrupted by a noticeable popping noise. Moments later, the hover lifted from the sand, and began to move forward across the water.

Sam stared out of the window, watching the island and Elliot get more distant. There was a louder than usual "pop" that succeeded in startling Sarah out of her slumber. Sam was equally startled as she almost leapt to her feet, lurching forward at the sound. It took her a few seconds to realize where she was and what was going on. It took another couple of seconds to notice that Elliot was not with them. She looked like she was about to start panicking again, so Sam put his hand on her arm to calm her.

"We're leaving. We're leaving Fervor. Where's Elliot?" she asked in dismay.

"Doing what he needs to do. Doing his own kind of fixing," Sam assured her. *"Don't worry, he'll find us again."*

And as Sam watched Fervor fade from sight, he truly believed that.

About the Author and Illustrator

Chantal Boudreau is an accountant by day and an author/illustrator on evenings and weekends. She lives by the ocean in beautiful Nova Scotia, Canada with her husband and two children. In addition to being a CMA-MBA, she has a BA with a major in English from Dalhousie University. She writes and illustrates predominantly horror, dark fantasy and fantasy and has had several of her short stories published, including her zombie tales "Palliative" and "Just Another Day" appearing in horror anthologies, and her e-novelette "Shear Terror". Fervor is her first novel.

-Chantal

BYRON REMPEL

visual artist
graphic designer
cool guy

www.byronjrempel.com

MAY DECEMBER
Publications

The growing voice in horror and speculative fiction.

Find us at www.maydecemberpublications.com
Or
Email us at contact@maydecemberpublications.com

LaVergne, TN USA
17 March 2011
220440LV00004B/5/P

9 781936 730056